A BRIGHT BLIGHT

THE BALANCING BRIGHTNESS TRILOGY

BOOK TWO

CHARLI NILE

ISBN: 979-8-9998437-1-5

Cover Illustration and Design by Amphi Studio

Nile House

To all the people who read the previous book, survived the cliffhanger ending, and decided a little more emotional torture would be a good thing.

Also to Pepper, never thought I'd say this especially in a fantasy book but that marketing scheme you came up with? Girl, you're out here singled handedly pulling an army together and you don't get enough credit.

INTRODUCING THE BAND

Members of The Boys

Open Role: Lead Singer, yet again recently departed
Reem Fontaine: Banjo, backup vocals, and band management
Fem Grantham: Fiddle and other miscellaneous instruments
Lent Bietoletti: Guitar and backup vocals

Explanation: In a world where technology and progress are worshiped, the arts and music have mainly died out. When people do hear music, especially at a concert, they lose their minds, much like an early Beatles concert. That's not to say The Boys aren't talented; it just gives some context to why the crowds are as insane as they are.

Music I Imagine The Boys Playing

Wait So Long - Trampled by Turtles
Codeine - Trampled by Turtles
Victory - Trampled by Turtles
Burn for Free - Trampled by Turtles

CONTENTS

PROLOGUE

To my brave and patient readers,

I should apologize for the place I left you at the end of my last story. If it is any solace, while writing this, I suspect I experienced many of the same emotions you may have while reading it. It may have been a bit cruel to leave you at that point with lovers torn apart and a life hanging in the balance. My wish is that you also feel hopeful because of the actions taken by that version of myself, as well as those I hold dear.

In reading this continued account of my life, I believe you will find plenty of joy. It is also my hope that you experience the feelings of love between two people who fought to be together. This story is certainly not without trials and tribulations, but I hope you will proceed bravely and know it will be worth it in the end.

As before, I have included diary entries and

summarized the notes of others who are important to me. Once again, I ask you to forgive any artistic liberties I take and reassure you that these people are happy for their story to be told.

Sincerely,
Chaosta

PART I

NOT AT ALL COMFORTING

I am slowly drawn toward consciousness despite my attempts to cling to the dark. I feel as though I am standing between worlds. One is dark, peaceful, and without pain. The other, which is currently pulling at me, is bright and loud. My lungs already ache as I'm drawn forward. Somehow, I know there is a significant amount of pain waiting for me.

I fight weakly to stay where I am.

Suddenly, remaining here is not an option anymore, and I'm pulled fully into a bright, drugged, pain-riddled existence. My presence here is part consciousness and part torpor. The drugs try to dull everything, but instead just make it harder to breathe. With my eyes closed, the light still seems to stab through my eyelids.

Through the agony, I hear a voice I recognize, maybe more than one.

I continue to try to gasp in shallow breaths. Fighting with my lungs, fighting with the dizziness from the drugs.

As I struggle, I hear one voice say, "Is this normal? It seems as though she's struggling to breathe."

A different voice says, "She's been magically sedated for nearly two months now. Her chest and abdomen were significantly damaged by the stab wound and the subsequent poison. The bastards nicked her lung when they stabbed her in the back. It *will* still be hard for her to breathe. Everything is still delicate and barely healed enough for her to be awake. We just need to give her some time."

"There has to be something we can do to help her," says the first voice. There is a note of desperation to the sound.

"We can help by *staying calm,*" says the second voice. The voice is quiet but somehow still forceful.

My chest, no longer willing to continue the farce of trying to breathe, rebels, and I cough. It's weak and wet-sounding. Pain splinters through me, and the cough turns into a sob.

"Easy Chaosta," the second voice says, still damnably calm. "Just take small breaths. I know it hurts, but please try to relax."

As I hear it said out loud, I remember my name. Something else tugs at my memory, and suddenly I have the feeling there's an important question I need to ask. A thing, a need, that feels almost as important as the oxygen I'm gasping for. I try to remember what it might be, but it eludes me.

Slowly, as I endeavor to take small breaths, the pain fades a bit. It is still higher than feels tolerable, but slightly less than before.

I finally managed to open my eyes slightly. Everything is blurry, and I blink a couple of times as I try to clear my vision. A face wavers in front of me. I blink again. My vision finally clears, and I see someone I recognize. I reach for a name, unable to remember for a moment as he looks down at me with open concern and caring on his face. Then it comes to me. His name is Malam, and the first voice belongs to him.

"Malam?" I grate out past cracked lips.

His jaw tightens as he stares at me, and there is a wild look in his eyes.

"Yes, Chaosta, I'm here. You are going to be ok," he croaks out. He sounds kind of breathless himself.

Something about his voice dredges up memories. Some memories I wouldn't have asked to relive if I could have chosen. Others I would.

"Lily?" I gasp.

He closes his eyes and shakes his head slightly. Then, still blurred thanks to my vision, I see him reach up and swipe his hand against his face. "Why were you there with her?"

"Instincts."

"I assumed some divine intervention since you shouldn't have known where the safe house was located. I'm glad she was with a friend at the end," Malam chokes out. After several more moments where I fight the tears and pain, he says, "Thank you for trying to save her."

I close my eyes, and in my memory I see the knife flying through the air, unerringly finding its target. She drops to the ground bonelessly, and a different pain splinters through me as I live through it all over again.

I concentrate on surviving again for a moment, conserving my strength as other memories slowly return.

"There was…something odd…about the…angels." I'm barely getting enough air to say that much.

"What?" he asks, his voice rough.

"I felt dizzy…weak as I fought them…vision blurring."

His eyes are piercing as he looks at me. Then he shakes his head slightly and says, "I'll see what I can find. Right now, you need to rest."

Happy to comply, I close my eyes and let unconsciousness begin to drag me into the dark place. Then the agony redoubles as I find the thought I was searching for earlier. I weakly, desperately gasp, "Dio?"

There is a pause where my heart beats as though it's trying to escape my chest.

"Don't worry," Malam finally says in a quiet, comforting tone, "he's not here."

The words threaten to unravel me. I try, almost involuntarily, to rise from the bed. I can't do more than tense my muscles, though, because pain immediately overcomes me. I gasp, which turns into another weak, wet cough.

I see movement through the blurriness in my vision as another demon reaches out to steady me. His touch feels like acid, and I whimper. "Easy, Chaosta, you need to be still," he says.

I realize it's Chiron. His is the second voice I was hearing. "What is it? Why did you just try to move?"

I fight to avoid another cough as he removes his hand. Pain flares in the base of my skull as my chest constricts. My lungs have almost entirely given up trying to breathe.

"She and Dio dislike each other. She must be worried he's going to scold her or something," Malam says.

"Whatever it was, we'll have to figure it out later. I need to sedate her again. We can't risk her pulling something right now," Chiron says.

I feel darkness trying to pull me away, even without drugs. I still somehow say, "Please…wait…"

In another life, I don't know the pain of his absence. Here, even with the physical pain trying to distract me, the deep pit of longing for him feels like too much to bear.

Somehow, through monumental effort, I manage to scrape my eyes open again. The two demons are leaning over me. Concern is clear on both of their faces. I use the last of my strength and gasp out, "In love…with him. Need—"

I feel someone, likely Chiron, pressing something against my lips.

I look past him, up at Malam's face. His eyes are wide as he stares at me.

I ignore Chiron's admonishment as he tries to drug me again and manage, between weak coughs, to say, "to know...he's ok."

When Malam nods, I let Chiron drug me again, more than willing to return to that dark, pain-free place as long as I know Malam will make sure Dio is all right.

ESCALATING SELF DESTRUCTION

A quiet knock on the door pulls me out of the drug-filled haze I was floating in. I lay still with my eyes closed, concentrating on breathing as Chiron curses quietly and goes to the door.

I have no idea how much time has passed since I was last conscious, but somehow I know that it has passed.

Then Dio's name cuts through the agony in my mind and body, and I fight to focus on the conversation happening outside the door. A conversation that I can now hear as Chiron begins to raise his voice.

"That's not fucking good enough. You don't know where he is or whether he's safe."

Malam is speaking more quietly, and I have to strain to hear him say, "I've done what I can by speaking with the coven just now. If his family sent him to a mental hospital, it was for good reason. I just don't want to upset her."

A whimper scrapes its way out of my throat, and I slowly and painfully push myself up onto my elbows. I don't know what my plan is, but I can't just lie here.

"No, you don't want to dig any further because you've never

liked him. Either that or you're too weak to see this through," says Chiron.

I roll onto the side and half slide, half fall off the bed onto my hands and knees. My vision goes grey, nearly black, as the impact jars my still barely healed abdomen.

"Take a breath, Chiron, let's think fo—"

"Don't you dare try to calm me down. Do you have any idea how close we came to losing her? The fucking least you can do is find the man she loves and make sure he's safe. It shouldn't be that difficult!"

I crawl slowly toward the door, half-dragging myself. I concentrate on the conversation to keep myself conscious.

"What if he doesn't care, what if he doesn't love her back?" Malam asks. His voice is raised as well now.

As I approach the door, I wonder for a minute if I'm losing my battle to remain conscious. Then I realize it's not my vision graying out, I'm seeing the dense shadows of demon magic seeping in through the crack along the doorframe. Unable to spare enough mental energy to try to figure out why, instead, I continue to drag myself toward the demons on the other side of the door.

"Even if he does love her, he's just a huma—"

I hear a loud crack. Then I'm at the door, and I press against it and half-drag, half-fall through onto the ground outside this room.

I catch sight of Chiron facing Malam, his hands in fists. One of Malam's cheeks is bright red, and his chest is heaving as he stares at Chiron. Some strong emotion crosses his face before he masks it.

As I fall through the door at their feet, their attention is suddenly no longer focused on each other.

Chiron, crouching beside me now, is swearing in their language. His voice shakes, and he rolls me gently onto my back. He begins to draw a rune over me, but I catch his wrist and, while he could easily remove my hand instead, he freezes and stares at me. Raw emotions, including fear, swirl across his expression.

"Is he at...Piquory?" I choke out. I feel moisture on my lips that I suspect is blood.

Chiron's head jerks to Malam. He opens his mouth to say something, but Malam holds up his hands in surrender. "I've got it," he says tightly. "I'll go now."

Just like that, he disappears in a swirl of shadow and wing-beats, and I release Chiron's wrist as he finishes drawing the runes that pull me into unconsciousness.

~

Despite the magic-induced sleep, I still somehow dream of a great force clashing, light versus dark. What catches my attention, though, is the space where the battle is taking place. While clearly outside, it is green. It is a stark difference from what I'm familiar with. There is more green than I've seen in my life, short though it may be.

Small trees and other large plants fill the space, and there are green growing things carpeting the ground. The stronghold that I am currently residing in looks like this, but it is a fraction of the space where this fight is taking place. Perhaps this is a different place, something in the past. Or maybe this is a memory of Malam's that has found me again?

I also dream again of shapes written in ash on a table-top. This time, I recognize them immediately as runes, but their purpose is still unclear. I study them carefully and hope that when I wake, I might be able to remember them.

~

EXCERPTS FROM MALAM

The following passage is from a summary of notes that were provided to me by Malam. Please indulge me for any inaccuracies, and know that they are an artist's liberties. Malam would want this to be as factual as possible. I would have avoided sharing this entirely, but it provides important context to the story that I wanted you, dear reader, to have.

My heart pounds as I materialize at this canopy farm. Apparently, the information I gathered when I met with the coven earlier wasn't enough to satisfy Chiron. It seems I need to find the location and confirm that Dio is safe if I want to be allowed back to the stronghold.

The stronghold that I'm supposed to be in charge of.

My stomach twists as I remember the look on his face. *Fuck, that isn't going to be something I can repair easily.*

As I stumble slightly, finding my feet, I reach up and touch my cheek. The impact from his hand still stings. I swear to myself as I square my shoulders. I could kill him for striking me. It's my right.

Of course I won't.

I look around, examining the canopy farm where I find myself. This farm, like all our others, fills the top floor of a massive building that rises well over 100 floors into the sky.

My nose wrinkles at the smell. I've always despised livestock. This particular farm raises goats and chickens. I breathe shallowly through my mouth as I begin to look around for the demon I came here to find. Eventually I see a form sitting cross-legged in the middle of one of the goat pens. I wince at the thought of it.

Vish is reading a book, casually defending the pages from the goats who are trying to eat them as though it's habit for him at this point. He has long, almost light colored hair, which is unusual among us. He is wiry, lean, and wearing a traditional black, sleeveless shirt and loose linen pants with bare feet.

He is so absorbed in the book that he doesn't look up as I get close. Needing his attention, I clear my throat, and he finally looks at me through the hair falling in his eyes. "Vish, I need to speak with you," I growl quietly.

He stands slowly and casually, and I feel myself starting to snarl at him. Vish is young for a demon, and he is also not as respectful as I would like him to be. However, since I have a favor to ask, I know it is not the right time to scold him. I need to get this done.

"I have a favor to ask," I say, a slight growl still creeping in as he stares at me as though I'm interrupting.

"What is the favor?" he asks, with a slight tilt of his head.

"I need to confirm the location of someone."

"A demon?" he asks, already beginning to look bored. He starts to pick at the dirt under his nails.

"No, a human," I say.

He sneers at his fingernails. Then, without saying anything

else, he turns, gesturing with his head for me to follow. I fall in behind him as he leaves the goat pen and walks to a small room in the corner. It was likely originally intended as a storage room, but he's converted it into one massive computer terminal.

As he sits and begins to tap on the screen, he says, "It's been a while since you were here asking me for information on that human girl. Is that who we're looking for?"

I don't correct Vish on his assumption that Chaosta is human. Most of my people don't know that I gave up some of my lifeforce for her, and I'd rather they not find out. Instead, I say, "No, I need information on Dio..." I pause a moment, trying to remember his full name. Then I recall and say, "Magnus, Dio Magnus."

Vish doesn't give any indication that he heard me, but his fingers continue their tapping, so I'm sure he did. I pace in the small space until he says, "Hmm, looks like he is at a hospital named Piquory Center. Isn't that where the girl was?"

My heart feels like it drops into my stomach. "Are you sure?"

"See for yourself," he says as he points at the terminal screen.

My heart pounds from what still feels like the vicinity of my stomach as I realize what that most likely means. If the angels used the center as a sort of prison for Chaosta, it's likely they are involved in this as well. That might also align with the fact that his brother was the one who committed him, as I learned from Reem earlier. The rest of Dio's family has long been involved with the angels.

"Can you trace where the commitment orders came from?" I ask.

Vish taps away at the screen. I'm already beginning to make a plan in case he confirms what I fear to be true. After a while, he says, "It looks as though someone named Alexander Magnus committed him. Must be a relation."

That confirms his brother had something to do with this however, despite the high likelihood that he was working with the angels, it doesn't confirm their involvement. "Are there any anomalies with the paperwork?"

Vish taps away again for a bit as my mind continues working on this problem. "No, everything looks like what I would expect with the paperwork..." He pauses for a moment and then says, "Actually, wait a minute, his status was updated several months ago when he arrived. Based on what it says here, he was initially sent there on a temporary family commitment, but his status was changed to a permanent, lifelong hold shortly after he arrived."

"Who made the order?" I ask, my heart pounding in my chest.

Vish again taps away for a while, this time before saying, "Oh, huh, looks like a court order of some sort. It says he was accused of killing some humans when he arrived."

As I look over Vish's shoulder at the screen of the terminal, I see him flinch out of my peripheral vision and realize belatedly that I'm snarling like some sort of animal. "Are you sure there is nothing odd with that paperwork?" I ask, trying to soften my voice.

Vish taps away again at the screen a little slower this time, and his shoulders are tense. "Nothing is out of place that I can find," he finally says.

I scrub at my eyes. The answer to whether the angels were involved won't be found here, but maybe we can at least verify if he's safe. "Is there any way to verify if he's alright?" I ask.

"Hmmm," says Vish, as he continues interacting with the terminal.

After a moment, he pulls up a video feed. The image from the camera looks into a white, padded room with a single foam pad on the floor. There is a man in view of the camera. He's lying on his back in the middle of the room, in a straitjacket, his legs tented.

He's lying so still that it's only the high resolution on the camera, allowing me to see him blinking, that verifies he's still alive.

It is clearly Dio. My heart sinks.

Vish says, "Fuck. Well, he's alive, but it looks like he's heavily sedated and being kept in solitary confinement."

"Has it been like this since he was admitted?" I snarl.

Vish flinches again, then taps on the screen a bit before saying, "Pretty much yes."

"Just sedatives," I ask.

"No, other mind meds too."

I swear, and the air begins to darken with the shadows of our magic. As I watch the video feed, though, it is clear that he is safe and being cared for, at least for now. Before I can pass the point of no return with Vish, I thank him and leave, transporting myself to the street outside Lily's apartment. When I find my feet again, I light up a cigarette and lean against the wall of the building. I need some time to think so that I can figure out how to confirm if the angels are behind this.

Fuck, I should have thought harder about what I was asking. Hours have passed since I made up this idiotic plan, and I've been pacing to kill time as I wait.

I decided that the most direct way to figure out if the angels are involved was to ask someone on the inside. So I sent a message to Bonum asking to meet here.

Bonum isn't a friend, but they also aren't exactly an enemy. They've been Rex, the High Leader's, right hand for as long as I've known them. They have plenty of other reasons not to be an ally to my people. Of course, they also have at least one significant reason not to support their own. However, at our last meeting, they led me to believe that they might be willing to act as a sort of informant.

That last meeting was less than an hour after I found Lily

dead and Chaosta mortally wounded. I hope that, in the state I was in at the time, I didn't misread their intentions. As I pace, trying to keep my mind away from my concerns about Bonum's potential loyalty, I consider the location where I currently find myself.

This is a place I haven't been back to since I laid Lily to rest. I've continued to pay for this apartment simply because I can't make myself clean it out. The pool of blood in her room somehow seems sacred. I also have no interest in cleaning or looking at the trail of poisoned, black blood that Chaosta left as she dragged herself to break the window and enlist a crow to get help.

I haven't been back here since I repaired the window. However, when I needed a place for this delicate meeting, I couldn't think of another neutral space. So here I find myself, pacing outside of the space where I lost the love of my life only months ago.

I've also just realized that I never did eat when I meant to, and my legs are beginning to feel weak. The beginning of a headache stabs behind my eyes, and I scold myself for not being more prepared.

Just as I'm beginning to think they are not going to show, Bonum walks around the corner. They are pale with light blue eyes and a scar across one cheek. Unlike last time I saw them, they are armed, a sword strapped to their hip. As I see the sword, I wonder if I did actually misread their intent at our last meeting.

Bonum stalks toward me, getting just slightly too close before leaning rapaciously against the wall of the building next to me. "What now, Malam?" they rasp.

I'm relieved to see that their hand isn't on their sword. I still hesitate a moment before asking them about Dio's commitment.

"You think our high leader has so much time on his hands

that he's concerning himself with a human?" It is clear they are angry, even with the lack of inflection in their ruined voice.

Not entirely sure what they might be, or not be, implying I say, "It seems as though it's too much of a coincidence and I am curious."

"You would risk my life on this question?" Bonum rasps as they stare blindly through me. The fingers on their right hand, their sword hand, curl into a fist briefly before relaxing again.

"Yes, it is more important than it might seem," I say tightly.

With that, Bonum nods and begins to turn away.

"Wait." When they pause, I say, "There's one more thing. Chaosta said something was odd when she fought the angels who stabbed her. She said she felt dizzy and weak. Do you know why?"

Without turning, Bonum says, "Why do you think I would know something like that?"

"I just thought maybe your people were doing something to her," I say as calmly as I can.

They roll their shoulders and then stalk off out of the alley without another word.

As they leave and the energy returns to normal, I let myself release the breath I hadn't realized I'd been holding.

LIVING AND LEARNING

When I next open my eyes, Chiron is leaning over me. My muscles tense.

"Don't," Chiron says harshly. "I'll keep you unconscious if I can't trust you to lie still."

I whimper, and my eyes begin to fill with tears.

"He's safe," Chiron says, and I feel his hand on my arm.

I stare at his face. He's looking at the closed door instead of me.

"Is he at Piquory Center?"

"Can I trust you to follow orders?" he asks a little less harshly.

I grit my teeth as I say, "I'll lie still."

He stares at me for a moment as though trying to decide if I'm lying. Then he says, "He is, but Malam confirmed that he's safe."

I close my eyes as the room spins. "We need to get him out."

"Yes, and we will, but we need you to accompany us. I don't think he'll trust us enough to go with us without you there, and you need to be stronger before we can bring you."

I'm trembling, and a tear runs down my cheek. I trust

Malam, but until I see for myself that Dio is safe, I feel as though I won't be able to rest.

Chiron curses, and I wonder if he's going to knock me out again. Instead, he brings me another blanket and tucks it around me. The gentleness of it is so at odds with his normal behavior that it settles me a bit.

"How?" I gasp.

"Rest and time," he says softly.

I sigh.

His shoulders relax infinitesimally.

"Do you think while I recover you can teach me some things?" I finally ask.

"Like magic?"

"Yes."

"I'm not the right person for that, I'm afraid," he says.

I open my mouth to try to convince him, but before I can say anything, he says, "I'll ask Malam if he would be willing."

I blink my eyes open and look at him.

He looks uncomfortable, staring at the door absently. "You need to get another couple of weeks of rest, and then I'll see if he'd be willing to start with some short lessons, alright?"

"Thank you, Chiron."

He glares at me as he says, "Now rest, or I'll change my mind."

Healing is slow, but as the next week passes, I'm gradually able to remain awake for longer periods.

I finally ask Chiron how long it's been since I was injured, and he tells me it's been three months. It's surreal to think about how, while I've been floating in the black, quiet place, everyone else has been healing from her loss. I haven't. Thinking of Lily is painful, and I try to avoid it because those thoughts make it hard to keep the tears at bay, and I can't do anything to make it harder to breathe.

However, the pain of remembering Lily is still less than the agony of worrying about Dio. Instead of dwelling on worries about his safety, I try to focus on happy memories. I remember watching him sing at a concert or imagine his arms around me as we slept on the floor of Lily's apartment.

Another week passes, and I get to the point where I can make it through the day with only a few naps. Chiron also allows me to sit up slightly, supported by carefully arranged pillows.

I'm so bored and desperate to do something at this point that when Malam shows up at my room with his arms full of books I actually shed a few tears.

When he sees my face, he freezes for a moment and says, "I'm sorry…I thought...I can come back later."

"No, please stay, I'm so bored, and I am just glad to see you."

He looks doubtful, but before he can do anything else, Chiron says dryly, "Yeah, don't leave or I'm going to need to start talking with her."

I actually laugh and then quickly regret it when it makes me cough.

That's more like the Chiron I remember.

Malam glares at him, but there's not much heat in it. He deposits the books in a messy pile on one of the counters in the room and pulls some pens out of his pocket. Then he settles himself on a chair next to me.

As Chiron returns to reading a book, Malam says, "I'll teach you this but only if you promise to tell me when you get tired, alright?"

"I promise," I say.

He stares at me for a moment as though ensuring I'm being

truthful, then he says, "There are three types of magic recognized by philosophers, dark magic, white magic, and black magic. White magic was fairly common thousands of years ago when my people first arrived here, but its use slowly died out. Black magic was believed to exist by philosophers, but I've personally never seen it used. Dark magic is the only practice that remains viable today. It is also the only type of magic that can be learned by anyone. "

"This is what the coven uses?" I ask.

"Yes, and group magic is just one way of practicing dark magic. It can also be practiced individually, and in combat, but we will get to that later." Malam studies my face as he says this, and I wonder about the sudden intensity in his expression. Then he opens the book he's holding, finds a specific page, and sets it on my lap.

Looking down at the open page, I see a list of runes and their specific effects. I turn the page and see that the list continues on page after page. There must be hundreds of runes marked on these pages.

Malam says, "All of the runes can be effective if drawn in blood, which is why it is so often used. However, there are also other specific mediums that each can be drawn with. It is important to memorize that list, since using the incorrect medium can cause damage to your surroundings or even the magic user themselves."

I flip the pages back to the start of the list and see that the first rune listed is called Ansuz, and that it can be drawn with the ash from cherry wood, concentrated tea, or blood.

"Today," Malam says, "I will begin by showing you how to draw the first few runes. The correct order for drawing them must also be memorized as there is a specific way to draw each."

"I'm going to draw them?" I ask, my heart beating a little quicker.

"Is that not what you wanted to learn?" Malam asks, a confused expression on his face.

"I thought I would learn more about magic, not that you would show me how to use it," I say a little breathlessly.

"Do you not want to learn?"

I consider for a moment before saying, "I would like that actually."

"Excellent, we will begin with Ansuz in that case."

For the remainder of the hour, I practice under Malam's close supervision.

After a while, Chiron chases him from the room, insisting I need some rest. I'd be annoyed if it weren't for the fact that I'm surprisingly tired from learning something that seems so simple.

Another week passes and each day we have our magic lesson. Each day, I also ask Chiron and Malam when we can do something about Dio.

Chiron continues to tell me that I need more time to heal and, despite the decrease in pain and discomfort I'm feeling, I trust him. However, it doesn't make it any easier to allow Dio to remain there.

SHARDS OF GLASS

An acrid smell fills the air on the street around me. It's light out, the dim light of late morning or early afternoon. The street is quiet, and there are no carriages flying past, however, I can hear them on the adjacent streets. My heart pounds. This is familiar somehow despite the gaps in my memory about how I got here.

Something seems to pull me forward, and I move further down the street. I feel the hair on the back of my neck stand up as I walk around a corner and see a scene that I suddenly remember. This is just a dream, or at least I hope it is. I've dreamt this before.

The acrid smell is stronger here, and as I stare, frozen, at the scene in front of me, I reach for a sword that isn't there. My heart pounds in my chest, and I try to run forward, but I suddenly can't breathe. As I fall to my knees I'm forced to watch as healers and guards run toward Dio who is surrounded by the bodies of several men. They're laying unmoving on the ground around him.

As the guards get to him, they overwhelm him and force him

flat onto the surface of the street. Unlike last time I dreamed this, he's suspiciously still and doesn't seem to be fighting them.

I gasp for air as my vision darkens.

I continue to try to push myself to my feet as I see a healer approaching him with a syringe.

I try to scream despite the lack of air in my lungs, and then everything goes black.

~

I wake with a scream, gasping for breath and trying to press myself up. My heart is pounding so loudly in my ears that I can't hear him until Chiron growls, "Chaosta, lay still."

I feel his hands on my arms and I force myself to relax.

"What happened?" he asks.

"I dreamed about what happened with Dio when he arrived at the Piquory Center."

"It was just a dream," he says calmly.

I'm sure this wasn't just a dream, it had the feeling of those visions I've had in the past that have come true. Only this time, I suspect that it has already happened. Instead of responding, I run my thumb along the place where Dio touched my hand in the carriage. It has become a habit recently.

Chiron seems to note it as he stares at me.

I wonder if he's going to ask more questions, but just then the door opens, and Malam steps into the room. He looks tired, and either doesn't notice or ignores the current tension in the room as he sets up his books.

Chiron opens his mouth, but I cut him off and ask, "Are you alright, Malam? You look tired."

"Training farmers to wield swords is slow work, but I'm fine. How are you?" he asks, clearly appraising me.

"I'm alright, just bored," I say.

By this point in my healing, I've been allowed out of bed. At first I needed support as I went even the short distance from to the door. More recently, I've been using a cane and can walk as far as the kitchen. My gait is more a shuffle than a walk, but it feels like progress. Still, I'm spending most of my time in bed at Chiron's insistence.

"When can we get Dio out?" I ask yet again.

I hear Chiron sigh from behind me as Malam's expression shutters. "You're still far too weak, and it will be a difficult enough task even when you're at full strength. We can't have you also be a liability."

"Also?"

Malam grits his jaw, and from behind me, Chiron says, "Dio is being given mind meds just as you were and will need to be managed carefully."

Malam looks at him over my shoulder and gives him the slightest nod.

I'm curious about the nod, but this seems as good a time as any to propose the idea I had when I woke up this morning. "Maybe instead of trying to sneak him out, we could get a lawyer involved? That man the boys enlisted to fight the case against me seemed talented."

Malam glances over my shoulder again.

I turn toward Chiron, moving carefully so I don't further damage the still healing wound on my abdomen.

Chiron is shaking his head slightly, but stops as I look at him.

I narrow my eyes at him, my jaw gritted as I ask, "Why not?"

Chiron remains silent, still looking at Malam, and I turn again.

Malam glances at me, seeming to assess my expression before saying tightly, "I was curious and did some digging after I found out that it was Dio's brother who had him committed. Alexander is the lawyer who got the charges against you dropped, and he is Dio's brother. He, like their late parents, is aligned with the angels."

It feels as though the floor drops out from under me. However, as I consider I remember feeling as though the lawyer looked familiar. Now that I look back on the memory, I realize that he looked like Dio. "Why did he sign the papers to commit Dio?"

"Dio has a history of addiction, and it seems the angels were able to convince Alexander that he'd relapsed."

I grit my teeth. It seems my prior suspicions about Dio's past were correct, but I'm confident that he didn't relapse. "If he got Dio committed, could he not also get him released?" I ask.

"He is unlikely to work against the interests of the angels. In fact, it was confirmed for me recently that it was their influence that caused him to have Dio committed," Malam says as he glances at Chiron past my shoulder again.

"But Dio is his bro—"

"I won't let you meet with someone aligned with that side," Chiron snarls from behind me.

I turn, a little too fast, to face him and flinch as pain burns in my abdomen. "Why would you think that I'll let you stop me?" I snarl back.

Chiron's eyes widen as he stares at me.

"I'll arrange the meeting," Malam says tightly, and I turn, more slowly, to face him.

I hear Chiron beginning to say something but Malam just shakes his head slightly and Chiron goes quiet.

"For now, let's have our next magic lesson," Malam says. His tone is overly casual.

Behind me, again, Chiron begins to say something, but Malam cuts him off quickly and says, "Chiron, how about you go check on Gaia. Didn't she twist her ankle yesterday?"

I turn to face Chiron again. He's glaring at Malam and, based on the intensity of his expression, I'm surprised that Malam hasn't caught on fire yet. Then, with a quiet curse in their language, Chiron leaves the room.

When I turn toward Malam again, he's brushing a hand over his face. He's slightly pale as he takes his normal place on the chair beside my bed. "I think you should know that just after you were injured, Bonum spoke with me. They were going to try to save Lily, but plans changed, and they were too late. I don't know why, but it feels important that I tell you that."

The bed feels unstable beneath me as I consider this new information. Then I remember Bonum stopping the guard who seemed to intend me harm. "Are they on our side?"

"I'm not quite sure," Malam says tiredly. "They did offer to act as an informant."

I consider silently for a few moments.

After a while, Malam says, "Perhaps we should get back to our lessons. Where were we? Oh yes, that's right. I think it is time to teach you about combat magic."

"Is this what the coven did in the street against those angels?" I ask.

"No, that was a creative use of weather magic. Combat magic is defined differently. It can't rely on single-use runes because of the nature of when and how it might be used. For combat, the magic user must permanently mark their body with the runes they might need in battle. That way they have immediate access to them. They then send energy to the rune, or runes, they want to activate to create effects in combat.

"Dio's tattoos?" I ask.

"Yes, Dio's tattoos are one such example of inscribed runes. Chiron has mainly branded runes, and I have some of both," Malam removes his shirt. Marks trace across his chest, abdomen, and one rune crosses over his right shoulder. There are a few raised scars, and two are tattoos.

"We must take care that we do not choose too many because the magic takes a great strength of will to hold back. This is especially true in times of volatility, such as when experiencing strong emotions or pain. For those of us who practice combat magic, there is always some amount of energy being used to hold back the runes we have marked upon us. The more runes, the more energy it takes to control them."

In my mind's eye, I see Dio, every part of his body I've seen, nearly covered in curling shapes, overlapped by scars. "But Dio is covered in runes."

"Yes," Malam says, "Dio has an extensive collection. He is also quite skilled at combat magic. In fact, to my knowledge, he is the most skilled combat magic practitioner alive today."

"Certainly you mean among humans?" I ask as my stomach flips.

"No, even among demons. Dio is particularly talented and driven when it comes to the use of combat magic." Malam is focused on me as he speaks, watching and gauging my reaction.

My world feels as though it flips on its axis with this new information, and I cling to the bed as though trying to stay upright. I sit in silence, trying to grapple with this new truth. "What happens if you can't control that energy for some reason?"

"It depends on how much control you lose," Malam says quietly. "If you're angry, for example, it could impart some pain on whoever you're focused on. With a larger loss of control, it could destroy an entire city block." After a pause, he says, "Or potentially worse."

I remember the feeling of glass shards scraping against my skin from Dio's glare. I also remember him looking away from me, trying to save me the pain of whatever strong emotion he was feeling.

Malam looks uncomfortable.

"What do you mean, worse?" I ask as my stomach churns.

"Without safeguards, if the loss of control was great enough and many runes were allowed to combine, it would create such a blast of magic that it could cause miles of damage. Especially if there were enough runes," he says.

"Safeguards?" I ask with a swallow.

The calm, slightly sorrowful look on his face fills me with fear as he says, "There is a rune that can be inscribed which will protect those around the magic user in the case of a full loss of control. That rune will end the life of the one it is inscribed upon before significant damage can be done. There will still be damage in a radius, but it will be significantly less than would be the case otherwise."

"The rune on the left side of Dio's chest. The one you traced when you saw it," I choke out as my heart pounds even harder.

"Yes," Malam says. "Many of us don't inscribe the Killswitch rune because we aren't willing to make that sacrifice. That day, when I saw how many runes he had inscribed, I was worried that he would be a liability until I saw it. It also spoke of the sacrifice he's willing to make for the cause, to see the balance restored."

I'm shaking, and there's a buzzing in my ears. The strain Dio must be under to control all that magic is clearly significant even under the best of circumstances.

The image of Dio catching my wrist as I traced the rune on his chest all those months ago plays in my memory. My shaking increases as I remember him withdrawing, intending to leave me, as he must have considered this a risk to me. It is clear that he has already accepted that risk for himself. My heart breaks yet again as I realize this was likely another reason why he tried so hard to keep his distance from me.

It's not fear for myself that makes me shake, that makes my heart pound, though. It's the fear of losing him. As tears slide down my cheeks and I struggle to breathe, I run my thumb over the knuckles of my index finger. Seeking comfort as I try to calm myself.

"You'll arrange a meeting with Alexander immediately," I say breathlessly.

Malam hesitates, but as I glare at him through the tears, he finally says tightly, "Alright. You'll need to have someone accompany you, and it can't be Chiron or me."

"Can you see if Fem will help?"

"Yes, I'll talk with him," he says.

"Thank you, Malam," I say.

When he leaves, I push myself out of bed and go for a walk with my cane. It is imperative that I'm ready for this meeting, and I know I need to continue to focus on building my strength. The movement is also one way to distract myself from the rising feeling of fear.

FAMILY TIES

I lay the small, leather bookmark along the page I'm reading and close the book in my lap. I scrub at my eyes, which have begun to blur. I've been staring at this page for hours, and I am no closer to being able to understand the writing in it than I was just over a week ago when Chiron delivered it to me.

When I decided to speak with Alexander, I knew there was a risk because of his alignment with the angles. As I tried to figure out how to approach that meeting without the risk of drawing nearby angels to me, as I have in the past, I remembered this book. The angel book I bought from that little shop, well over a year ago now.

Chiron was kind enough to fetch it for me from my room when he was at the mansion for magic practice. I didn't tell him what it was for, since I suspected he might not be so willing if he knew that it was going to help facilitate the meeting with Alexander.

Some of the book is written in my language, but there are also sections in a language I don't recognize. Unsurprisingly, when I asked Chiron, he, with a grimace, told me that it's the language of the angels.

Two illustrations stand out to me. Why I'm drawn to them, I'm not quite sure. However, I know there's something important here. I don't know why I think that I'll figure it out by continuing to stare at it. I also don't know how else I might get the answer I seek. Besides, this is one way that I've been trying to distract myself while waiting for the meeting with Dio's brother.

Malam told me a few days ago that the meeting has been scheduled and Fem is willing to accompany me. Unfortunately, that meeting is still a few days away. On one hand, that has continued to give me time to get stronger. On the other, it has given me ample time to imagine worst-case scenarios regarding Dio.

To that end, I know I'm pushing myself to get stronger more quickly than Chiron approves of. While he's around, I try to go easy and listen to his direction. However, each evening when he goes to the boys' mansion for magic practice, I take advantage of his absence to push myself harder.

Within the last week, I have progressed from limping slowly with the help of a cane to walking greater distances. Over the last couple of days, I've been able to get rid of the cane entirely.

That is, at least when Chiron isn't here.

As I wait for the meeting, I begin to slowly and carefully practice the footwork for sword fighting. It's slow and painful at first. I can't help but collapse on my bed and cry after the first night, when I can barely make it through the first few forms, but I keep at it.

On the second night, while I'm trying to add in some more slow, painful steps, there is a sudden pain in my back, along my shoulders. Or rather, pain may not be the right way to describe the feeling. Perhaps a strong, sudden feeling of energy would be more accurate.

As I realize that I'm staring at the wall, unmoving, the ache suddenly moves to my head. My eyes blur, and my vision darkens. I realize I haven't been breathing and gasp for air.

When my vision returns, I'm suddenly drawn to the book, which is resting in its familiar place by my bed. I open it to the page I have marked. As I look at the words, I'm surprised to find that I can now understand their meeting.

Then, I reverently thank every deity I can think of because this changes everything. Thanks to the book and this sudden understanding of the language, I now see how I can use the power of the wings to temporarily hide myself from the angels. If I do it right, I'll just look like any other angel, a forgettable entity in a sea of bright-winged beings. While it only lasts for a few hours at a time, that should be enough for when I need it.

I read through the passage several times and fall asleep that night, practicing the steps. All I can wish is that I had figured it out sooner and avoided some of the violence.

Finally the day dawns when I'm scheduled to meet with Alexander.

Malam and Chiron have both attempted to talk me out of this at least once, and Chiron tried forbidding me from going. Malam knows better than to try that particular tactic, but he looks pale, and they're both tense.

As I get ready to leave, Chiron tries one more time to talk me out of going. He reminds me that I'm already being targeted and walking into their domain to meet with Alexander, especially as weak as I still am, doesn't seem wise. I nod along without really listening. I tried to explain to both of the demons how I can now use the wings to hide from the angels, but I don't think either of them believed me.

Trying to ignore the fear and worry on both their faces, I make my way slowly to the waiting carriage. As I get closer, I see Fem sitting inside. When I struggle slightly with the steps, he helps me. He's dressed in a suit, his short brown hair neatly combed.

I, on the other hand, am wearing one of the demon's long-sleeve black shirts with the sleeves rolled up to my wrists and a pair of their black linen pants. They had to hem the pants to be short enough for me. The clothes are loose enough not to press on the still-healing wound on my abdomen. They also cover my scars.

Chiron braided my hair for me and helped me pin it up on my head so I'm not a complete mess. Of course, I don't have my sword, and I feel anxious and twitchy without it, especially now that we are out of the demon stronghold.

As I slowly, and stiffly, settle myself on the seat opposite, Fem's green eyes study me closely. "How are you doing, Chaos-ta?" he finally asks into the silence.

"Much better, Fem. It is so good to see you," I say as tears prick at my eyes. I hadn't realized how much I'd missed seeing the boys until just now. "Thank you for accompanying me. Malam was worried about allowing me to go by myself."

"I'm happy to attend the meeting with you. How can I help?"

"I think Malam was worried I'd get into trouble, or maybe that I would collapse or something," I say with a slight smirk. "I'm meeting with Alexander to see if he'll agree to help get Dio released. I don't know if you'll be able to help with that, but maybe you can speak to Dio's mental state?"

"Of course, I would be happy to," Fem says with a slight smile. "I'm fairly certain he wasn't using again when the healers showed up with paperwork from his brother. I don't know how his brother would have known even if he was," he says, the words rushing out of him. "I know they aren't close. It seems odd."

"You're right. I wouldn't tell you, but I know you're aware of more than the others already, so it somehow seems fair."

He nods at me, meeting my eyes, his face serious.

"According to the information Malam found, the angels arranged the commitment papers and manipulated his brother into signing them as a way to hurt me," I say.

"Damn," Fem says tightly.

"I don't know what reception we'll get from Alexander, but I'm hoping I can convince him to help, without mentioning the angels."

I'll keep my mouth shut unless you need me then," he says.

We spend the rest of the trip in silence. He continues to glance at me as I stare out the window.

When we eventually come to a stop, I take a breath, close my eyes, and lean my head back against the seat. Centering myself, I repeat the steps of the ritual that I need in order to hide myself. I'm glad when I feel a slightly electric feeling pass through my body from the top of my head to the soles of my feet, and I hope that means it worked. "If we get in there and I get arrested or attacked, just promise me you'll leave immediately."

Fem grits his teeth, but he nods. "I'll leave and make sure Malam and Chiron know," hc says tightly.

My heart pounds a little too fast as I leave the carriage, leaning on his arm as I take the steps to the street. I move haltingly, with the use of the cane, up to the door with him walking at my side.

I realize as I look up at the building, that we are not outside the angel stronghold. I relax slightly, hoping that may mean that there won't be any angels here.

As we get through the front door, I let Fem take the lead since he knows where we're going. He sticks close, allowing me to set the pace, and leads us to the lift. Once inside, he looks at something he's drawn on his hand and presses a button for floor 103. A quiet ding sounds moments later as the doors open on the appropriate floor.

We walk out into the hall, and I momentarily pause as I see

bright wings everywhere. Fem of course can't see them. The people here look like humans to him, so he continues on, leading us at a considerate but confident pace down the hallway.

The angels seem to be going about some sort of business. Some walk in pairs, talking. Others carry paperwork or small crates. I feel their eyes on me, but unlike my past experiences, facing predatory stares, this time, they just glance and look away. They do, however, clearly note Fem. I realize there must not be many humans who have business here.

We walk down a few hallways, and I continue to feel poised for sudden violence but the angel's eyes continue to pass over me.

Eventually, we get to a dark metal door with a name plaque on it that says, *Alexander Magnus, Attorney at Law.*

Fem opens the door without knocking, and I step in after him. Looking around, I see that we are in a small reception area. A woman I recognize sits behind a desk. *Roxana is her name,* I remind myself, as she looks up at us.

Her eyes pass over Fem and fix on me. She steps out from behind the desk and strides forward with her hand out. "Chaosta, how nice to see you again," she says, her voice friendly, a smile lighting up her face.

As I shake her hand, Fem says, "We're here to meet with Alexander."

With the smile still on her face, she holds out her hand to Fem next and says, "Roxana, and you are?"

"Fem, I'm a friend of Chaosta's," he says as he shakes her hand.

"Very nice to meet you," she says. Then she moves towards a door in the wall beside her desk. "Come with me, Alexander is ready for you."

We follow her into a large and well-appointed office. Comfortable brown chairs sit across from a massive desk, and the man I recognize as Alexander sits behind it. Large windows let in dim light behind him. Now that I know who he's related to, the resemblance is striking. It also makes my chest hurt with the ache of missing Dio.

Alexander immediately notes my cane as he walks around the desk and holds his hand out to me. As I shake it, he asks, "Get into another fist fight?"

Fem glances quickly at me.

"Not this time," I say as mildly as I can, careful to keep my face as pleasant as possible. "I just got into an accident. Thankfully, I have been healing well."

"Glad to hear that," he says as he nods to Fem, and then he returns to sit behind his desk.

I sit at the edge of one of the chairs as Fem settles onto the other. I'm glad for the break from standing. My legs were beginning to feel wobbly.

As Alexander sits down and waits for us to settle ourselves, he says, "What can I do for you?"

"It's about Dio," I say, and his expression darkens.

"Is he related to the *accident* you got into?" he asks, the darkness fills his voice now as well.

"No," I say quickly. I choke down sudden anger at the question and carefully mask my expression. It won't do for me to anger Dio's brother, especially not when I'm asking for his help. Bracing myself for his reaction, I say, "I'm in love with your brother."

His eyes widen, and he chews on a thumbnail as he considers me silently.

Before he can respond, I say, "I found out that you had him committed to a mental hospital. I wanted to discuss why. I'm sure he wasn't using again."

He just shakes his head, looking tired. "You clearly don't know him that well," he says. "Dio has had a problem with drugs for most of his life. In fact, the last time I talked to him, when he asked me to represent you, he seemed as though he was teetering on the edge of falling back into that addiction."

I grit my teeth. I don't know how close Dio is with his brother, but Alexander seems like a bastard.

His voice is overly calm and kind as he says, "When I heard the news that he'd slipped again, it was an easy decision to sign the papers to help get him support. Unfortunately, when he arrived at the facility, there was an incident. He has been accused of killing multiple people. It was just a matter of time, really. The psychiatric hospital really is the best place for him."

Malam had told me that Dio's commitment had been changed to a permanent hold, but didn't tell me why. Based on my dream, I suspected that he might have injured some guards, but I didn't know until now that he'd been accused of murder. My jaw is so tight that a muscle begins to spasm. I'll have to talk with Malam later.

I'm angry that Alexander was willing to make this decision to sign the papers without even visiting Dio to see if he was actually struggling. However, getting into an argument with a man who is on the side of the angels, and the relative of the man I love, doesn't seem wise.

I belatedly realize that Fem is speaking and focus back on the conversation to hear him say tightly, "Accused? Was it proven that he killed someone?"

"There is a video of him lashing out, I think throwing punches, as he was led to the center. A few guards and a healer collapsed and were later pronounced dead. He hasn't been to trial yet because the date continues to be delayed. However, it is unlikely that he will be found innocent," Alexander says. He sounds tired and, in an oddly familiar movement, he runs his hand through his hair.

I bite my lip, looking away and blinking at the tears that suddenly prick at my eyes.

Whether Dio hit them or, as I suspect based on my dream,

lost control of his magic, I'm not surprised that those men ended up dead, and I'm just thankful the Killswitch rune wasn't activated.

"Also, if you hoped I might be able to help him, unfortunately, it would be a conflict of interest for me to represent him," Alexander says, speaking to me this time.

I sit silently for a few moments, willing myself to come up with another solution. Finally, I say, "Do you know another lawyer who could help?"

"I can give you some names, but until the date for his trial is scheduled, there isn't much that can be done. I'm so sorry, Chaosta," he says with a kindness that makes me grind my teeth. "I'm glad that Dio has someone who loves him. I understand that you'd like to save him, but he is a danger to those around him. I'm just glad he never hurt you. All I can wish for him is that he was able to experience that love before he got himself into this situation."

"He knew," I say, my voice breaking slightly. Even as I say it though, I wonder if he did. I certainly didn't tell him I loved him. I remember waking up beside him, reaching out to brush the hair out of his eyes before the instincts drove me from the apartment.

Suddenly, I can't hold back the weak cough as my chest constricts.

Alexander's face falls, "Are you sure you're alright?" He worriedly glances at Roxanna, who's standing behind us.

"I'm fine," I say tightly. Suddenly feeling as though the ground might collapse from beneath me, I gulp in a quick, shallow breath, steadying myself. I know I can't come apart here, not with the gauntlet of angels facing me outside of this door.

Instead, I rise, pushing myself up with heavy reliance on the cane. I step forward, holding out my hand to him. "Thank you so much for meeting with us, and again, thank you for your help in getting the charges against me dropped."

"Of course," he says as he stands and shakes my hand. "If anything should come up in the future where you need legal representation, please let me know." His face is still full of concern, but he doesn't try to stop us as Fem, and I leave his office.

I can't focus as we bid Roxana farewell and thank her for her help. Later, I only vaguely remember Fem getting the names of a few lawyers from her.

I'm thankful for Fem as he accompanies me back to the carriage. His shoulders are tight, his face drawn as he glances frequently at me.

When we arrive outside the doors of the demon stronghold, Fem helps me out of the carriage but doesn't follow me through the doors. I limp slowly to the lift and then past Chiron and Malam, who are waiting on the upper level, without speaking.

"I'll go talk to Fem," I hear Malam say quietly from behind me.

When I get back to my bed, I curl up in a ball and try to figure out a plan to get Dio out. I can hear Malam and Chiron's voices in the background as they talk quietly to each other in their language. At this moment, I'm glad not to know what they're saying.

FRAGILE LIKE A BOMB

Something is irrevocably different when I wake up the next morning. The map in my head, which was willing to listen to Chiron. Willing to wait, rest, and heal is now pushing me to get stronger, faster. It's a cruel master, and I haven't been able to rest until, exhausted, I fall into my bed in the evening.

I've picked my sword back up, despite Malam and Chiron attempting to keep it from me. I have been practicing until my hands bleed, until my lungs ache. At times, I can't stop coughing.

Chiron stays close, observing me, until one day I'm bent over, struggling to breathe as I cough up blood. "I'm not fucking doing this anymore. I didn't spend the last three months putting you back together just so you could tear yourself apart," he shouts, his chest heaving. I feel the sting of his glare against my skin, the physical pain of his combat magic, driven to the surface by strong emotions. Then he spins and strides out of the clearing.

I flinch, and tears build in my eyes. He's not wrong, but I can't afford to remain in bed. I need to build my strength and not only to rescue Dio. Something big is coming. I can feel it hanging over me, an amorphous threat that seems poised to strike.

Thankfully, my skill with the sword comes back fairly quickly. My strength is another matter.

On this day, Malam finds me as I'm practicing the sword-fighting forms. I'm focused on my footwork as always. My hands are wrapped because I haven't been able to get the skin to heal quickly enough. My pink hair is tangled around my shoulders, some of it stuck to my face with sweat.

I'm taking a break, leaning over with my hands resting on my knees to keep myself upright. My throat feels raw from gasping for breath.

At least that's some improvement, I think to myself.

I look up as I start to get my breath back and see that he's watching me closely. He opens his mouth and then shuts it as he pinches his nose between thumb and forefinger. Then he takes a breath as though readying himself to speak.

"Don't," I say before he can utter a word. I straighten and walk past him, sheathing my sword. "Don't even try to stop me. There's no other way, so I'll do it myself."

As he follows me he says, "So what, you're going to go storming into a psychiatric hospital, cut down all the healers with breaks to get your breath back? Then what? Dio is in no state to walk out of there on his own. Are you planning to fucking carry him?" His voice is full of anger, but the words are shaky.

I know he's scared for me, but it still stings. It's hard enough to believe in my ability to accomplish this. I can't take someone else doubting me right now.

I turn to face him suddenly, and he doesn't expect it, so he almost walks into me. I don't step back, so we stand nearly touching as I glare up at him, "Did you know why Dio's commitment was changed to a permanent hold?"

A confused expression crosses his face. "He killed some people. Did I not tell you?"

For a moment, I just stare, unable to find words. Finally, I say, "No, you didn't."

He presses his lips together. "I'm sorry, I guess I forgot," he finally says.

"You're telling me that you forgot to tell me that the man I'm in love with is accused of killing multiple people?"

Malam shrugs. "They're just humans. By the time this is done, we'll all have far more blood on our hands."

My jaw drops slightly as I stare at him. Despite their deaths not impacting me personally, it somehow feels important. However, I'm sure I am not the one to try to convince a demon of the importance of human lives. Instead, I return to firm ground as I say, "If you have any suggestions about how I should be preparing to rescue him, I'll be happy to hear them. Until then, you can keep your opinions about how likely I am to fail to yourself." My voice is quiet but infused with violence.

I spin on my heel and stride towards the room they've moved me into now that I don't need round-the-clock medical care.

Malam continues to follow me, a little way back, as he mutters something in his language that sounds like a prayer.

I stop before opening the door to my room and turn to face him. "What is it?" I snap.

He takes a deep breath and then says, "I do have an idea."

I attempt to compose myself. "What's your idea?"

"It hinges on getting Chiron to help. If he agrees, I could transport you in. When we get there, I can summon Chiron. Then, if you can convince Dio go with us, Chiron could transport him back here while I take you," he says.

Even as he says it, a route on the map in my head fills in. I can't help myself as I step forward and wrap my arms around him, tears filling my eyes.

Now breathless for a very different reason, I mumble, "Thank you, Malam."

He awkwardly pats the back of my shoulder and then steps back, putting some space between us. "Don't thank me yet," he says. "We still need to convince Chiron."

"I'll talk with him," I say confidently, and Malam relaxes. I nearly laugh at the relief in his face that he won't be the one to have that conversation.

I turn and walk toward Chiron's room. "You coming?" I ask when I don't hear him following me.

"Now?" he asks.

"Yes," I say firmly and hear him sigh. Then he begins to follow.

Hours have passed, it's later in the evening, and I'm still dressed in the clothing I was wearing earlier. My hair is still a mess. After talking through the plan with Malam and Chiron, we believe my appearance will be perfect for the path we are taking.

Chiron was not easy to convince. However, when I firmly told him that I would be getting Dio out either way, and the alternative included me marching in the front door and fighting my way to him, Chiron finally relented. Whether to save the healers from me or me from myself, I couldn't tell.

We're gathered now in one of the small clearings as we prepare to leave for the center. Malam is dressed as a healer, in clothes he previously stole when he was here to rescue me. Seeing him wearing them now brings me back to standing on my bed, ready to flee when he was there to bring me home.

Chiron is dressed all in black, including a long-sleeved shirt and tailored pants. He has a cowl hood pulled up, concealing most of his face. There is a sword strapped to his back. It's mine.

If it comes to it, he'll use combat magic as he's more proficient in its use.

Malam's expression is grim, Chiron's is more akin to irritation, but I ignore them. If this goes the way we have planned, it won't take long. I'll have plenty of time later to seek their forgiveness.

"Ready?" Malam growls at me, a grimace on his face.

I nod, and he steps forward and grasps my upper arm. As his fingers close around it we are surrounded by shadow and the sounds of wingbeats.

When my vision clears, we're standing in a street, surrounded by darkness. My heart pounds in my ears, and I'm shaking, but I don't do anything to settle myself as Malam drags me forward. He directs me through the familiar front door and then past the front desk with a healer sitting at it. I allow my heart to beat and my body to tremble. Looking anxious will help with my disguise.

While we were back at the stronghold finalizing our plans, I finally convinced them that I can use the magic of the wings to blend in with the angels. I completed that ritual before I left. However, the woman sitting behind the desk is just a human.

As we pass, I catch movement at the corner of my vision, but I stick with the plan and allow Malam to continue to pull me along. She begins to say something, but Malam doesn't hesitate as he pulls a random, folded-up piece of paper out of his pocket. Without looking at her, he says simply, "Outside orders," in a confident tone as he continues to drag me toward a closed door.

"Wai-" she starts to say, which is cut off as Malam runs into the still-closed, and apparently locked door. The crashing of my heart increases, and I hear a low growl from Malam.

"Sorry, I tried to warn you. There has been an increase in security after a recent incident. We have limited access, and I need to check you both in and verify your identification," she says from her position behind us. Her tone is apologetic.

My heart pounds in my throat. We certainly don't have identification or actual orders to be here.

Malam remains where he is for a moment, his back still to the healer. With wooden movements that are somehow still gentle, he pulls me in front of him and, pressing me against the door, growls under his breath, "Stay." Then he turns toward the desk, leaving me trembling slightly.

As I peer out through my tangled hair, I see the healer's face go white as Malam stalks toward her. "Please," she says as she reaches under the desk for something.

I expect her to pull out a weapon, and the fingers of my left hand curl into a fist, wishing for a sword I don't yet have. I realize suddenly how vulnerable I am without my sword, especially right now as pain and weakness twist through me.

Malam, however, is fully capable of violence. Closing the distance, just as a loud sound begins to blare overhead, he grabs the top of her head and slams her face into the desk. I hear a crunch, and my stomach twists as her body slumps to the ground.

I close my eyes, fighting the bile in my throat, as Malam begins to search the space around her, presumably for a key of some sort. After a few moments, he swears in his language. "Come here Chaosta," he says tightly.

I crack my eyes open, focused on the floor as I walk across the room. As I get to him, he grabs my arm, his movements tight.

"We probably could have just knocked her out rather than killing her," I mumble.

I'm not sure if he doesn't hear me, or simply ignores me, but without responding, he holds a hand out toward the desk and twists his fingers slightly. His chest stops moving for a moment and then resumes in panted, harsh breaths as fire blooms on the desk and the healer's body. An acrid scent, not related to the fire, fills my senses.

Malam takes a step to the side, around the desk, pulling me behind him. With a slight squeeze, he releases my arm just as another tone begins to blare overhead, clashing with the first. I resist the urge to cover my ears with my hands.

Then water begins to pour from the ceiling. I can just see the previously locked door swing open from my place, mostly behind Malam. He moves forward and, without prompting, I follow close behind. The water quickly soaks through my clothing. I can barely see through the curtain of hair that now sticks to my face. However, following him feels nearly innate.

As we clear the doorway, I hear footsteps and stop moving just as Malam does. All I can see from my position is the sudden tension in the set of his shoulders. Again, his breath pauses and then increases in pants briefly as I hear two loud thumps. Another wave of that acrid smell reaches me. He moves again. As I follow, I'm forced to step over the bodies of two guards who are now slumped in the hallway.

Malam directs us to the right, down a hallway. I remain close to him as I continue to struggle not to vomit. I concentrate on breathing through my nose and trying to settle myself.

He turns us down another hallway and then tucks us into a dark alcove. He presses me against the back wall and says, just loudly enough for me to hear over the continued alarms, "Stay there." Then he steps back to put a yard or so between us. "Chiron," he says quietly, and the other demon instantly materializes between us in a swirl of shadow.

He freezes for a moment, facing Malam, his shoulders tense as water from the ceiling rains down over his large form.

"Slight complication," Malam growls. "Apparently, they've increased security."

"Slight?" Chiron snarls as he turns to me, unbuckles my sword from his back, and hands it to me. His expression is irritated, sodden curls hanging in his eyes, but as he sees me, he pauses. There is worry on his face, warring with the irritation.

Malam must pick up on Chiron's concern because he moves so he can look at me. When I meet his eyes, Malam says, "We can try this without you if you aren't up for it?"

I shake my head as I strap the sword to my back, already feeling better as its familiar weight settles against me. I won't risk Dio's rescue to demons whom I know he doesn't fully trust or even like.

I step past the two of them and manage to choke out, "We'll be quick."

Malam will be staying in this alcove while Chiron and I find Dio. As I walk into the hallway, I can only barely hear them say something to each other. Then Chiron falls into step behind me, and I let out a breath.

We had a basic idea of where Dio was being kept when we planned this. Now that we're here, the map in my mind has taken over despite the din of the alarms and the water raining down.

I walk as confidently as I can down a couple of hallways. I move steadily, peering around corners, careful not to be seen. Chiron, still behind me, is doing something with magic that's adding shadows to these otherwise brightly lit hallways. Whether or not it will cover our movement, it's certainly making this space more comfortable for me. It mutes the brightness that seems to try to crawl beneath my eyelids.

Eventually, we reach the correct door, and I freeze when I see it's cracked open. As we get closer, I hear voices inside. "We'll need to knock him out fully if we have any hope of getting him out of here for the fire procedure," says one loud voice. They're nearly shouting over the din of the alarms and the heavy flood of water falling from the ceiling.

Before I can freeze up, I push the door open and walk through it. There are three healers surrounding Dio, where he lies on the ground in this small, fully padded room. One has a syringe in their hand and is crouched over him, bringing the needle to his neck. The other two restrain him, as though he's not already lying completely still.

A flash fire burns through my veins, and a predatory feeling takes over. I stalk forward, already unsheathing my sword. I'm vaguely aware of Chiron pulling the door closed behind us as I slice through the neck of the healer with the needle. I'm blind with anger, but it doesn't seem to matter. I hear screams that are quickly cut off, and by the time I can see again, there are three bloody bodies lying fanned out around Dio.

The water is already beginning to spread the blood across the floor as I start to wipe my sword clean.

Chiron, in a choked voice from behind me, says, "Let me."

I hand the sword back to him without turning and lower myself to a crouch next to Dio. He is struggling weakly against the straitjacket. I vaguely note the blood from one of the healers that is splashed across his body.

I carefully brush his, now long, soaked hair out of his eyes as I say, "Easy, Dio."

He stills and says, "Chaosta?" His voice trips over my name. He's quiet enough that I have to strain to hear him over the alarms. It looks like he's having trouble focusing on me.

I allow the predatory feeling to continue to beat through me because the alternative would be falling apart. I know I can't do that right now. My heart thrashes in my chest, and the rune on Dio's chest plays in my mind as though it's burnt into the back of my eyelids. This is fragile, and I know it. I'm terrified that all of this will be too much for him and he'll lose control of his magic.

Calmly, quietly, I say, "You're ok. We've come to get you out."

Over the top of my words, he slurs, "I really didn't think they'd ever kill me. I hoped you weren't dead, but if that's what it took for me to see you, I guess that's ok."

My chest tightens, my breath freezing in my throat as tears build in my eyes. The sound of the water spraying from the ceiling is the only thing I can hear other than the pounding of my heart in my ears. The man I love is so close and yet still so far. I close my eyes for a minute, trying to center myself as emotions threaten to tear me apart.

Finally, I grapple the emotions back under control. "We're both alive, Dio," I say, "Can you trust me for a few minutes?"

He blinks, staring at me, seeming confused.

I flinch as I note the water hitting his face and lean over him to shield him from it.

He tenses as he says, "That can't be. Is this a dream?"

We're running out of time, and this isn't the place to try to help him understand, not in his current state. Instead, my chest tight with unshed tears, I say, "Yes, Dio, I'm here in a dream. Can you stay with me for a little?"

He nods, his body relaxing.

I look away before I can lose my grasp of the strength that still fills me. I gesture to Chiron to join me beside Dio. I make the mistake of glancing at the demon's face as he crouches opposite me and almost lose control as I see the sorrow on his normally harsh face.

I quickly look back at Dio, focusing on his jawline and the beard that now covers it as I say, "You remember Chiron, right?"

Dio doesn't look at the demon but he nods.

"He's going to transport you somewhere safe where we can spend some time together, ok?"

Chiron holds something out to me, and without looking at him, I take the tablet. We decided it was too much of a risk for Chiron to try to de-materialize with Dio when he's in this state. I'm used to the feeling of being dissolved and rebuilt by the demon's shadow magic, but they've never brought Dio anywhere. I wanted to avoid giving him anything, but Chiron convinced me that it would be the safest option.

"I need you to take this for me, ok, Dio?" I say and finally hear my voice break, my control beginning to fray.

He lets me put it in his mouth. He chews and then his eyes shut and his breathing evens out.

Before I say anything else, Chiron lifts him into a sitting position and wraps his arms around Dio's torso. Then shadows surround them, and they're gone. Suddenly alone, still crouching among the bodies, I see my sword, now clean, lying on the floor beside me and scoop it up, sheathing it.

In my mind, I can still see Chiron's eyes looking at me as he disappeared, and the memory of the pain in them nearly snaps my control. I choke back a sob and rise to my feet. My knees shake, but I force them to carry me as I walk back to Malam.

My sword doesn't remain sheathed for long.

As I step out of the room, I immediately hear footsteps. Glancing down the hallway, I determine they're between Malam and me. I move down the hallway, toward the sound of movement, and draw my sword.

A voice yells, "Don't just go rushing ahead, didn't you see what happened to Pen and Rissa?"

Even as I hear the last word, two more guards round the corner. For a moment, they freeze, staring at me through the water that still pours from the ceiling. Then they each pull a weapon from their hip. These aren't swords. Blocky, square, handheld weapons of some sort are pointed at me. Thankfully, the instincts guide me, and I know somehow that they're projectile-based. That same instinct also tells me that I certainly don't want to get hit.

"Drop the sword!" a female guard yells.

"Who the fuck is that?" the other guard says more quietly to his companion.

My fingers tighten around the hilt in my hand as I take a step forward.

"I mean it, DROP THE SWORD," she barks.

I pull numbness around me like a blanket, and the sound from the alarms fades into the background. Reaching out on a thread of consciousness, I ask for aid from the deity responsible for these instincts.

I take another step forward.

Even as a pop rings out, I subconsciously twist sideways without taking my eyes from the guards. The small projectile flies harmlessly past me. Through the numbness, I'm only just aware of a percussive rapping sound. The projectile seems to still be attached to the weapon somehow.

The eyes of the guard who discharged her weapon are wide.

I stride forward, the muscles in my abdomen already tight and sore.

"SHOOT NOW, you idiot," she barks at the other guard.

He, however, seems to be completely frozen. He stares at me without moving as I close the distance.

The instincts guide me to tuck and roll towards them as the first guard reaches for the second's weapon. The breath freezes in my lungs as pain from my injury cuts through me, trying to steal my focus. The loud pop echoes in the hallway, and I'm vaguely aware of the projectile passing over my head as the percussive raps attempt yet again to be perceived over my numbness.

I sweep the legs of the second, less competent guard, flinching at the pain from the movement. His body hits the ground hard, and I hear the satisfying sound of the breath being driven from his lungs.

In the absence of the predatory feeling that burned through me when I saw the guards around Dio, I suddenly realize that I don't want to hurt or kill these people.

I shakily rise to my feet, and the competent guard takes a step back, staring at the sword in my hand with a white face. I close the distance and, in a quick movement, knock her out with the pommel. She crumples as the other guard scrambles to his feet with a whimper.

"Ple—" he begins to beg. It's cut off as I plant my knee in his gut. I grit my teeth, struggling to retain the remains of my focus as the pain increases. The air wheezes out of him again as he falls to his knees. Then I knock him out as well.

I keep my sword out, moving as quickly as I'm capable of at the moment, as I return to the alcove where Malam is waiting.

When he sees me, his shoulders tighten. I realize the water hasn't completely washed the healers' blood off me as he says hoarsely, "Who's blood?"

"Healers, they were hurting him," I manage before sobs begin to break me apart.

Malam steps forward quickly, wraps his arms around me, and then we're surrounded in the comfort of shadow and wingbeats as he brings us home.

THE PHOENIX BURNS

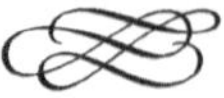

My heart pounds, beating so hard in my chest that it feels like the delicate, not-yet-fully-healed muscles across my sternum might burst. I push myself rapidly through the final two sword-fighting practice forms before my knees give out and I fall to the ground. I lean forward on my fists, my sword still grasped in my left hand. I try to focus on the cool earth beneath my knees and hands.

Instead, the only thing I can focus on is the closed door across the room.

I can see it now through the tangled curtain of hair that hangs in front of my face. Even as black spots cross my vision from still-weak lungs, I can't tear my eyes away.

After a few more gasped breaths, I sink back to sit on my heels. My vision slowly clears, and I look up at the ceiling above me. The bright light of day filters in, creating halos around the trunks of the trees where they rise through the ceiling into the open air above. I close my eyes, my heart slowly steadying.

Feeling the strength of the sun on my face is still a rare gift.

It's not the sun that is drawing me like a beacon right now, though. It's that closed door, or rather, it's the man behind it. I heave in another breath, my jaw tight as I swear quietly in a shaking voice.

A few days have passed since we got back to the stronghold with Dio. Since then, he has been kept sedated. He's had a fever, and even the sedation hasn't been able to keep the dreams entirely at bay. In the brief moments I've been able to visit him, seeing him struggle in his sleep is a special kind of torture. Seeing him like that, I feel the weight of every unsaid word between us. The pain somehow echoing in the space and time since we last saw each other.

While I'd love to say that I have been strong enough to continue to be there for him, I can't. Instead, Chiron has been by his side constantly, and I have been pushing myself to get physically stronger. Well, to get stronger and to try to distract myself from the emotional agony.

It's not as though the distraction is working, I think to myself as I realize I'm staring yet again at the closed door.

Earlier today, Malam found me in my room and shared that my description has been given to the government in association with the attack on the mental hospital. I still don't regret knocking those guards unconscious rather than killing them, but it does mean there were witnesses who shared my description. Unfortunately, the three employees Malam killed, the three employees I killed, and the two whom I "assaulted" mean that the government is rather actively hunting me. Well, me and Dio.

Since Dio is supposedly on the run with me, Malam notified the boys that they would likely have government officials showing up at their door. I was worried about the disruption, but Malam shared that he'd put a ward on the mansion when he first began working with the coven. That ward will apparently keep angels, or those aligned with them, out of the apartment without an explicit invitation. However, Chiron canceled his sessions with the coven for the next fortnight just to be safe.

This morning, I've been pushing so hard that I have already vomited once. At least this time there wasn't any blood in it. I took that as a sign to keep pushing. Hence, my current state.

I'm pushing myself to get quicker and quicker with the forms, and I have been through them twice just now. Perhaps it was a bit further than I should have pushed, but I needed something, anything to distract me from the fear of what will happen when we wake up Dio.

I finally force myself to turn away from the door. I push myself up on wobbly hands and knees and slowly rise, using my sword as a sort of cane, a technique that would likely be frowned upon. Thankfully, Demonforged steel is strong enough that it serves this purpose without issue.

Standing on wobbly legs, I clean the blade and sheath it before walking shakily to my room. Someone, likely Malam, left a tray of food on the table next to my bed. After stripping out of my clothing, I sit down and force myself to eat before I close my eyes. When I lie down, I fall asleep almost immediately.

~

I dream a familiar dream, but with a different context. It has been a long time since I last saw this image, and as it plays in front of me, I wish I had some power to leave this place. I'd like to remove myself from this dream and the pain that I'm already aware it's going to leave me with.

In the dream, Malam stands with his back to me, his broad shoulders shaking. The shadowy wings that I'm so familiar with are nearly corporeal here, and they beat slowly as though pain powers them.

The scene plays out just as I remember from last time as he turns to me. His eyes are bloodshot and dark, and his face is wet with tears, his arms full of the body of a tall young woman. This time, I recognize her as Lily.

She hangs limply, her only movement coming from him. Her light, curly hair is sodden with blood that leaks from an open wound at the center of her face.

Then I see the dagger flying towards her as I fail to defend her.

This time, instead of Malam speaking, Lily opens her eyes, looks right at me, and gasps, "Don't forget me."

I fall to my knees, and even as everything goes black, I scream out at the pain from her loss.

Whatever sends me these dreams doesn't seem to feel that I've had enough yet, and it pulls me on to the next, another familiar dream.

There are roses, the petals dripping with blood. The sky is still white, and the sadness in me is a memorable and almost palpable pain in my head. I see the small, familiar figure moving, but this time I don't run to it, instead moving slowly and reluctantly, my feet leading me to him without conscious intent.

When the little boy turns to me, I'm greeted with the familiar sight of his eyes dripping with blood. This time, only one of his arms and one leg are missing, but there is still a hole in his chest that frames several of the roses.

In this version of the dream, his blank eyes immediately recognize me and examine me carefully. As those blood-covered, white orbs inspect me, he nods slightly, and then from his bloody lips a familiar, deep, powerful, masculine sound emerges.

"I see that my creation has developed a steel backbone," the incongruous voice says. "Yet we, all of us, are still too far from balance. The brightness is like a blight on this land."

He steps forward, closer to me, and I flinch as the copper tang of blood floods my senses even in the dream. Seeming not to notice my discomfort, he reaches towards the hole in his chest and grasps something hanging just in front of it. Something I didn't notice because of the violent carnage surrounding it. He holds his bloody hand out to me and, lying in the middle of his palm, is a small, silver pendant on a chain.

I glance back up at his eyes.

"You will need that steel in your spine in the coming days, little one. The additional trials you face may seem senseless at the outset, but there remains an impetus, whether you can understand it at the time or not," the ancient voice says.

I note the oddity of a small boy calling me little one.

"You tread a razor's edge between doing what is right and selfishness. I offer a boon, or perhaps a test. There will be a singular opportunity to do what is needed for balance or to answer the call of a burning heart. Choose well," the mental voice grates out just as the vision of the boy turns to a flock of ravens that fly directly at my face.

~

I wake, soaked in sweat. The sheets are tangled around my legs as though they seek to tie me to the bed. Even now that I'm awake, my senses are filled with the scent of copper. I lay for a few minutes getting my breath back and banishing the emotional pain from Lily's loss yet again.

After some moments pass, I pull myself firmly to the present and push myself off the bed. As I stand, I feel the familiar and unwelcome sensation of my consciousness being commandeered by those instincts that have been a part of me since my creation. In some ways, it feels like I'm still dreaming, going through pre-determined motions with no chance of resisting.

I go to the communal showers and get myself cleaned up and dressed in some of my own clothes for the first time since my injury. I even brush my hair, working the knots carefully out.

Why those instincts care, I'm not sure, but my thoughts on the subject don't matter at this moment.

My palms begin to sweat as I strap my sword to my back. I can hope that it is incidental, and I can't say I'm disappointed to be armed. It is the potential need to wield a sword, especially in my current state, that makes my heart pound a little too fast.

As though watching my own life from behind a screen, my feet tread a path to the lift. The demon guards watch me, their expressions a little strange as I press the button, but neither of them attempts to stop me. After I enter the lift, I watch my hand press the button for the roof, one floor up from the stronghold. When the doors open, I step out into the blue expanse at the top of this tower of a building.

Here I find Malam. He is in a clearing in the middle of the forest of trees, practicing his own sword work. The instincts momentarily pause in their pursuit, and my actions are my own again as I watch quietly from the edge of the shadows.

He has his shirt off, the inscribed runes standing out against olive skin, as he flows through movements I know by heart. I realize that I've never seen him wield a sword before, as an awareness hits me that the steps, branded on my consciousness, were put there by him.

Without pausing his movements, he says, "Are you going to join me, or just watch?"

I step forward out of the shadows and say, "I should know better than to believe I could hide in the shadows around a demon."

He chuckles, still not pausing.

Closer, as I am now, I realize with a start that I recognize the sword he's wielding. "When I summoned you at the concert, you lent me your own sword, didn't you?" I ask.

Now he pauses his movements and looks at me. As he brushes sweaty hair off his forehead and out of his eyes, he says, "You deserve nothing less." He bows his head slightly to me.

Guilt hits me over what I'm going to ask him next, despite not yet knowing the words that are going to leave my mouth. Then I hear myself ask, "May I ask where Lily's body is?" My voice is calm even as my heart begins to pound in my chest.

Malam's face instantly changes to a cold mask. "Her body is in the central city mausoleum," he says, and then his voice cracks as he says, "per her wishes."

"I'm so sorry, Malam," I say tightly as tears prick at the back of my eyes.

He doesn't respond. Instead, he turns away from me and returns to his sword work. It's a tactic I'm familiar with.

Then the instincts take over again, and my feet direct me back to the lift where I press the button for the bottom floor. While I wait, I go through the steps to hide myself among the angels.

Eventually, I arrive in the main entry hall and leave through the front doors. It's odd to be on the street calling a carriage after all this time. Even more odd, as I give the carriage driver an address that my memory has no connection to. At this point, if this were not a familiar feeling, I believe I would be terrified. As it is, I sit back against the seat of the carriage and simply wait.

Eventually, the carriage comes to a stop, and I step out into a version of hell.

The slums are somehow both familiar and not. The windows of the buildings surrounding me are covered in some flat black material, and the streets are clogged with detritus. The carriage driver quickly drives off, likely not wanting to risk waiting for the unlikely chance that someone here might be able to afford a ride.

I make my way down the street, feeling eyes on my back. However, the gaze of the people surrounding me seems to hit my sword and bounce off, and thankfully, no one approaches. I soon arrive at a small brown door and knock with a confidence that I do not feel. I wait for a moment before I hear the sound of a loud, masculine voice yelling from inside the space.

Those instincts still driving me, I push open the door into a small apartment. The loud voice leads me through another door, and then I see him. A large, bald man wearing only a short-sleeved linen shirt and dirty trousers is facing away from me. Sweat stains his shirt, and this room smells and looks as though it hasn't been cleaned in a long while.

My eyes catch on the small figure I can just make out on the other side of him. Despite not being able to see him well, I immediately recognize him as the boy who had a part in my creation.

The fingers on my left hand twitch, and I draw my sword. However, I don't seek to leave the little boy without a caretaker, nor do I want to traumatize him. Instead, I call out, "What's going on here?"

The large man spins toward me, but the initial surprise leaves his face as he gets a look at me. He spits and then says, "You ask what is going on here as you seek to rob me, bitch? I'm sorry to tell you, there is nothing here worth stealing." His eyes pass up and down my body, and his expression changes as he leers at me. "Lucky for me, you're a pretty one," he says as he charges at me.

I step aside out of his way, avoiding his ill-timed lunge without much effort. As he crashes past me, I trip him with a toe, hooked around his ankle. As he goes down on his knees, I kick his shoulder and knock him onto his side. I feel the muscles in my sternum pull and realize that perhaps I've overdone it. He's not light, and my body is already fatigued from sword practice earlier.

I mask a flinch and level the sword at his throat as I say, "Answer my question. What reason would you have to raise your voice to this boy?"

He barks a laugh at me and begins to move as though to rise.

With a flick of my wrist, I slice a shallow cut against one cheek before leveling the sword at his throat again. "I won't ask again," I say, my voice harsh. My arm is shaking slightly with the increased pain in my abdomen.

He claps a hand over his cheek, and his expression slowly turns from confidence toward fear. "He's as worthless as the rest of the things in this slum, and yet I feed him. I should be rewarded for that, not punished for raising my voice," he snivels.

"Perhaps it is not the boy who is worthless but the man who brought him into this world," I snarl at him. "If I EVER hear that you raised your voice or spoke unkindly to him, I will come back and see that you pay for it."

He pales, shaking and blubbering about not doing anything of the sort.

"Get out," I bark at him, removing the blade of my sword from his throat. He scrambles up and out of the room, and I turn to the little boy who is watching me with a curious light in his eyes. I expected that, perhaps, he would be scared, but he doesn't seem particularly upset.

Gesturing at my sword, I ask, "Do you happen to have a rag I could clean this with?"

He leaves the corner and walks through a small door, and I follow. I recognize this room from my first waking moments in this world. I hesitate slightly, remembering the agony I was in as I sat against the wall while Malam told me that I should leave before this boy woke.

"Will this work?" the boy asks. He's holding out a small piece of cloth.

"This is perfect, thank you." Taking it from him, I carefully clean the tip of my sword, scrubbing the blood off before sheathing it again. I flinch at even that slight movement and realize that I have certainly re-injured something.

He continues to watch me curiously, that same odd light in his eyes.

"Are you alright?" I ask.

"I'm ok, only you seem familiar somehow," he says thoughtfully.

Malam's warning echoing in my head, I say, "I don't know where I would have met you, but it is nice to make your acquaintance."

"Did you come here to save me from him?"

"Actually, while I'm happy to have been able to discourage him from further ill treatment, I'm here for a different reason. I've been led to believe that you might have something I need." Again, the words leave my lips before my mind seems to think them.

He looks even more thoughtful, but opens a drawer in a small desk, pulls out a small wooden box, and hands it to me.

When I open the box, I see a small, silver necklace not unlike a locket lying within. It is the pendant I remember from the dream with the gory version of this boy.

Removing the necklace from the box, I examine it closely. It is silver in color, and the pendant looks like a solid piece of metal with a small hole in the center, no larger than a pin could fit into. Nothing about it seems odd. While I'm no expert, there doesn't seem to be anything magical about it. "What's this for?" I ask as I glance at the boy.

He shrugs, "I'm not sure. The idea came to me in a dream, and I made it. There are working elements within, but I don't know what it might be used for."

Realizing that I don't need to know anything beyond that I am meant to have it, I clasp it around my neck. "What can I pay you for this?"

His eyes snap closed before I even finish speaking, and he pales as though he just saw a ghost.

"What just happened? Are you alright?" I ask quickly.

He shakes himself slightly as though chilled, and then, with some color slowly returning to his face, he goes to his bed and removes a wooden carving of a rose from beneath it. He hands the wooden rose to me. "Just pay my respects," he says. He stumbles over the words as though he didn't expect to say them.

Now it's my turn to go pale as I take the rose from him. For a moment, I don't know what to do, and then I say, "Thank you."

Before anything else odd can happen, the instincts pull at me, and I wish him farewell and leave.

Walking out through the rest of the apartment, I wonder if I'll see the large man, but he is nowhere to be found. I'm thankful since my hands are shaking badly and the pain is blooming through me in a way that I'm confident will soon be intolerable.

Once on the street, I hail another carriage. When the instincts force me to ask the carriage driver to take me to the central city mausoleum, I'm somehow not surprised.

This trip takes a while, and I rest, closing my eyes and leaning my head against the back of the carriage. The numbness of letting the instincts take over has calmed the swirling emotions, but I'm exhausted, and the emotional numbness doesn't do anything for the pain.

Eventually, we arrive, and I step from the carriage, only just catching myself as my knees threaten to give out. I take a breath and step forward into a large white opening that leads into a cool, shadowed, stone hallway. The room is wide and disappears in front of me with no apparent end. There are three rows of stone slabs on either side with gold plaques on their surface.

I walk deeper into this crypt until I find myself in front of a stone slab with a golden plaque that says, *The love of my life's final resting place. Rest well, Lilith.*

Tears threaten to spill from my eyes as I read Malam's words. I rest my forehead against the cool stone, fortifying myself for whatever action I'm here to take.

After a few moments, a few breaths, I push myself back. I'm glad when the instincts take over again. I slide my sword from its sheath and slice a shallow cut on my arm. Swearing quietly, I trace the rune for silence in the air in front of me. Then I trace another rune on the stone with my own blood. As I step back, I send energy into it and watch as the stone cracks and falls to the ground nearly silently.

Inside, there is a body wrapped in white silk. As I see her form, I can't believe how much I miss her. Emotions bubble up again, my throat thickening and threatening to limit my air. Tears begin to spill from my eyes. With little time for mourning, though, the instincts guide me to set the carved rose on the stone slab beside her body. "I haven't, and won't forget you, Lily," I say. "Also, a new friend sends his respects."

Then, still not understanding what exactly is happening, I step back and draw a few more runes to mend the stone slab and push it magically back into place.

The trip back in the carriage blurs, and I'm thankful when I find myself in front of the doors to the building the stronghold is in. As I take the lift to the level with the medical rooms, I decide that it is time to check on Dio.

Immediately, when I enter the medical room, Chiron says, "What happened?"

"What do you mean?" I ask, unable to pull my eyes away from Dio's form. There is sweat on his brow, and his jaw is tight, even though he's unconscious. I hope he's not having nightmares. Again, the sharp pain of missing him despite standing so close tries to drag me to a dark place.

"Why were you doing blood magic?" Chiron asks as he glares at the cut on my arm.

"I had an errand," I say tightly.

He doesn't push me for more of an answer, but he rises and directs me to stand near the cabinet. He digs through a drawer and then begins to clean the cut.

"When will you allow him to wake up?" I ask.

"Hmmm?"

I glare at Chiron as he continues to focus on my arm.

"This is deeper than it needed to be," he says. He drags his focus to my face, and I catch a slight flinch as he meets my eyes.

"When will he be recovered enough to wake up?" I ask again.

"His fever just broke a few hours ago. I'd like to give him one more night. If he is stable in the morning, we could try waking him up then."

I bite my lip, looking over my shoulder at Dio again. My attention is pulled to him as though there is a magnetic draw. One that I have no hope of fighting.

"I know that what Malam told you has you scared that he'll lose control, but he's stronger than you may think," Chiron says.

I drag in a breath, fighting to calm my erratically beating heart.

"Malam told me how Dio found out about your injury. Did he tell you?"

My focus is dragged back to Chiron. "He didn't," I say, and the steel sound is back in my voice.

Rather than flinching, his lips quirk into a crooked smile. "Bastard demon," he says.

I can't help but laugh.

He grows serious again and says, "Malam was in a dark place after laying Lily to rest, as you can well imagine. He was less… *tactful* than may have been appropriate. In his defense, I also don't think he had reason to believe there was a relationship between the two of you."

I nod. My palms sweat, and I drag them against the skirt I'm wearing.

"Malam told me that he blurted out that you were gravely injured or perhaps even dead in front of the band. He recalled Dio falling to his knees."

I can only imagine myself hearing that news in place of Dio, and the pain of that thought is excruciating. A lump forms in my throat, and my heart pounds, feeling as though it's full of shards of glass.

Now, Chiron does flinch at whatever expression he sees on my face. "I tell you this not to cause you more pain but to share perspective. If Dio's feelings for you are what I believe them to be, and he was able to manage the emotions and magical energy then, I suspect his control is far better than Malam assumes."

My focus is pulled to the runes branded on Chiron's arms. The raised skin is mottled, and I briefly consider how painful it was to have done. "How hard is it for you to control them?" I ask, gesturing at the runes. My voice is tight as I fight past the lump in my throat.

Chiron seems to consider how to respond for a moment before saying, "It is a constant output of energy, but it becomes a sort of habit. Strong emotions seek to interrupt that control, but after so many centuries of practice, it is like second nature. It may be different for Dio, especially with so many inscribed runes. You should ask him when he's awake."

The reassuring words from Chiron seem to cut through the fear. I heave in a breath. "Can I stay and read in here with you?" I ask.

"Of course."

I leave the room to take a quick and distracted shower and change back into the overly large linen clothes from the demons. Then I collect a few books from my room. When I get back to the medical room, I see that someone has brought me some food. I sit on the floor in the corner and, yet again, force myself to eat. Then I attempt to focus on reading under the watchful eye of Chiron.

I struggle through half a chapter, re-reading sentences over and over as I try to understand words that blur or seem to leak through cracks in my memory. Finally giving up, I close my eyes and rest my head back against the wall.

I don't remember falling asleep, but as I feel Chiron's hand on my shoulder, I realize I must have.

I groan and wrap an arm around my abdomen as I try to move and realize how stiff and sore everything is. I'm vaguely aware of Chiron scolding me as I press myself slowly to my feet to check on Dio. I begin to move toward the bed. My progress, however, is halted by an angry demon.

"You're not fucking healed enough to be sleeping on the godsdamned floor," Chiron nearly yells.

I try to sidestep him again, but he throws an arm out, halting me.

I snarl at him, and he snarls back.

After a few more moments, the two of us at an impasse, he sighs and runs a hand through his hair. Mumbling something about "Malam's influence" and "stubborn blood," he drops his arm to his side and steps out of my way.

I walk to Dio's bedside, my arm still clutching my abdomen. I relax as I see that he's sleeping as peacefully as ever.

"There, see? He is fine. Now that you've satisfied your curiosity, I selfishly need you to go get some sleep in an actual bed."

I turn and glare at him.

"What do you think Dio will do if you are in rough shape when he wakes up?" he asks more quietly.

I heave in a breath and cough tightly as the stiffness and new pain halt the intake of air. "Sorry, Chiron," I say breathlessly. Then I leave the medical room and go to my quarters. The pain keeps me awake for a few hours, but eventually exhaustion wins, and I fall asleep.

~

I'm surrounded by sound. Cheering and jeering people stand shoulder to shoulder, pressing against me. Idly, I realize there's no pain. Then I look around and realize that I'm standing at the edge of a ring, in the crowd, watching a boxing match. Dio's back is to me, and I'm cheering him on. Even as I realize this is a dream, ill ease twists in my gut. Something is wrong.

I turn around, scanning the crowd for angels. As I search for bright wings, I hear the final bell and turn just in time to see the official hold Dio's hand up in victory. His back is still to me, so I can't see the joy on his face.

That twisting feeling in my gut increases tenfold. Feeling sick with it, I turn again, scanning the crowd.

"Hey, baby," he says from behind me as he leaves the ring. I'm still distracted, searching for the threat that something tells me is approaching. Then he grabs my chin and turns my head. I still don't look away from the crowd. I'm unable to drag my eyes away from the search for a threat.

Then his lips are on mine.

I close my eyes and kiss him back, his tongue toying with the roof of my mouth.

Bile suddenly rises in my throat, and I pull back and open my eyes only to see that it's not Dio.

The man, or rather the angel, looking at me is Rex, and his face is far too near mine. "Told you I'd win again," he says with a smirk as angels suddenly surround me.

I struggle, but they restrain me, fastening manacles to my wrists. I spit at him, and he wipes his face with a sneer as he says, "You'll never escape me."

~

I wake with a cry and make it to the small attached bathroom just in time to vomit.

At least I'm confident this isn't a prophetic dream. Rex would never want to kiss me, nor would I allow it if he did. With that thought, I press myself up shakily and brush my teeth for several long minutes.

After what happened yesterday, the pain in my abdomen is much worse than it has been. I just want to go back to bed, but today is when Chiron will wake up Dio, and I won't miss it.

I pull on fresh clothes. Then I leave my room on my way to the medical wing.

DISLOCATED INTENSITY

Time seems to move oddly, both too fast and too slow, as I walk to the medical room. Either that or it's the push-pull of the way I feel about waking Dio up. Despite Chiron's words of comfort, I'm terrified that this will all be too much and he won't be able to retain control. At the same time, there is a crack, gaping through my soul, and only having his arms around me again will close it.

Then I'm at the door and out of time.

I open it and step through into the room. I feel Chiron watching me as I move to the side of Dio's bed. I clench my fingers into fists to stop my hands from shaking.

Chiron moves to stand on Dio's other side, opposite me. "I'll draw the runes to wake him up," he says as I avoid looking at him. "I'll give the two of you some space, but I'll be near. I will knock him out instantly, magically, if you tell me to."

"Thank you," I say, hearing my voice break.

"Do not doubt him. He is stronger than you know," Chiron says, and I finally look up at him and meet his eyes.

It's not worry I see when I meet his eyes, but instead a quiet confidence. A look that somehow settles me. Thusly armored, I nod at him and watch as he draws three runes on the bed. In the moments as I wait for Dio to wake, I can't help but remember Lily nursing me while I recovered from my time at the Piquory Center. Fresh pain over her loss blooms through my chest.

Then Dio's chest expands with a larger breath, and his eyelids flicker. He swallows, his throat bobbing, and I suddenly remember struggling to swallow as I was recovering.

"Dio," I say without touching him, "it's Chaosta."

His eyes open. His face is drawn, and he's staring at the ceiling as though he's scared to look at me.

"Dio, please look at me," I say.

His eyes dart to me and then close again. "Where am I?" he chokes out.

"We are both alive and safe. We're in the demon stronghold." I still don't touch him. I tighten my fingers, my nails biting into my palms. I've been starving for him, in agony without him, and I fear that the lack of contact with him now will irrevocably damage something in me. Yet, I know something of what he might be experiencing, and so I hold myself back. Giving him some time and space.

He looks around the room slowly.

I realize, as he does, what an insane place this is for him to be coming off psychiatric medication. The smoke is thick in the air as always, and the smell of incense is strong when you aren't used to it. There may not be trees here, in the medical room, but it is dark. The walls are painted black, and the lighting makes it look as though anything might emerge from the smoke at any moment.

"Malam said you were dying or might be dead," he chokes out.

"I was badly injured, but thanks to Chiron, I survived. I've been healing, and I'm alright."

Dio opens his eyes and looks at me. I can tell he's struggling to focus on me.

"You were at a hospital for a while, but they weren't caring for you well. We got you out, and you're going to be ok," I say, my voice breaking.

He tenses and closes his eyes, licking his lips, and I wonder what he's thinking. I see his fingers move slightly under the blankets. Remembering the straitjacket, I pull the blanket back to free his hand. Watching his face and moving carefully, I finally run my fingers along his arm, down over his wrist, and then twine my fingers gently with his.

He closes his hand around mine firmly, and his lips move like he's praying. At least I hope it's that and not spell work.

"Dio?" I ask, focusing on modulating my voice and not letting that panic creep in.

He turns his head slightly again to stare at me, and then he reaches towards my face. I bend toward him, closing the distance as my abdomen screams at me. He runs the pads of his fingers along my jaw, his thumb running over my lips. Then, before I realize what's happening, I'm sobbing, and he has his arms wrapped around me. I don't remember climbing onto the bed next to him, but I'm suddenly there, in his arms. He's shaking slightly against me.

Unfortunately, the movement of climbing onto the bed and my position, curled against him, makes the freshly pulled muscles in my abdomen scream with pain. I bear it for a while, but as my sobs begin to cease, I can't ignore it anymore. I try to adjust my position and can't help the whimper that escapes my lips.

Dio stiffens, and I swear quietly.

"Chaosta?" His voice is tight and sounds strained.

I stay still, stalling, as I try to figure out what to do. I breathe through the pain, trying not to upset him.

Then Chiron is at the side of the bed. "She's fine, she must just have overdone it with her sword practice," he says. Annoyance and doubt are warring in his voice.

I pray that Dio doesn't pick up on the doubt.

Those prayers are not answered as Dio presses himself up on his arms and knees. He gently half-lifts, half-drags me to lie on my back on the bed as he leans over me, carefully not putting pressure against any part of me.

"Care—" Chiron begins, but cuts off as Dio swears. At me, Chiron, or himself, I'm not sure.

My vision greys out slightly, but I can still see Dio's expression and the intensity in it as he stares down at me. He no longer seems to be having difficulty focusing on me. Instead, that familiar look of utter intensity burns across his expression.

Thankfully, in this position, the pain lets up enough that I can breathe more easily.

My vision is beginning to clear as, without looking away from me, Dio asks, "Where is she hurt?"

"I'm—" I start to say, but Dio cuts me off.

"Going to keep your mouth shut," he growls at me. His arms shake slightly, and with a curse, he sits back on his heels, still straddling my legs. He pins Chiron with a glare, and I close my eyes.

I have a moment to remember how I felt as I was recovering from the mind meds and wonder how he can be capable of any of this.

Then Chiron says, "They stabbed her in the back. It's her abdomen."

I feel Dio touch the fabric along the bottom of my shirt.

I reach up and wrap my fingers around his wrist, stopping him before he can lift it. "I'm fine," I say without opening my eyes.

He doesn't fight me. Where our skin touches, it feels warmer than it should, as though sparks connect our nerve endings. I open my eyes to see him looking at Chiron again. "Is she?"

Chiron looks at me, and I see him considering. I start to shake my head slightly, trying to convey that I don't want to worry Dio. As though that decides him, he meets Dio's eyes and says, "She overdid it yesterday. It's likely fine at this point, but I haven't checked it since."

I feel the blood leaving my face as I stare at Dio.

He closes his eyes and heaves in a breath. Then he pulls his hand gently out of my grasp and leans over me again. I feel as though I might be consumed by the intensity of his expression as he stares at me. The familiar golden specks in his eyes seem to pin me in place.

I'm barely breathing as he runs the backs of his fingers along my jaw, then his thumb along my cheekbone. He brushes a tendril of hair behind my ear. "You're going to let Chiron check your injury," he says, his voice just louder than a whisper.

I shake my head, opening my mouth to respond, but he cuts me off again.

"Either you let me check it, or Chiron will. There's no third option where you get to avoid this."

This feeling, this caring from him, transcends anything I've felt before. The beautiful intensity of him as he focuses on me as though nothing else exists, makes the breath scrape at my throat. His want for me to be all right crashes in my chest, electrifying nerve endings and pushing my heart past its normal rhythm. I momentarily lose the ability to form words.

As though he can read my thoughts, his mouth quirks up slightly. He sits back on his heels again, and without looking away from me, he says, "Chiron? You're more qualified."

Without hesitation, as though worried that one of us might change our mind, Chiron lifts me gently. He carefully extricates my legs from beneath Dio and carries me out of the room as Dio settles himself back on the bed shakily.

"Told you he'd be fine," Chiron says with a smirk in his voice as he closes the door behind us.

I swallow down the wild laughter that tries to emerge and relax in his arms.

WITCHING HOUR

Chiron swears viciously when he gets me to another medical room and takes a look at my abdomen. When he pokes and prods around the wound, I grit my teeth and the breath stalls in my lungs.

After thoroughly examining the entry wound on my back as well, his verdict is that I likely tore some of the previously injured muscles. When he pulls my shirt back down, and I go to press myself up to climb off the bed, he snarls, "Absolutely not. You're going to stay here, where we can keep an eye on you for at least the next couple of days."

"What about Dio?"

"I'll talk with him," he says. He glares at me as though daring me to challenge him.

I'm beginning to sweat from pain again, though and close my eyes and lie back. When he offers me a sedative, I accept it, glad to have a break from the discomfort.

When I wake next, the light is dimmed, and I'd guess it is late at night. There is a form sitting on the cot along the back wall, but I'm sure it isn't Chiron.

"It's Elling," says the familiar demon as he sees me staring.

I relax. "Where's Chiron?" I ask, my voice thick with sleep.

"At the mansion, teaching the coven."

"Dio?" I ask.

"He's resting, as you should be," Elling says firmly but kindly.

"What time is it?" I ask

"Early hours of the morning, I think around three," he says softly.

I pause, suddenly curious. "Chiron's still at the mansion?"

"Of course," he says. He seems surprised by the question.

Before I can pry further, he asks, "Would you like another sedative?"

"No, but some water would be nice."

"Alright, but you have to promise to lie there and not move while I'm gone, or Chiron will hang me by my entrails when he returns." There is no humor that I can read in his flat inflection.

I stare at him. Finally realizing what he's waiting for, I swallow and say, "I promise."

He rises and leaves the room.

I try to relax, but the bed is uncomfortable, and the freshly injured muscles are painful. I can't figure out if it was only pain that woke me up or something else. If it was a dream, I don't remember it.

When Elling returns, I drink the water he brings me. Then I close my eyes and drift off again.

When I slowly drag myself to waking next, I hear Chiron's voice say, "Are you alright staying with her for a bit while I go get cleaned up and get some rest?"

As I try to figure out how long I've been asleep for him to be asking Elling to watch me again, I hear Dio say, "Yeah, I can do that."

At the sound of his voice, I feel as though I can breathe again for the first time in a long while. It was different somehow when he was unconscious, as though he wasn't really *here*.

There's a long pause, and then Dio says, "It's ok, go get some rest. We'll be fine."

After another moment, I hear the door open and shut.

Quiet footsteps draw closer to the bed. "Pretending to be asleep so you can spy on me again?"

I snap my eyes open and look straight into his.

Instead of the anger I expect to be present, though they're sparkling. There is a slight smile drawing his lips up as he searches my face.

He is just as beautiful as I remember. Dark brown eyes, with those flecks of gold, threaten to steal the air from the room as he fixes me with a look of utter intensity. His hair is longer, but that, and the start of a beard, still don't hide wide cheekbones that would seem at home on a sculpture or as inspiration for art. I should know.

"I didn't want to distract Chiron," I mumble.

"That was thoughtful of you," he says. He seems to barely be breathing.

Silence hangs between us for several long minutes. I shift slightly, trying to get more comfortable. He watches closely and then, with a quiet, mumbled curse, he gently moves me to the edge of the bed and climbs up next to me. He's careful, and while the ache increases slightly with the movement, it stays manageable.

Dio arranges himself on his side, his body lying along mine. "You're supposed to be sleeping."

"These beds are uncomfortable," I groan. "I don't know how the demons ever get any rest."

Dio chuckles and shrugs a shoulder. "They're not so bad."

"I'd have thought you, of all people, would expect more comfortable accommodations," I grumble at him.

His expression darkens, and he looks away from me quickly.

"I spent too long being thankful for the sleep I was able to get, even if it was on the street or on the floor of someone's spare room. I'm no longer that picky."

A lump forms in my throat, and I reach up and brush a piece of longer hair away from his face.

He glances at me but looks away quickly. Still, in that brief moment, I feel the familiar sting. Now that I know it's emotions causing a minor loss of magical control, it feels less like a personal attack.

"Sorry," he mumbles.

"No, I am. I guess there's a lot about you I still don't know."

"I'd say something about having plenty of time to figure it out except I learned my lesson last time," he says. He fixes me with a stare that no longer stings. "No tempting fate this time."

I laugh without thinking and then whimper as the muscles on my abdomen twinge with pain.

Dio swears, looking away from me again. He runs a hand through his hair. The movement is tight, and he shakes slightly. "Do you need something for the pain?"

"No, it's fi—"

"No," he cuts me off, "it's not." He swallows. "I was so sure I'd lost you," he chokes out. "When I came to, you were there right next to me, and I couldn't quite believe it. Then I heard you whimper, and I thought my heart was going to stop."

"I really have been healing," I whisper.

"Chiron told me that you re-tore some muscles."

"Bastard demon," I mumble.

Dio glares at me, a muscle ticking in his jaw. He clearly doesn't find it funny. "I'm not going to allow you to continue to commit to your own self-destruction."

"Dio, I—" I cut myself off as he shakes his head.

He sighs and looks at the back of his hand as he makes a fist. My gaze travels there as well, and I see the scars layered over his knuckles. "You think I haven't seen it, haven't experienced it myself?" His voice is a quiet growl. "If we have any hope of this working, I need you to take better care of yourself." He stares at me.

I open my mouth to tell him that I don't have full control over my fate, but the words are trapped in my throat. I try again, and the sudden tightness feels like invisible hands attempting to strangle me. I fight back tears as I realize that whatever it is that guides me won't allow me to share this.

Dio's eyes narrow as he watches me.

Before he can say anything, though, I change course and say simply, "I promise I'll try to take better care of myself."

"Hmm, I guess I'll accept that for now," he grumbles. "I expect earnest effort and not just a half-assed 'try, ' though."

I can't help but grin at his tone. Despite learning about him sleeping in the streets, he's no less the haughty prick than I remember.

He notices the grin and glares at me. Then his attention moves to my lips, and suddenly, there is more heat than anger in his expression. After another moment passes, the air thick with something charged, he groans, "Fuck."

Then he's leaning over me, and his lips are on mine. The kiss starts out gentle. However, while he carefully avoids my abdomen, it grows into something that is anything but. It is deep and searching as though seeking to repair something that was damaged irrevocably when we were forced apart. The darkness in both of our souls seems to attempt to claw its way back to joining again.

I reach for him, pressing my hand under his shirt and against his abdomen. I brush the raised scars with my fingers, his skin hot. My touch travels up to his collarbone, and I feel his chest heaving. His tongue is pressing into my mouth, his hand around the back of my head. Pleasure dances up my spine as I submit fully to the kiss, moaning into his mouth as he takes what he wants.

After another moment, though, I gasp shakily for breath, and Dio pulls back quickly. He grumbles a curse, his eyes scanning down my body as though he can see my aching lungs through layers of cloth and flesh. Then, as though he somehow indeed confirmed for himself that I'll live, he relaxes and lies down on his back beside me. I feel his fingers brush along the inside of my arm, and he takes my hand in his.

We lay in silence for a minute as I catch my breath.

"I had all these weird dreams last night," he finally says.

"Like what?"

"Lots of odd things. I dreamed those men in the alley who were trying to mug me were angels," he says.

I close my eyes and squeeze his fingers gently as I say, "They were angels."

"Why would angels mug me?"

"They weren't trying to mug you. They were trying to disable you. Kill you, kidnap you, I don't quite know," I say. "I think they were hoping to hurt me by hurting you."

"You killed them," he says. "You killed two angels."

"They were hurting you," I say. I hear that steely sound in my voice. "I couldn't let them do that."

He's silent, his body so still that I wonder if he's breathing. I turn my head to look at him and see a thoughtful expression on his face. "I guess that might explain why my magic didn't hurt them the way it should have," he says.

I continue to watch him as he considers.

"I also dreamed that you killed some healers," he finally says as he turns his head and meets my eyes. Before I can respond, he says, "That wasn't a dream, was it?"

I shake my head, flinching slightly as I wait for him to scold me, as I wait for the condemnation to fill his face. Instead, I feel his hand on my jaw as he tilts my face toward his and then his lips are on mine. This kiss is gentle and brief. His movements are tight as he pulls away as though he's fighting himself and only barely winning.

We lay in silence for a while. Finally, I say, "I was so scared when I found out you were at Piquory. It killed me to leave you there while I recovered."

Dio's fingers tighten around my hand. "After sending you there without your consent, it was probably the least I deserved. I'm just sorry I didn't take out more of those bastards before they drugged me."

I lift his hand and gently kiss his knuckles. He meets my eyes and, at the look in them, elation fills me. He swallows and looks away, his throat bobbing, and I return our joined hands to the bed between us.

We lay silently for a while. After some time has passed, I move again, trying to find a more comfortable position. Even the slight movement aggravates the freshly injured muscles.

I manage not to whimper this time, but at the audible, sharp intake of breath, Dio tenses. He squeezes my fingers gently and then releases my hand and leaves the bed. I watch as he goes to the counter and comes back with a glass of water and a tablet.

Looking from the tablet to his face, I say, "I don't need a sedative. I just can't get comfortable."

Dio continues to stare at the wall, not looking at me, and my chest tightens. "Take it for me then?" he asks.

I sigh, accept the pill from him and swallow it, forgoing water. As he climbs back into bed and curls up alongside me, his arm resting over my hips, the sedative pulls me away from the pain.

I wake slowly, pressed against a warm, firm form. It takes only moments this time for me to realize where I am and who has their arms wrapped around me. I also realize I'm the first to wake this time as I hear Dio's even breaths. Not ready to get up just yet, I carefully curl myself tighter against his sleeping body. My abdomen twinges slightly, but the pain is far less than it was.

I feel the moment when he wakes, his whole body going tense, his back arching slightly. My heart aches as he silently struggles. I tuck my face against his abdomen and take a breath against him. He finally relaxes as his arms tighten gently around me.

Because he's Dio, he just says, "Did you sleep alright? How are you feeling?"

"Fine. The pain is less," I mumble sleepily as I continue to press my face against his chest.

"This is adorable," I hear Chiron say in a flat voice, "but you should both go get some breakfast and get out of my hair for a while."

Dio untangles his limbs and then presses himself up and slides off the bed. "Shouldn't Chaosta stay in bed longer?"

"The muscle tear is a setback, but since she's had a couple of days of bed rest, she can and should get back on her feet." I hear Chiron moving, and then he's at the bed beside me.

I rise carefully so that I'm sitting on the edge facing him.

"I won't try to keep you from your sword practice, just promise me that you'll keep the strenuous activities to a minimum," he says tightly. He glances at Dio over my shoulder as he says it.

Annoyed that he's roping Dio into this, I glance over my shoulder at him. I'm surprised to see open amusement on his face. I turn and glare at Chiron again.

I make a rude gesture at the demon and hear him grumbling quietly as Dio chuckles, and then I slide carefully off the bed and walk to the door. I hear Dio behind me, and with that reassurance, I walk out into the open expanse of green.

I take a path around the edge of the trees, walking slowly. Dio continues to follow—I can feel him at my back as though a cord of ether connects us. The energy between us feels as volatile as it ever has.

The only difference is that I'm no longer avoiding it.

The awareness of him makes what feels like flame rush through my veins. I focus on breathing evenly and pause for a moment to catch my breath.

He closes the narrow space between us, his focus entirely on me. "What's wrong?" he asks, his voice slightly breathless. His eyes scan over me, pausing on my abdomen before he looks away.

"I just wondered what you thought of the trees?" I ask, trying to buy myself a minute as I look anywhere but at him.

Dio glances in the direction of the small forest and then away. His gaze brushes past me as he does, and I feel the sting of it. I'm wondering what the strong emotions are as he says, "They're nice, kind of majestic, I guess."

I realize suddenly how strange it is to see him in the clothing the demons wear. Even more incongruous to his normal appearance, the shirt is short-sleeved, showing far more of his arms and all the inscribed runes than I'm used to.

I tear my eyes away quickly. Swallowing is difficult, and my pulse is feathered. I can feel it fluttering in my neck as though trying to take flight. I manage to heave in a breath. Then I lead him to the small kitchen.

FRACTURED AND FRAGMENTED

I press the door to my room open and step inside with Dio close behind me. We're both carrying trays of food.

As I step into the space and look around, I suddenly realize what he's going to see, and my stomach flips. The entire room is a mess. Clothes are everywhere, and my sword is hanging haphazardly from the end of my bed. Pillows and blankets are scattered across most surfaces. Worse, I have several sketches tacked to the walls, many of which are of him. I feel my cheeks light up as though they're on fire as he walks into the room.

Before he can say anything, I grit out, "Sorry, it's a mess."

When I turn to him, his eyes are passing over every inch of the room, pausing on the sketches.

"Sorry," I say again.

Instead of responding, he sets his tray down on a shelf, closes the distance, and wraps his arms snugly around me. He's shaking slightly as he holds me.

Eventually, I feel him reach up and wipe at his face. Then he takes my tray and sets it beside his before he leads me to the bed. "How did you get stabbed?" Tightly wound emotion fills his voice, and he's staring at the wall behind me.

I hesitate, trying to process the sudden topic change, suddenly not sure if he's up to the retelling of it. Realizing I can't exactly keep it from him, even if I wanted to, I say, "I was defending a friend from a couple of angels. They got past me and killed her. When I was distracted, they stabbed me in the back."

"Can I please see it?" Strong emotion spills over in his voice.

His hands are on my shirt, and this time, I allow him to remove it. He takes my shoulder, pressing me back gently while supporting me until I'm lying on the bed. He stares at my abdomen. His eyes are dark pits, and fury seems to spark in his expression."What's this from?" he asks after a moment, his voice tight. I feel him trace a line from the stab wound.

Without having to look, I know what he's asking about. "That's the poison from an Angelforged blade."

He looks into my eyes, and the potency of his rage hits me. Somehow, his eyes don't cause pain as they meet mine, and I realize how tight his control must be to regain it this quickly with such a significant amount of magic. Especially through the emotions he's clearly feeling.

Still, as though at the edge of what he can handle, he looks away. His throat bobs as he swallows. "Malam really wasn't sure if you were going to survive or not," he says. It's not a question, and I see the pain hit him as though it's a fresh wound.

"None of them were," I say, "I was in a magical coma for over two months."

Pain fractures his expression, and he swears colorfully. Then he lies down and wraps his arms around me. After a few moments, he says, "I always wanted to see this place. I didn't realize it would take something like this, or I may not have been so interested."

Laughter escapes my lips as I curl against him, and he hugs

me tighter for a moment. Silence stretches on. Finally, my heart in my throat, I whisper, "Malam told me about the Killswitch rune you have tattooed."

His arms wrap a little tighter around me, and he seems to stop breathing. "My control is better than you might think," he finally says. His voice is tight. "Still, I would have kept you away from me if I could."

I pull back until I can see his face. He reluctantly relaxes his arms enough to allow it. "That assumes I don't get any say in this," I say.

He closes his eyes, and a muscle in his jaw tics. "Did Malam share that you're in constant danger of me losing control?" he asks tightly. "Even with the Killswitch rune inscribed, a loss of control would be catastrophic to anyone around me. Just like with those people I killed on the street outside Piquory Center. A complete loss of control means my death. I avoided you for as long as I did because I didn't want to put you in danger."

"Yet again, it seems I need to remind you that I'm not exactly some innocent girl." My voice is harsher than I mean for it to be, and I flinch even as he does. "I certainly bring my own danger to this. You were attacked, badly beaten, and locked up because of me. It will hardly get better."

I can feel a flush rising in my cheeks as I control a wave of frustration. "When I said I didn't need someone to save me, I meant it. I'm just terrified of losing you."

Dio heaves in a breath. Finally, he says, "Noted." His voice is quiet. He pulls me back against his chest.

After a few minutes, he rises. I whimper quietly as he leaves the bed, and I just catch his smirk as he picks up our trays and brings them over. We eat in silence until he says, "I thought the band ate well, but that's nothing compared to this. Makes sense, I guess, with their involvement in producing food."

My eyes are caught by his hand as he tears a piece of bread. I suddenly remember him neatly cutting everything into bite-sized pieces at the mansion. Demons don't seem to believe in utensils, but Dio seems just as comfortable without. He still eats neatly, tearing the bread into small pieces and neatly scooping up dip and the ground meat that is common in the demon's cooking.

Distracted as I watch his precise movements and the muscles bunching in his forearms, I awkwardly blurt out, "Yeah, and they make my favorite bean dip." I blush as I eat another piece of bread, and when I glance up, I see him staring at my lips.

He's not eating, nor maybe breathing. He brushes his thumb against the corner of my mouth, and electricity seems to jump from his skin to mine. Heat blooms in my abdomen. Still not looking away from my face, he sucks the dollop of bean dip off his thumb.

I lick the corner of my lips where he just touched.

He closes his eyes and looks away from me with a quiet, tortured groan. The sound of a man who is at the edge of his control.

I close the distance between us, on my knees on the mattress in front of him. My tray of food crashes to the floor beside the bed. I twist my fingers into his hair and pull him into a kiss.

His mouth is hot and insistent on mine. There's another crash as his tray joins mine. He pulls my hips firmly against him and moans into my mouth. A spasm flutters deep inside me. Calloused fingers trace up each side of my ribcage.

Too soon, he ends the kiss, holding me slightly away from him. I growl at him, my body seeming to ache from the lack of contact.

"Chiron sai—"

"Fuck him," I snarl.

He curses, quietly under his breath, in Latin. Then he relaxes, and I press myself forward again. I kiss and suck along the column of his throat, and his back arches as he groans.

The energy seems to change, becoming even more charged.

His muscles tense as he presses me back again. This time, though, he does so to drag my leggings down, off my hips.

He presses his fingers against my clit, and my hips buck, pinning his arm between us.

He tangles his fingers in my hair and pulls my head back. Then he's sucking and biting the side of my neck. I gasp for air as my heart pounds in my chest. He pauses, releasing my hair.

I open my eyes to see his, searching my face. He chuckles quietly at whatever he sees there. "Look at you already coming so undone for me," he says hoarsely.

He places the hand he just had tangled in my hair against my lower back, splayed against the base of my spine. He traps me against the hard planes of his abdomen. I feel his hard cock pressed against me through the fabric of his pants and whimper. Then he presses a finger into me.

My back arches, and I moan.

"Nuh-uh, you're going to be so quiet for me," he grates out. "No need to advertise what's going on in here to all those demons. Besides, those sounds are mine, and I don't share."

I grit my teeth as he adds a finger. This time, I manage to mostly stifle the sound of a moan. Heat builds in my abdomen, and my legs begin to tremble.

He kisses along my neck, and then his teeth scrape along my jaw as he draws his fingers slowly in and out of me.

I reach for the top of his loose linen pants. He releases my back, catches my wrist, and pins it behind me, holding me flush against him again. "You're not ready for that," he says, his voice rumbling against me. He presses his fingers deeper into me and holds pressure there as I moan breathlessly.

"Please," I gasp.

"Fuck, you're gorgeous when you beg," he grates out, tightening his fingers on my wrist slightly. Then he curls his fingers inside of me, and my hips buck again, my back arching and spots floating across my vision.

"Dio, please," I whimper as quietly as I can. Then I bite my lip hard to keep silent as he adds another finger and presses his thumb to my clit.

"Mulier est hominis confusio," he groans as his thumb circles my clit and he works his fingers in me.

I can't tell if I'm unable to understand because he's speaking Latin again, or if I just can't concentrate on anything except his touch.

Then I see stars, and my release builds in me until my whole body shakes, my legs boneless. Just before my climax bursts through me, he releases my wrist and clamps his hand across my mouth, muffling the scream that tears out of me.

He chuckles as his fingers keep moving in me, prolonging the orgasm. His other hand is still covering my mouth.

"Pretty sure they heard that one," he taunts, his voice a quiet growl. He removes his fingers, and the loss of his touch makes me whimper. Then he guides me gently to sit, leaning against the wall, boneless and still panting.

He shifts away from me, and I whimper again. "Remember how we aren't greedy?" He rises and walks into the small attached bathroom. I hear the faucet and realize he's cleaning up.

I close my eyes and rest my head back against the wall while I wait for him, aftershocks of pleasure still filling me and making my limbs slack.

As though he timed it on purpose, just as he gets back into the room, there is a knock on the door. "Everything alright in there?"

"Chiron?" Dio asks quietly.

"Mmhmm," I mumble.

"Everything's fine, Chiron," Dio calls out.

"Remember what I said," Chiron calls out, irritation clear despite the closed door.

I'm slightly breathless, not only because of what Dio just did to me but also because I can see his erection clearly from where he's standing beside the bed.

"Eyes up here," Dio says.

I feel my cheeks flush as I meet his eyes.

He's grinning, but then his expression turns serious. "Are you actually alright?" he asks.

I assess for a minute before saying, "I'm sore but no more than I was before."

His shoulders relax. "Is there a place where we can get an actual shower?" he asks.

I nod, "I'll take you. Probably a good idea for me to get cleaned up, too."

A smug look flashes across his face. Then his expression tightens again as I wince, climbing off the bed. Before he can also try to play nursemaid to me, I walk to the door and open it.

The showers are a little way and are in an open room. I find the soap and other supplies I like from the shelf at the edge of the space. Then I strip, step under one of the faucets, and turn on the stream of water.

I'm partway through washing my hair when I feel hands on my arms. I jump slightly, a squeak escaping from my lips before I realize it's Dio.

His gaze is heated as he looks at me.

He's also naked, and I can't keep my eyes off him. I realize it's the first time I've actually seen him without any clothes on. I've had plenty of time to imagine where he's tattooed. I see now that they do, indeed, continue down his groin, over his corded thighs, and down his shins.

My focus catches on his dick. He's partially erect, and as I stare, the world around me goes slightly fuzzy. Feeling it was one thing, as I see it, I can't help but wonder how that might ever fit.

Then he pulls me closer to him and takes over washing my hair, pressing my forehead against his chest as he scrubs his fingers against my scalp. "The showers are public?" he asks, and his voice sounds choked.

It takes a minute for my voice to work again. "Yes, but they aren't busy. When I shower, I'm usually by myself," I finally squeak. I can feel the hard, velvet length of him pressed against my stomach, and I feel flushed.

He growls in response. After a minute, I hear him mumbling quietly to himself. I can't bring myself to care about what he's mumbling, though. Fire tears through my veins, flaming despite the water falling around us.

After a few minutes of silence, as he washes my hair, he asks, "What's this?" He traces his fingers along the silver chain to the pendant hanging around my neck. There is a note of something dangerous in his voice.

"I got it from an old friend," I mumble.

I wonder if he's going to say something more about it, but he doesn't. As he finishes rinsing my hair, he hands me the bar of soap and tells me to finish up.

As I wash my body, I'm distracted, unable to tear my eyes off him as he washes his own hair.

He's blocking me from anyone else's view, I realize, and don't know if I'm annoyed or even more turned on.

The minute I'm finished washing, he pulls me gently out from under the water and wraps a towel around me. Pointing to a bench near the exit he says, "Sit."

I hesitate for a moment, and his jaw tightens. I'm just about to tell him that I'm not his property when I realize how much pain I'm in. Instead, I settle for sitting down while glaring at him.

He either doesn't notice my expression or doesn't care, because without another word, he goes back to finish his shower.

Irritation is quickly driven from my mind, though, as I watch him. *Fuck, the man is pretty.*

The muscles along his back and shoulders flex as he finishes washing himself. With his back to me, I note the tattoos on the backs of his thighs and calves. One particularly wicked-looking brand covers the outside of his right leg, the scarring clearly apparent even from this distance. I flinch, again imagining the pain of having that done.

Eventually, he finishes his shower and wraps a towel low around his narrow hips. Then he turns and walks to me. I feel his eyes on me, but I'm too distracted to look at his face right now.

"Chaosta?" he says, and I hear that self-satisfied smirk back in his voice.

"Hmm?"

"Where can I get supplies to shave?" he asks.

I finally look up and meet his eyes. Eyes that twinkle back at me with amusement. I shake myself slightly and realize that I've never seen facial hair on a demon, nor have I ever seen them shave. "I don't think demons have a need for those things. I'm sure they'll get them for you, though," I say.

He sighs and runs a hand over the beard covering his jaw.

As a way to distract him, I say, "Let's go get something to eat since we didn't finish our last meal. We should also see if we can get some supplies to clean up that mess in my room. We can talk with Chiron about getting some shaving supplies later."

"Ok, food first then," Dio says, his eyes still on me.

I get up to leave the showers, grabbing my clothing.

"You don't have a robe or anything?" Annoyance is clear in his voice.

"No, the towel will be enough. We don't have far to go back to my room."

Dio grumbles but doesn't try to stop me as I lead us back.

TOO MANY NURSEMAIDS

I move slowly through the forms in a small clearing. My only audience are the trees around me and a few crows who watch me closely with beady eyes. I idly wonder if one of them is the crow who brought Malam when I was near death in Lily's apartment.

A drop of sweat drips off my eyelashes. I ignore it. The perspiration is more from pain than exertion at this point. My body is trying to tell me that I should be resting.

It's evening, and Chiron took Dio out to pick up shaving supplies. I decided to fill the time with some sword practice. I told myself that as long as I went slow and didn't push, I'd be fine.

After a while, I feel the energy change and realize that I'm being watched by more than just crows. I finish the last few forms in this set before I stop to catch my breath. As I look around, I see Malam leaning almost casually against a tree, his eyes focused on me.

"Want to spar?" he asks.

Surprised, but also pleased, I nod, feeling a grin split my face.

I take my place and ready myself, but he says, "Not with

that," as he gestures at my sword. He tosses me a wooden practice blade instead.

I catch it carefully with my right hand and, sheathing my sword, switch it to my left. I wonder if Chiron has spoken with Malam about my freshly injured muscles. For a moment, I consider telling him that I should probably rest and heal a bit more. However, the mental peace from sword practice is like a siren call, and I give in.

He's wearing linen pants and no shirt. His hair is trying to flop into his eyes, and I wonder if he needs a haircut even as I realize that I probably should have tied up my own.

Ah well, sometimes it is good to practice with distractions.

He takes his place across from me, and for a moment, I have a strange feeling as though I'm looking in a mirror. We begin moving through the forms, and all other thoughts are pushed from my mind as I go to that familiar, quiet, focused place.

We are unsurprisingly well-matched, and we get through an entire set without either of us getting a blow in on the other.

Panting, I step back and see that the grin on my face is mirrored on his. Beads of sweat roll down his torso, and he shakes out his sword hand. I note the movement and can't help but grin.

"Worth giving you life just for that," he says between breaths, his eyes sparkling.

My chest feels tight, my muscles sore, and I know I should rest. Instead, I ask, "Faster?"

He nods, a gleam of challenge in his eyes.

We're midway through the second set when the pain begins to cut through my focus. My lungs are also punishing me for asking for the faster set of forms. My hair is crawling into my eyes, stuck to my forehead with sweat, but I look past it, eyes trained on Malam's movements and the blade in his hand.

Our blades crash together, and I feel the familiar reverberations run up my arm and into my shoulder. My hand is numb by this point.

Then suddenly I hear something that pulls my focus. It is the slightest distraction, but we are perfectly matched, and it's enough for Malam to get through my defenses. He scores a blow on my ribs. I'm sure he pulls the blow, it will bruise, and the wind is momentarily knocked from my lungs, but I'm confident he didn't hit me with his full strength.

I lean over, coughing, eyes tearing from the pain as he steps back, no more apologetic than I would be if it had been me who struck him. As I struggle to regain my breath, I realize belatedly what I heard, and the hair raises along the back of my neck.

That acrid smell, far stronger this time, assaults my senses as a vine that was previously attached to a nearby tree wraps around Malam. Dragging him backward, it pins him by the chest and throat to the tree behind him. I hear the sound of the impact, a loud thump in the sudden silence.

My vision grays out as I attempt to stand too quickly, and I bend over, still gasping for breath. I hear footsteps and manage to lift my head, blinking to try to clear my vision. Through a fringe of hair, damp with sweat, I see Dio rapidly closing the distance as he strides toward Malam, his chest heaving.

Then Chiron is at my side, his hand on my arm. I'm vaguely aware that he's asking if I'm hurt, but I can't drag my eyes away from Dio. He's standing so close to Malam that it's as though there isn't any air between them. I can hear a quiet bass and know that he's speaking, but I can't make out the words.

Malam's expression is calm despite the fact that he's clearly fighting to breathe past the grip of the vine around his throat. Then his eyes widen slightly at something Dio says, and he struggles for a moment.

Dio's hands are in fists, but otherwise he looks deceptively calm, his breathing even. He has a hip cocked, and his shoulders are relaxed.

Then Chiron moves in front of me, blocking my view of them as he places his hands on my arms. "Look at me," he growls.

I wobble, and he steadies me as he swears. I meet his eyes, and he searches my face. "Did he hurt you?"

"I'll be…bruised," I say between tight breaths. "My fault… overdid it."

He releases me as he swears in his language. His glare pricks against my skin.

"How is she?" Dio calls out. The hair on the back of my neck stands at the sound of his voice. It's quiet and controlled, but there's violence dripping from it.

Without another word to me, Chiron joins Dio. I hear them conferring quietly as Dio glances at me. In the background, Malam glares at them both, still seeming to struggle to breathe past the vine around his throat and chest.

Then the vine drops to the ground. Dio turns and walks toward me. Malam rubs his throat. He's glaring at Chiron, who's glaring back at him.

I start to say something to Dio, but stop when he fixes me with a glare that feels as though it might rasp the skin from my bones.

He swears and closes his eyes, and then he takes my arm gently and leads me from the clearing. As we walk through the trees, we're suddenly surrounded by demons. They're completely silent, staring at Dio with slightly wide eyes. None of them tries to stop us.

When we get back to my room, Dio presses me gently to sit down on the edge of my bed. "Give me that," he says, gesturing to the wooden practice blade.

I hand it to him.

As he moves to set it on the shelf in my room, I try to find words to tell him why I was pushing myself beyond my limits again. Trying to figure out how to explain why I broke that promise to him, but the words aren't there.

He returns to me, standing close enough to touch without doing so. His expression is shuttered as though he's not quite fully there. "You promised," he says.

"I'm sorry, Dio."

He nods and then brushes sweaty tendrils of hair out of my face. The rough feeling of his callused fingers against my skin feels as though it breaks a dam, and a tear tracks down my cheek.

He notes it, his jaw tightening. "I need to go talk with the two of them. I think I have some mending to do with those relationships." He runs a hand through his hair, his expression still slightly absent. "Will you promise to stay here and get some rest, please?"

I nod, my throat too tight to speak.

"Need anything?" He asks tightly.

I shake my head.

"I'll be back soon. Just rest, please, alright?" Then he's gone, out the door, which he closes quietly behind him.

I lay on my back, staring at the ceiling as time passes. After a while, I'm feeling bored and desperate, so I get cleaned up as well as I can in the sink.

As another hour passes, though, I begin to worry about why he's not back yet. I'm just about to leave and try to find him, suddenly scared that the demons might have hurt him, when there's a knock on the door. "Come in," I call.

Chiron cracks the door open, and my heart crashes in my chest.

I push myself up to sit as I ask with a shaking voice, "Dio?"

"He's fine," Chiron says quickly. "Malam took him to the mansion to talk with the others about moving you back in there."

Relief floods through me, and I lie back again.

Chiron sits down on the bed next to me. He's facing away, his shoulders slumped. He's silent for several long minutes, and then he says, "I have some idea of how tough it is to be who you are and in love with a human. They're more delicate than we are, and their emotions are much more volatile."

He glances at me, and I feel another tear track down my cheek as I meet his eyes. Chiron grimaces slightly and then says, "You really do need to be more careful with his heart. It wasn't easy for him to break down those walls he built up over so many years in order to let you in. He needs to be able to trust you."

"Did he tell you that?" I ask, my voice shaking only a little.

Chiron looks away and sighs quietly. "No, but I guess I can sort of relate, even though he's human." Then, without moving or looking at me again, he asks, "How are you feeling?"

"Sore, but mostly I think it's just fatigue and some bruising where Malam struck me."

Chiron pats my shoulder gently. "Get some rest so that you're feeling better when he gets back." Then he rises and leaves the room.

I'm relieved to know that Dio is all right. At the same time, the agony in my chest at the pain I caused him cuts like a knife. Chiron's point is well taken, and I commit to myself that I'll work harder to take care of myself for Dio's sake, even if not for my own.

DIO'S JOURNAL - ENTRY 1

The following is an entry from one of many journals provided to me by Dio. It is shared without any of my own edits and is a direct recounting of his thoughts and feelings at the time he wrote it. I have notated this and other entries to fill in gaps and provide another voice to the narrative that I share with you, dear reader.

Annum:5615
Entry 1 - Agitatio

After what happened with Malam, I realized that I need to work on processing again and asked Chiron for a writing book. He seemed a little caught off guard, but he came through, so here I am writing in a new journal.

I don't know quite where to start. I don't remember

much about the last several months. Apparently, it was the angels who got me committed at that mental hospital. It's not as though I forgive Alexander for his part in it though. He's too much of a bastard and there's too much bad blood there for me to believe he didn't enjoy signing those papers.

There are random things I can remember from my time there, but I just can't tell which were real and which were dreams. I do remember, before I got committed, the agony of Malam saying that Chaosta was injured and may not survive. She was basically all I could think of in the rare moments when I was lucid. I really thought I was going to lose control when I finally saw her. I was so sure that we were both dead, and I didn't want that for her. It felt like my heart was being torn from my chest.

Seeing her again was like the first breath of air after having the wind knocked out of me. An experience I'm all too familiar with from my experience boxing. I honestly don't know how I was able to keep her away from me for as long as I did. The anguish of being apart from her felt like my soul was shredding itself. I have a lot to atone for because of my past behavior toward her, that is clear. Also, to be in a position to want to keep her safe but also know that I'm a significant threat to her feels nearly untenable.

Being here at the demon stronghold has been... intense, I guess. It certainly hasn't been like I expected. I've barely looked at the trees. I've been too busy looking at her.

When I first saw her, I thought she looked shockingly good. Since then, I have seen and heard her pain and had a chance to see her injury. Fuck, the amount of strength it's taking me to not walk into the high leader's hall and unleash everything at him feels nearly unsustainable. Of course, that can only end one way, and I don't want to cause her pain, so I've been attempting to distract myself.

She's not exactly helping. I've asked her to take better care of herself, but she continues to push too hard. Things were going pretty well until I walked in on her and Malam sparring. In front of my eyes, Malam got a blow in. Even though I knew they were fighting with wooden practice blades, seeing him hit her in the abdomen was like watching that bastard angel stab her in the fucking back.

I pinned Malam to a tree. He was fighting me magically, or trying to, but I barely felt it. I guess I hadn't realized the true power difference between us. Well, that and he's clearly out of practice. Chiron would have put up more of a fight, I think. Speaking of Chiron. He seemed to side with me, actually. He was angry with Malam for not being more careful with her and engaging in sparring in the first place. He told me he spoke with her after, and I'm hoping maybe he was able to get through to her and convince her to get more rest.

Anyway, after Chiron confirmed that she would be all right, I was able to make myself let Malam go. I got

Chaosta back to her room with instructions to rest. When I got back, Malam apologized to me. I'm still surprised about that. I guess I know how arrogant he is, and it's clear that he doesn't much like me. I don't know what Chiron did or said to get him to apologize, but I'm honestly glad I wasn't there for that conversation.

Then the three of us talked. It was a surprisingly cordial conversation. We decided that it made sense to see if she and I could move back into the mansion. Chiron thought it might be good for her to be around her friends again. He thinks she's pushing herself because she's bored. We're hoping that, once she can help with research again, it will be easier for her to rest.

I know it won't be like old times. Chiron told me that the band replaced me as lead singer, and I honestly can't find it in me to care. It was splitting my focus anyway. I don't know exactly where we are with the cause, but I offered to help, and Malam accepted. At the very least, I owe it to my old friend to keep helping with this work. He fought so hard to solve the issues with our government. I can't let his sacrifices, including training me, be in vain.

I was surprised when Malam asked if he could train with me. He wants help with his combat magic. I think Chiron might have had something to do with that as well, but I was hardly going to say no. He does need help, and I'm willing to teach him as long as he doesn't act arrogant with me. He's also going to spar with Chaosta once she's had a bit more time to heal. I wanted so badly to forbid it, but it isn't my place to do so. I also know that she needs to build her skills just like the rest of us if we are to have any hope of surviving a potential future conflict with the angels.

When I got back after speaking with Reem and the others and saw the bruising on her ribs, I just about marched out of there and confronted Malam again. Instead, I got some salve from Chiron and took care of her. I need to be careful. The possessiveness and the strength of this rage I'm feeling at those who hurt her could consume me if I'm not.

I need to be able to handle this stuff so I can fight at her side and protect her when it's needed. I can't fall apart at every little thing if I want to be able to keep her safe.

Also, I've had some time to think, and I have some concerns about the viability of combat magic against the angels. Since it happened, I haven't been able to stop thinking about that fight in the alley and how my magic didn't seem to do much. I think being in the mansion and having access to some help with research will potentially facilitate a solution.

PART II

OUT OF THE WOODS AND INTO THE BACHELOR PAD

Buildings fly past outside the window of the carriage. The energy is tense. I glance at Dio and see that he still hasn't moved. His head is tipped back against the seat behind him, his eyes closed.

My eyes track down his jaw, which is still covered in a coarse beard, to the column of his throat. My mouth waters as I stare at him.

Then Pepper, who's sitting on the seat next to Dio, says, "It will be so fantastic to have a woman around again! Those guys are such bachelors, and the mansion needs a woman's touch." She's nearly vibrating with energy.

I flinch. "It's going to be great to see them again. Thanks for all your help, Pepper," I say. I hope she can't read the complete disinterest in providing a "woman's touch" in my tone.

When I risk a glance at Dio, one corner of his mouth is quirked up. I force myself to look out the window of the carriage again, snarling silently to myself.

After a few more minutes, I feel his eyes on me. When I meet them, he searches my face. I can only just hear him sigh past the sound of wheels over cobblestones. It is a quiet but tortured sound.

Heat flushes through my cheeks, and I look out the window again as Pepper says, "You too, honestly, Dio. You're so neat compared to them."

He responds, but I tune it out before I'm tempted to ask her not to sit so close to him.

Hoping I might be able to distract myself, I think back to when Dio returned after speaking with the boys.

I'd been dozing on my bed, but I woke up quickly when he walked through the door to my room.

"Chiron let me know that he spoke with you about moving back to the mansion," he said.

"He did," I said, my voice tight.

"You're alright with that?"

"Of course, as long as Reem will allow me to live there?"

He ran his hand through his hair in a tight movement as he said, "I informed Reem that you would be allowed to return to the mansion before I was committed. I spoke with him last night, and he said that it still stands. Of course, if you'd rather we find our own place, we can do that."

I shook my head before saying, "I would like to live in the mansion again. With you."

A smile tugged at his lips, and then he pulled me against his chest. It's quickly become my favorite place in the world.

"Besides," I muttered with my face pressed against him, "now that neither of us has a job, I don't know how we would afford our own place."

He pushed me back from him slightly and tilted my chin up so that he could look into my eyes. "You don't know?"

"Know what?" I asked, irritation clouding my voice.

He relaxed slightly, his arms softening around me.

"What?" I asked as I pushed back slightly so I could see his face.

He shook his head slightly, joy twinkling in his eyes, arms still loosely around my shoulders. "When my parents died, they deeded me their fortune. My ass-of-a-brother likes to remind me that it was a mistake. A fact I'm sure is true since I'm the fucking black sheep of the family. There is no way they intended for all that money to go to me instead of him.

"Whatever the intent, the result of it is that I'm rather hilariously wealthy. I couldn't help but wonder if it drew you to me as it has with women in the past. Judging by the way you just responded, the last doubt I had was just put to rest."

I've never cared much about money, so I just shook my head and said, "No, I didn't think of it, I guess." Then I focused on the part of that story that hit me in the chest and asked, "You don't get along with your brother?"

Confusion flashed across his face. Confusion that quickly turned to anger as he said with a growl, "No, if I never needed to speak with the asshole again, it would be too soon."

"I went to see him about getting you out of the center," I said.

"Hmm," he grumbled. "Glad he didn't get to have the pleasure of holding that over me for the rest of my life."

My throat felt tight. "But you asked him for help getting the charges against me dropped?"

Rage flashed across his expression as he glanced at me and then quickly looked away. "Don't look at me like that."

"Like what?"

"Like it was some heroic, self-sacrificing act," he said. His voice was tight, and he wasn't looking at me. "It was the bare, fucking, minimum, and I waited far too long before I did even that."

"Don't do that," I whispered. "I'd still be there if not for you."

He hugged me tighter but didn't say anything, and I didn't bring it up again.

"I did think he was kind of a bastard," I said quietly. Dio's arms tightened around me.

The next few days consisted of packing and making arrangements, mostly with Pepper. The boys had kept our rooms for us and planned for us to move back into them. However, when Pepper found out we wanted to share a room, she worked it out with the band, and they cleaned out one of the empty, larger rooms for us.

Malam and Chiron fussed endlessly and sent many supplies with us, including enough healing supplies for an entire army. I tried telling them that both Dio and I were fine, but they didn't seem convinced. I heard Malam mumbling something that sounded like, "The human and my creation are so delicate."

The only thing that settled them was my reminder that Fem is very qualified to keep an eye on us. Well, that and the fact that they'll both be at the mansion often. Chiron, to continue to work with the band on group magic, and Malam to practice combat magic with Dio and to spar with me.

This morning, the day of the move, we packed the last of our things and made our way to the lift. Malam and Chiron accompanied us, along with a couple of demons, their arms full of crates.

As we arrived at the main floor and were walking toward the front door, Dio suddenly coughed out a laugh.

Malam glanced at him and asked what that was about.

Dio just shook his head and refused to answer.

I was going to ask about it, but then I was pulled away to help supervise packing the carriage. As I remember now, I make a mental note to ask him about it.

Pepper watched Chiron and Malam help pack the carriage with her mouth slightly open.

Before we left, I gave each of them a hug. They awkwardly and stiffly each accepted.

Dio said a few quiet words to each of them and clasped hands with Chiron. As we climbed in the carriage and got on our way, Pepper asked breathlessly if either of them was single, which made Dio snort rudely.

I let her know that neither of them was likely interested in dating.

It didn't seem to sour her mood for long.

U*nfortunately,* I grumble silently to myself as she continues to try to chat with Dio. By the time the carriage stops outside the mansion, his expression is full of amusement.

I wrinkle my nose at him, and he brushes a hand across his mouth as though wiping the amusement from his face. "You ready?" he asks.

"As ready as I can be."

He steps out of the carriage first but remains close, offering me a hand. I appreciate the support it provides as I make my way down the steps. Then, without releasing my hand, he guides me after him toward the front door of the mansion. From my place behind him, I hear him greeting the boys. His voice is reserved.

Then he gently tugs on my hand, and I step around him to see the others.

Fem and Lent immediately step forward to greet me, but Dio pulls me back against him, his arms lying over my shoulders and crossed in front of my torso. That and, perhaps, whatever it is they see on his face makes them hesitate.

With my back pressed against him, desire suddenly makes my knees weak. I wobble a moment, but I don't want to be rude.

When I move toward the others, he lets me go with only a moment of reluctance.

As I step forward, Fem says, "Welcome back, Chaosta. It's so good to see you looking well. I was worried after the meeting with Alexander."

Dio makes a tight, angry sound behind me.

I ignore him as I say, "It is good to see you again, as well, Fem. Thanks again for helping me out with that meeting."

Then Lent steps forward, a broad grin on his face made even more brilliant in contrast with his dark skin. His hair as grown and hangs nearly to his chin. I'd forgotten how tall he is and I realize suddenly how much I've missed him.

He holds an arm out, inviting me into a hug.

Before we can though, Dio's fingers wrap around my arm, pulling me away. Dragged along toward the entrance to the mansion, I grin at Lent and say, "Nice to see you as well."

There is a crazy smile on his face, and he gives an awkward salute before heading to the carriage as Pepper puts them to work carrying crates.

Dio and I run into Reem on the steps to the front door of the mansion. His blond hair is slightly mussed. His expression is composed, but he doesn't seem particularly pleased to see either of us, his blue eyes hard as he glances between us.

"Dio," he says as he nods a tight greeting to him. As he looks at me, he says, "Welcome back, Chaosta." His voice grinds, making it clear that he's gritting his jaw.

Dio offers his own short greeting, barely slowing his path as he pulls me past Reem and into the entry hall. I briefly see a man I don't recognize who just gapes at us. Then we're at the door to Dio's room, and he pulls it open, drags me inside, and shuts it firmly behind us.

I find myself in the middle of his room, slightly breathless.

He has his back to me, and his shoulders are tight. "Fuck," he says under his breath. He rests his forehead against the door with a slight thump and swears quietly in Latin.

I hesitate for a moment. The last time I was in this room was when he first saw my scars. I remember reading his emotions then as disinterested or hostile. Now I know it was actually anger from not being able to protect me. That same possessiveness is written into the lines of his body now.

I close the distance between us and note that he's shaking slightly."Dio?" I say but he doesn't turn.

Without thinking, I reach under the loose linen shirt that was given to him by the demons. It is still so strange to see him in something other than his normal, crisp, button-up shirts. I can't say I hate being able to see more of his arms. I press my hand against his back, his muscles tight under my fingers. His skin is hot and seems to sting slightly against my palms.

He shudders at my touch. Then he slowly turns to face me. He keeps his eyes on the ground at my feet, and I'm sure it's to protect me from the pain of his magic. He traces his knuckles against the bare skin of my arms, and goosebumps follow the touch. A chill tracks down my spine. "Tell me I didn't hurt you as I dragged you in here," he says. His voice sounds pained.

I reach under his shirt again, tracing the hard ridges and planes of muscles. I want to memorize every inch of the man in front of me, know every line of his body, but right now the desire I'm feeling for him eclipses that.

"Chaosta," he says, a quiet warning in his voice.

I've never been much good at listening to his warnings, I realize as I run my hands higher up his chest.

Standing on my toes, I go to work his shirt over his head. He resists slightly, but I don't stop, carefully pulling it over his head. I drop it on the floor beside us and run my hands over his shoulders and down his arms, tracing the muscles and veins of his forearms that I can see in my mind's eye at this point.

"This isn't..." he starts to say before I'm curling my fingers around the waistband of his linen pants and pulling them down over his hips.

Whatever is causing him to hesitate, it's certainly not a lack of desire for me. As I pull his pants down, I free his erect cock, which I felt against my back just moments before when he pulled me against him outside of the mansion.

Still, I check with him. "Want me to stop?" I ask.

"No bu—"

I press one hand against his abdomen and wrap the fingers of the other around the velvety length of his cock. His skin is hot, especially there, but no longer stings against my skin. I explore, running my hand up his length and over the tip.

His eyes are closed, and the breath huffs through his slightly parted lips.

I drop to my knees in front of him, lean forward, and run my tongue up him, tasting the saltiness of his skin, the veins and heat of him sliding against my tongue.

He moans my name, it has a warning tone again, but the sound is also tortured, and his hand tangles in my hair.

I wait for him to pull me away, but he doesn't; instead, he follows my movements, seeming to guide me. A hoarse sound, almost a whimper, crawls out of his throat as I lick up his length again. Then, guided by some memory that's not mine, I run my tongue around the crown, tasting the precum that leaks from the tip.

As my tongue touches him there, his fist tightens in my hair, and he pulls me slowly away, tipping my head to look up at him. "Tell me," he says breathlessly.

Heat pools between my thighs. I know the words he wants to hear, but I've always preferred action. I take him into my mouth, and he grunts out a tormented exhalation as I show him that he has sole possession of my desire.

I continue my movements, stroking the hot ridges of him as I take more into my mouth. I glance at him through my eyelashes and see that his pupils have taken over his irises as he watches me, a sea of black staring back at me.

His fingers twist tighter into my hair, and his hips buck against me before I can get used to the feeling of him. I gag and pull back slightly.

I hear him muttering something, but before he can change his mind, I go back to licking and sucking while I wrap my fingers around the base, working with my hand what I can't fit in my mouth. I steady myself, gripping his thigh with my other hand. The ridges of that raised scar press against my palm.

Memories again seem to guide me, and I take him deeper again and swallow against him. His hips buck again, and I feel the tension building in him, and then, with a deep groan, heat hits the back of my throat as he comes. I swallow, feeling like I'm claiming some part of him as mine.

His hands slowly release my hair as he moves them to the wall behind him, stabilizing himself.

I stay where I am, on my knees and look at him. It's like looking at the fucking sun. He's come completely undone, his body arched, his head thrown back against the door behind him. Sweat-dampened tendrils of hair stick to his face across his eyes.

He looks like a god because of me.

After a few moments, where I continue to stare at him hungrily as I wipe the drool from my chin, he presses himself fully upright, and his eyes meet mine. Then he grasps my jaw, his grip firm, but not overly rough. I rise as he guides me, and he crashes his mouth onto mine. His lips and tongue take me apart slowly and neatly, just as with everything he does. It feels as though he wants to consume some part of me.

He finally pulls back, his chest heaving. "Gods," he says, "Please don't tell me where you learned that."

I'm not sure where I would have learned how to do that.

Maybe it's similar to how I know how to fight with a sword, I think to myself. I'm just glad that he seemed to enjoy it.

As I stare at him, drinking in the sight of him, my body aches with need. However, the pain in my abdomen is shortening my breath, so I move to sit on the edge of the bed.

He closes the space between us and tucks a tendril of hair behind my ear. Then, with a finger under my chin, he guides my face up toward his. "Are you sure you're alright?"

I press into his touch and close my eyes, enjoying the feel of his thumb resting against my chin, just below my lips. "I'm just a little sore," I say breathlessly. "You really need to stop treating me like glass.

"Hmmm," he grumbles as he continues to search my face. Whatever he sees must reassure him because he releases me and walks to the bathroom. I hear him cleaning up at the sink. When he rejoins me in the bedroom, I can't help but stare.

I ignore the smug look on his face as he says, "I haven't had a chance to shave yet, and I'd like to shower."

"Alright," I say as I stand, only wobbling a little and still not able to tear my eyes away from him. "I'd like to get my room cleaned up."

He looks away from me, running his hand through his hair.

I bite my lip.

His eyes fasten on it, and he closes the distance between us and frees it gently from my teeth. I meet his eyes as he grumbles something quietly to himself in Latin.

"I'm not used to this," he finally says.

"This?"

He sighs, and the silence stretches for moments before he says, "Being with someone while not using. Last time I was in a relationship, it didn't end well for either of us."

"You weren't using when your brother sent you to the Piquory Center, were you?" I ask.

He seems slightly surprised by the question. "No, I wasn't," he finally says.

Returning to the topic, I ask, "What can I do?"

He seems to consider, and it is as though he's fighting some internal battle. Finally, he says, "I don't quite know. The only thing I would ask isn't fair to you."

"What's that?"

He shakes his head slightly and then closes the distance between us again. He takes my head in his hands, thumbs running over my cheekbones.

"Just tell me you're mine," he barely whispers.

"Just yours," I say, my throat tight.

He kisses me gently. It still steals the breath from my lungs. When he steps back and releases me, I wobble slightly. I catch his grin before he turns and walks back into the bathroom.

I leave the room on wobbly legs and head to my old room.

As we were arranging to move back here, Pepper let us know that they weren't going to do anything with our old rooms until we got here. The boys have offered to help us move into the larger room but they wanted to wait for us to be here to help with our things. Now that I'm here, I figure some cleaning would be prudent before anyone else sees my mess.

The route to my room leads me through the entry hall and past the dining room. As I walk past, I smell food, and my stomach growls. Realizing that it's likely around lunch time, I walk, hesitantly, into the dining space. Trepidation fills me at the thought of being here, almost as though nothing happened when I feel like I am so different. However, I quickly relax as I look across the table and see Lent shoveling food into his mouth.

The familiar sight settles my nerves enough that I'm able to go to the sideboard and fill a plate while he says through a mouthful of food, "How are you settling in? Anything I can get you?"

I take my food to the table. "I don't need anything yet. I was just going to clean my room."

"If it is anywhere near as messy as mine, that might take a while," he says with a grin before going back to shoveling food in his mouth.

I grin back at him, *thank all the dark gods for Lent.*

We eat in companionable silence for a while before I hear footsteps and see that Fem has joined us.

He glances at me before taking a plate, filling it with food, and finding his own seat. His face is thoughtful as he says, "You brought rather a lot of healing supplies with you. Will you need medical attention?"

I can't help but grin as I say, "No, that was just Chiron and Malam fussing."

"How's Dio?" he asks.

As he says it, I catch Lent grimacing slightly from where he sits opposite me at the table.

"He's fine," I say, "He's still just a little weak, I think." Glancing at their slightly pale faces, I say, "I'm so sorry that our return here is putting all of you in danger."

Lent shakes his head and says, "We knew we were taking a risk with the cause. Now that we know more about how integrated the angels are into city government, we realize we'll always be hiding something. At least with the two of you here, we have a bit more firepower." He chuckles, and Fem throws a cloth napkin at him.

Feeling slightly surprised at how well they're taking this, I say, "Thank you. We both thought it would be better to be here than at the demon stronghold, but I know you didn't need to allow that. I know it is a risk."

Lent shrugs, "Honestly, we missed both of you. Besides, I trust the stronger wards that Malam and Chiron worked on before you returned. As long as none of us invite those bastards in, we should be fine. Reem is struggling with the risk to the band, but he'll get over it."

I'm unsure if that's correct. I'm somehow unable to imagine Reem forgiving me for everything that's already occurred, much less this. Instead of sharing those thoughts, I just say, "Thank you, Lent, I've missed you all as well."

"Just promise you'll let me know if either of you needs anything," Fem says.

"We will, thank you, Fem," I say.

Fem digs into his lunch as I go back to mine.

I'm just finishing my meal as Lent stands up and clears his plate. As he does so, he says, "Really good to have you back, Shorty. Will you be joining us in our research again?"

"I'm always happy to help when books are involved," I say with a grin, and he tousles my hair with a laugh before leaving the room.

As I stand to clear my plate, Fem says, "With you and Dio both accused of killing people, there is rather a lot of danger in having you both here, isn't there?"

"Yeah, neither of us should be seen outside the mansion."

Fem's face is filled with concern. Instead of asking any more questions, though, he says, "Probably best not to share any of that with Reem."

A smile tugs at my lips. "Thank you, Fem, you have been so good to us." He smiles at me and awkwardly pats my arm.

Walking into my old room feels like walking into a different time. It has been so long since I've been here, and so much has changed with me while this room still looks the same.

The first thing I take care of are the old medical supplies and bloody bandages that I had stuffed into a drawer in the dresser. Not exactly advisable, but at the time, I was more focused on trying to avoid anyone finding out how badly I'd been hurt. Then, suddenly, I was forbidden from returning.

I bundle them up and bring them to the trash. Then I organize my clothes. The clean items I haphazardly fold, flinching slightly when I realize that Dio might not be particularly fond of living with me and my mess.

Finally, I make piles of my books. I carefully tuck the many sketches, mostly of Dio, in between the pages of some of the books to hide them.

With that done, I take one small pile of books and go exploring. I want to see where we will be staying. After wandering for a while, I find our new room on the second floor. As I look around, I note that the boys have neatly stacked the things from the carriage on the floor near the center of the room. My sword is laid across the large bed.

The mansion is large enough that, other than the room I used to sneak away to practice sword-work in, we primarily keep to the first floor and basement, so this isn't a room I'm familiar with. There are large windows that look onto the street. There is even a small sitting area in the corner of the large room with a couple of chairs, a small table, and a bookcase. I poke through the closet, which is empty, and then find the door to the bathroom. It is larger than those in our current rooms, and it even has a large bath. Before I leave, I set the books I brought with me on the bookshelf.

Then I go to the kitchen and dish up a plate of food for Dio before heading back to his room.

DIO'S JOURNAL - ENTRY 2

Annum:5615

Entry 2 - superstitio mentes occupavit

Out of what is likely a ridiculous superstition, I'm going to continue to use this notebook to document my thoughts instead of returning to the journal I was using before I was taken to the center. It seems unwise to open those pages somehow. It's not as though I'm going to burn it or something. Maybe someday I will want to look back, or it will be used for something.

Anyway, onto the topic at hand. I knew it would be good to get Chaosta back to the mansion. Also, I figured she'd do better around friends. I knew it was going to be tough on me, but I guess I didn't realize quite how difficult until the other guys were there in front of me, wanting to welcome her back. We'd barely stepped onto the street in front of the mansion when we were surrounded by Lent and Fem. They were there to greet us, or rather to greet Chaosta. It's not like they were actively disappointed to see me, but Chaosta is who they were there for. It's not like I can blame them.

I did all right with Fem, but fuck, when I saw Lent getting ready to hug her, I just couldn't make myself allow it. I mean, he should realize by now that she's not available for his flirtatious advances. I will put my foot down more firmly with him if he doesn't drop it. I need to be careful not to damage my relationship with him, though, because unfortunately, I think I need his help with that research on how to make combat magic more effective against angels.

I've always been possessive. Then, when my last relationship imploded, I guess it hurt more than I realized. Since then, I've avoided getting close to anyone. I was doing a damn fine job of keeping to myself until I met Chaosta. At any rate, I guess I need to figure this out.

That last relationship was prior to when when I began practicing combat magic. It was also when I was still high most of the time. At least then, I wasn't dealing with those volatile emotions from the magic. Actually, that relationship ending was what led me to get clean.

Since then, there was only one other time when I got close to someone. They were still dealing with an active addiction, and I nearly stumbled in my recovery. If not for my dear friend, I likely would have. At the time, if not for him, I don't quite know what I might have done. Dealing with the volatility of a relationship on top of the magic and not having him here to confide in brings the pain of his loss back tenfold. Also, I would have liked to tell him about Chaosta. Actually, I think they might have gotten along.

Anyway, back to the topic at hand, it's not like I'm proud of myself. When Lent looked at her like that my emotions began to take over. All I could manage was dragging her into my room. I don't know what I was going to do once I got us there. Knowing me, probably put my fist through the wall and traumatized her. Then she...well, she sucked me off. Gods damned, that mouth that I was already obsessed with on my dick. I wish there were some way I could have captured it more firmly than in my memory. I'll never stop thinking of it. Someone taught her very well, and I'd love to be able to thank them and kill them at the same time.

At any rate, it settled the possessiveness a little. I took a shower and meant to get rid of this beard, but she got back to the room with food before I could get that far. I can't possibly have done enough in my life to deserve her. All I can promise is that I'll work hard every day to earn this undeserved affection that she's gifted me.

Since then, things have been a little calmer but certainly awkward. Cal, my replacement, is pretty quiet and seems to keep to himself. I've heard him singing, and he's decent. Honestly, I'm just glad they don't seem to expect me to start rehearsing with them. I hardly *have the time or interest at this point.*

Things were uncomfortable with the other three. Less so with Fem, maybe because I confided in him before I was taken to treatment. I'm sure part of that awkwardness is the risk we're causing by living here again. Chaosta has historically brought trouble, which is why Reem kicked her out all those months ago. Now, of course, we're both being hunted by the government for the people we've hurt and killed. I'm sure it was disruptive when the city officials showed up at the mansion. Thankfully, it sounds like the wards the demons have in place weren't needed. Still, answering a bunch of invasive questions couldn't have been easy. Luckily, because the band is famous, I'm sure the city officials attempted to limit the disruption.

Also, the mansion turned into a mess while we were gone. I've seen the guys sleeping on couches in communal spaces, sometimes in various states of undress. Clothes, instruments, books, and other things are littered about. I even found old food left out. I don't know if the house employees are understaffed or just tired of the bullshit, because it seems so unlike them to let those things slide. I'm sure the other guys felt my judgment of the mess, and that's certainly not helping. I understand now what Pepper was on about in the carriage. I hope they don't actually think Chaosta is going to play housemaid. If they try to rope her into cleaning, I'll be firmly setting them straight.

It seems Cal also took my place in the coven. That's

a role I think the other guys would like me to take back, but I haven't felt up for it. Instead, I plan to focus on my combat magic practice. Chaosta told me that she asked Malam for a week for us to settle before he shows up to practice with me. I know she's hoping to spar with him then as well, but I don't know that I'll be strong enough to let her. I'm working on it, but I don't have long to figure it out before he will start showing up. I don't want to argue with her, but I am terrified that he is going to hurt her. Especially after what happened last time.

Anyway, that's why I am writing about it. It's not like I can go boxing right now with how weak I still am after my stint at "treatment."

DOMESTIC FRUSTRATION

I wake slowly, a few days later, against a familiar, warm wall of muscle. He is still asleep, his chest rising and falling slowly with the steady breaths of a deep sleep, his arms and legs tangled with mine. I nuzzle against him and let myself doze for a short while longer. Finally, though, I grow restless and carefully remove myself from his embrace.

I know he wouldn't normally sleep like this, but I remember how much rest I needed after my stint at Piquory. In my absence, he grumbles in his sleep, wrapping his arms around himself. Once he settles again, I tear myself away.

I look around his room, trying to figure out how to cover myself so that I can go to breakfast. We still haven't moved, so my options are limited. I finally pull on a button-up shirt that I find in his closet. It's large enough on me that it goes to my mid-thigh like a short dress. It also smells like him, which fills me with a sense of peace. Rolling up the sleeves slightly and buttoning it, I decide that I'm covered enough to get some food.

Leaving the room, I pad, barefoot, to the dining room. Lent and Fem are already there, and they grumble their "good mornings" as I pour myself a cup of coffee. Fem starts loading a plate with food at the sideboard as I sit next to Lent.

I feel his eyes on me as I settle onto the chair and note that he tenses slightly. When I glance at him, I see that his eyes are on the doorway. "Is Dio still sleeping?" he asks, his voice still hoarse from sleep. There is something else in his tone as well.

Is he worried?

"Yeah, he's ok," I say reassuringly. "I think he just needs some extra rest right now."

"I'm sure he does," Lent says, his eyes passing over me again. "Is that one of his shirts?" he asks. The teasing note is back in his voice.

I glare at him as I say, "Yes, all my things are still in the other room. I think we are going to get moved in today, and then I can wear my own stuff."

He raises his hands like he's surrendering. "You just look cute, that's all," he says.

I relax and go back to focusing on my coffee as I realize he isn't going to call me a slob or grumble at me for wrinkling Dio's clothing.

Fem sits down across from us at the table. He's staring at me as well, his eyes slightly wide.

"What?" I ask.

He just shakes his head and then focuses on the food on his plate.

We all sit in silence for a minute, and I finish my coffee. Feeling a bit more alive, I rise and go to the sideboard to get a second cup and fill a plate with food.

As I sit at the table again, I catch sight of a small, odd-looking bruise on Lent's arm among all the small scars from working blood magic. "What's that?" I ask, gesturing at it. "You ok?"

Lent quickly pulls his sleeve lower and pales. "Ah, that's

nothing. I think I must have just burned myself or something," he says quickly.

I glance at Fem and see that a corner of his mouth is lifted in a lopsided smile.

Glancing between the two of them, neither of whom meets my eyes, I say, "What? Am I missing something?"

"Just nice to see the two of you resuming your friendship," Fem says, his mouth full.

Somehow, I'm doubtful that there's not something else going on, but as long as Lent is fine, I'm not too worried. Fem certainly doesn't seem worried about the burn, and he tends to be pretty cautious with medical stuff.

"It is kind of starting to feel like old times," Lent says quickly.

I don't miss that he looks again, almost nervously, at the door.

"Yeah," Fem says, "We have a concert coming up in a fortnight, and it looks like our research 'bookclub' is getting back together."

"Are you researching today?" I ask, suddenly realizing how much I missed our group reading time.

"Yeah, Fem and I are going to be reading in the flower room. We would love to have you join us," Lent says as he grins at me.

"Maybe in more clothes though?" Fem says. His voice squeaks slightly.

"You are both being ridiculous," I grumble as I carefully rise from my seat. I go to the sideboard to scrape my plate.

Fem says, "What help do you need to get moved today?"

I start loading a plate of food for Dio, and after thinking for a minute, say, "I'm not quite sure. I'll talk with Dio and let you know what we need."

"Just let us know," Lent says, rising from his place at the table to clean his own plate. "We're meeting to read after lunch. Hopefully you can join us."

"I'll be there," I say with a grin.

Then I turn and leave the dining room and head to Dio's room with food for him and another cup of coffee for me.

As I open the door, he's just pushing himself up, his eyes scanning the space. The expression of concern on his face quickly changes to relief when he sees me. I move into the room and set the food down on the table beside the bed. He's staring at me, and when I glance at him, I see that he's looking up and down my body, his eyes wide.

"You wore that to breakfast?" he asks. It sounds like he's struggling to say the words.

"Yeah, I didn't have any clean clothes in here. Sorry, it is probably a little wrinkled," I say, wondering if he's going to get grumbly about it.

His expression turns hard, and he rises and stands near the edge of the bed. He holds out a hand. "Come here," he says breathlessly.

I take a step toward him, and he wraps his fingers around my wrist and pulls me carefully but firmly against him.

His voice rumbles in my ear as he says, "Please tell me the other guys weren't at breakfast."

"Lent and Fem were there, why?"

With his fingers on my chin, he directs me to look up at him. "We need some ground rules," he chokes out.

I just blink at him, not quite sure where he's going with this.

"This is the single sexiest thing I have seen you in, and there is some fierce competition. I just can't stand the idea that they get to see you like this. At least not right now," he says, emotion strong in his voice.

I feel a spike of anger that he is trying to tell me what to do again. At the same time, I can't ignore the pleading note in his voice, so I nod in agreement.

He swallows and closes his eyes for a moment before asking, "The demons didn't send you with any of their things, did they?"

"No, but I have my own clothes here. They're just in the new room."

"Alright, I guess that will have to do. After I eat, I'll go get some of your clothes and bring them here for you to change into. Then we can start moving," he says. He slowly relaxes as I allow him to hold me.

A few more minutes pass before I prompt quietly, "I brought you some breakfast."

"I'm not really hungry," he says.

I push myself back, and he lets me go. I pick up the plate and hold it out to him. "You need to eat. I want you to get your strength back."

He sighs but takes the plate and, sitting on the edge of the bed, starts eating woodenly.

When I'm sure he's going to continue, I ask, "Can I start packing your things while you eat?"

"I can help," he growls.

"I know," I bite back, "but it will give me something to do while you finish eating."

"Alright," he says more softly.

I start with his clothes, which I fold as carefully as I can. I can feel him staring at me, but despite the fact that I'm sure I'm wrinkling them, he doesn't say anything. Occasionally, I glance at him. Every time I do, he's still eating, but his eyes never seem to leave me.

At the look on his face, I'm slowly distracted from my task. My heart beats faster, tension beginning to build low in my abdomen.

A few more moments pass, and I try to remember what I was doing. I feel a little like I'm floating, and my heart is beating strongly enough that I can hear my own pulse. I'm glancing around, trying to figure out what to do next when I see him set his plate down.

He strides toward me and before I can say anything, he

scoops me up by my thighs and lifts me so that my legs are wrapped around his waist. I expect that he's going to take us to the bed, but instead he presses my back against the wall behind me. His movements are rough, and my head bumps against the surface as my back hits and the breath halts in my lungs.

"Fuck," he says, his voice full of heat. "Are you ok?"

The muscles in my abdomen twinge, but I barely notice. "Mmhmm," I mumble, my eyes on his.

He nods, and then from where he is holding my thighs, I feel him lift one of his hands up, between my legs. I gasp as his fingers brush against my entrance, and he freezes.

"You're not wearing anything under this," he says. A statement made in a low and dangerous tone.

I can't respond, jaw gritted and chest heaving as he stands there pressed against me, not moving. I meet his eyes, struggling to focus.

The heat in his eyes changes. "Fuck, you're wet," he mumbles breathlessly. Before either of us can say or do anything else, there's a knock on the door.

We both freeze.

He whispers, "Not a godsdamned sound," to me as he removes his hand and gently sets me on my own feet. His hands around my waist steady me.

I swallow a whimper at the loss of his touch.

"What?" he bites out at whoever knocked.

Reem's voice calls, "I just wanted to check in on moving. We offered to help, but we have a busy day, so I need to know your plans."

"Shit," Dio whispers, rubbing the hand he didn't have between my legs through his hair. "Can you stand on your own?"

I whisper, "I think so."

He steps away, eyes trained on me as though making sure I didn't lie to him. I wobble but manage it by clinging to the wall.

I see a corner of his mouth quirk up before his eyes close, and he growls, "Fuck, you are going to destroy me."

"We're just getting dressed," he says as he glares at me for a moment, "and then we will be ready to start moving my things."

Reem calls through the door, "Will fifteen minutes do it?"

"It will."

As Reem's footsteps fade away, Dio closes the space between us again. He wraps his fingers along the side of my neck, thumb pressed under my jaw as he tilts my head up to meet his eyes. "We might have been interrupted, but I won't forget that we need to resolve the whole no-panties-thing."

Mute for a moment, I just nod against his hand. Seemingly satisfied by that as a response, he steps away and begins to get dressed. After a few moments, he points to the bed and growls, "Sit and stay there until I get back."

I move meekly to the bed, my legs less wobbly but still not quite as strong as I would like. As I sit, curling my legs under me, he nods as though grading me on my behavior and then leaves the room.

He returns quickly and hands me a pile of my clothes. I change while he continues to pack his things. Once I'm dressed, I help him pack and we work in companionable, if heated, silence for several minutes.

I continue folding his clothes as he opens his cabinet and removes a false back. He pulls a great number of magical supplies out, packing them carefully in crates. The knife I helped him choose to buy at the magic shop is there, as are many small pots and wooden boxes. All are labeled in his neat handwriting.

I eventually finish folding clothes, and begin to help him with the other items until we have a few of the small crates full of items.

"I'll get Reem so we can get this over with," Dio says. Before he leaves, though, he closes the distance between us and presses his lips to mine. The kiss is hungry, almost desperate. It leaves me gasping, starving for more as he steps back. When I open my eyes, I see a smug expression on his face before he turns and leaves.

I get control of my breathing, after a long moment, and manage to return to packing. He returns with the others, and they begin taking crates out of the room.

Dio directs the others to take his hanging clothes and bring armfuls up to our room. I note with a grin that between those and his clothes I've folded he has far more than I do.

Eventually, everything except the last crate, which I just finished packing, is removed. I reach to pick it up, but Dio says, "Absolutely not." Then he takes it and hands it to Reem.

As Reem takes the crate and leaves the room, I feel Dio's intense stare on me again. I glance at him and feel my heart rate begin to race.

Then Lent walks into the room.

Dio's back is to the door, standing between Lent and me. He tenses.

"Lunch is nearly ready. Will you two be joining us?" Lent asks. Then he catches sight of whatever expression must be on my face and Dio's tight shoulders and goes awkwardly quiet.

Dio closes his eyes, and his fingers clench into fists as he grits out, "We'll be right there."

Lent doesn't move and continues to stare at us. His cheeks are pink, and he seems frozen in place.

Dio says, "Can we help you with something else, Lent?"

"I'm fine," Lent manages as he finally turns and leaves, clearly understanding that dismissal at least.

Dio heaves in a deep breath, and I see his lips moving. I'd guess he's counting. "Are you hungry?" he finally asks.

"For food?" I ask, and a corner of his mouth quirks up slightly.

"I think they are going to be a nuisance until they practice this evening, so yes, unfortunately, for food," he says tightly.

"Yeah, I guess I could eat," I say.

With a sigh, he turns, and we walk together to the dining room.

As we fill our plates, I feel his eyes on me, the heat of his focus pricking along my skin. I finish first and sit on my normal chair next to Lent.

Dio sits in the chair on the other side of me. I'm just lifting a bite of food to my mouth when he reaches out, grabs the chair I'm sitting on, and yanks it closer to him. I let out a squeak as my body jerks at the sudden movement of the chair.

Reem's eyes widen as he stares from his seat across the table. Fem, who paused as he was plating up food for himself, recovers quickly and sits down next to Dio.

I reach for my plate and catch a brief glance of Lent, who is a little pale.

Under the table, Dio's hand wraps around my thigh. I glance at him, but he's eating his food, seeming to ignore the others completely.

My focus is anywhere but the food on my plate. As I try to force myself to eat, I hear a stilted conversation start up between Reem and Fem about the upcoming concert. I'm listening to them talk about some arrangements that Pepper is making and whether everything will be ready on time.

As I continue to make myself eat, I eventually hear Fem say, "How's it going, Dio?"

He pauses mid-chew, his fingers tightening slightly on my thigh. Then he says, "Fine."

"Well, that's good," Fem says, his tone sarcastic.

Dio's whole body goes tense. Then, with a sigh, he says, "It's been tough adjusting to being back here."

"I can only imagine," Fem says. "I wanted to make sure you

knew that my offer from before still stands. You ever want to talk, I'm here."

Dio seems to stop breathing, his fingers still tight against my thigh. After a moment, though, he relaxes and lets go of me as he continues eating. I miss his touch immediately, but it makes it slightly easier to concentrate.

We're joined then by the new band member. I study him as he dishes up a plate and settles at the table across from me. His hair is tousled, and his eyes heavy. He has delicate features and, other than Lent, who is long and lanky, he is the least muscled of the boys. He looks younger than the rest, but I can't tell if it's because he's less muscular or if he's actually younger.

After a bit, Lent asks, "Hey Cal, did you just wake up?"

"Insomnia was shit last night," the new man, who's apparently named Cal, says.

"Want some coffee?" Lent asks. When Cal nods, Lent thoughtfully goes to the sideboard to pour him some.

As he does Cal says, "Were you also struggling to sleep last night, Lent? I thought I heard you moving around in your room."

There is a crash from behind us as Lent drops something. We all turn to look at him, and I see that he's frozen, his shoulders tense. Then he swears and grabs a cloth napkin to try to blot up the spilled liquid.

"Don't Lent, you'll cut yourself. I'll go get the house staff to clean it up," Reem says as he leaves the room.

Lent returns to his place at the table and drops inelegantly onto his chair with a mumbled apology to Cal about the coffee.

"That's ok," Cal says. "You alright?"

"I'm fine," Lent says quickly. "Just annoyed that I fumbled and broke something."

The remainder of lunch is quiet and awkwardly strained as the house employees clean up the mess behind us.

As everyone finishes eating, Fem asks, "Chaosta, you still feeling up to doing some reading with us?"

I feel Dio tense briefly beside me before drawing in a breath. He glances at me and then says, "I'm tired and should probably get some rest. You should read with them."

I can hear the reluctance in his voice, but he does look tired.

"You sure?" I ask.

He nods, a calm look of acceptance on his face.

"Alright, I will," I say with a grin to Fem.

Dio rises from the table, taking both of our plates. He brings them to the sideboard behind me, and I hear him scraping the remaining food. The others stand as well to take care of their plates. Only Cal remains sitting, finishing his meal and glancing up at me almost as though he didn't realize Dio and I were here until just now.

A few moments later, as I finish the last of my coffee, I feel Dio's hands brush against my shoulders from where he's standing behind me. His fingers gently trace up my neck to my jaw, and he tilts my head back. He leans over and kisses me, hot and needy, his tongue pressing into my mouth. The kiss is even more intense at this angle, his beard, which he still hasn't shaved, pressing against my cheek and nose. As he pulls back, his fingers brush over my throat, and I pull in a breath, eyes still closed.

"Join me when you're done," he grates out and then turns and leaves the room.

I lift my head from the back of the chair, and when I glance across the table, I see Cal's wide eyes on me, his jaw frozen mid-chew. "Fuck that was hot," he says after a moment. Then, blinking, he goes back to eating as I feel a blush heating my cheeks.

I want nothing more in this moment than to follow Dio, but I know he won't rest if I'm there.

I also miss my friends, and we haven't had much of a chance

to get caught up since I've been back. So instead, I rise and head to the floral room for what I'm sure will be a distracted afternoon of books and time with friends.

DIO'S JOURNAL - ENTRY 3

Annum:5615
Entry 3 - castus

I think there are going to be lots of gods damned entries in this journal while I get control of my emotions. It's almost painful to see the guys around Chaosta right now. The last thing I want is to be controlling with her, but I'm struggling to handle the possessiveness I feel. I need to figure this out before I drive her away. Fuck, seeing her in my shirt earlier and then finding out she wasn't wearing a single thing underneath it. Even now, hours later, I can't stop thinking about it. I trust her, but I certainly don't trust them, especially that sneaky shit, Lent. I shouldn't have pulled her chair toward me like that, but fuck, she was sitting so close to him.

I came back here to try to sleep. My emotional regulation is worse when I'm tired, the monster closer to the surface, and it doesn't take much to exhaust me right now. I laid in bed for a while before I couldn't take it anymore and decided I needed to get my feelings out on paper. I'll admit, this doesn't feel like it's helping much at the moment. Fuck. I need to believe it's worse right now because I wanted her for so long and wouldn't let myself have her. Well, that, and the fact that she's still hurting. I'm trying not to smother her, but it's hard not to worry.

Damn it! That's it, this isn't doing anything other than increasing my frustration. I'm going boxing. I'm sure it isn't a good idea in my current state, but I'm crawling out of my skin, and maybe some controlled, and socially acceptable, violence will help.

MESSY

Researching in the floral room with Lent and Fem is both as I remember it, and not. The familiar dim light filters in through the windows, highlighting the pastel shades on the walls. The only sounds are wisps of turned pages and the scratches of pen on paper. However, the room has gotten messy. Not only are there piles of books, notes, and writing materials lying everywhere, there are also plates with crusts of bread and old food. Pages of paper cover the walls, tacked over the flowers, creating an even more chaotic background.

When Fem sees me looking around, he winces slightly before saying, “We haven’t been letting the staff in here. We’re worried they’ll throw away notes.”

“It happened before,” Lent says as he throws himself down on a couch and picks up a book.

“We probably should clean up a bit, though,” Fem says, biting his lip as he looks around at the mess.

I walk to the couch where Lent is sitting, picking up a book on the way. I start to sit next to him, but he stiffens and leans away from me, pointing at the other couch. "Absolutely not," he says, his voice higher than normal. "Sit over there."

I hesitate, looking from him back to Fem as I try to figure out what's going on.

Fem must see my confusion because he says in a teasing tone, "I don't think Lent wants to die today."

I still hesitate.

Fem has a corner of his mouth quirked up as he watches me.

Then I remember Dio pulling my chair away. I sigh and move to the other couch. "Don't be dramatic," I scowl as I sit and open the book, "I'm sure he wouldn't kill you."

Fem makes a scoffing noise, and Lent's face is pale. He meets my eyes for a moment and shakes his head. Then he leans back against the couch, opens the book in his lap to a marked page, and begins to read.

"Anything specific we're looking for?" I ask.

"We believe we're still missing something," Lent says.

"While you were gone, we told Chiron about the stone we found," Fem says. He's standing, looking at some of the notes tacked to the wall. "He thinks we are still missing something with the stone in order to create the magic we want."

"And that's if the stone is actually magic, as the others keep reminding me," Lent grumbles.

"I'm sure it's what you need," I say, and both of them quickly turn to me.

"How could you possibly know that?" Fem asks, but he sounds curious and not accusatory.

"I guess you could call it a vision," I say, my voice lifting at the end.

Both of them are openly staring at me now, and Fem asks, "Do you have many of these visions?"

Remembering how they have doubted me in the past, I hesitate.

"It's ok, Chaosta," Fem says as though he can see what I'm thinking.

"It happens fairly frequently," I say.

"Hmmm," Fem says. He goes back to his notes, still clearly considering.

Lent is still staring at me from the other couch. "How do these visions come to you?"

"Often I see things in dreams, but sometimes when I'm awake, I'll see something or hear something and just *know* it's important. That's what happened at the magic shop with the stone."

"Do you know anything else about it? Are we missing something?" Lent asks.

"When I saw the stone in the shop, I knew it was important to what you're doing, but that's all."

"You could have saved me a lot of grief if you'd said something sooner," he grumbles, but his tone is teasing.

I stick my tongue out at him, and he laughs as we all return to reading.

A few hours pass, and I'm stretching, my back and neck stiff from hunching over books for that long. As if on cue, I hear the door behind me open.

As Reem walks into the room, he asks, "How's it going in here?"

"Fine," Fem responds grumpily, "We're not making much progress."

"We did find out that the stone is the real deal, though," Lent says proudly.

"How did you figure that out?" Reem asks.

I flinch as Lent says, "Chaosta had a vision."

Instead of doubting me, though, Reem just says, "Well, that's one less thing to worry about, I guess."

"You came to get us for dinner?" Fem asks, and Reem confirms.

Fem moves to sit on the table in front of me and says, "We need to grab dinner early so we can get some band practice in before Chiron shows up."

"Is he here every night?" I ask.

"Yes, or at least he has been ever since Dio recovered enough for him to leave again," Fem says.

I hope I'll get to see him. His absence has felt odd after spending so much time around the demons.

"Did he tell you that Malam will be here to practice with Dio and me in the evenings?" I ask.

"He didn't," Reem says. "Where will you be practicing?"

"I thought maybe in the room upstairs that I used to practice my sword in?"

"I didn't realize you cleaned out a room," Reem says thoughtfully. "I guess that will work. We just can't have you disturbing our rehearsal or magic work. We're on a tight timeline with the upcoming concert."

I flinch at that, irritated by his tone, but I don't want to get into an argument with him, so I nod. "We'll stay out of your hair."

When I straighten, I see Fem glaring at Reem as he rises. As the three of them leave the room, I hear Fem saying something to him about being rude.

I rise and stretch out carefully, realizing I should check on Dio and see if he would like to get dinner with me. When I get to his room, the bed looks slept in, but he isn't there, and my heart stutters in my chest. I glance around, wondering if he's already at dinner. Then I see a note lying on the pillow.

> *Needed some air. Went boxing. I'll be careful.*
> *-Dio*

My heart races.

He wasn't supposed to leave the mansion.

I scoop up my sword and strap it to my back, quickly grabbing a hood to pull over my hair.

I stride downstairs and toward the front door. As I'm nearing it, though, the door opens, and Dio walks in. He flinches at whatever expression must be on my face. He holds his hands out in a placating gesture, but all I can focus on is the bandage wrapped around the knuckles of his right hand. "Where did you go and what happened?" I snarl at him.

"I'm fine," he says. Then closes the distance between us and wraps his arms around me. I stand stiffly for a moment before relaxing against him, the beating of my heart beginning to calm.

"I just needed to get some emotions out. I'm a bit bruised, but it was good." He rests his head against mine and mumbles, "I feel better."

I sigh and wrap my arms around him gently. "Just promise me you'll get some sort of mask to wear if you are going to leave the mansion again."

"Alright," he says. "Do I smell dinner?"

"Are you hungry?" I ask. I'm surprised because I've noticed that he hasn't had much of an appetite since he's been back.

He cups my chin gently and kisses me before saying, "Yeah, I am kind of hungry actually."

When we get to the dining room, it's empty. The others must have already finished or taken their plates elsewhere. I'm glad for the privacy and not having to answer questions as I unstrap my sword and set it on the table.

We sit close together and enjoy a quiet meal.

I note that he's nodding off as we finish, and this time I take care of our plates before leading him to our new room. I hang my sword on the hook by the door and then help him undress.

I bite my lip when I see already colorful bruises covering his ribs and one side of his abdomen, still clearly showing between his tattoos.

Dio frees my lip from my teeth. "I thought I told you that you aren't allowed to chew on those," he grumbles sleepily at me as he yawns.

"Fuck Dio, you are covered in bruises."

He looks down at his ribs and shrugs. "That's not that bad," he says casually and then freezes.

My voice is tight as I say, "Not that bad, what do you mean not that bad. It's been worse in the past?"

"Easy Chaosta," he says. "The activity, and the pain, ground me sometimes."

"Lay down, let me put some salve on them," I finally say. My voice is tight as I struggle to speak past the sudden lump in my throat. I go dig through the medical supplies the demons sent with us. Finding a small pot that I recognize, I return to the bed.

He's already lying flat, quickly falling asleep. His eyes are half closed as he watches me. I sit down next to him and gently spread the salve over his bruises. Soon, his eyes close, his chest rising and falling evenly. When I finish, I pull the blankets over him, brushing his still long hair off his face.

Feeling restless, I look around the room. I could start unpacking some things, but I don't want to disturb him. I'm still too filled with adrenaline to rest, so instead I grab my sword and head to the familiar, large room to practice.

If I want to continue to recover and be capable of giving Malam a challenge, I need to keep up on my practice. Also, there's no better way to wear off this adrenaline than sword work.

ATTEMPTING TO SHIELD

The ballroom is dark, even with dozens of candles lighting the coven's workspace. All those flames gutter as the door to the ballroom opens and Cal joins us. He's the last one here.

It's been a few days since I started researching with Fem and Lent again. Earlier, when we were in the floral room reading, Lent asked if I'd like to attend their magic practice. I quickly accepted. Other than in dreams, and the alley where we fought angels, I haven't seen them work magic. After all the time I've spent researching for this cause, I'm glad to finally be invited.

Over the past few days, while we've been reading, the boys have been taking some time to fill me in on The Cause. Both what they're working toward and how much progress they've been making. I knew from helping research that they were working on recreating ancient weather magic, and I'd guessed that they intended some sort of large action against the government. Until now, though, I didn't know the specifics.

They shared that the goal is to destroy a large swath of city. The demons will then regrow that area and return it to nature as quickly as they can. While the storm is not a direct attack on the angels or humans, Malam and the coven expect that many people will lose their lives. Because of that loss of life and loss of city, they are confident that it will break the truce between the two immortal races. Of course, that will likely cause the angels to attack our group. From what Malam has told the boys, the demons will then attempt to hold off the angels for as long as possible while they continue to regrow the land.

I remember the dream of the two armies clashing and the significant imbalance. Yet again, my gut churns. I hope that Malam has considered the numbers and that he has a plan to address any imbalance.

Pulling myself out of the memory, I glance up to see Lent and Fem have just finished drawing runes and a massive circle on the floor with chalk. Reem is talking quietly with Chiron in the corner, and Cal joins him, apologizing a little breathlessly for being late. He looks like he just woke up. His hair is messy, and his shirt is wrinkled.

As he talks with Chiron, Reem unbuttons and strips off his crisp, button up shirt, revealing a short-sleeved undershirt. Cal and Fem just roll their sleeves up neatly as they participate in the discussion.

Lent turns and walks towards me. He's shoving his sleeves up his arms, where they bunch and wrinkle above his elbows. There is a brilliant smile on his face as he says, "I'm glad you were able to join us. Little different than in an alley against a bunch of angels, huh?"

"I guess I could go get my sword," I say with a laugh.

"Nah, you're our guest. I can't wait for you to see what we're working on," he says, still grinning.

"You do weather magic here, in the basement?" I ask.

"Yep! You'll have to just wait and see how," he says with a wiggle of his eyebrows.

I growl at him, and he laughs. "Where's Dio tonight?" he asks.

"He went boxing again." My voice sounds tight. He's been covered in bruises since he began going regularly again, just over a week ago. I can't imagine what shape he's going to be in when he returns to the mansion tonight.

As I think of it, Rex's face, far too close to mine from the dream of him boxing, flashes in my memory, and I flinch.

"He'll be fine," Lent says, clearly noting the flinch. "I know Pepper got him some masks so he won't be as easy to identify when he's out."

I just nod, unsure what to say. As I do, the others call for him.

"It'll be all right," he says quietly to me before he turns and walks away, joining them at the edge of the circle.

After a few moments of hushed conversation, the four coven members step into the circle, careful not to smudge the line as they step over it.

Chiron uses a small blade to make a shallow cut on his arm and then traces the blood into runes on the floor along four points at the outside of the circle. Then he steps a little way back, and I see his lips move slightly. The breath suddenly huffs out of him, and he breathes more heavily for a few moments. As that happens, the air around the coven seems to shimmer slightly from the floor to the high ceiling of the ballroom.

"Ready?" Reem asks, and Chiron grunts. That seems to be enough of a confirmation because the boys each use small, sharp knives to make a shallow cut on their arm and then begin to trace runes on the ground around their feet.

Chiron watches them closely, staring at Lent as he traces his runes. "Careful to close the points on Berkano," Chiron growls at him.

Lent's shoulders tense, but without a word he slowly makes the correction.

They each stand as they finish that task. Lent is placed across from Cal, and they seem to focus on each other as Reem and

Fem, across from each other, do the same. Their lips begin to move, and I hear a quiet, almost mumbled chant.

Chiron slowly walks around the circle, watching them closely. From my position, sitting on a crate a few yards away, I can just hear him occasionally saying something. He seems to be giving them feedback on intent or energy.

As he walks behind Lent, I hear him growl, "Focus, Lent."

For a while, nothing else seems to happen. Then they all stop chanting at the same moment. Silence hangs in the air. I catch movement from Reem. He's made a small cut on his other arm and is tracing additional runes around the first. His chest is heaving slightly as though he's been running.

One by one, the others do the same. I note that their breathing is also heightened. Sweat glistens on all their faces. Even though there doesn't seem to be anything else happening as they each trace their runes, their movements are precise. Between tasks, they remain focused on the coven member across from them.

As I wonder what might come next, I watch one of Lent's sleeves slide down his arm. I wince as I realize it's going to be stained with blood.

Then Reem begins to chant. As he does, rain begins to fall around them. I suddenly realize what Chiron's magic did as I see that it is contained within the circle, the air still shimmering slightly at the edges.

Next Fem begins to chant. The sound clashes against Reem's words, but the magic is clearly working together because the rain picks up, seeming to grow more volatile.

They're all soaked through quickly, their hair hanging in sodden tendrils against their cheeks or in their eyes, but they hardly seem to notice.

Cal begins to chant, and a bolt of lightning strikes the ground in the center of where they're standing. I jump at the sudden, loud sound, my heart beating hard against the walls of my chest.

Chiron is standing directly behind Lent now, and his shoulders are so tense, tight against his shirt that I wonder how he hasn't ripped it. I hear him growl something, but I can't hear the words over the sound of the rain.

I can hear Lent though as he begins to chant. As his voice adds to the others, the wind suddenly begins to whip at the rain, beating it sideways against the protective circle. The boys are somehow maintaining their feet despite the strong force that's battering against them.

The hair on the back of my neck and my forearms is standing on end. I realize I'm gritting my jaw as I begin to fear for the safety of men who are like family to me.

Chiron says something to Lent again, nearly shouting, and I flinch.

Why is he so angry at Lent?

The wind continues to strengthen, and Chiron takes a step forward as though he wants to join the others. Then the movement of the rain begins to change. It begins to churn in a sort of circular motion. The four boys are fighting even harder against the strength of it.

After a few more moments, Chiron shouts, "That's enough!"

They all gradually stop chanting, one by one in reverse order to how they began. The weather effects finally cease. As they each crouch and erase the runes at their feet, Chiron does something to banish the effect that caused the shimmering in the air. He steps forward then, nearest to Lent. I can tell that he's saying something, but it's too quiet to make out the words.

I realize I'm shaking slightly as I watch them debrief whatever just happened.

After several minutes, Fem gathers towels and passes them to the others. They're each shaking slightly as they dry their hair. They talk for a while longer, and then Fem walks over to where I'm watching. "What did you think?"

"That wasn't quite what I expected," I say with a tight laugh.

"Yeah," he says as he brushes damp hair out of where it's flopped again into his eyes, "It's getting pretty intense, and this is nothing compared to what we'll need if we're going to take out a large enough chunk of city."

My chest tightens as I imagine it.

Lent joins us and, with a grin, says, "It's thanks to you that we've accomplished what we have so far."

"We owe you our sincerest thanks, really, Chaosta," Fem says.

I feel a blush rising in my cheeks. "I'm always happy to help."

From where he's talking with the other two, Chiron calls out, "Let's get back to it you two. Chaosta, you're a distraction now. Why don't you go check on Dio."

"Grumpy demon," I say to the boys.

Fem laughs and looks at Lent, who grins crookedly at him. Then they rejoin the others as I make my way out of the basement.

I return to our room to find Dio already asleep. He still hasn't shaved. I haven't said anything to him about it. I'm not sure if it's a sign that he's struggling with something or if he just wants to keep the beard. At any rate, I trust that if he is struggling with something, he'll tell me when he's ready.

When I pull back the covers, I note that he is, indeed, covered in even more bruises. I sigh and undress and then curl up carefully against him. Still mostly unconscious, he wraps his arms around me, and I relax as sleep quickly claims me.

~

ain pours down around me, dragging my hair into my eyes and making it hard to breathe. I'm gasping for air, and my arms are aching. The acrid scent of combat magic is so strong that my eyes are tearing with it.

I swipe the hair out of my eyes with my forearm and suddenly, breathing becomes even more difficult. I'm completely surrounded by angels. Across the sea of brightness, Dio is staring at me as he falls to his knees. Instantly, he's surrounded by bright wings.

An agonized scream tears its way out of my throat. It tastes like death, a dirge of copper against my senses.

Then my view of Dio is blocked by a form. I somehow know who it is even before I look up to see Rex's face. I'm shaking, and my knees feel weak, but I fight to remain standing. He grins at me, all teeth and smirking arrogance.

I step toward him, holding my sword in a shaking hand. Before I can get far, I feel an impact and look down to see the painfully familiar sight of a sword protruding from my abdomen.

When I look back up expecting Rex, instead Lily is standing in front of me. Her face is white. "Help me," she gasps as blood drips down the bridge of her nose from the familiar wound on her forehead.

I open my mouth to scream again, but no sound emerges, and everything goes black.

~

I wake, fighting against restraints that are trying to bind me.

Then I hear Dio's voice. "Chaosta, it's me. It was just a dream. You're alright."

I go still, gritting my teeth to keep from screaming. My lungs fight for air, breath heaving through my nose. I slowly relax as he holds me.

"Just a dream," he says. His fingers are splayed against my back, and he's gently caressing the skin there with his thumb.

Slowly, my breathing evens out.

"Want to talk about it?" he asks after a few minutes.

I shake my head.

He sighs but doesn't ask again.

"What time is it?" I ask.

"Late night or early morning," he yawns. "Want some water?"

I nod.

He detangles himself and rises, leaving the room for the kitchen.

The bed feels cold without him, and I lie on my back, trying to relax and slow my still rapidly beating heart. When he returns, I drink some water as he disappears into the bathroom. As he gets back to bed, he wraps his arms around me again I somehow manage to return to sleep.

A few more days pass, full of books, research, and friends. Lent even teaches me how to make coffee. He's quite good at it. When I ask where he learned, he shares more about how, in a roundabout way, it relates to why he joined the band.

It turns out that his goal when he was younger was to open a small food shop. He worked diligently, and at a remarkably young age, he opened his own little store. He was wildly successful for a couple of years. People traveled great distances to get his pastries and other baked goods.

Eventually, though, the cost of food and the space he was renting increased beyond what he could afford. Instead of giving up, he began to research why the cost of food was so high. When he did, he unearthed resources that aren't readily available to the general population and discovered the truth that so few know. Demons produce all of the food to support our world, and the space they have to farm is limited to only the canopy farms. When he realized how dire the situation was, he found a group that was trying to find a solution. That was where he met the prior lead singer and Reem.

During the hours we spend researching, I also get to know Cal a bit better. He seems uncomfortable around me, but opens up a bit when he's around the other boys. He shares that he's starting to feel more comfortable working magic. I have to smother a grin when he talks about how gruff and moody Chiron is.

Magic is something we can compare notes on. The few times we do end up chatting, we mostly discuss the difficulty of learning magic. It's nice to have someone else to talk to about learning something new.

Finally, the day that Malam will be here to train with us dawns.

The day drags on. Dio opts not to go to the gym to save his energy for the evening, and I decided to skip research because I'm sure I wouldn't be able to concentrate. Instead, we rest in our room, and he tells me about boxing and the opponents that he fights.

The gym sounds nice. I guess I hadn't realized how structured it was, much like sword work. I had pictured people punching each other while an audience made bets, like the dream with Rex. However, Dio tells me that's not what it's like.

Mostly, though, I struggle to concentrate on what he's telling me. Between research and practicing the sword, I feel like I've barely seen him except when I stumble to bed at night. We've both been sleeping more than normal, still, as our bodies continue to heal.

My mind feels fuzzy with his arms around me. As my fingers slide against hot skin and the ridges of well-defined muscles, I can't help but wonder how I'm going to be able to concentrate well enough to make it through a sparring match with Malam.

It's not until we leave our room, headed for dinner, that I realize we didn't talk at all about tonight. Thinking about Dio sparing makes my stomach churn. I'm scared of Malam hurting him, but mostly I'm scared that he'll lose control of all that magic and activate the Killswitch rune. Maybe someday that fear will let go of me, but right now, so soon still after learning of the danger to him, it has me tightly in its grip.

Dinner is quiet despite all of us sitting at the table together. Dio and I haven't been making it to meals at the same time, and his presence seems to mostly shut down the easy conversation I'm used to. However, I'm not that disappointed since it feels like all I can focus on is keeping my food down.

Glancing at Dio, I see that his shoulders are tight, his expression guarded, and I suspect he might be feeling similarly.

Eventually, it's time for the demons to arrive and I rise, bidding the others good luck with their magic as they head to the basement. Then I follow Dio into the entry hall. Catching his hand, I pull him into the office.

"We need to wait here. Malam doesn't know where to go tonight," I say tightly.

His jaw ticks, and he's avoiding my eyes. Knowing I can't make this better for either of us, I keep my mouth shut. My knees bounce, and I watch the door, sitting on one of the leather chairs. Dio remains standing, leaning against the wall near the entrance.

Eventually, I hear the front door open, and we leave the office to see Malam and Chiron entering the mansion. Malam is carrying two wooden practice blades and has a linen bag over his shoulder.

"Good to see you, Dio, and you, Chaosta," Chiron says.

Dio greets him back, but I can't quite make myself speak. With a nod to me and a searching look, Chiron walks toward the door to the basement.

I go to Malam and hold out a hand for the swords. He glances over my shoulder at Dio and simply tightens his grip on them. "Nice to see you, Dio," he says.

"You too," Dio says. His voice is tight.

"So, ballroom?" Malam asks, as he looks at me. His voice is almost forcefully casual.

I shake my head, "I don't want to bother the others, and Reem will make a fuss if we interrupt their work. I have a room cleared upstairs that I think we can use."

"Lead the way," he says.

I turn and head up the stairs with Dio walking close at my shoulder. His face is still pale and grim-looking, but he lifts one side of his mouth in a grimace-like smile when he glances at me. I return it shakily. As we walk through the door into the large room, I say, "This is it. Will this work?"

Malam walks around, examining the space. He looks over the few piles of furniture still covered in dust-cloths that I moved out of the way so long ago. Searching through one of the piles, he frees a small table and a chair and sets the linen bag and wooden practice blades down on the table. "Who's first?" He asks.

My chest tightens when Dio says, "I'd like to go first."

"Excellent," Malam says. "Come here, Chaosta."

Dio's hand tightens on mine.

Malam doesn't seem to notice Dio's hesitation as he focuses on removing books from the linen bag.

I squeeze his fingers and then turn and, on tiptoes, pull his head down to me and kiss him. It starts out gentle and close-lipped but quickly turns hungry. His other hand cups my back at the base of my spine. He releases my hand to trace his fingers gently into my hair. His touch is reverent, at odds with the heat of the kiss. Somehow, my heart calms in my chest as heat blooms in my abdomen.

Eventually, I pull back, and Dio blinks his eyes open, meeting mine. The gold specks seem to dance like flames as he looks at me. “Fuck,” he says as he runs a hand through his hair.

“Please be careful,” I say in a quiet voice, and he blinks at me. He looks slightly surprised, as though he didn’t realize I’d be struggling with this too.

Before either of us can say anything else, though, Malam says, “Chaosta?”

I walk slowly, dragging my feet, to join him at the table.

As I approach, his eyes search mine. He doesn’t say anything until I get to the table, and he hands me a book. “I thought we could make the best use of our time and you could focus on learning some history while I spar with Dio,” he says.

There’s an expression on his face that tells me he knows exactly what he’s doing. I sigh and grumble, “Demons,” at him before I take the book and sit at the table as he chuckles.

He pushes a pen and some paper toward me and says, “Start on page 143 and fill that paper with notes. I’ll check your work when we get done here.”

I grumble at him but nod, open the book, and start reading. My attention is split, though, as he returns to the center of the room to join Dio. Unable to do much reading, instead I listen to I a quiet conversation between the two of them, the words not fully audible. It goes on for long enough, though, that eventually I forget about them as I’m pulled into the book.

Much of what I read is familiar. As though some part of me lived through events from thousands of years ago. Of course, that’s impossible.

I guess that’s what happens when an immortal being shares some of their life force with you.

My focus is then fully captured as I read about how mythical creatures once lived in peace across a wild world. I feel my jaw drop. I didn't realize there was ever anything other than demons, angels, and humans.

The book has explanations and drawings of beings such as pegasus, dragons, phoenixes, and other humanoids such as mermaids, fairies, and sirens. As I read, I find out that angels and demons existed as well, but they were inaccessible, living in their respective shadow realms. When humans began to increase in numbers, there began to be a conflict between them and the humans.

Then my attention is pulled away from the book as something tugs at my awareness. I hear a thump and see that Malam has fallen to his knees. His face is red, and the air is filled with the now familiar, acrid smell of combat magic.

Dio is standing a few yards away and says calmly, "If you need air before you figure it out, just tap out."

Malam shakes his head slightly, and I see that his fingers are moving and his chest heaving as though he's fighting against some force.

"We've got to work on that tell," Dio grumbles as he watches Malam's fingers. He's relaxed, unmoving, and his posture is almost lazy.

Suddenly, the air begins to glimmer in front of Dio, and I open my mouth to say something. Before I can make a sound, though, a corner of his mouth quirks up, and the glimmer suddenly disappears as he says, "That's not going to help you here. You're running out of time to figure this out. Unless you want me to let up?"

I blink.

He didn't even move. I briefly remember Malam using combat magic when we were breaking Dio out, and the effort it seemed to take.

My mouth goes dry.

I risk a glance at Malam and see that he's shaking his head slightly, even though his lips have a bluish tinge to them.

I glance at Dio again and see that he's looking at me. He has a smirk on his face as he says, "Chaosta, you're supposed to be reading."

My heart speeds up, and I have to force myself to look away and go back to my book.

I struggle to concentrate for a bit, especially when I hear Malam gasping and coughing as Dio says, "When you've caught your breath, we'll try again. If you need help, just say so, and I'll show you how to do it."

Eventually, the book captures my attention again as I read that the angels got greedy and decided they wanted to rule. They arrived from the bright realm and began to mingle with humans, blending in and hiding themselves, and winning the humans over. As technology and industry began to take over the wild spaces, the demons finally realized they couldn't remain in the shadow realm any longer.

Unfortunately, they realized what was happening too late and, while they initially tried to endear themselves to humans, the angels had too much influence. They had made life easy with advances such as running water, and they were keeping them safe. Thanks to that power, the angels were able to skew the narrative to portray demons as evil instead of as an important part of balance. That forced the demons into hiding.

Demons eventually made a deal with the angels to handle farming and grow food. Because of the structure of those farms, though, they are spread thin over the entire world, while the angels are able to concentrate in the city centers. Apparently, the angels have also integrated themselves into politics over the years, and this has been causing the world to slide further, quicker, into a significant imbalance.

According to the author of this book, because of all the

advances in technology, angels don't use magic anymore. What they are extremely skilled at is combat.

I have just about filled up two whole pages of notes when I realize Dio is approaching me. "Hey," he says. He looks tired and slightly pale, but I'm glad to see that he seems all right. In fact, other than a tendril of hair stuck to his temple with sweat, he seems no different.

I stand and close the distance between us, and he cups my chin firmly with calloused fingers. "Are you sure you're feeling up to this?" His eyes are pinning me with a focused intensity that I'm familiar with.

My skin where he's touching me feels warmer than it should. I drag in a breath, attempting to pull my focus to the thought of sword fighting and not the man standing so temptingly close to me. "I'm fine. I'll be fine," I somehow manage to say.

"Your turn, Chaosta," Malam calls.

Dio tenses, his fingers tightening slightly. I feel as though his eyes might burn me alive. "It's alright if you want to go to our room and go to sleep early," I mumble.

"I'll be staying," he says tightly.

I wrap my fingers around his wrist. "You going to kiss me?"

"I'm considering," he says, but a corner of his mouth quirks up, and his shoulders relax. Then he does just that.

Malam clears his throat.

Dio growls into my mouth, and as he pulls back, he nips at my bottom lip, making me gasp.

I slowly blink back into awareness, and when I can trust that my legs won't give out, I step around him and join Malam. As I approach, he hands me a wooden practice blade. As we set up to spar, I realize that while Dio might have looked a little tired, Malam looks exhausted. His shirt and hair are soaked through with sweat, and he's pale.

"You alright?" I ask before we get started.

"Oh, I'm fine," Malam says. "It was good for me to spar like that again. I've not practiced combat magic in a while, and it showed. It will be good to get more practice."

My heart rate picks up slightly as I'm reminded that they'll be sparring again in the near future. Then I take the position of the first sword fighting form. As Malam mirrors me, we start on the first set.

DIO'S JOURNAL - ENTRY 11

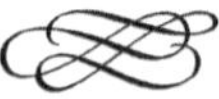

Annum:5615
Entry 11 - praedonius

As I write this, I'm watching Chaosta sleep peacefully in our bed. I should be there with her. I'm exhausted, not only physically, but mentally. Combat magic, especially with so many available runes, is tiring, and I'm sore all over from their use.

Malam was fine as an opponent, I guess. I got a feeling for his skill level when I went after him at the demon stronghold. I knew he wouldn't be a match for me, but, honestly, he was worse than I thought. At any rate, I'm glad to be able to help him improve a bit. Anything I can help him with will pay off in the future. Honestly, I don't know why Chiron hasn't tutored him. As I mentioned previously, I'm fairly certain I could still best Chiron, but he would certainly put up more of a fight. It seems like he would help Malam get better, but perhaps there is bad blood between them. Anyway, it is good to have an opponent to spar with magically again after all this time.

I must admit Malam is growing on me a bit. I wouldn't have thought to distract Chaosta with something. Honestly, because of my own fear of her getting hurt while sparring with him, I was so unfocused that I didn't realize how scared she was to watch me. Then I saw her face when she clung to me as we walked into that room. I feel bad that I hadn't checked with her sooner.

Thankfully, Malam thought about it and came prepared with a history book and some homework. She only got distracted once when I first stole the air from him. After that, she seemed too focused on the book to pay much attention.

I wished, as she went to spar with him, that I'd thought to bring something to distract myself. I think watching her and Malam was alright only because I was still tired from my session with him. Well, that and the fact that I was a bit distracted by how fucking gorgeous she is. Every movement was efficient, graceful, and wasted no energy. Malam never once got through her defenses, even when they did a second, faster round. She got him once, which she owed him.

Despite my fear she would get hurt, I can't believe how proud I am of her. Also, I can't believe how much I wanted her. If she hadn't clearly been sore when they finished, if we both hadn't been so tired, I doubt either of us would be sleeping right now.

I only vaguely remember her fighting the ~~muggers~~ angels in the alley. I was bleeding and in quite a bit of pain, and there was a dead ~~guy~~ angel nearly on top of me that she had just stabbed through the back. Shock doesn't quite describe how I felt. I also think her skill has increased since then. I hope it has. I can't quite reconcile that at some point in the future, we will almost certainly have cause to be in combat together. All the more reason for me to continue to get my shit together. Next time we have a reason to fight those bastards, I want to be standing at her side.

The darkness of the upcoming action is still weighing on me, but maybe my soul being in ruins is all right when she's becoming woven into the fabric of it.

That reminds me, I need to talk with Lent soon. Not now, obviously, right now I need to get to bed. At any rate, there is plenty of time to worry about potential future battles when the love of my life isn't asleep in our bed waiting for me.

CLAIMING

The first thing my senses pick up is the strong smell of antiseptic. It's so strong that it burns my lungs. I cough and agony splinters through me, focused primarily on my wrists. Sharp pain radiates down my arms, skin and tendons abused as I hang from them. The metal of the manacles digging into sensitive skin. My fingers tingle, and my shoulders ache.

I scrape my eyes open and see that I'm in a familiar bright room. I'm disoriented trying to remember why this is familiar. I know I've been here before.

Was it a dream?

Then, further disorienting, the dream seems to move back instead of forward, and I feel as though I'm dragged through a wall into a dark space. I'm naked and bound. The floor is hard beneath me, and my head aches. The room grows darker until I'm in near total blackness.

As I look around, trying to figure out where I am, I realize I'm no longer bound, and I'm dressed. I blink and realize that I'm holding a knife and carving a twisting shape into the skin on the underside of my wrist.

My vision twists, and the room is suddenly bright again.

Not a room, a hallway maybe?

A massive group of angels is running toward me and, despite the sword in my hands, I have a feeling that they're going to win this time. As my heart races in my chest and aches as though it is going to break, the rune carved into my wrist is suddenly covered in flames, and I scream and thrash against the pain.

~

I wake roughly, clawing out of a dark hole.

I can't breathe.

When I open my eyes, I see Dio's face near mine from where he's leaning over me. I'm gasping for breath and soaked in sweat. I look down at my wrist, and I'm glad to see the skin is unbroken.

"Were you dreaming again?" he asks, his voice still hoarse with sleep. Despite that, I can clearly hear a note of fear. "I woke up to you screaming and thrashing around," he says as he pulls me to his chest.

"It was just a dream," I say. A lie not just to him but to myself. A lie I'd like desperately to believe. I'm too used to these dreams now, and the pieces from this will come true. I don't know when, and I don't know where, but these were windows into a future I will experience.

As I try to relax, caged by his arms, I remember falling into bed late last night. We were both exhausted after our time with Malam and barely able to undress. I remember thinking that Dio got up at some point before returning to bed with me, but the memory is vague.

Eventually, he releases his firm hold on me, and I feel him stretch. "Looks like we must have slept in a bit. We should get up so we don't miss breakfast," he groans.

I snuggle closer against him, and he chuckles. Then he rises and, scooping me up in his arms, carries me into the bathroom. Setting me on my feet, he goes to the shower and turns on the water. I glance at myself in the mirror and see tangled pink hair resting against particularly pale skin. I flinch slightly at my appearance.

He takes my hand and leads me into the shower. As he cleans himself while I wash my hair, he asks, “Do you need to wear that necklace?”

“What do you mean?” I ask, suddenly nervous that he’s going to want more information about it.

“It’s just...how much do you like that friend?”

I smirk slightly without being able to stop myself, but since I’m facing away, he doesn’t see it. “The friend is quite young, certainly less than half your age. It was just a thoughtful gift,” I say as I turn to face him.

He looks satisfied but says, “I’d like you to wear something I got you.”

Joy perfuses every atom of my being as I say, “I’d like that too.”

A smile spreads across his face, and he kisses me gently. Then, before we can get distracted and miss breakfast, he steps out of the shower.

I can hear both of our stomachs growling.

Dio brings me a towel, his already wrapped around his waist. I dry off as I watch him looking at himself in the mirror and examining his beard. I step into the other room, dress myself quickly, and soon he is dressed as well.

We make it to the door into the dining room just as Reem is leaving. He stops us and reminds us that the concert is later. Thanking him, I begin to push past him, my nose drawing me to the smells of breakfast. However, he continues to block the door as he looks at Dio and says, “Actually, there is something I’ve been meaning to ask you. I should have before today, but we had another option fall through just a short while ago.”

"What's going on, Reem?" Dio asks. He sounds annoyed, probably with hunger.

"We're short a few security personnel for the concert tonight," he says as he draws his hand over his chin. "I wondered if you would mind being a bouncer for us?"

Dio pauses for a moment before saying, "Alright, and Chaosta too." It's a statement and not a question.

Irritation fills Reem's face, and I carefully school my expression. "Alright, I guess she can come too," he says tightly.

"I think you misunderstand me," Dio says, his voice firm. "Chaosta will take one of the bouncer spots."

Reem's eyes widen further as he glances from me back to Dio. "Alright, if that's what you want. Just—she hasn't done that work before, and she always gets in trouble, so you'll have to be responsible for her."

Dio grimaces, his expression suddenly stormy as he says, "Were you not there when those angels attacked us, and she helped fight them off?"

Reem flinches slightly. I'm no longer able to keep a smile off my face as he glances from Dio to me and then back. Finally, he says, "Alright, I guess that will be fine. Actually, it will take care of another spot that I need to fill."

Dio drawls, "All set then? We'd like to get breakfast while it's still hot."

"Sure, yeah, that's all," Reem says as he moves out of our way and walks off, mumbling quietly to himself.

I glance at Dio and see a self-satisfied smirk on his face as he takes a plate and starts loading it with food. We settle at the table, and he rests his hand on my thigh as we eat.

I can't wipe the smile off my face.

. . .

The rest of the day falls into a familiar pattern. I join the others for research after breakfast, and Dio leaves for the boxing club.

After a few hours, however, I'm surprised when Cal joins us in the floral room since he usually keeps to himself during the day. He sits down next to me on my normal couch and starts asking questions as we read.

I'm about ready to tell him to be quiet when Lent jumps up with a gasp and walks over to sit on the other side of me. Holding out the book he's been reading, he points to a passage. "What do you think of that?" He asks, his tone full of excitement.

I'm reading the passage when the door behind us opens. Out of my peripheral vision, I see Fem glance at it.

He freezes.

Suddenly worried, I turn and see Dio standing in the door. For a moment, I wonder why Fem reacted that way when Dio doesn't seem to be hurt. Then I notice the unbridled rage in Dio's expression as he stares at Lent's back.

Lent must feel the change of energy in the room because he also turns. When he sees Dio, he quickly pushes himself away from me, but the damage is already done.

I open my mouth to say something, but before I can, Dio strides forward. As he gets to the couch, he grabs me under my arms and hauls me over the back of it.

Fem says, "Wait a minute, Dio. Let's talk, alright?"

It apparently falls on deaf ears.

Dio drops me on my feet and then picks me up and throws me over his shoulder. He wraps his arm possessively around my thighs, and the breath squeaks out of my lungs. I'm hanging by my hips and not my abdomen, so clearly he has enough control of his emotions to be careful with me. Despite that, anger rushes through me as he treats me like his possession.

As he strides out of the room and up the stairs, I try to tell him that Lent was just showing me a passage in the book, but he doesn't seem to hear me. I clench my fists, my heart pounding hard in my throat as I hang upside down in his hold. My hips are pressed against the muscles of his shoulder, and suddenly rage isn't the only thing heating my blood.

He carries me into our room and slams the door behind us. I flinch from where I hang, face pressed against his back, and it seems to be enough to start to pull him out of whatever rage he's in. Still clearly far from calm, he drops me roughly onto the bed.

I spring up and, standing on the bed, close the distance between us. I react before I can think and slap him as hard as I can. His head snaps sideways, and the sound reverberates in the room.

He slowly turns to face me again, his cheek bright red. His chest is heaving. He's clearly still angry, but there is also a ravenous heat in his eyes as he stares at me.

My palm stings and my chest constricts. I hate whatever made me strike him, yet I'm still angry with him. "I'm not your belonging," I snap, glaring at him. Even with anger pounding through me, I'm aware that I'm not fully able to keep the hunger from my expression.

"Then why do you melt like that?" he asks as a corner of his mouth tilts up, and he gestures at me.

Heat blooms in my stomach. "Don't do that," I nearly shout. "You don't get to just drag me in here and act like I wanted it."

He closes his eyes for a moment, and I see his chest heave with a breath. When he opens them and meets mine, he says, "You want me to stop, just tell me." His voice is husky.

I hesitate, but shivers of pleasure roll down my spine. I step back, putting space between us so I can think for a minute.

He stays where he is, still staring at me with a desperate sort of heat in his eyes. The anger seems to have cooled, leaving just that volatile cord of ether that connects us. His expression is anything but apologetic. However, I know with a core certainty that if I ask him to stop, he will.

The problem is, I don't want him to.

The sight of him, standing there with that ravenous expression, a hip cocked, and the imprint of my hand on his cheek does indeed make me melt. "Don't," I say. "I'm sorry I slapped you."

"I don't want you to apologize. You're not wrong," he says as he drags a hand through his hair. Then he pins me with a look. If I thought he looked at me with intensity before, it's nothing compared to now as he says hoarsely, "I want you whimpering with my hand around your throat as you fall apart for me."

I can't swallow. I want to be his. I want him to claim some part of me.

He remains where he is, still waiting for me.

I step forward and climb off the bed, closing the space between us. I move to kiss him, but he puts a hand on my stomach, keeping me back, unable to touch him. I moan as my heart races, and the fear that I went too far crashes into me.

"I need to hear you say it," he says huskily as his eyes search my face.

"I want you to claim me," I say, my voice only a whisper as desire dances through my core.

A deeply reverent expression spreads across his face, and then he leans forward, and his mouth is on mine. The kiss takes my breath away as heat cascades through my body. It's not a gentle kiss, and he bites my lip as he pulls away. At the warm sting, pleasure courses through me.

He picks me up then by my thighs and, walking forward a few steps, drops me just as roughly back onto the bed. He stares, searching my face for a moment.

"I'm fine," I croak.

He relaxes and then walks to the closet, where he digs for

something. Climbing onto the mattress, he straddles me and pins my hands. I feel him wrapping something around my wrists, and then he pulls it tight.

He sits up on his knees, and I try to move to see what he did, but my hands are bound to something. I crane my head up and see that he has me tied to the bedpost with a couple of his silk ties. A whimper involuntarily escapes, and my core spasms.

Before I can catch my breath, he presses his thumb against the corner of my lips, and I open my mouth. He rests something against the corners of my mouth and fastens it around the back of my head.

He made a gag with another of his ties.

"Your noises are mine," he says as he smirks at me. Then he moves lower, where I can't see him without craning my neck.

I don't need to wonder for long what he's doing, though, as he drags my leggings off. He pauses, and I'm just about to move so I can see him when he says in a choked voice, "Do you ever wear panties?"

I open my mouth to respond, but remember I'm gagged. My skin pebbles in the cool air, and I moan, the sound seeming to crawl out of the depths of my being.

"Fuck I love when you make that sound," he groans.

He straddles me again, and I whimper as I feel his hard length pressing against me, the cloth of his pants frustratingly still between us. He leans over and searches for something in the drawer of the table beside the bed. However, the breath freezes in my lungs when I see the knife I helped him choose from the magic shop.

He must see my expression because he growls quietly, "I'm not into that, I just need a way to get this shirt off you. Now don't move."

I force myself to lie still as he moves against me. He shears through my shirt, first down the center and then up either sleeve. The small, sharp knife cuts through the cloth like butter, and I can't help the shiver that travels down my spine.

Then he sets it on the table, and his mouth is on my body.

He starts with my nipples, and my back arches against the bed. My muscles convulse, and a whimper tears through me as he licks and then nibbles on one sensitive bud while he gently pinches the other.

He moves up to my throat and, tangling his fingers in my hair, he tips my head back further, baring me to his mouth. He sucks and bites the sensitive skin there, and I moan again, seeing stars. His mouth is hot and drugging, and the sting of his teeth makes my breath hitch.

Pleasure coils through me in increasing waves. I feel possessed as, wracked with pleasure, I grind against him with whatever small amount of movement I can gain. My jaw is tight against the gag, and I feel tears in the corner of my eyes as the sensitivity heightens to the point of pain. I need him inside of me.

"Please," I try, but it comes out garbled.

"Gods, you beg so pretty for me," he says as he nips along my collarbone and then stands over me and begins to strip off his clothes.

The absence of him and his touch is devastating, and I feel additional tears make slow tracks down my temples. I curse at him past the gag, the words unrecognizable, and he chuckles.

His shirt is finally off, and then he slowly unbuttons his pants and unzips the zipper. Of course, because it's Dio, he is neat and precise as he removes and folds them. Finally, he slowly strips out of his boxers. Unmoving for a moment, he stares down at me. His expression is ardent as he says, "I grew up surrounded by the finest works of art. None of it holds a candle to this."

The breath freezes in my lungs, and the next tear that drips down my temple isn't from oversensitivity or frustration.

Finally, he lowers himself back over me, not touching me with anything but his eyes as they devour me.

Frustration builds in me again, need burning painfully through my core. "You're a fucking prick," I try, the words still garbled.

His eyes still on my body, he says, "Careful or I'll leave you like this."

A sob bursts out of my chest, and he chuckles again.

He lowers himself between my legs, but he doesn't touch me where I want. Instead, he sucks and bites his way along my inner thighs, his beard scraping along already sensitive skin.

I'm just about to kick him in the balls when he grabs my legs and presses them apart, pinning me to the bed. "Nuh-uh," he growls at me.

Not for the first time, I wonder how he read me that well.

Finally, though, he puts his head between my legs, and I feel relief and ecstasy flood through me as his tongue runs over my clit. Still, though he teases me, bringing me right to the edge and then backing off as he nibbles, sucks, and bites his way along my hip bones. I feel him inhale against the skin there, as though I'm as crucial as oxygen to him.

"Dio, please," I try. The sound still comes out garbled. I try to growl at him, but it comes out more like another sob.

He chuckles darkly but finally moves higher, nudging my legs further apart with his knees as he lines up with my entrance. My whole body is shaking at the amount of pleasure burning through my nerve endings.

The head of his cock rests at my entrance, and, involuntarily, my hips buck against him. He growls at me and pins them, his hand splayed against the hollow space beneath my navel. Then he starts to press into me, and I whimper. The feeling of him stretching and filling me infuses me again with ever-building ecstasy.

He moves slowly, so slowly. His exhale sounds tortured as he watches me, reading when it's too much and easing up.

Garbled noises escape my throat, emerging past the gag.

"If you want this, be a good girl and make that sound you know I love."

I moan, deep in my throat, and he reaches up and presses his hand over my mouth before he begins to drive into me more firmly. I cry out into his hand, as the coils of desire take hold, continuing to unravel me.

He fucks me so hard that I see stars, his hand moving from my mouth to my throat, but his fingers just skim along my jawline, his thumb cupped around my chin.

At that, the clear but gentle ownership of his touch, I splinter apart for him. I come with a cry as shockwaves of pleasure crash through me.

He follows quickly after with his own guttural moan.

We lay, intertwined, where he fell partially on top of me, his dick still pulsing in me, still filling me. After a few moments, he turns his head and gently kisses the underside of my arm before pressing himself up and pulling out of me. I whimper, and he chuckles again.

From his position above me, he stares at me with yearning in his expression. "*Ab imo pectore* Chaosta," he says.

With no energy left to ask the meaning of the words, and the gag still in my mouth, I let my eyes close and lay boneless, somehow finally feeling like I can breathe.

He gently removes the gag and then unties my hands. I rouse slightly when he picks me up and carries me to our bathroom. He runs a bath for us, again cradling me in his arms as he waits. Just like in Lily's apartment, he lowers me into the water. This time, various places on my body sting, and I can't help but grin as I realize I must be covered in bite marks.

"You like that?" he asks as he climbs into the water with me, arranging me so I'm lying back against him.

"Mmhmm," I mumble.

He pulls me back against his chest and rests his nose and mouth against the top of my head. The hot water relaxes the slight pain in the muscles of my shoulders, and after a few minutes, he starts washing me.

I'm nearly catatonic by the time he's done, so by the time he lifts me out and wraps me in a towel, he needs to carry me to bed.

"You only have an hour before we need to get ready for the concert," he says, kissing me on the forehead.

Even though it is only the afternoon, I'm so relaxed, so sated that I'm tired and I eventually doze off.

DIO'S JOURNAL - ENTRY 12

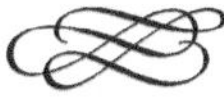

Annum:5615
Entry 12 - postulatus

I'm again, watching Chaosta sleep peacefully, but under very different circumstances. We should be getting ready for the concert, but she did so good for me. I know I wore her out, so I'm glad she's taking a nap and getting some rest, now while she can.

I went to the boxing gym earlier, but I kept it short. I knew I'd need my energy to work at the concert as Reem requested. On the walk back, she was all I could think of. I got cleaned up with a quick shower and then went to find her.

When I opened the door to that room, where they research, I thought I might lose control and burn Lent alive. He was sitting cuddled up right next to her, and Cal was there on her other side. The monster in me was so close to the surface at that moment. There was an acrid taste in my mouth, my magic rebelling at the thought of them touching her. The fucking bastards looked way too comfortable there.

I tried to get control of myself, I really did. I don't want to be this person, but at that moment, with everything we've both been through, I just couldn't handle seeing them like that.

I dragged her back to our room. I was starting to calm down. Then she slapped me, and pride overtook all of it. If she wasn't already so skilled with a sword, I'd see if I could get her to come to the boxing gym with me, I think she'd have some talent for it. My cheek still hurts from the strength of her strike. Fuck I wanted her, but I didn't want to force her. When she confirmed the feeling was reciprocated, I finally let that side of me go a little. I may have gone overboard marking her as mine. She's got bite marks all over. Still, I can't quite bring myself to feel guilty.

At any rate, once I got both of us cleaned up and she was napping, I went out to confront the guys. Well, initially I went to apologize, but by the time I found them in the ballroom, packing up the instruments, that resolve had fractured. I lost it and nailed Lent in the gut. The others dragged me off him, but I wasn't really fighting them anymore. I got control of myself after the one hit and I at least had the presence of mind to pull it.

Fem, ever the diplomat, was trying to get everyone

settled down, and Reem was yelling at me about the concert tonight and how I was going to "ruin everything." Finally, I shook them off me and got back in Lent's face. He surprised me. He stood there, white-faced, and just took it while I yelled about how he had to know that he was in the wrong. I was berating him for how he's been flirting with her and trying for something he can't have. I told him he was getting too close to something that was mine. Finally, I just came right out and told him that he needed to let it go, that she'd chosen me.

He actually looked a little surprised, and when he got a word in, he told me that he likes hanging out with her and everything, but he's not into women. I was so shocked, I just froze up. I told him I doubted it, that I knew he'd been flirting with her since I joined the band, before, for all I knew. He just laughed, but it wasn't unkind. Then he repeated that he isn't into chicks. That she's nice and all, but he isn't attracted to her. Fem started to say something, but Lent cut him off. I need to ask Fem about that now that I think of it.

Anyway, I apologized to him for overreacting, hoping it wasn't too little too late. I feel bad, actually. I knew I should have talked to him sooner. It would have saved both of us from all that. He accepted my apology, even gave me an awkward hug, and told me he was happy for me and that he plans to still be her friend. I agreed. Fuck, even if it's hard on me sometimes when they're male, she could certainly use more friends.

To break the awkwardness, I took the opportunity and asked him if he might be able to help me with some research. I've been meaning to speak with him since we got back. While this was hardly the ideal moment, I figured asking for his help couldn't hurt.

I've had a lot of time to think about what happened in that alley when I tried using magic against the angels, and it didn't work the way it should have. I did some of my own digging and learned that magic isn't as effective against angels or demons since they're immortal beings. Effects that limit movement, or affect the world around them, are still useful, but effects that would cause damage in a human are muted in immortals.

I'm hoping Lent might be able to help me find a solution. If not, all this combat magic shit I've worked towards might be nearly useless in the end. While I might be able to slow them down, if I can't damage or kill them, it will be of limited effectiveness in a battle.

I felt even worse for my outburst, though, when Lent agreed without hesitation to help out. I owe him, I guess. I'll do what is needed to mend this.

Shit, I should go wake Chaosta up now. We really need to get ready for this concert so we aren't late. If we are, I wouldn't be surprised if Reem decided to throw both of us out at this point.

STAR OF THE SHOW

I'm woken gently by Dio, and for a few moments I can't quite recall why he's fully dressed while I'm sleeping, and why my shoulders and wrists are sore. Then it comes back to me, and I can't keep the grin off my face.

He notices and chuckles at me. "Come on, we don't have much time for you to get dressed and ready to go."

I'm quite sore, and I can't hold back a slight groan as I get up. I catch him hiding a grin. "Prick," I snarl, but there's no heat in it.

He continues to grin as he holds out my clothing.

As I get off the bed, I vaguely wonder how I'm going to make it through an evening on my feet, wobbling slightly as I get dressed.

There's a knock on the door. "Leaving in ten!" Pepper's voice calls out.

"At least she's more cheerful than Reem," I grumble.

Dio helps me braid my hair, and I pull on my boots and strap my sword to my back. I remind myself to ask him later where he learned and if he can teach me. Before we leave the room, he pulls a sleeve of stretchy fabric over my head so it falls around my neck. I note that he has one too.

"What are these?" I ask, running my fingers over his.

"The masks that Pepper got for me. You'll want one for the concert," he says.

"I can hide myself from the angels," I say. "I shouldn't need it."

"Ah," he says, "you may be forgetting what happened the last time you were at a concert. I doubt that fans of The Boys are very fond of you at this point."

Remembering the interruption, kiss, and ensuing riot, I feel myself blush.

His eyes are suddenly full of heat. "Gods, you're gorgeous," he says and captures my chin, kissing me until I don't have any breath left.

I hold onto his arms to keep myself standing. As he pulls back, I say, "My knees were already wobbly, you prick." I can't keep the smile off my face.

He chuckles and, with heat in his voice, says, "Watch your mouth, or I'll make doubly sure that you won't be able to stand through the concert tonight." Then he scoops me up by the thighs, and with my legs wrapped around his waist, he carries me to the street outside the mansion.

Reem glares at us from where he's standing just outside the carriage.

It's larger than normal and seats more than six. Despite that, Dio keeps me seated on his lap.

As we sit on the wide bench seat, I suddenly feel awkward when I remember what happened the last time I saw Lent, Fem, and Cal.

When Lent looks at me, though, and I mouth, *I'm sorry,* he just winks at me with a grin on his face.

Slightly confused by his ambivalence, I glance at the others. Fem is eyeing Dio with a reserved expression. Cal is white-faced, looking out the window, but I suspect performance jitters more than any reaction to what happened. Reem is focused on a book with some notes on it in his lap, and Pepper grins at me, innocent and perky as always.

Glad that things don't seem too awkward, I lean against Dio and close my eyes, happy to relax and rest in his arms.

I doze slightly, in and out of consciousness. With the carriage still moving, Dio finally says, "We're about ten minutes out. I wasn't sure how long you needed to hide from the angels."

"Thank you," I mumble, and then I go through those steps. A few minutes after I finish the ritual, the carriage stops.

We let everyone else exit first. While they leave, Dio lifts the top of the stretchy tube of fabric, pulling it over my nose and concealing most of my face.

"It's kind of hot in here," I mumble to him.

"Try boxing in one," he grumbles from behind his own mask as he pulls the hood over my head, concealing my pink hair.

He keeps his hand in mine, steadying me as I climb down the carriage steps. When we get inside the venue, he pulls me to the side, my back against the wall.

Meeting my eyes, he opens his mouth as though to say something, but freezes. Even under the mask, I can see his jaw tighten. Then he leans close to me and growls quietly into my ear, "By all that is unholy, don't look at me like that or we're not going to make it through the night."

I close my eyes, feeling my heart racing and heat in my belly.

His face still near, he says into my ear, "Reem had all sorts of directions while you were asleep and I swore that I'd tell you. The important pieces are that we will be near the stage to stop anyone from trying to approach the band. There was some other stuff for after the concert about a fan club, and backstage passes, but we'll figure that out when we get there."

He grabs my arm and squeezes gently as he says, "I need you to promise me that you'll stay close." Searching my face, he says,

"No matter what goes down, I need to be able to see you, promise?"

Hanging between us, so powerful that the air almost seems thick with it, are the unspoken words that he'll protect me above all else. He's asking me to help so he doesn't feel the need to, so he doesn't risk hurting innocent fans.

"I promise, I'll stay in sight."

He squeezes my arm again and releases me and proceeds toward the stage. I stick close, following him through an already packed space. Thankfully, with the band not playing yet, the crowd is fairly docile, and they allow us through with only minor grumbling.

When we get to the front of the stage, I'm glad to see that there is a rope barrier between the crowd and us. I'm also glad to see Pepper on the stage. She grins at us and hands us both cotton for our ears and badges of some sort to hang around our necks. Badges that seem to denote us as security. "You look kind of scary like that," she says with a wink.

I grin at her, my smile stretching the cloth covering my face.

We take our stations, facing the crowd at locations across the front of the stage.

I can't stop glancing at Dio, and I feel him doing the same. As time passes, I slowly become both bored by our task and hot and flustered with him standing so far away and yet so close. My knees are still weak and my body still wonderfully sore from what he did to me just a few hours ago, but I already want more.

He's standing, feet slightly spread, hands crossed in front of him, dressed all in layers of black just like I am. It is so unlike his normal neat, buttoned, and pressed appearance. The mask and hood make him look like an assassin or the warrior prince from one of the books I read while staying with Lily. His shoulders stretch the fabric across them, and I can see the ridges of muscles through his shirt. As always, he's wearing long sleeves to hide his tattoos, but the sleeves cling to his forearms.

Heat dances across my nerve endings. Ragged breaths drag at my throat as I finally manage to pull my eyes away to scan the crowd again. I suddenly remember the guards he hired for me, all those months ago, blushing and staring at him, and I chuckle at myself for pitying them back then.

Then, The Boys walk out on stage as the concert gets started, so I have more to focus on.

Watching the crowd surge and hearing them scream from this angle is intimidating. I watch them carefully, eyes scanning across the massive group of people to make sure no one tries to push through the barrier.

While I'm watching the crowd, after the initial intensity subsides, I have to admit that listening to The Boys perform again brings back so many memories. However, despite Cal being an excellent singer, I miss hearing and seeing Dio perform.

As I think of it, I glance at him again.

He looks over and meets my eyes briefly.

For a moment in my memory, I'm standing in the crowd, opposite the stage, as he appears in front of me and brushes a tendril of hair behind my ear, then our lips meet. Joy fills me, and I nod at him, grinning under the mask.

He nods back and then brushes his fingers over his lips before going back to his role of stoic security.

Concentrating on the job at hand is suddenly more difficult.

How does he read me so well, I wonder yet again.

There are a few minor incidents as the concert proceeds. First, someone trips or is pushed into the barrier near me. I step forward and steady them. As I do, I give the crowd a warning that it is not to happen again, or they'll be removed. As I'm warning them, a shoving match breaks out. I raise my voice further, barking at them to cut it out, and things settle.

I have to admit that I'm surprised when Dio remains where he is as I handle the situation. I feel his eyes on me, but he doesn't intervene.

Then, someone tries to push through the barrier, close to Dio, presumably to get to the stage. I watch from my station as he handles it smoothly. When he puts them in cuffs, I can't help the shudder that runs through me. After he gets it resolved, handing the subdued fan off to one of the other security guards, he glances over at me and winks.

I quickly turn away before I entirely lose track of my role as a guard. I heave in a breath, trying to settle my heart as it tries to beat out of my chest.

Then a fan spills his drink, very purposefully, over me. He tries to pretend that someone bumped into him and it was a mistake, but it's clear that's not the case. As I drag the guy past the barrier, force him to his knees, and cuff him, Dio moves slightly toward me. Before he gets far, though, he stops and settles back at his station. The guy struggles a bit, but he's either drunk or not that strong. I'm able to keep him restrained until one of the other security guards comes to collect him.

When I glance over at Dio, he seems to be focused on the crowd, but I can see the tension in the lines of his body. After a few minutes, he looks over at me, and his eyes hold a question. I just nod, unable to communicate anything else with the distance and noise. Thankfully, he must understand that I'm all right because he stays where he is, and his shoulders relax slightly.

I'm tired, flustered, soaked in some sort of cold, sticky drink, and even more ready for this to be over.

Finally, the concert wraps up, and the band leaves the stage. I follow Dio's lead and remain where I am as the crowd slowly begins to filter out of the venue. Most of the fans leave, but I'm surprised to see that a rather large group remains behind. As they move closer to the barrier, I note that they all have badges around their necks as we do. Their badges identify them as members of *The Boys Fan Club*.

One of them starts to move the barrier, and I'm glad they're closer to Dio as he shakes his head and says, "Not yet, you need to wait."

The man backs off, and a few minutes later, Pepper walks across the stage toward us. "Welcome, fan club members," she calls out, and the group cheers. "I will be taking small groups back to meet the band. You will have a security escort," she says, nodding at us. "You have all received the rules of what constitutes inappropriate behavior and will be removed from the fan club and banned from future concerts if you don't follow them."

With that, she calls out a number, and several people walk forward. Dio checks the back of their badges and then gestures to me to follow him. As we accompany them backstage, two security guards take our place, watching those who remain behind.

My legs wobble, and without prompting, Dio reaches behind his back, holding out a hand for me. I take it and steady myself as we walk up some steps and through a door. He gestures for me to stay, and I firm up my legs and stay there, using the wall for support, while he follows the fans further into the room.

I'm surprised to see banners that have The Boys fan club written on them, along with the twisting shape of runes. Reem, Lent, Fem, and Cal greet the group. Pepper stands nearby offering refreshments, and Dio posts up near them. From where I am, most of the conversation is too muted for me to make out words, but I'm surprised to occasionally hear discussion about runes or magic.

After a bit, Pepper leads the group back out the door. I watch as she gathers the next group and brings them back to meet and talk with the band.

The night stretches on, and I'm thankful for the mask since it makes it a bit easier to conceal my yawns. Eventually, finally, the last group of fans leaves. Dio talks with Pepper and then walks to me. Without a word, he scoops me up against him, my legs wrapped around his waist. I don't resist, glad to not be standing anymore. I lay my head against his shoulder and close my eyes.

He carries me outside to the street and hails a carriage.

"We aren't going to wait for the others?" I mumble sleepily against him.

"No," he growls, his voice rumbling against me. "I'm getting you home to get that alcohol washed off you."

I'm thankful to relax in his arms as he carries me to the carriage.

DIO'S JOURNAL - ENTRY 13

Annum:5615
Entry 13 - fautor

Gods, my whole body is sore and stiff. I feel like I went ten rounds instead of being on my feet for hours. Of course, I went boxing yesterday, but mostly I'm tired from standing for so long at that concert. I can't even imagine how sore Chaosta must be today. Clearly, neither of us is fully recovered yet.

Last night, after I washed off the alcohol that bastard at the concert spilled on her, I got her to bed. We both slept in this morning, but I woke up first and brought her food in bed. After she ate, she went back to sleep while I finally shaved and then left the mansion and got a haircut. It's nice to be feeling more like myself. I don't know why it took until now. Probably just superstitious junk again.

While I was out, she joined Lent and Fem for research, so for now I have our room to myself. I was going to go boxing, but I wanted to record more about what happened at the concert last night while it was still fresh, plus, it's always tougher to write after I've been boxing.

Yesterday, during the carriage ride, while Chaosta rested, Reem and Pepper filled me in on the newest tactic for the cause. Pepper had the idea of forming a fan club for The Boys. Not just a fan club, though, a group with a purpose. The band has been identifying fans who are sympathetic to the cause and recruiting them, even sending a newsletter with lessons on runes and basic magic. It was Pepper's idea initially, but Chiron was on board, which shocked me. He's even involved one of his people who's a hacker to ensure the group isn't infiltrated by anyone who supports the angel scum.

I learned that it's been several months since they formed the fan club, and already they have hundreds of members across the region. Of course, it was a more limited number who could attend the concert last night. Those who can get cheaper tickets, a chance to meet the band, and additional in-person lessons on magic.

After learning about the concept in the carriage, I was able to observe in my role as security. I was surprised and impressed by how smoothly the whole thing went. The covens were formed and already had some practice with using runes. Most were even able to recreate several minor magical effects. The coaching on group magic work was done well. Pepper really is an impressive assistant, and Reem is surprisingly a great teacher. After seeing the additional people on our side last night, I feel a little lighter somehow.

This morning, I offered the band my assistance with that project. Reem and Pepper took me up on it and have asked me to help create lessons for the newsletters. I'm not looking forward to writing basic magical lessons, but it will be good to have one more way to contribute. Fem offered to help me with the first few, so I'm going to meet with him once I finish boxing.

It's going to be a busy day since we'll be sparring with Malam again this evening. Speaking of that, I'd better leave so I can get a few rounds in before meeting with Fem.

THE SECRET

I have my nose buried in a book about history and the ancient use of magic. The dim light is filtering in through the windows, casting shadows across the pages.

A few days ago, I took it upon myself to supervise the house staff, and we got this room cleaned up a bit. The wall is still covered in pieces of paper with notes, but at least the food and other clutter have been cleaned up.

Dio wasn't much pleased when he found out, but he isn't the one spending all his time here. He was apparently frustrated because, in his words, "as a female you're automatically tasked with cleaning."

To distract him from his frustration, I asked him more about the fan club, and he shared the information with me. I wish it were work I could help with, but Dio reassured me that I'll be helping by continuing my research.

That reminds me suddenly of what I was doing, and I focus on the book in my lap again. It is very dry and written in flowery, nonspecific language, which is why it hasn't been read yet. I volunteered for the task, and I am finding it far more fascinating than I probably should.

My ability to focus on this book might be at least partially influenced by my interest in avoiding a conversation with Fem. He saw the visible marks on my neck and looked worried. He didn't say anything at first. However, when he saw the bruises on my wrist, he went pale and asked if I would like to talk about it privately.

I declined and tried to reassure him, but I think I just made it worse. He has been watching me like a hawk ever since, especially when my legs nearly gave out and deposited me on the couch across from Lent.

Unlike Fem, Lent just had an almost conspiratorial smile on his face. At one point, when he caught my eye, he even winked at me.

Thank the gods for Lent.

I'm still pretty sure that something happened between him and Dio, but he seems fine. He still isn't sitting next to me, but he doesn't seem any more worried about spending time with me than he did before. A fact that I am resoundingly thankful for.

Time passes slowly, and the conversation is stilted and awkward as I continue to try to avoid meeting Fem's eyes. I'm thankful when one of the house staff stops by to let us know that dinner is ready. Standing slowly and stiffly, I stretch out some tension in my neck and shoulders. I expect that Fem might try to stop me again, but he doesn't.

The three of us go to dish up food, and we are soon joined by the others.

Dio gestures at me, and after setting my plate on the table, I follow him to the side of the room. "How are you doing?" he asks me, his eyes scanning as though looking for some serious injury.

"Sore, but I'll live," I say with a smile.

He leans down and kisses me gently. It still takes my breath away, and I hear a whistle. When I turn, I see Lent watching us with a wide grin on his face.

"Don't encourage them," Reem grumbles, and Dio chuckles.

"I'm going to be working with Fem on a project for the fan club newsletter. I'll meet you in the entry hall in a few hours for Malam's arrival."

"I'm going to eat my dinner and then go get a nap, I think," I say, still slightly breathless.

Dio nods and then gently kisses my forehead before filling his plate with food and following Fem out of the room.

I sit at the table and eat, but I barely taste it. I'm suddenly so tired that I can't stop yawning. Finally, after finishing about half of what's on my plate, I give up. Leaving Lent and Cal in quiet conversation, I head for bed.

The stairs take me a moment, my sore body protesting, but I make it to our room and undress quickly. As I climb into bed, naked and chilled, I catch sight of myself in the mirror, and it triggers a memory. I realize suddenly that the mark I saw on Lent's arm looks just like the marks I have covering my body. I can't keep a grin from my face, wondering who the lucky person is. His wink makes more sense now, and I fall asleep full of joy for my friend.

~

In this dream, a strange vision surrounds me. Dio and I are standing together, shoulder to shoulder, with only a railing separating us from a massive amount of water. Feelings of wonder overtake me as I look over the expanse without a hint of land in sight. The water moves and rolls, looking not unlike the crowd during one of the boys' concerts.

"We are so close to achieving our goals," Dio says, some strong emotion shining in his eyes. "I wasn't sure if we would ever stand here together like this, nearly ready to achieve what felt unachievable, but here we are."

He leans forward and kisses me passionately, and I return it. Joy, love, and agony from the heat of the flames in my chest flood through me as the phoenix beats its wings.

"*Ab imo pectore* Chaosta," he says, and even in the dream, the phrase seems vaguely familiar.

"I love you too, from the bottom of my heart, Dio," I say and feel tears glistening in my eyes as the dream leaves me.

~

As I open my eyes, I see Dio, his hand on my arm as he gently wakes me. "Chiron and Malam just showed up. Chiron and I talked, and he wants to check your injury to make sure you're still healing well."

I grimace but let him help me up. I dress in clothes appropriate for sparring as I blink the sleep from my eyes. Dio waits for me, leaning against the wall near the door, his hands in his pockets.

"Want me to stay with you?" he asks.

"No, go ahead and start with Malam," I say. "I will be alright, and he'll get grumbly if we make him late," I say with a grin.

Dio doesn't seem convinced, perhaps worried that Chiron won't be thorough enough if he isn't there. However, when we get to the stairs, he parts from me, heading to the large practice room.

As I walk down the stairs, I see Chiron leaning against the wall in the entry hall. He seems to immediately notice the marks on my neck, but, unexpectedly, the corner of his mouth quirks up. "Chasota," he says, with a slight bow of his head, as he gestures to the door of the office.

I walk into the familiar space and stand near the couch while he closes the door and sits on the short table in front of me.

"Looks like you and Dio are having a good time," he says brusquely as he stares at my neck. His voice is free from judgement but there is a question there, and I realize he's making sure I'm ok.

"We are," I say with a grin.

An actual smile spreads across his normally serious face. "Let's see it then," he says.

After a thorough examination of my abdomen, he says, "Everything looks fully healed, and there's no sign of any remaining poison. You seem to have recovered well." I note the look of relief on his face.

"Thank you, Chiron," I say. "I don't know if I've really thanked you before for saving my life and taking such good care of me."

Strong emotion is written across his face. Before either of us can say anything, though, there is a knock at the door. Chiron glances at me, and, seeing that I'm fully dressed again, he says, "Come in?"

The door opens, and Lent strides into the room. "Cal said you were in here. What are you..." He freezes. His cheeks go pink when he sees me, and it looks like he's struggling to find words.

Unsure what's going on, I glance at Chiron, who also looks oddly awkward. "I was just checking to make sure Chaosta is on track with her healing, *Lent,*" he growls. He's staring at Lent as though trying to share something unsaid.

Glancing between the two of them as the air in the room seems to prickle with something, a realization suddenly hits me. "The two of you?" I ask, my voice squeaking slightly.

Both of them snap their heads toward me so quickly that I'm surprised they don't break their necks.

Lent's face is suddenly beet red, and Chiron's is pale.

Chiron runs his hand through his hair and glances from me to Lent and back.

He looks as though he's just about to say something when

Lent steps forward with his hands slightly raised and says, "It's not what it looks like."

Chiron's focus snaps to Lent as he snarls, "It's not?"

I know a reason to leave when I hear one.

Glancing between the two of them, I say, "I'll just leave the two of you to talk through this."

Lent's face goes from red to white in the time it takes me to walk to the door, and he's stumbling over an apology as I close it behind me. I vaguely hear Chiron's reply, his voice raised enough that I can hear it through the closed door.

As I head toward the stairs to the upper level, Fem walks through the basement door. When he catches sight of me, he asks, "Have you seen either Chiron or Lent? Reem is on the warpath about keeping things on track."

"Um, they're talking in the office," I say hesitantly.

"Ah," he says wisely and scrubs a hand along his jaw. "So you know?"

"I only just found out," I say with a grin, and Fem grins back. "Do the other guys know?"

"No, I think it's just the two of us now," Fem says.

"Have they been together for a while?"

"I don't know exactly when it started. I found out about it shortly after Chiron began teaching us again following your injury," Fem says. Then he sighs. "Well, I guess I need to go distract Reem so he doesn't go looking for them."

As he turns to leave, I say, "You're a good friend, Fem."

He laughs softly. "Friend or keeper of secrets?"

"Same thing?" I say with a grin before heading upstairs.

As I get near my destination, though, I feel my stomach flip. I open the door carefully, worried about what I'll find on the other side, but Malam and Dio are just talking. Dio is saying something about technique, but cuts off as I enter the room.

They both look at me. "Everything alright?" Dio asks.

"Chiron is happy with my healing," I say with a smile.

"I brought more homework," Malam says before Dio can respond.

I grimace and head to the table without needing any additional prompting. As I do, the two of them go back to whatever conversation they were having.

I sit at the table and take the new book, which seems to be about weaponry. I open it and begin to read. I'm glad for a topic that immediately captures my interest.

This book was written within the last hundred years, which makes it one of the more modern books I've read recently. It expounds on information I already knew, such as that Angelforged and Demonforged blades are the only weapons that can "easily" kill immortals of the other side.

It turns out that the poison I've experienced was rather minor compared to what would happen to a demon. According to the book, once the poison from an Angelforged blade hits the blood of a demon, it instantly begins to spread. It is only in rare cases that death is avoided. If death occurs, the same poison will cause the body to turn to dust over the span of a couple of days. The same is true for the opposite.

I remember Alexander telling me that the angels couldn't produce the body of that first guard I killed, and I realize it may have turned to dust. Of course, that would have meant I killed that angel with a Demonforged blade. Since I found that sword on a random carriage, it seems unlikely. I decide to ask Malam about it when I have a chance.

Because the book was written so recently, the author doesn't seem to realize there are still angels and demons living among us.

Occasionally, I glance up at Dio and Malam to watch them spar. For the most part, there isn't much to see. There's a lot of conversation, and it seems as though this time Malam is trying to get through Dio's defenses. From what I can tell, he hasn't been able to yet, or at least I haven't heard him curse this much in the time I've known him.

Eventually, Dio makes his way over to me, and we swap places. Yet again, he looks only slightly tired. Dio gently brushes my arm before taking a seat.

As I join Malam in the center of the room, wooden practice blade in hand, he asks, "Did you learn something?"

"I think so, but I have some questions for you," I say. As I get a better look at him, I decide that letting him have a break isn't a bad idea. He is soaked with sweat and shaking slightly.

"Why was I able to kill that angel, so long ago now, with the sword I found on a carriage?"

"I kept meaning to share this with you, but I never found the right moment," he says with a sigh. He brushes sweaty hair out of his face. "It turns out that the sword you located was actually a Demonforged blade. One that had been missing from our armory for many years. After it was determined that the blood on you was from an angel, a few of my people went out and located it."

I must look surprised because Malam says, "I don't think I really knew what would happen when I created you. That was one of the first things that showed me how critical you are to restoring balance. The chance of that exact scenario happening was infinitesimal. Something about you seems to innately weave fate into a pattern of your choosing. It was one small sign of what I believe is still to come."

Reeling slightly at the weight of what he's expecting of me, I ask, "The author of that book and the history from the other night both postulate that angels don't know magic and instead focus on sword and other weapon fighting, but that seems unlikely."

"You are right to doubt it," Malam says, a look of pride clear despite his exhaustion. "Angels can and do use magic, they just don't typically have a need to because of the technology they have access to. I have some information that they're trying to create weapons that can cause similar effects to combat magic. Unfortunately for us, if they succeed, they'll be able to mass-produce the effects of combat magic without the risk that one of us takes by inscribing runes onto our skin."

Another section of the map in my mind seems to fill in. Where it will lead, I don't know at this moment, but another piece of information has been added. Outwardly, I flinch at the thought of what that means for the difference in power they might wield compared to the demons.

"This is why it is so important for the demons to learn to wield swords. We can not count on magic alone to win if we were to end up in a battle against the other side," Malam says, his voice now dark.

Neither of us speaks again as we take our positions and start on the first set. As always, the effort of the familiar steps and the reverberations up my arm as I defend and strike out calm the dark thoughts in my mind.

PICKPOCKET

The door crashes open, and my head snaps up from the book I'm reading to see Lent and Cal walking into the floral room. They seem to be in high spirits. Lent nudges Cal with his elbow, and they drag laughter behind them into the quiet room.

They make their way over to where Dio and Fem are sitting at a table in the corner. Their backs are to me as Cal carefully takes a couple of items from a bag hanging over his shoulders and sets them on the table in front of Dio.

Lent watches him closely, mischief warring with pride in his expression.

"What's this?" Dio asks tightly. I can only just see him between the two boys. He briefly meets my eyes, a corner of his mouth lifting slightly before he concentrates again on them. "I'm in the middle of something here," he grumbles.

I can't help but smirk at what a prick he is as I go back to reading my book. I just finished reading a passage about how to combine water and wind in magic. The book postulates that the two combined are more powerful than either on their own. It immediately reminded me of Lent's role in the weather magic I witnessed. Suddenly, Chiron's actions that day make more sense as I realize he was being protective of Lent.

I hide a wide grin behind the book.

I can vaguely hear Dio, Lent, and Cal talking, but my attention is on the next paragraph.

This microcosm of weather magic can be extrapolated to great effect if additional water is added to the mix. The larger the body of water that is combined with the magic, the larger the impact. This is thought to be driven by the interaction between water and land and the temperature differences that exist there. However, large bodies of water can also cause changes in air pressure, which can create irregular effects. These must be guarded against carefully, and the runes Burmatx and Trisap must be used in the tethering to ensure the magic user remains—

My attention is suddenly pulled as I hear Dio say loudly, "You did what?"

I look up to see that Cal's back is stiff with tension, but Lent is looking at him with an expression of pride. "Tell him, Cal, brag a little. It's damned impressive, man," Lent says.

Cal glances sideways at Lent. Then he looks back at Dio and says, "I nicked them from the central library for you."

From what I can see of Dio's expression, mostly concealed between the two of them, his jaw is tight. He looks down at something on the table in front of him. "These aren't small and must be exceedingly valuable," he says tightly.

"See, I told you it was impressive," Lent says joyfully. As always, his emotions seem to rise above the tension present between the others.

"And you think these will have the answer I need?" Dio asks.

"Should be as good a place to start as any," Lent says.

"Where'd you learn this?" Dio asks, his attention now on Cal.

Cal's shoulders tighten even further, and he looks pleadingly at Lent, who shrugs. Cal sighs and then says, "My parents kicked me out when I was a teenager, and I learned how to pick pockets and steal stuff to survive. After a couple of tough years, I befriended some musicians, and they housed me. That band eventually dissolved, but the guitarist introduced me to Reem."

Fem glances at Dio before looking back at the book in front of him. I'm about to do the same, uncomfortable with my unintentional eavesdropping, when Dio says, "Sorry, man." He runs a hand through his hair. "I guess I can relate. Not sure what happened in your case, but that's an inexcusable thing for parents to do."

Cal shrugs, his movements still tight. "If they hadn't, I guess I wouldn't have learned about all this shit with our government. And I wouldn't have joined the work these guys are doing. I guess it's also been pretty interesting to learn magic."

The door behind me opens again, and Cal jumps as Reem says, "What's going on in here?"

Cal and Lent turn to face him, and I notice that Dio slides two ancient-looking tomes under another stack of books on the table. His movements are concealed from Reem by the other two.

"Just helping Dio with a project," Lent says.

I glance at Reem in time to see his eyes narrow slightly. He opens his mouth to say something, but Fem cuts in. "Time for rehearsal already?" As he asks the question, he stands and stretches.

"You're all five minutes late, actually," Reem grumbles.

I fight back laughter at Reem's complete focus on the band, and carefully pull my own focus back to my book.

The other band members follow Reem out of the room as I try to concentrate on the passage about weather magic again. It seems as though it might be useful, but I don't know what the author might mean by a "body of water." I decide to read on and see if I can figure it out.

PART III

THE PHOENIX RETURNS

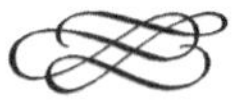

The mansion is quiet, the only sound is the quiet scrape of pages as I read that same, dry history book I've been working my way through.

I'm deeply absorbed in this book and researching magic even without the normal companionship of Lent and Fem. They're not reading with me this afternoon because the band is preparing for another upcoming concert. I'm not sure where Dio is, but he's likely working on writing magic lessons for the fan club or out boxing.

I shift, stretching slightly. My shoulders and arms are tight and sore from sparing the previous evening. I'm just shaking out my left hand when that familiar feeling of my deity-given instincts takes over. It feels as though an invisible rope is attached to my spine, through my neck, and the top of my head. It draws me up from the couch, the book no longer important, and directs me from the room. I don't even fight it at this point, despite the bile in my throat and twisting feeling in my stomach.

This time I'm allowed enough autonomy to go to my room,

pull on a dark hood, and one of the masks. I also strap my sword to my back.

I'm surprised when, instead of dragging me out of the mansion, the instincts direct me to the cabinet that holds Dio's magical supplies. I sort through until I locate and remove a few thin sticks of some sort of wood and put them in my pocket.

I also manage to control my actions just enough to leave a note for Dio that I'm running an errand and will be back soon.

I leave my room and make my way silently out the front door. As I walk past the office, I attempt to call out. I'm not sure if Dio is there or not, but if he is, I would like desperately to talk with him. However, my body doesn't hesitate, and I remain mute as I'm led by those invisible shackles toward the front door.

Once on the street, I flag down a carriage. As I give the address that I remember from several months ago, I feel shock perfuse me. The address is to the building where I went to protect Lily. A vision of the knife hitting her in the face stabs through my subconscious, and a strangled sob escapes my lips.

As the carriage moves toward its destination, I clench my jaw and try not to vomit. Memories of that fight make my hands shake and my heart pound. I finally manage to return to some level of calm and go through the ritual to hide myself from the angels just as the carriage comes to a halt.

When I step out onto the street, the sound of carriage wheels racing over the cobblestone street and drivers screaming at each other threatens that internal calm. I draw in a breath as my feet move me unerringly toward the entrance to the building. I take the steps, jogging up the flights with those instincts seemingly uncaring about the burning of my lungs and shaking of my legs.

As I arrive on the appropriate floor and move toward the door to Malam's safe-house, a flashback plays like an overlay in my mind. The memory seems to eclipse my current reality. That horror burns through my nerve-endings, a taste of acid paints across my tongue. The mental agony and sadness of Lily's loss combine with memories of the physical pain of my injury until I feel dizzy.

I realize, as my hand settles on the doorknob, that I don't know if the apartment is still vacant, but the instincts don't seem to care, and I attempt to turn the knob. It sticks, unmoving, and I feel a moment of hope before I'm guided to kick up a corner of the doormat. A smile tugs at my lips for a moment as I see that Malam, unimaginatively, stores a spare key here. Then the momentary delight dissolves as I watch my hand take the key and unlock the door.

I open the door and step into the space. As the door closes behind me, the instincts release me. Emotions threaten to choke me as I see the trail of black, poisoned blood I left as I dragged myself to the window. Someone has patched over the broken window, but otherwise nothing has changed.

Except, of course, that Lily's body now lies in the mausoleum.

As I step forward, I see the bloodstain from where she took her last breath. Unable to control the twisting feeling in my stomach any longer, I make it to the bathroom just in time to vomit. Wiping my mouth, I lean back against the wall and press my temple against the cool tile. When I can stand, I clean my face at the sink and rinse my mouth out with water.

As I return to the dining space and see the table, it's as though I'm transported into a now familiar dream. I can nearly see the shadow of Lily standing behind the table and the runes drawn across it. It feels as though that image is imprinted across the back of my eyelids.

The breath crashes out of my lungs as I realize why I'm here. I pull one of the small sticks I took from the cabinet in our room out of my pocket. Then, I trace the rune for fire in the air in front of it, and the end lights with flame. I let it burn until I have a few inches charred. Then I painstakingly begin to trace the runes onto the table top, carefully tracing out the scene that I can see so clearly in my mind.

The instincts seem to guide me on the correct way to trace each rune. As I do, I realize I don't know these runes and certainly don't know what might happen when I combine them. I also have no idea what tracing them in this particular ash will do.

Remembering Malam telling me about the catastrophic results of doing this very thing, I'm suddenly glad I'm here alone, far away from those I care about.

Without seeming to care about my own safety, the instincts continue to drive me, not giving me much time to worry about dying in a magical explosion.

After lighting the stick on fire a few more times, I finally complete all the runes. As I finish tracing the last, I step back, holding my breath as I wait for some large magical effect to take place. Instead, nothing happens.

I study the runes again, trying to think of what I might have done wrong, what I might have missed. As I consider, I have a sudden memory of Dio's hand. It is a shape I've sketched and admired so many times that I can remember every line and curve, every scar. What I can't figure out is why this memory showed itself now. Then, suddenly, I realize.

I need the rune from the dream of his hand tracing a shape in blood.

I take a knife from the block in the kitchen, carefully avoiding thinking about the one empty space on the block and where that knife is.

I make a shallow cut on my arm, drag a finger through the blood, and trace the appropriate rune on the floor near the table. The moment the rune is complete, I'm dragged into the most vivid dream I've ever had.

~

It's the smell of earth that hits first. It's reminiscent of the demon stronghold, but much stronger here.

I blink my eyes open, but darkness surrounds me. I blink again, peering into the gloom and attempting to let my eyes adjust. I'm just about to trace the rune for fire when my eyes finally adjust enough to show me something that looks like a blank terminal set in a stone wall in front of me. There is a set of buttons just below it.

Unsure what to do, I look around and realize that I'm in a small stone chamber with no apparent exit.

Without another clear path, I step forward and press the middle button. As it clicks, a scene begins to play in front of me as though I'm watching a video feed on a terminal.

I feel my jaw drop as I watch the vivid images playing in front of me. There are various mythical creatures living in a green and wild place. I recognize many of them from the drawings in the book I read while Dio and Malam sparred.

There are sirens, griffins, mermaids, unicorns, dragons, and many others, many of whom weren't represented in those drawings. I watch as they farm, play, fight, and find love. I feel sadness as I watch their lives, knowing that these beings no longer exist in our world.

Then the vision changes. A group of mythical beings is standing in a large stone chamber. The group includes individuals who seem to represent the various races. The stone chamber is massive and has large, arched windows. There are large skylights allowing in bright sunlight. The clothes the beings wear include bright colors in many brilliant shades. It is far more colorful than I am used to, with the typically muted tones we wear today.

The vision seems to have dropped me into this place in the middle of the gathering, and the mythical beings are mid-conversation.

As I try to center myself, A man with goat-like legs wearing nothing but a long green tunic steps forward into an open space near the middle of the room and says, "The humans and angels outnumber us too greatly. If we continue to fight to protect the land, our kind will be lost."

A beautiful woman dressed in a black silk gown with snakes for hair then steps forward and says, "What else is there for us to do? Our people need the land that was taken from us if we want to survive. I also can't continue to watch as my people are slaughtered."

"Perhaps there is another way," says another woman with wings of fire upon her back. She is wearing a beautiful, grey gown with a gold belt. As she steps forward, I feel the hair raise on the back of my neck. She looks just like Lily.

I feel myself wobble slightly and have to lock my knees to remain standing as she says, "We have all seen what the angels did with the war horses. They have continued a bloodline by crossing pegasi and horses. Those beings will live on because they are *valuable* to the humans and angels."

"What is it you are suggesting, Philomena?" says a man who seems to have tree bark for skin.

"What I'm suggesting," she says, "Is that perhaps survival is more important than winning."

"My people simply will not give up this land," says the woman with snakes for hair.

"What exactly have you Seen?" asks the man with goat-like legs.

She shakes her head slightly, and silence falls over the room. When she speaks again, her voice is deep and powerful and doesn't seem to be her own. "There is a blight taking over the land, one of brightness. There will come a time, far in the future, when the land might be regained. However, if we continue to fight the brightness, we will cease to be." She shudders and wobbles as though she is about to fall, and others step forward to steady her.

There's silence as they all look at each other worriedly before Philomena coughs and seems to revive. "This isn't the first time I've had this vision. I believe our best chance is to hide what we are, to be with the humans, dilute our blood, and live among them. We should allow ourselves to conform to their ways until all forget we exist."

"I refuse to do any such thing," says the woman with snakes for hair, and she turns with a curse and leaves the stone room.

Everyone begins to speak over each other, and a loud din begins to fill the room. After a few moments, though, the room suddenly goes strangely quiet.

"This is not helping anyone," Philomena says so softly that we all need to strain to hear her. "If we are to survive the coming days, at the very least, we need to stand together as one."

"I see the value in this, but what about those of us who can't form relationships with humans?" I look around for where the voice is coming from, and when I find the speaker, my heart jumps in my chest. Near the middle of the group is a large being whom I recognize as a griffin.

Whispers and quiet laughter fill the room, but I'm too shocked by seeing a griffin to pay much attention. Just as I'm regaining my equilibrium, there is a loud scraping sound, and a massive, reptilian head emerges through one of the large windows.

The din takes over the room again. It seems I'm not the only one surprised to see a dragon.

The mythical beings scramble to clear space for the massive form, but eventually, the room settles, seeming poised at the edge of something.

Then the dragon opens their mouth and says, "My people possess the ability, with our magic, to transfuse blood magically. We have done so successfully on a few occasions. We believe that we may be able to use that magic to help those of you who are interested in Philomena's plan."

The room is so still, for so long, that I begin to wonder if the vision has ended. Just as I'm trying to decide if I should push a different button, Philomena steps forward, nearing the head of the dragon. As she closes the distance, she sinks into a deep bow. "Ancient one, you honor us. You would help in this way?"

"We would," the dragon says, "for you are correct. If we are to survive, we need to act as one."

Quiet whispers break out across the room.

Then a beautiful woman, wearing nothing but jewelry, steps forward. All eyes are on her as she says, "I see the value in this, and despite having Lured plenty of humans to a watery grave, I am willing to make this sacrifice and join them instead. What I don't understand is how we will be remembered and found if we hide so fully, diluting our blood with the humans, and forgetting ourselves?"

As the siren finishes speaking, Philomena looks directly at the screen as though she can see me, and says, "I have seen that a balance bringer will be born. She will know what to do."

As I meet her eyes through the screen in front of me, the world splinters into fragments of black.

~

My chest heaves, gasping for oxygen. I choke and gasp, rolling onto my side and clinging to the floor. The bright light hurts my eyes, and I squint through a significant amount of pain in my head. Blood from the cut on my arm sticks to the floor slightly as I press myself up to sit.

I rest, regaining my equilibrium, for as long as I can before the instincts again drive me to my feet. Before they can regain total control, I go to the bathroom and wash the cut and cover it with a bandage. Then I allow myself to be guided out of the apartment. As I leave, pulling the door shut behind me, I notice that the runes I drew on the table have disappeared entirely.

Once on the street, I hail another carriage. When the instincts cause me to ask the carriage driver to take me to the central city mausoleum, I feel only a modicum of surprise. The trip takes a while, and I rest, closing my eyes and leaning against the cushioned seat. I feel dizzy, and the pain in my head is increasing, stabbing at the back of my eyes.

Eventually, we arrive, and I step from the carriage, only just catching myself as my legs wobble. The pain in my head is bad enough that it makes my eyes blur as I walk toward the large, white opening. I blink to clear them and continue on, into the cool, shadowed, stone hallway. This time, I know exactly where to go and walk directly to Lily's resting place.

Arriving at Malam's plaque for Lily once again, I check to make sure I'm alone. Then I trace the rune for silence in the air in front of me and go through the steps to break the stone slab. It falls, and I see the familiar sight of a body wrapped in silk, this time with a carved wooden rose lying beside it.

Yet again, sadness fills me as I see her body but there is no time for me to dwell on it as the instincts guide me to take the carved rose. Then, with no conscious control over my actions, I remove the bandage from my arm and watch with a morbid fascination as I paint the rose in my own blood.

With that done, I trace the rune for fire in the air. As flames light on the rose, I set it on top of Lily's body and magical fire rises up and begins to consume her form.

Panic floods through me as the instincts finally release their control of my actions. I quickly search for any memory that might help put out the fire, but I can't think of a single rune that might help me here. I grit my jaw and try not to cry as I watch flames spread.

What will Malam do when he realizes her crypt has been opened and her body burned?

There is a pop, and a shape rises within the flames. It is somewhat the shape of a bird. It raises its wings and turns to look at me. As it stares at me, framed by wide wings of flame, it opens its mouth in a silent scream, and then suddenly it's gone.

When I blink, the fire is gone. Strangely, a form still lies beneath a clean white silk sheet. I blink again, wondering if this was another dream, a waking one this time.

Then the body beneath the sheet moves, and my heart threatens to stop beating.

Swallowing down a scream, I step forward and pull at the sheet, untucking it from her body. As I pull it back, Lily blinks up at me, the skin of her forehead unbroken.

MENDING

I take another sip of coffee. This is the best I've had so far.

I probably shouldn't tell Lent, I think to myself.

"Where did you learn to make coffee?" I ask Lily.

"Oh, the doctor at the clinic where I used to work was picky, so I figured out how to make it like that so he'd be less grumpy," she laughs.

My heart soars at the joyful sound.

Our eyes are both still red from the cry we had once we got back to her old apartment. I wasn't sure at first if her space would have been rented out to someone else. We decided to check and were thankful to find that Malam hadn't done anything with it either.

After I helped Lily out of the compartment at the mausoleum, I noticed that the wooden rose was still there next to her. Surprised it hadn't burned, I gave it to her. For what purpose, I don't know, but it felt right. Then I used the mending rune to fix the stone slab again. My hope is that no one will have a reason to go digging for her body.

When we arrived here, I was surprised at the sudden rush of emotion as I remembered the time I spent with Dio before I was injured. Of course, Lily, being Lily, she saw that I was struggling with something and told me to sit down at the table while she got us refreshments. She made coffee and located some frozen pastries, which she put in the oven as I told her about what had happened since I last saw her.

I shared how I'd been mortally injured and was able to enlist a crow to get help. I told her how Malam showed up and transported me back to the demon stronghold just in time to save my life. She asked for details about the stronghold, and I learned that she hadn't ever been there or met any of the other demons. I told her about Chiron and how he cared for me and helped me heal.

Finally, I told her about the vision I had of the mythical beings and the fire. I told her about the phoenix made of flames as her body burned.

I had wondered at first if she and Philomena were the same person, but it turns out that the resemblance was just uncanny. After I finished telling my story, Lily told me about her very human parents and how she grew up in a nearby part of the city.

"If what you saw in that vision is true, it must mean there are more of us out there," she says as she stares into space.

"I think there are more, and if Philomena's vision was correct, it means that I must be the balance bringer. If so, that must mean that a chance exists for your people to help even the balance."

She stares at me without speaking for a few moments, and then says, "Is that the work you and Malam are involved in?"

"Yeah, and I think if you can help find more people with mythical blood in their veins, it would help with that work."

"I'd be happy to help, but Malam didn't tell me much. What exactly is the work you're doing?" she asks.

I consider for a minute, wondering what I can share. However, it is clear that whether or not it was Malam's intention, Lily is now an important part of this. This is information she needs to have if she's going to be able to help locate and prepare her people.

I tell her first about the angels' power and their roles in government and leadership, and how that gives them power. I share how the smog in the air and food shortages are caused by that imbalance, and that they will continue to get worse until we weaken the angels and the brightness they represent. I tell her how we're quickly approaching a turning point where, if no action is taken, demons will no longer be able to survive here and will need to return to the dark realm. If that happens, because food will no longer be produced, humans will also no longer be able to survive.

"That doesn't even consider what might happen to those of us with mythical blood," she says.

I wonder suddenly if I've said too much, but she continues to watch me calmly, so I continue.

I tell her about the coven and the work they're doing with weather magic. I share how the storm they plan to create will clear some land to allow the demons and fan club to begin to regrow nature. Finally, as gently as I can, I share that once the demons take that action and break the truce, the angels will have a reason to attack.

She is pale by the time I finish, but she seems to be thinking. After a few moments, she says firmly, "Malam can't know I'm alive."

I open my mouth to disagree, but she interrupts me.

"If he finds out about me, it will distract him from the work he's doing. He's never wanted to lead, and it will be too easy for him to lose focus if he finds out that I'm alive. He must not know."

I see the pain on her face. I know how much she loves him

and how hard it must be for her to say this. “Ok,” I say, “it will be our secret for now.”

She nods, the motion seeming to be aimed at herself more than me. Then she stands, and I follow her as she begins to pack her things. “I can’t stay here in case he ever comes back.”

“How can I help?” I ask.

“You have done all that you can for me. Now it is my turn. I will find an apartment nearby and figure out how to locate my people. I will ensure they are prepared, however they can be, to assist you when the time comes to defend the land and the demons.”

I hug her, unable to speak, suddenly as tears tighten my throat. “Thank you, Lily,” I eventually say tightly.

As we pull apart, she gestures at my abdomen and says, “Can I see it?”

I nod and lift my shirt. She steps forward, running her fingers over the scar. Without looking up, she says, “I’m so sorry.” Tears shine in her eyes.

I lower it and take her hand in mine. “This is not your fault, Lily. If anything, it is me who should apologize for leading the angels to you and failing to defend you.”

“You have nothing to apologize for,” she says as she scrubs the tears from her eyes. “Promise that you’ll keep him safe for me?”

“Malam’s quite capable of protecting himself, I think,” I say. “However, if there is ever a need, I will indeed do what I can to protect him.” I feel tears shining in my eyes.

She hugs me, and I relax into her embrace even as the pain in my head increases. Suddenly, my stomach twists as I realize how much time has passed. “I need to get back, or Dio will worry,” I say, my voice tight.

“Dio?”

“Oh, I guess I haven’t told you,” I say with a grin even as my vision blurs again. “Dio and I kissed at a concert. Since then, we..." Suddenly realizing that we're both standing on the rug that Dio and I slept on that first night, I trail off.

"Ah," Lily says wisely. "I'm happy for you." She has a broad grin on her face and hugs me again.

"Can you help me with one more thing?" I ask as I pull back slightly.

"Of course."

"I cut my arm for blood magic, but I think I cut a little too deep again. Do you have a bandage?" I show her the cut on my arm with the dried blood.

"Let me get some supplies, and I'll get that cleaned up and bandaged."

I sit at the table while she collects what she needs. When she gets back to the table, she sits down next to me. "What did you cut yourself on?" she asks.

"One of your knives."

She tuts at me. "I did keep those knives rather sharp," she says with a quiet laugh.

I can't help but laugh at that.

"Ok, that should be it," she says as she finishes covering it in a fresh bandage. "You should go now before I distract you further. I don't want Dio to be worried."

"Take care of yourself, Lily," I say tightly, already missing her. Then I turn and leave the apartment.

As I get to the street, it is apparent that more time has passed than I'd thought. The lighting, which is always dim through the smog, is the deeper dark of late evening.

I'm able to hail a carriage fairly quickly, but as time passes on the ride back, my stomach is in knots. The pain in my head continues to stab into the back of my eyes. As soon as the carriage stops, I walk, as quickly as I can on shaky legs, toward the mansion. My heart stutters as I walk into the entry hall and see everyone in the house, other than the staff, waiting for me.

Reem leaves after giving me a cursory glance. He directs the rest of the coven to follow him. Fem hesitates, but after a moment follows.

Dio is staring at me with that familiar, focused intensity, his hands in his pockets as he leans against the wall. I can't read his expression.

Malam looks worried and seems to want to say something.

Before he can, though, Chiron steps forward, his lip curled, and his eyes on the bandage on my arm. "Why are you bleeding, Chaosta?" he snarls.

I glare back at him. "I cut myself, but it's bandaged and fine," I snarl.

Malam says quietly but firmly, "Chiron, I'm sure the coven is ready to get started."

Chiron glares at him, but finally, without speaking, he turns on his heel and strides angrily downstairs.

In his absence, the room somehow feels even more tense. Malam looks from me to Dio."I'll give you five minutes to talk, then I'll expect you both upstairs," he says firmly.

As he leaves, Dio steps closer to me. He reaches out and gently runs his fingers over the bandage. "Why don't you ask for help?" His voice is quiet but tight.

My heart aches. Yet again, I can't tell him that my actions were controlled by something outside of myself, likely a deity. Instead, I say, "Because I didn't need help."

His fingers clench into fists. He takes a breath and relaxes, slightly at least. "Thank you for leaving me a note," he says.

I glance up, meeting his eyes. I'm surprised that he's letting it go this easily.

Then he pulls me into his arms, fastening me into a tight hug. "Just tell me you're alright?" he asks.

"Yeah, I'm good," I say as firmly as I can while another round of dizziness hits.

"You sure you're ok to spar?" He asks, pushing me away from him and looking into my eyes.

"Yes, I swear I'm fine." Even as I say it, I'm thinking of all the times I spent pushing myself, coughing up blood, while I drowned out the terror I was feeling about what might be happening to him.

"Alright then," he says, and he leads us upstairs.

I'm glad when he takes the first turn again, and I can sit and pretend to read. The stabbing pain in my head behind my eyes feels as though it's getting worse. I'm also exhausted, far beyond what I should be. I suspect it has something to do with drawing and using all those runes.

By the time it's my turn, my vision is worsening, but I blink it clear as I take the wooden sword and move to stand in front of Malam.

We make it through the first set, and I manage to defend and not receive any hits. As I gasp for breath, though, I suddenly feel the contents of my stomach twisting and run for the closest restroom. I make it just in time.

I hear Malam's voice in the doorway saying, "I'll get Chiron."

Dio crouches next to me, his hand on my back. "Tell me what happened, Chaosta," he says, a warning in his voice.

I shake my head, but it just makes the pain worse. I push myself back against the wall, again resting my head against the cool tile with my eyes closed.

Soon, I hear Chiron at the door saying, "Get out, Dio."

"I'm not going anywhere," he growls.

"Don't be an idiot, kid. Get. Out." Chiron snarls back.

Dio stands and moves to the door, blocking my view of the demon. "I'm. Not. Going. Anywhere."

The space is charged with tension, and it feels like, even without magic, lightning might hit and incinerate everything in its path.

Malam swears and says something in their language.

Another beat of silence passes, but then Chiron says, "What are her symptoms?"

"She's pale and has a fresh injury on her arm. She was sparring with Malam when she ran in here and vomited," Dio says, his voice tight.

"Was she doing magic?" Chiron asks.

Dio curses as he crouches beside me again. I keep my eyes shut as another round of dizziness hits. "Look at me," he says. I comply, and he tips my chin up and peers closely at my eyes. "Fuck," he says as he runs a hand through his hair. "You were, weren't you?"

"Yeah," I mumble as I close my eyes again.

He releases my chin. "What fucking sort of magic did you perform, that you're experiencing magical overuse?"

I stay quiet. Even if I wanted to tell him, I'm sure the instincts wouldn't allow it.

Dio gently scoops me up despite my mumbled protests. As he carries me out of the bathroom, Chiron asks, "Do you have any wine here?"

"I don't think so," Dio says tightly.

"I'll get some," Chiron says, and I hear wingbeats.

Despite my head pounding and the waves of dizziness, it feels like home being here in his arms. I relax, resting my cheek against him. Dio curses quietly and then says, "Please tell me you're still conscious?" His voice is full of worry.

I open my eyes and glance up to see that he's staring at me as he carries me toward our bed. "I am," I mumble.

"Well, try to stay that way for a bit, alright?" There is a note of desperation in his voice.

"I'm fi—"

Dio cuts me off as he says, "Yet again, you're going to keep your mouth shut. Just focus on staying awake, alright?"

Dio lays me on our bed and then leaves our room. In his absence, I arrange myself, trying to get comfortable and pulling a blanket over myself.

A few moments later, I hear footsteps and open my eyes to

see Dio walking toward the bed with a mug of something in his hand. Chiron is standing in the doorway, watching me. Dio gently lifts me up so that I'm sitting against him. I whimper as the pounding in my head increases. "I know, but you need to drink this," he says.

He presses the cup to my lips, and I take a sip. The liquid burns as I swallow, and I cough. "What is that?" I gasp.

"Wine," he says. His tone makes it clear that it should be obvious.

I turn my head away when he tries to press the cup to my lips again. He takes a deep breath and says, "You need to drink everything in the cup. It will help your head and protect your body from additional damage while it heals."

I sigh and let him help me drink the rest. As I finish the last of it, the pain in my head is already beginning to lessen.

He sets the cup down on the table beside our bed. "When you're feeling better, one of us is going to teach you more about the risks of magical overuse and how to handle it if it ever happens again," he says.

Then he wraps a blanket around me, and I quickly fall asleep as he talks quietly with Chiron.

DIO'S JOURNAL - ENTRY 15

Annum:5615

Entry 15 - perterrefactus

The amount of fear I felt when I returned from the boxing gym and saw Chaosta's note was painful. Somehow, I kept calm and tracked down the others to ask if they'd seen or spoken with her. I was hopeful that maybe she'd gone out with one of them, but they were all here, and none of them knew she'd left.

Fem seemed a little worried, but the others were pretty unfazed. I couldn't imagine what errand she would have left for. I know how independent she is. I know how good she is with a sword. I also know the stakes.

Also, I couldn't stop thinking of what happened last time she disappeared unexpectedly.

It's clear that she's keeping some secret from me. Or rather, she's keeping some secret from all of us, because when the demons arrived, and they learned she wasn't here, they were both worried as well.

Thankfully, they hadn't been here long when she showed up. I thought my heart was going to break free from my chest when she walked through the door. I was able to relax a little when it was clear she didn't have any major injuries. I just don't understand why she doesn't ask for help. I'd burn the world down for her. I hope she knows that.

I still felt shaky as I joined Malam to spar. I was slowly regaining my equilibrium, thankfully, and it was good to have something to focus on. We worked on magical control this time. Malam has been grilling me about how I manage it, especially when I'm in pain or my emotions are elevated. I couldn't make myself use the example of when he told us that Chaosta was mortally wounded. Instead, I used boxing as an example and explained how it's a constant background noise to control that energy, especially when opponents come at me hard. It's so habitual at this point that it feels as though it takes minimal effort.

We also worked again on minimizing his tells. He still has trouble isolating the mental energy work completely from the physical movements that we all use as we're learning.

Then it was Chaosta's turn, and I couldn't make myself sit. I also couldn't leave, so I just found a spot against the wall. I was thankful that I had the wall there to stabilize me. I knew something was off, but I just couldn't tell what it was. Now that I know what tough shape she was in, I can't believe I couldn't tell. She is incredibly strong to have made it through a full set against Malam, who is an extremely skilled swordsman.

As they finished the set, I saw her wobble. I was going to her, needing to reassure myself that she was all right. Then she took off out of the room.

We followed her to a bathroom where she was vomiting. Malam fetched Chiron while I stayed with her. Chiron told me to leave, but there was no way I was going to do that. For a moment, we were in a standoff, and I was prepared to incapacitate him if I needed to. Then Malam said something in their language that seemed to call him off.

I must say, I'm glad Chiron was there. I must not have been thinking clearly because I hadn't even considered magical overuse until he brought it up. Then again, I didn't realize she knew enough magic to be able to overextend herself. I can't even imagine what she must have done to cause symptoms that severe.

Once we figured it out, Chiron went to get some wine, and I got her back to our room. I was thankful all over again when he arrived with the bottle. I'll need to teach her how to handle this in case she does overextend herself again in the future. I should talk with the demons to see if I can get a bottle to have on hand.

When she wakes up and is feeling better, I'll get an

answer on what caused this. I'm not going to let this go. If she's out of the mansion working magic like that, it certainly risks discovery, and that could lead the angels back to us and the work we're doing. That would be disastrous for the cause. More importantly, I can't allow her to risk herself like this.

I guess I didn't realize how painful loving someone would be.

BRIGHTNESS LOOMS OVER HER

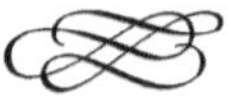

I wake slowly, a sharp, acid tang on my tongue. When I open my eyes, Dio is leaning over me. He rests his hand along the side of my face and runs a thumb gently along my temple. "How are you feeling?"

"A little achy," I say hoarsely, "but my head doesn't hurt anymore."

"How about the dizziness?"

I shake my head slightly. "The dizziness seems like it's gone."

"Good," he says as he sets a tray on the table near the bed.

I wrinkle my nose as I see that it's bread with bean gravy again. "I'm not really hungry," I say.

"Well, you need to eat something. If you don't think you can keep this down, I can get you some broth?" He looks searchingly at me.

I sigh, "I'll eat that." I push myself up to sit, leaning against the wall.

He kisses me on the forehead. "I'm going to go work with Fem on some magic lessons for the fan club. Unless you want me to stay?"

I shake my head again as I take the tray and begin to eat.

He leaves the room, closing the door behind himself.

I eat methodically, cleaning my plate despite not wanting to. As I take the last few bites, I'm already yawning again and barely able to keep my eyes open. I set the tray on the table beside the bed and curl up, pulling the blanket over my face.

~

I open my eyes to the familiar sight of two great armies clashing. I'm looking down from above as though I am in the clouds. Just like last time, the bright far overwhelms the dark. In fact, the massive difference between the two is nearly unfathomable, and I feel fear fill me. In the middle of an enormous sea of bright white wings exists a small island of darkness.

Then the dream shifts, and I see four men working some sort of magic together. I blink and realize it's Fem, Reem, and Lent, along with one other man whom I can't quite see. It's as though he's covered in shadow.

In the sky above them, the clouds swirl and condense, the wind increases, and the sky darkens. As they chant, the storm grows to massive, unbelievable proportions.

Curiously, I move toward the boys, feeling like I'm disembodied and floating as sometimes happens in dreams. As I get closer, I can see a small object floating in the center of the circle. It seems held aloft in the air by what can only be magic.

I seem not to be interrupting that magic, so I move closer to get a better look. As I do, I see the hagstone I recognize from the magic shop with the boys. It is a simple, small, black colored stone with a hole in the middle. In this dream, there is a small filigreed stake through the middle of it. Both are rotating slowly, and the map in my head highlights the golden stake. It is important.

Then the dream pulls me back to the two forces, clashing

in the middle of a green space. I am at the front of the dark force. The massive number of angels seems to glow with the light of all those wings until it hurts my eyes to look at them. As I feel despair filling my chest at the sheer difference in numbers, the angels begin to level weapons at the demons behind me.

These are not swords; they look like the weapons the guards had at Piquory Center. They are handheld and blocky and, just as the instincts guided me then, something tells me they are projectile weapons.

As I stand by, unable to do anything to stop this, blasts emerge from the ends of the weapons and bright lights of pure energy flash toward the army of demons. I

can't help the tears that run down my cheeks as I turn and watch demons fall quicker and in greater numbers than they should, even with the already unfair advantage. As they fall, their bodies are already turning to dust. Pain stabs through my heart at the loss.

Then Malam and Chiron step forward, and as the bright lights flash toward them, I scream.

Suddenly, I'm pulled out of the dream by a loud noise. I realize belatedly that it's coming from me as I swallow down another scream to Dio, shaking me.

His eyes are wild, but his voice is calm as he meets my eyes and says, "You're dreaming again. You're ok."

I gasp down a sob, and he wraps his arms around me. I'm shaking, my whole body tense and aching with the agony from the dream.

He holds me until I calm down. "What were you dreaming about?" he asks, pushing himself back to meet my eyes.

I shake my head slightly, knowing without trying that I

won't be able to tell him. Instead, I say, "It was a nightmare. Those I care about were dying."

He kisses my forehead and then says, "Well, your day of rest is off to a rough start. How are you feeling otherwise?"

"Not too bad," I say. "I still feel achy, but I think mostly better."

He moves so that he's sitting on the edge of the bed, near me. "Despite feeling better, with the significance of your symptoms, you need to rest and take it easy today." He runs a hand through his hair and looks away from me. Recognizing that he's fighting for full control of his magic, I remain quiet. "I'm not going to ask now, while you're still recovering, but once you feel better, I need to know what happened."

"I can't tell you that," I say, and I can hear the note of desperation in my voice. I want him to understand that I mean it, it's out of my control.

His shoulders tense, and he says, "I'm not going to accept that as an answer."

I swallow down words of frustration and remain quiet. *Maybe if I don't make a fuss about it, he'll forget.*

"What do you need to keep busy while you rest here?" he finally asks into the continued silence.

"Could I get some books and my things for sketching?"

"Of course," he says softly and then leaves the room.

I close my eyes, still trying to shake off the horror of the dream. Luckily, it doesn't take long before he returns with his arms full of books, a thankful distraction. He sets them on the table next to the bed.

I look at the books, trying to decide if I'll be able to focus on something so dry. Realizing I most certainly won't be able to focus on history right now, I take one of my sketchbooks and some pens. I'm opening the book to a blank page when I realize he's hesitating.

"What is it?" I ask.

He's focused on the sketch book on my lap. He reaches into his pocket and pulls out a well-worn, folded piece of paper and hands it to me.

I unfold it carefully and am surprised to see one of my sketches of the two of us kissing in the alley after the concert. "Where did you get this?" I ask.

"I took it from that apartment when I woke up, and you were gone. I've had it with me ever since, other than when I was at Piquory Center."

He says it quietly, but I'm barely listening at the end. I brush the books off the bed and, rising to my knees, move to the edge of the bed in front of him. I grasp the back of his neck and crush my lips to his.

He kisses me back hungrily, seeming to pull all of the oxygen from my lungs. I feel his hand against the side of my neck, fingers curled around the back of my head. He kisses me until I'm gasping.

We eventually pull back to catch our breaths, "This isn't resting Chaosta," he growls quietly, but his lips are lifted slightly in a smile.

I hold his eyes as I strip off the shirt I'm still wearing from when I saw Lily.

"You need rest," he says, but his voice is a husky, low rumble, and I feel like his eyes might set me ablaze as he stares at me.

"Mmhmm," I mumble, as I strip out of my leggings.

I see that his eyes are dark, all pupil as he stares at me. He still doesn't move. I consider unbuttoning his shirt, but somehow I think he might choose that moment to make me rest.

Instead, I drag my hand between my thighs and touch myself. My body is on fire with need, so with barely a brush of my fingers, my back arches, and a needy sound scrapes its way out of my throat.

"Eyes on me, gorgeous," he orders.

I snap my eyes to his as I reach up with my other hand and play with my nipple.

His eyes drop to the hand I have between my thighs.

I can barely control my breathing. I whimper, unsure what noises I make as I pinch and toy with myself.

Lust floods across his expression.

Instead of stepping closer to me, though, he takes a couple of steps back. His eyes close, and he exhales, his body tense. Then he opens them and sits on one of the wooden chairs in the corner of the room."You're supposed to be resting, darling," he says quietly but firmly from where he sits, so far away from me.

Frustration stabs hot and burning into my abdomen, like claws digging into me. A quiet, breathy growl escapes me. I rise on my knees and step off the bed, closing the distance between us.

He swallows, his throat bobbing, as his eyes travel over me.

Desire for him is a need, embedded in my core.

I close the distance and, before he can stop me, pull his shirt open with no regard for the buttons. He smirks at me, his eyes smoldering as they meet mine while I unfasten his belt and then his pants. Grabbing the waistband, I tug on it to get him to rise.

He does so without further argument, grunting slightly as I pull his pants down, freeing his erect cock.

He shrugs the rest of the way out of his shirt.

I press my hand against his chest until he sits again. As he does, I crawl onto his lap, straddling him.

His arms curl around me, calloused fingers running along the small of my back and around my hips. I moan as he shifts so that I can more easily grind against him. His breathing is erratic, his chest heaving.

I lick and nibble along the base of his throat where it meets his chest. I feel the need to mark him, to claim him as mine just as he did with me. I suck and bite the skin there, and I feel his back arch.

He moans, the deep sound rumbling against me.

I move my mouth along his neck, right along his collarbone, and bite again, my teeth scraping over his skin.

As I do, he runs his hand around my ass and lifts me gently. I keep my teeth against the skin of his neck as he guides my hips, slowly sheathing himself in me. The sensation of him filling me makes me bite down harder, and he groans.

I grind against him, unable to get purchase in this position to do more than shift my hips. Then his hands brush down my thighs and grasp my knees, giving me the ability to ride him the way I want and effectively tethering himself.

I grasp his shoulder to balance and begin to do just that. As I do, I tangle my other hand in his hair and tip his head back, baring his throat so I can continue to mark him with my teeth and tongue.

"Fuck darling," he moans like it's a prayer.

Unable to take it any more, I release his hair and let my head tip back, sweat sticking my hair to my forehead as I ride him until pleasure crests over me.

Slowly, he lets go of my knees, and my legs drape to either side of him. He's still grinding slightly against me. Then he rises, holding me tightly against him. His movements against and inside of me make me whimper as heat rushes through me again.

He carries me a few steps and pins me against the wall. Then he starts driving into me. I moan again as my tension builds again in my abdomen. My eyes drift open to look at him.

"Don't look away until you fall apart for me again," he gasps. His expression looks like it could burn the world down without even using magic.

My legs shake as pleasure continues to build and then crests over me again.

Moments later, he gasps, and his head falls forward against the wall, his temple against mine.

Eventually, he slowly and almost reluctantly sets me onto my feet, stabilizing me against the wall. We both catch our breath, resting against each other for a minute.

I'm just beginning to shiver, as the sweat on my body cools, when he scoops me up and carries me to the bed. "Remember how you're supposed to be resting," he says, but there is a self-satisfied smile on his face. He sets me down gently on the mattress and then settles next to me. Looking at him, I can't keep a smile off my face as I see the marks around the base of his neck. I've left him a collar of bruises.

"What's that smile for?" he asks.

I just shake my head and curl tighter against him. I'm nearly asleep when he asks, "Tell me you won't leave me?"

I open my mouth to respond, but the instincts wrap around my consciousness like a cage. I suddenly know that I will leave him, but not of my own free will. However, from the prison those instincts create, I say, "No Dio, I won't leave you." Carefully, desperately, I swallow down tears, my throat so thick with unreleased sobs that it hurts.

He wraps his arms around me tighter.

Even as I struggle to breathe past the weight of emotion in my chest, I feel his breathing grow steady, and his arms relax as he falls asleep.

I want to scream, want to rage and throw things, but I know it won't help. Whatever my destiny is pulling me towards won't be stopped. Instead, I pull a blanket over us and try to relax in the safety of his arms. My brain tries to solve the puzzle that the map just presented, but it was just a feeling, a knowing without any details. Eventually, against the warmth and comfort of Dio's body, I can't remain awake any longer, and I close my eyes as sleep takes me.

We nap for a little while before we both get restless enough to get out of bed and clean up. He insists on bringing me lunch in bed, and I'm happy to do whatever he wants.

The emotional pain continues to tear at me, threatening to rip its way out of my throat in a sob at any moment. Eventually, unable to remain in the room any longer, I convince him to let me move to the floral room to read with the others. He reluctantly agrees when I promise that it will give me something quiet to do and help me rest.

Once he brings my books and ensures I have everything I need, he goes to the boxing gym, and I settle in for a quiet afternoon of reading.

DIO'S JOURNAL - ENTRY 16

Annum:5615

Entry 16 - pugna

Godsdamned fucking stubbornness. I wish for once in my life that I could have forgotten something, let something go. Fuck I'm a bastard.

I feel even worse because of how Chaosta responded when I shared that I'd been carrying that sketch with me. Dark gods that was hot. Afterwards, I was focused on getting her to rest, and I knew if I left her in bed, she'd be less likely to sleep, so I stayed and even dozed off. When we woke up, she asked to go to the flower room they use for research, and I allowed it.

I was feeling more possessive than usual, so after I got her settled, I went boxing to burn off some steam. I figured it was particularly important since we've paused sessions with Malam until she's had some time to recover. We don't need her to be tempted to spar with him until she's no longer dealing with these symptoms.

I thought I was feeling better after boxing. When I got back to the mansion and got cleaned up, I finally caught sight of what she did to me in the mirror. She left me a necklace of bruises. Somehow, seeing them settled me and also made the possessiveness and worry worse. I have this gut feeling that she was lying to me when she said she wouldn't leave me. I know it's stupid, she certainly doesn't seem like she will, but my gut isn't so sure.

It was with those thoughts that I went and found her. She was curled up on the couch, with her nose buried in some massive book. She had these large, dark circles under her eyes. My heart stuttered when I saw her there, looking so tired. I was suddenly irate that I'd let her initiate like that. I should have known better. Magical overuse is serious, and it's important that she get some rest to recover from it.

I asked the others to let us have the room. They cleared out pretty quickly. She asked if I was all right, and I didn't know what to say. I felt like I couldn't breathe. I finally managed to get some air and asked her what she'd been doing with magic. Her look of worry turned into a pointed glare. Despite being so delicate looking, it's not a small thing to be the sole recipient of her anger like that. I remember it well from before she saved me in the alley. Then I saw her clench her jaw, refusing silently to respond, and my worry turned into anger. I told her she didn't want to make me ask again. I regretted the words the moment I said them.

She slammed her book shut and leaned forward into my space. I had this flash of memory of the concert where she threatened to fight back if I attempted to drag her. At the time, I was so confident that I would have had her on the ground in a moment. I'm no longer so sure of that. I had to work to remain impassive. I wish now that I'd seen the wisdom in withdrawing, but my damned stubbornness just took it as a challenge. She spoke softly, but there was poison woven into the words as she told me that she's not my property, that she doesn't answer to me, that she won't have me smothering her. I was shaking with adrenaline and anger. I realized later that I hadn't protected her from the magic leaking from my expression, but she didn't even flinch.

I fought back and told her that she clearly wasn't capable of taking care of herself, so she was forcing my hand. Then I said something unforgivable. Words I know will always haunt me. I said that if she didn't tell me what she'd been doing, I'd confine her to the mansion for her own good.

Her expression changed. I don't know how to explain it. Hurt and anger were at war in her eyes as she looked at me, but there was something else. I'd have called it hope? As though she was begging me to follow through, but that can't have been it. Then her expression shuttered and, without another word, she stood and walked to the door. I nearly said something to her. Now I wish so badly that I had called her back. Without turning around she told me that she was going to get some rest and that she didn't want to see me until I was willing to take back what I'd said.

That's why I'm here in this ugly-ass room with the awful flowers on the walls, getting ready to sleep on the couch. I don't know what I need to do to remedy this, but I'll do it.

Fuck. I'm sure I won't get any sleep tonight. I keep running my fingers over the marks she left on my neck.

I'd go see if I could catch a late-night boxing match, but that certainly won't help repair this, and that's the only thing that matters. No, I need to get some rest so that I can think clearly tomorrow and have a serious conversation with her after she's had a little time to cool down.

TRAPPED IN A DREAM

I wake in the dark, soaked in sweat and tangled in blankets. I know I was dreaming, but I can't remember what it was about. For a moment, I panic when I realize Dio isn't in bed with me, then I remember what happened.

Fuck, the man is stubborn.

Then again, so am I.

I can't believe that he said he'd confine me to the mansion. I can't help but wish he would. There was a moment where I wanted to ask him to, but then the deity or whatever, controls me took over again, and I couldn't.

I consider whether I should go check on him and make sure he's all right. As I push myself up, untangling the blankets from my limbs, though, a path on the map closes in around me. It's as though thinking of that control summoned it. Under its influence, I am again dragged along without choice.

A sudden memory of what I was just dreaming hits me. It was the now familiar vision of me carving a rune into the skin on my wrist.

The breath freezes in my lungs.

The influence of those instincts force me to take Dio's dagger from the drawer in the table beside the bed. I go to the cabinet where he stores his magic supplies and find an ointment with the smell I recognize from the dream. Bracing myself, I dip the tip of the blade into it and, with care this time to keep it shallow, trace the rune into the skin on the underside of my wrist. It stings more than it should. I'm sure it's something to do with the ointment. As my hands take the action, guided yet again by that invisible puppet master, I note that this is not a rune I know.

I wrap the new wound in a thin bandage, half expecting the flames from the dream to appear, but they don't. I clean the dagger, return it to the drawer and then dress myself, putting on boots, pulling on a hood, and strapping my sword to my back.

As I leave the room, I try to regain control to stop, hesitate, leave a note for Dio, anything really. This time, the instincts don't allow me even enough autonomy to do that. My gut screams at me of finality, of endings, and my cheeks begin to grow wet with tears. Whoever has control is undeterred, forcing my movements with enormous strength.

As I settle myself in a carriage that I'm only vaguely aware of having flagged down, I begin the ritual to hide myself from the angels. As I think of what that might mean, I begin to sweat, fighting to breathe.

My eyes still burn with tears.

The carriage ride feels as though it takes an eternity as I continue to struggle with everything in me to break free from this control. However, when the carriage stops, I still have no autonomy.

I exit down the steps onto the street and look up to see the door to the angel stronghold. My heart nearly stops, so much fear crashing into me that my vision darkens for a moment. Uncaringly, my feet lead me without pause through the door, down the main hallway, past angel after angel. Yet again, it seems the ritual worked, as most of them don't even glance at me.

Finally, I arrive at a lift and watch my hand press the button for the 111th floor. I have a few minutes to come to terms with whatever is going to happen. I would love to say that I think of the boys, Lily and her people, and the demons and how important balance is to keeping them safe. I wish I could say that I think of how, whatever mission I'm being led on, might help the people I love. Instead, all I can think of is Dio.

Eventually, the lift halts and, with a ding, the door opens, and I step out into a long white hallway. As is familiar to the angel stronghold, the lights are so bright that my eyes hurt.

My feet lead me unerringly down the hallway to a door that looks like all the others in this space. As I put my hand on the knob, I half expect, or maybe hope for, it to be locked. Instead, the door opens into a dark space.

After the bright hallways, I'm nearly blind as my eyes struggle to adjust. Before I can second-guess myself, I flip on a light, and the small apartment is illuminated by a single remaining bulb. It's messy and clearly well-lived in. I'm more confused than ever as my feet lead me to a closed door. Again, the door opens easily, and I walk into a scene that makes my stomach churn.

A small light is on in the corner, and it clearly, if dimly, illuminates a messy bedroom. Bonum is lying on the bed and they are covered in sweat. Blankets are tangled around their legs and waist. They're either having a nightmare or a seizure. My gut tells me it's the latter. As I walk to the bed, I see syringes and bottles of alcohol.

Still unable to control my actions, I take a knife from the kitchen and, returning to the side of the bed, make a shallow cut on my arm. I drag my fingers over it and trace two runes onto the bed. I don't know the runes or what they might do, but it is quickly apparent as Bonum quiets. Only the motion of their chest as they breathe tells me they're still alive.

My chest aches for them. I would help them of my own accord if given the option. They protected me from that guard, and they tried to save Lily. Their actions toward me have been kind or, at worst, neutral. They may be an angel, but by helping me they have set themselves apart from the others.

I go to the bathroom, wash the blood off my hand, and dampen a small towel that seems clean enough. Returning to the bed, I begin to wipe the sweat from their skin. They're covered in scars that are not runes, and it's clear they were either creatively tortured or have seen a significant amount of combat. Their ribs stand out through the skin on their chest, and their cheekbones are more hollow than I remember.

I pull the blanket off their bed and find a clean sheet to cover them with. Then I sit down on the floor, resting against the wall and close my eyes. I drift off for a bit into an uneasy meditation of sorts that certainly isn't sleep.

I'm still not in control of my actions, but at this point, I'm not fighting them anymore. I'm aware it's wasting energy, and a feeling of futility weighs heavily on my chest.

After some time passes, my eyes open of their own accord, and I rise and move to the side of the bed. As I close the distance, Bonum opens their eyes to stare at the ceiling, flinching as they realize I'm in the room. "You came," they rasp. Their voice is more grating than normal, and as though emphasizing that fact, they cough.

I bring them a glass of water, which they accept after slowly dragging themself up to sit. "I didn't have a choice," I say. I want to say more, but no other words are available to me at the moment.

"Ah, but free will would be such a bore, would it not?" they ask.

I swallow thickly, not sure I agree with that sentiment. They drink the water and then hand me the cup. Without needing to be asked, I fill it for them again. "How long were you like that?" I ask.

"What day is it?" they ask. When I respond, their eyes widen slightly, seeming to highlight that scar on their cheek, just under their eye. I wonder idly how they received that injury, as they say. "That would make it just over a month."

I gasp. "How can that be?"

"As an immortal, I cannot be easily killed. Take enough shit, though, and my body shuts down," they rasp.

"And if I hadn't helped?"

"Eventually, perhaps another would have thought to check on me," they say. There is a blankness to their words that tells me they don't find it likely. They close their eyes and rest their head back against the headboard, baring their throat. After a few more moments of silence, they croak dryly, "Speaking of free will…"

Finally, they lift their head, and their blue eyes stare right through me. "Apparently, it is time for me to share my tragic story with you."

I wait silently, not sure what to say.

"A few centuries ago, I fell in love with a beautiful man. He and I were like two halves of the same soul. He was fierce in his love, and we spent several exquisite years together. He also happened to be a demon," they rasp.

My eyes widen as I consider what that would have meant for the two of them. As far as I know, the two sides have been at war, even if it is currently a war of attrition, and not of battles, for thousands of years.

Bonum continues as though they didn't notice my surprise. "We were careful, but eventually our luck ran out, and our people found out. Through some arrangement, I ended up in the hands of the demons, and he was taken to our prison here."

They cough weakly, and I go to get them more water. Other than taking the glass from me when I return, they don't move. "I cannot speak to what he experienced, although I believe both of us have some idea."

I flinch, remembering my time imprisoned in the angel stronghold.

"I can speak to what I experienced," they say. "I tell you this not because I seek to sway you to the side of the angels but because it is information you are to know. I am compelled to share this with you, little bird, and for that I am sorry."

"You see, as easy as it would be to believe that one group is evil and one group is good, we are simply two sides of a coin. One in shadow, one in light, both making decisions they feel are the best for their own kind. Both sides are willing to commit atrocities for what they believe to be right."

I watch Bonum's face as they continue, my heart pounding hard in my chest.

"Of course, it took centuries to accept that. I was tortured brutally while in the demon stronghold, and I lost my sight. It takes a lot to break the body of a being such as us, and yet they did that to me."

Tears begin to slide down my cheeks. A crack seems to split through me at the thought of those I consider family taking part in that atrocity.

"It was Malam, their leader, who eventually told them to release me. What truly broke me, though, was being freed only to discover that the love of my life had not survived."

Complete silence hangs between us. I'm barely breathing, my chest tight with silent sobs. "I am so sorry," I gasp.

Tears begin to slide down their cheeks. "Rex likes to remind me it was not he who killed my beloved, but after centuries of quiet research, I know he was there. He did not stop what they did, and, as a leader, that means he had a hand in it."

"What was his name?" I ask.

"Kai, his name was Kai," Bonum says breathlessly. "I have existed for many centuries now, despite my wish to join him in the afterlife, only because I am ordered by my leader to live. Then you showed up."

I bite my lip as I scrub tears off my cheeks. I wonder where they're going with this.

"When I was tasked by Rex to bring you before him, I was irritated, but then I saw you talk back to him and something changed."

My expression hardens involuntarily as I say, "And yet you watched while they tortured me."

Bonum flinches and then says, "I, like you, am not in full control of my destiny. I'm sure it is a feeling you are familiar with. Besides, I think both of us know that any larger action would have been futile. Instead, I attended as a witness to keep watch over actions I did not support. I hoped that I might be able to stop them if they moved to take it too far."

Anger still fills me, but there is truth to the statement. While I don't have the strength to completely forgive them for the lack of action on their part, I can recognize the futility of it all.

"I can only imagine how painful that was for you to witness."

"Do not minimize your pain for me, little bird. You deserve my apology for the agony my people caused," they rasp.

Then, almost as though snapping out of a dream, they swipe the tears off their face and take another drink of water. They are even more pale as they look at me and say, "I must recover from this and do not need you to stay and play nursemaid to me."

"Are you sure?" I ask. I want nothing more than to leave this place, but something is still holding me here.

"Yes, you are no longer needed here," they say tightly.

I'm preparing to leave when words emerge from my mouth that are not my own. "Will you dance with us when the time comes?" I hear myself ask.

A look of surprise crosses their face, but they nod and say, "I will, little bird."

I hesitate for a moment, unsure what that might mean.

They continue to stare through me.

Finally, I force myself to leave. As I turn and walk to the door, hauntingly from the room behind me, they rasp, "We will see each other soon, I think."

PART IV

THE IMPOSSIBLE CHOICE

As I walk through the door and into the same cold, overly bright hallway, I wonder what time it is. There were no windows in Bonum's apartment, but I suspect hours have passed.

A sense of panic seizes me. *I need to get home now.*

I can think of nothing else.

Everything is muted by thoughts of Dio and how worried he must be. I wonder if I might be able to get back before he wakes. Some feeling in my gut twists at the thought, but my feet carry me on, back to the lift where I press the button for the first floor.

Resting against the wall of the lift, my heart beats rather too fast. *The pain of the story Bonum told me must still be hanging over me.*

Eventually, the door opens, and I step forward only to realize that I'm still on the third floor. Even as my stomach clenches and my heart pounds at the sudden realization I didn't do anything to hide myself from the angels, I see them.

There are two of them, standing just on the other side of the open door. Their eyes widen as they stare at me. Worse, looking past them into the massive room, I see at least ten more pairs of bright wings. The angels turn, as one, to look directly at me.

The only sound in this moment is the beating of my heart. It echoes in my ears.

Whether it's instincts or simply the realization I have no other options, I lift my hands slightly, away from my sides, surrendering.

They move forward quickly, hands grasping my arms and the back of my neck. They force me onto my knees and then flat onto my stomach on the floor of the lift. They speak in their language, giving orders, and I feel one of them cutting the straps of my shoulder harness and taking my sheathed sword. More angels continue to flood into the lift, pressing me roughly against the ground and making it hard to breathe.

There are so many of them pressed into the small space that panic rises, and my body finally rebels, fighting back. Their voices get louder, words I don't recognize. As I continue to struggle against all that immortal strength, I feel a sharp stab against the side of my neck, and then everything goes black.

I wake on a hard surface in the dark. It's different from anything I've experienced in the angel stronghold so far. The floor under me is rough stone. I'm shaking badly, but I'm unsure whether it's from the drugs or the cold in this space.

I push myself up to sit, leaning against the wall and find that my hands are manacled together in front of me, and my ankles are also bound. My clothes are gone. The only possession they left me with seems to be the necklace, which I can feel resting cool against my chest.

Why they left it I can't begin to imagine. As it rises to my consciousness, this item, which should be innocuous, instead causes my heart to thrash in my chest. I try to figure out why, and suddenly, the dream with the ancient version of the little boy plays in my mind again, and his words echo through my head.

"I offer a boon, a singular opportunity to do what is needed for balance or to answer the call of a burning heart. Choose well."

I sob at the fresh pain in my chest, folding forward, crushing my hands against myself. Gasping through the agony, I consider the options. This is an impossible choice, and while I already know the answer, the pain of it causes me to delay.

I feel as though I might die from this. As though I will be slowly, agonizingly, consumed by it.

Finally, with tears streaking down my cheeks, I reach up and take the small silver pendant and put it between my teeth. What guides me to do so, I don't know, all I know is that it is the action I must take.

Biting down, I realize vaguely as I'm pulled away from consciousness that my body jerks, my head hitting the wall of the cell.

~

For a moment, everything goes black, and then I'm in front of Lily.

She's standing in a small, cozy kitchen. There are a few people sitting at a table behind her, drinking out of mugs. They are giggling at something. The simple joy and peace of the scene stabs through my heart.

Lily gasps when she sees me and drops something which shatters on the floor in front of her. "Chaosta?" she cries out, her voice full of fear.

Looking down, I see that I'm translucent but appear as I actually am. That's to say, I'm naked with ankles and wrists manacled.

"I don't have long," I gasp. The pain is still reverberating through my chest and now my head. "I need you to run. You need to go to the southern coast with those of your people whom you've already found. You need to find more and quickly."

Lily begins to sob. She reaches toward me despite the expression of futility on her face.

"Please, Lily, you need to go now and not look back," I gasp even as the scene disappears and I find myself back in the dark cell.

I collapse sideways onto the floor. The necklace is now nothing more than a slim chain around my neck. I used up my chance, my one opportunity for outside communication. I used it for the cause, to share the message that strange intelligence says is imperative.

I didn't use it to save the love of my life.

A strangled cry escapes me, and I sob Dio's name over and over again. I'm confident that without communication, he will attempt to find me and try to save me despite the futility of it. Despite the fact that when he does, he will most certainly be killed.

I didn't even get to say goodbye.

Eventually, the door to the cell opens. I don't even move as I hear footsteps approach me, too overwhelmed by grief. Then I feel another sharp stab against my neck, and yet again everything goes black.

DIO'S JOURNAL - ENTRY 17

Annum:5615
Entry 17 - ignotus

It's been less than a day and already I'm writing again. If you think that can't mean anything good, you would be right.

I woke up this morning feeling disoriented until I remembered why I was sleeping on a couch and not in our room. It was still early in the morning, and I didn't want to wake Chaosta too early after everything she's been through, so I used the shower in my old room. Fem is also an early riser, and I borrowed shaving stuff from him.

While I got cleaned up, Fem and I talked. I told him what had happened and what I'd said. He was appropriately disappointed in me, but he stayed and talked. I guess I hadn't realized until this moment how much he cares, how much they all care, I guess. I'm not used to it. He didn't have any real solution for me other than talking to her and apologizing, but it was still good to have someone to talk with like that.

After I got cleaned up, breakfast was served, but I couldn't eat. Fem encouraged me to share with the other guys what had happened and, after some hesitation, I did. They all agreed I'd messed up. For a moment, I thought it might have been better if I hadn't told them, but then they all had good advice. Lent even offered to talk with her first. I declined, but it was a kind offer and, if I can't mend things on my own, I may ask him for help.

Finally, Fem told me to just go see her. I was in agony at that point, but I listened to him and made my way to our room. I knocked, and there was no answer. I waited, giving her a moment, and then knocked again. There was still no answer, so I opened the door only to see that she wasn't in bed.

Fear tore through me like a tempest. I checked the bathroom and then searched the mansion. When I didn't find her, I looked everywhere for a note and even enlisted the others to help me look. Despite not finding one, I actually think I responded pretty well. I came back here to our room to pace and try to be patient. Just because she didn't leave a note this time doesn't mean she isn't coming back.

Since then, I've been focused on the words she told me just over a day ago, her voice echoing in my head, *telling me she won't leave me. I need to believe those words. I can't stop running my fingers over the bruises she left me. She marked me as though she was claiming me, and I have to believe that it also meant something.*

It isn't the first time she's disappeared, and she's always come back after no more than a few hours. At least other than that one time.

Fuck

FRANKLY, I DON'T GIVE A DAMN

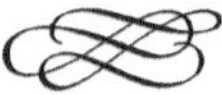

I wake, hanging, my arms manacled and chained to a hook in the ceiling. Only my toes reach the ground, and I press onto them, trying to relieve the pain in my wrists. I'm unclothed, and the room is a cold, bright expanse. The familiarity of it from the dream I had is eerie.

I can hear the movement of angels behind me. There is a blank, white wall with a closed door at its center in front of me. The space smells of harsh cleaning formulas strongly enough that my eyes water.

As I blink at the door, trying to ignore the pain in my shoulders and wrists, it opens, and Rex walks in with Bonum in his wake. I focus on Rex, who moves into the room and stands in front of me.

He has an indolent smile on his face, and he props a hip, looking rather casual about standing in front of someone hanging by their wrists from the ceiling. Someone who I'm sure is about to be tortured.

His eyes give him away, though. He looks at me with the gaze of a hungry predator. Gesturing at me he says casually, "Looks like the torture already started."

For a moment, I don't understand what he means and then remember that I'm still covered in Dio's marks and I have a couple of fresh cuts on my arm.

I don't react quickly enough to mask the snarl that contorts my face, and his eyes darken.

Lifting his chin slightly, he says commandingly, "Flog her."

Without a chance to prepare, the pain of the impact crashes through the nerves of my back, and I cry out. The whip impacts my back twice more.

I'm seeing stars as Rex says, "Enough." He steps forward, his expression still dark, and grabs my chin. He tips my head to face him, his fingers tight enough that it feels like my bones might break.

I whimper but meet his eyes.

"How are you feeling about the side you chose now?" he taunts. "Want to reconsider?"

"I didn't choose a side," I gasp.

He shakes my head side to side by his grip on my chin and then, directing my eyes back toward him, he calls out, "Again."

He continues to make eye contact with me as my body jerks when the whip strikes my back. The metallic scent of blood surrounds me and bite back a sob without looking away from him.

"I'll give you another chance to answer my question. Take care to answer honestly this time," he says, a deranged grin spread across his face.

I remain quiet for a moment, but then realize there's no good reason to pique his irritation. Instead, I say, "I didn't choose a side, I chose to fight for balance."

"It's a pity that you continue to lie to yourself and me," he says with a chuckle. "You're lucky you're more valuable alive than dead. Whether that be as a bargaining chip, a point of pain for the evil in this world, or because you are a singular being, and I am curious how you work. Whatever happens, you must not be in the hands of our enemy."

He releases my chin and takes a step back, examining his fingernails thoughtfully as he says, "That doesn't mean you must remain unharmed, though. Besides, I know who raised you, and they wouldn't have taught you not to lie. If you are to become one of us, it will be an important thing to rid you of. Consider this your first lesson."

Glancing at me briefly with a self-satisfied smile on his face, he then turns on his heel and walks towards the door. As he walks away, he calls over his shoulder, "Flog the skin off her."

As the whip begins to slice across my back again, I see Bonum, from where they're standing against the wall in front of me, flinch, ever so slightly. Shortly after, I lose consciousness again, more than happy to slide into the comforting blackness.

IS THIS A TRAGEDY?

When I wake again, I'm lying on my stomach on a firm surface. I'm in agony. My back feels as though it is actively on fire. I focus on lying as still as I can and breathing shallowly through my nose. There are others moving around the room, maybe two people. I keep my eyes closed, hoping that if they think I'm still unconscious, they will give me a little more time to recover before I'm tortured again.

As I lay, barely breathing, and hoping that maybe I will lose consciousness again, I hear the door to the room open.

There is quiet for a few moments, and then a familiar, raspy voice says, "There was an accident involving multiple carriages, and medical assistance is needed. They are calling all the healers to help." Bonum's voice sounds even rougher than it did when I saw them last.

Two sets of footsteps leave the room. Another moment passes, and then a single set of footsteps move to the side of my bed, the side my face is turned to. "Chaosta?" Bonum asks. I hear them mumble something in their language that sounds like a curse. "Tell me you are conscious."

"What?" I gasp.

Bonum lets out a breath in a sigh and then says, "I don't have long. It is a risk, but I can get a message out for you."

I don't hesitate before gasping out the message. Words that I spent hours deciding on in case I was ever able to reach him. I formed the message carefully, knowing that if I do anything other than drive him away, I will risk his life. Still, my heart splinters into shards as I share the words with Bonum.

There is silence for a moment, and I feel tears begin to drip over my nose and pool along my cheek. I open my eyes to see that their expression is full of pain. They take another deep breath and then turn and walk out of the room without saying another word.

Sobs begin to crawl their way out of my throat, and with them, the physical pain increases in my back until I soon lose consciousness again.

EXCERPTS FROM MALAM

My feet are beginning to hurt from pacing in this clearing in the demon stronghold. I'm trying to decide if I should pick up a sword and get some practice in, but somehow that reminder of Chaosta feels like it would hurt too much right now. I beg time to pass quickly so that I can transport myself to the mansion again and hopefully find her there, safe.

A week has passed since the evening when I showed up at the mansion to find Dio waiting for me. He was remarkably calm when he told me that she'd been gone since earlier that morning.

I was less calm, but I hid it from him as best I could. However, I could taste his fear when I confirmed that I didn't know where she was.

I was surprised to see the bruises on his neck. It took me a minute to realize what they were, but when I did, and saw him brushing his fingers over them, my chest got so tight I couldn't breathe. Dio isn't alone in loving someone known for leaving marks like that.

I made him show me to their room, where I looked around,

trying to find anything that might be a clue to where she went or what happened to her. Even with my heightened senses, I couldn't find anything out of place. When I asked if he had woken when she left their bed, he said they had been in a fight, and he slept on the couch.

That was when I really started to worry, and not just about her. Of course, she is also critical to the work we are doing, but she has become so much more than a weapon, so much more than a tool to mend the balance. We all need her to be all right.

On top of that, Dio is too important to risk, and I can only imagine what this fear is doing to his control. If we don't find her soon, or worse, get bad news, I worry that he won't be able to manage.

Since then, I have returned here during the day, trying to focus on the work I need to be doing. Instead, I have been spending most days simply passing the time until evening, when I can show up at the mansion again.

Chiron has been irritatingly calm for the most part, but I can tell he's actually worried. His words have been sharper than normal, and I feel bad for anyone who needs his healing right now. He certainly has even less patience and worse bedside manner than normal, and for him, that is already in short supply.

Suddenly, interrupting my reverie, I hear fast footsteps and look up, hope and fear at war. One of our guards is running toward me, and as she sees me, she gasps out, "There is a situation at the lift. You are needed."

I feel myself pale as I bolt after her. The memory of Chaosta lying on the floor in a pool of black blood plays on repeat in my head.

As I approach the lift, I see a crowd of at least thirty demons grouped together, some with weapons drawn. "Get back," I bark as I get close, terrified for what I'm about to see. As they step back, though, I'm not sure if I'm thankful or even more terrified. Bonum is in the middle of the group, kneeling, bound and gagged, their face paler than normal.

Casey stands at their side, the fingers of her hand digging into Bonum's shoulder firmly enough that they're white. When she sees me, she says quickly, "We found this *angel* in the atrium. They were attempting to use the lift."

In the background, I hear one of my people mutter something about Bonum, "needing a reminder."

Bonum's eyes flash up to pierce through me, and they try to say something past the gag. I step closer to them and undo the cloth tied behind their head.

"What is it?" I growl as I glare at my people over their head.

There is a wild look to their expression, so unlike their normal predatory stillness as they gasp, "Please, can we talk somewhere private?"

Memories of the last time they would have been here play behind my eyelids. I nod before barking, "Release them."

No one moves, and when I glance around, I see wide eyes looking at me. "NOW," I order, and Casey slowly begins to undo the angel's bindings.

Some of the others try to talk to me, but I hold up a hand to silence them. Once Bonum is untied, I reach out to help them up. They ignore me and rise gracefully to their feet.

I escort them to one of the empty medical rooms, which are the closest private space I can think of. Once inside the room, I round on them, "What is it? Where is she?"

"We have her. She is being tortured," they rasp.

Without thinking, I drive my fist into their torso. They don't seem to attempt to move or block it. I hear the gratifying sound of breath rapidly leaving their lungs, and they bend over, gasping and coughing weakly.

I step back, shaking my hand out, my knuckles aching, but the pain is somehow grounding.

"Well, this brings me back," they rasp out between gasps, and I nearly hit them again.

Instead, I grit my jaw and clench my fists, waiting for them to say whatever else it is they came to tell me. I find myself wishing I hadn't struck them so that this would happen quicker.

Eventually, they get their breath back and stand, mostly upright, with a hand across their torso. Their eyes stare through me again. "I told her I could get one message out, and she gave me words for you to tell Dio."

I feel my heart crack open.

"She said to tell him that she left because she couldn't take his possessiveness anymore, and he needs to let her go."

I feel the crack widen.

"She said to tell him not to look for her, that she has decided to focus on her work, restoring the balance."

I feel as though my heart might break open. I'm clenching my jaw as though if I grit my teeth hard enough, I can hold in the pain. "Can we not get her out?" I ask.

Unfortunately, I know the answer even before they say, "Would you throw away everything she has worked for by attempting a suicide mission here and now?"

Despite knowing they can't see, I turn my face away from them to hide the tears sparkling in my eyes. "Do you know what they intend to do with her?"

"I do," they rasp.

I'm ready to demand that they tell me, but the haunted look on their face stops me. Instead, I take a breath and wipe another tear from the corner of my eye. "You risked a lot to come here. I can only guess how hard it must have been to return to this place. You have my thanks."

They take a breath, staring straight ahead. After a moment passes, they ask, "Will I be allowed to leave?"

I flinch. "I will walk you to the lift. You will be allowed to leave."

Their jaw tightens as they nod.

As we walk to the lift, we pass a gauntlet of my people. They swear at Bonum and glare at me as I walk past them, but no one moves to stop us. I won't allow the angel to be held or harmed, and not just because they are more valuable as a spy than a prisoner.

Once they are safely in the lift, I stride back through the group of demons. They ask me questions in a cacophony of frustrated and angry voices. Stopping in the midst of them, I look around, meeting as many eyes as I can as I say, "I owe you an explanation, but this is not my priority right now. I need you to trust me as your chosen elder. I will have answers for you, I just need some time."

Most of them nod, soothed by my response. A few are still clearly angry, but the crowd disperses.

I go looking for Chiron and locate him in a medical room. He's caring for a demon with a leg injury. He freezes when he sees my face. I shake my head at him slightly and then step out of the room and wait.

Several minutes pass before he walks through the door. He runs his hand through his tousled curls, his normally olive skin pale. "What is it? How bad is it?" he growls quietly. There is acceptance on his face before I even open my mouth.

I relate to him what happened.

Chiron looks away from me, his jaw tight, and I'm reminded again how young he is for a demon.

He wasn't living in the stronghold back when I discovered that some of our kind were holding and torturing Bonum. It is a part of our history, though, so I know he recognizes the name.

"Fuck," he says, looking toward the sky as though he's swearing directly at one of our deities. After a few moments of silence, he asks, "What do we do?"

"We have to hope that this is all part of her purpose. We need to trust that she knows what she's doing. There is nothing else we can do other than share her message," I say, not liking the note of hopelessness in my voice.

"We both know what might happen if we just share that message with Dio and then leave him to his own devices," Chiron growls at me as though this is somehow my fault.

"What else can we do?" I ask angrily.

He brushes the curls out of his eyes, his movements tight and angry. He opens his mouth but closes it again without speaking. He looks at me, his eyes searching, and finally says, "If we're going to show up and tell him this, at least let me get Lent out of the mansion."

"Why Lent? Do you think Dio will target him?" I ask. Then, as I consider, I say, "Actually, why not get the whole coven out?"

He pales and looks away from me, and I see his throat bob. "I can ask Lent to talk to them," he says finally.

"What?" I ask, suddenly confused.

"Lent and I..." he runs his hand through his curls again.

"You and Lent what?" I ask.

He scowls and then looks me in the eyes and says, "Lent and I are involved."

"In what?" I ask, even more confused now.

He curses at me colorfully in our language, the darkness of his magic thickening as it swirls around us. My head grows muzzy and painful with it until I snap at him to stop.

"We're in a relationship," he snarls at me. Then, more softly, the words hesitant, he says, "I think I love him."

I couldn't be more shocked if the floor suddenly dropped out from under me. Humans may not be quite as off-limits as angels, but it's a near thing, a matter of degrees. I've always been terrified my relationship with Lily would have been discovered. Not just by the angels, and the danger that would have meant, but by my people.

"Since when?" I choke out. It isn't just surprise flooding through me at this moment.

"Since shortly after Chaosta asked me to take your spot teaching them magic."

I choke on nothing and start coughing.

"Look, don't get weird about it, alright," he says, his tone irritated. "I only shared because I won't risk his safety, despite having faith that Dio will be able to handle this."

I manage to get control of my coughing. Before he can say anything else, I reach out and draw him into a hug. He's stiff for a moment, but then relaxes and hugs me back. "I'm happy for you," I say, emotion flooding my voice.

As we pull back, he meets my eyes and asks, "Hey, you alright, Malam?"

I quickly scrub the fucking tears from my cheeks and say with a growl, "Fine, let's get this plan moving."

He looks as though he would like to ask more questions, but then seems to think better of it.

"What's the plan for speaking with him?" I ask quickly before he can dematerialize.

He shrugs, "Just share her message and be prepared to transport ourselves out if he seems like he can't control the magic, I guess."

"And if he decides to try to go after her anyway?"

A hopeless-sounding laugh emerges from Chiron's lips. "We'll do our best not to let him. If we need to try to subdue him and bring him back here, I guess we can do that."

"You think we have any hope of doing that?" I growl. I've felt his strength and seen his skill firsthand. The very idea of attempting to even hold our own against him fills me with hopelessness.

"Not alone, but maybe if we work together," he says with a sigh.

"Alright, go arrange things. Let's get this over with," I say tightly.

Even as I finish the sentence, he disappears in a swirl of shadow and wingbeats.

THE PAIN OF HEART THAT'S BROKEN FREE

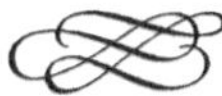

This time, when consciousness returns, I am sitting with my wrists bound to the arms of a chair in one of the bright rooms. I'm slumped, but there isn't a back to the chair, so I'm hanging by my arms again. I weakly pull myself forward so I am sitting nearly upright. I'm glad that the wounds on my back aren't resting against anything. The burning agony across the skin there still feels fresh, and I'm sure not much time has passed. Certainly not the fortnight for healing that I'm used to from my past experience.

There are others in the room behind me again. Angels or healers, I don't know, but the awareness of them where I can't see them makes the hair on the nape of my neck stand up.

I concentrate on blinking away the spots darkening my vision and try to breathe shallowly to not pull at the fresh wounds. Then the door in front of me opens, and Bonum enters and moves to stand along the wall off to the side. Out of my peripheral vision, I see them barely dip their chin in a subtle nod.

Tears begin to crawl down my cheeks as the realization that they delivered my message hits me.

Anguish pulses through my chest, and I start to shake as I realize that not only did I not get to say goodbye, I also never told Dio I loved him. I close my eyes, struggling to control myself, struggling to be strong. As I do so, I feel like the bright flame that has been alive in my chest, the phoenix and the love it represents, gutters and then dies down to the smallest flame.

I'm shaking so hard that my restraints are rattling against the chair I'm sitting in. Because of that, I don't realize that the door has opened again until I hear footsteps draw near.

I open my eyes to see Rex, crouching in front of me so he's at eye level. When my tear-filled eyes meet his, he purrs, "Now that is better."

He stands and watches me clearly coming apart for a few minutes and then says, "Because I also believe in balance, I will give you a choice. You can choose to remain obstinate and support the wrong side. If so, I will torture you and hide you away in a small cell, away from the daylight, to be forgotten by all. We will also hunt down that human male you love so much and kill him."

Despite knowing it's what he wants, at the threat to Dio, I can't control myself anymore. I scream and throw myself at him. As I fight my restraints, I feel the wounds on my back split open.

"When you act like that, you look like one of them," Rex says, wrinkling his nose and watching me calmly as I continue to fight with everything in me to get to him and kill him.

Finally out of breath and nearly unconscious, I lean forward, toward him. I'm resting heavily against my arms, gasping for air. I feel a hand on my chin again, and I don't have the energy to fight anymore. I close my eyes as tears continue to track down my cheeks.

"Look at me," Rex commands, and I drag my eyes open, spearing him with my gaze. Seeming unaffected, Rex says, "Alternatively, you can choose to transfer your support to the correct side, the side of all that is good, and work alongside us. If you do this, there will still be some pain since you must atone and be taught not to lie. However, if this is what you choose, the human man will be allowed to live, and your torture will be reduced."

My hands clench into fists as bile rises in my throat. Unsure if the one controlling me will even allow it, I gasp out, "I will support you and the angels. Just let Dio live."

A lazy grin spreads across Rex's face, and he releases my chin and takes a few steps back.

As he moves away from me, I finally feel the blood dripping down my back. My vision starts to darken, and I grow dizzy.

He looks at whoever is behind me and then turns to Bonum, "This is what leadership looks like. When others don't get the job done, sometimes you need to do it yourself."

Bonum's posture is relaxed, their eyes passing through Rex.

Those behind me say, "Thank you, High Leader."

Bonum remains quiet and unmoving. Rex turns to glare at them. After a few moments of tense silence where I wonder what danger Bonum might be in, Rex turns and strides out of the room.

Shortly after, Bonum leaves as well without another look at me. Even as their footsteps fade, my vision goes fully black, and I give myself up to unconsciousness yet again.

EXCERPTS FROM MALAM

I'm pacing again, wearing a track in the earth as I wait for Chiron to return. Finally, he appears between the trees, the magic of our people leading him directly to me.

As I meet his eyes, he says gruffly, "Lent didn't want to leave. He wanted to be there for Dio. I managed to convince him, though. He's going to make up a story about a magical item the coven needs to pick up. He'll get them as far away as he can."

My chest is so tight it's painful. "Thank you, Chiron, I know Chaosta would be thankful."

He nods, scrubbing his hand through his hair, and then mumbles something about needing to get back to work as he turns and heads back towards the healing rooms.

The day strangely drags and flies by at the same time. I have never dreaded anything more than this conversation. I feel for Dio, but at this moment, I'm more worried about what will happen if he decides to try to rescue her. If he does, not only might he risk her safety, but it could also lead the angels to strike back against my people. If they do now, while we're still not fully prepared, it will be even more of a slaughter.

Of course, there is also the risk to both of us that Dio will lose control before we're able to transport away. That fear tears at my own control until I pick up my sword and put myself through the forms until my muscles shake.

When they threaten to give out fully, I finally stop and sit on the ground, leaning against a tree. I close my eyes, but all I can see is a vision of the look of pain on Chiron's face as we're hit by an explosion of magic.

With a curse, I open my eyes.

Suddenly realizing how long it's been since I've eaten, I get some food and go to my room. Somehow, I manage to eat, knowing that if I don't, I will risk negative effects from any magic use.

After trying to distract myself for a while with some reading, I finally hear a familiar knock on my door. Bracing myself, I rise, open the door, and step out into the open space where Chiron is waiting for me.

"Ready?" he asks gruffly.

I just nod, unsure what to say.

"When we get there, let me speak with him," he says roughly.

"No," I say, and his eyes flash to mine. I clench my fingers into fists to conceal the shaking of my hands as I say, "I won't risk you when the man you love is out there waiting for you."

Chiron is frozen, staring at me. His throat bobs as he swallows and looks away. He finally nods tightly and then, in tandem, we transport ourselves to the alcove outside the mansion.

It's tight with two of us in here, but after the past weeks, we are practiced at it and no longer trip over each other. Chiron, braver than me as always, leaves the space first and strides towards the front door. I follow just behind, my heart pounding in my chest.

As we walk through the front door and cross into the entry hall, I see Dio waiting for us. I'm surprised to see Fem standing nearby.

Chiron's shoulders tense. "*Fem*. Dio," he greets with a nod of his head. His tone as he says Fem's name makes his displeasure at Fem's presence clear.

Fem glares at him, but his face is white.

I step around Chiron and say, "Let's talk in the office."

Dio's eyes are wild. Still, he follows Fem and me silently into the room.

The hair at the back of my neck prickles at the feeling of all that barely controlled magic behind me.

Once in the office, I turn to face him. Chiron enters the room last and closes the door silently. I suddenly realize the wisdom in having him there, behind Dio, and hopefully momentarily forgotten.

Fem is pale and standing near the couch, a short distance from all of us. I briefly wonder what Chiron might have already shared with him.

"What have you come to tell me?" Dio asks. His voice is tight but still relatively calm. Despite that, the energy of his magic burns through the air, making goosebumps rise along my arms. He's brushing the fingers of his right hand over the base of his throat, just above his collarbone.

I feel a bead of sweat slide down the back of my neck as I say, "Chaosta asked me to give you a message."

Dio's glare sears against my skin like a brand, and my heart beats in my throat.

"She wanted me to let you know that she has moved on. She said that she needs to focus on her work, restoring balance, and couldn't risk the distraction of being in a relationship with you."

His jaw tightens, the air now painful to breathe with the massive amount of magic burning through the room.

Fem coughs. His human lungs must be struggling even more than mine.

I glance briefly over Dio's shoulder to see Chiron take a silent step forward. He's surrounded by the shadows of demon magic.

Pulling my focus back to Dio, I swallow and say, "She also wanted me to tell you that she couldn't handle your possessiveness, and that she doesn't want you to go looking for her. She doesn't want to be found by you."

He blinks, unmoving other than his eyes, which search mine. "How long has she been in the hands of the angels?" He asks, his voice calm, but the pain of his magic as he glares at me continues to build.

I fight to keep from flinching as I say, "What makes you think that this has anything to do with the angels?"

He takes a slow step forward, and suddenly, there is seemingly no oxygen in the room. My lungs struggle involuntarily against the magical force around my chest as he steals the air from me.

"Answer my question, Malam," Dio says darkly.

Can't, I mouth.

"Chiron?" Dio asks without turning.

Chiron freezes from where he's now standing, just a pace behind Dio. He begins to trace a rune in the air, the rune for sleep, but before he can finish it, he drops to his knees, his back arching as he cries out.

There is half a moment where I am filled with wonder at the delicate control Dio has over the magical energy of all those inscribed runes. He hasn't moved beyond the step toward me. No movement of his fingers or lips. Everyone tries to minimize those tells, but no one else I know is so entirely free from them.

Also, it was one thing when we were sparring, and it was just the two of us. However, for him to control two different effects like this, and at the same time, speaks of such consummate skill that I can't help but study it even as I slowly suffocate.

Then Chiron cries out again. The pain in it pulls my attention to him and makes my already tight chest burn further.

The pressure against my lungs finally lets up, and I drag in a breath. Despite the hopelessness of it, I quickly flood the appropriate runes I have inscribed and use them to drag the rug out from under Dio. I gasp, chest heaving as doing so steals energy from my body.

He stumbles for a moment but quickly rights himself. His eyes are dark, but there's a wry grin on his face as he says, "Look at that, you're getting better."

"Please stop, all of you," Fem says tightly.

Chiron whimpers. He's still frozen, on his knees, back arched.

"I'll start breaking his bones," Dio says as he glares at me. He either hasn't heard Fem or doesn't care.

His voice is blank of emotion, and I feel another bead of sweat trickle down my scalp. I glance again at Chiron as I say, "They've had her since she disappeared."

Chiron, suddenly free from Dio's magic, straightens slightly, still on his knees. He coughs, glaring at Dio's back.

Dio's chest is heaving. He closes his eyes, and I only just catch movement behind him as Dio says, "Don't."

There is a quiet snap, and Chiron bites back a curse as he drops his hand into his lap. His index finger, the one he was using to again attempt to draw the rune for sleep, is bent back at the wrong angle.

Dio wobbles and clutches his chest. I'm not sure if he's grasping at his heart or the Killswitch rune.

The magical energy in the room is so thick that I can taste it. The acrid tang is so strong that it makes my eyes water. My lungs burn with pain as they breathe in air that is thickly polluted with magical energy.

Fem dissolves into a fit of coughing. I have no time to worry about him, though, as Dio drops to his knees and leans forward, his forehead pressed to the floor.

I stop breathing and take a step back. Chiron rises to his feet slowly and quietly, and I see tendrils of shadow snaking around him, matching mine, as we prepare to transport ourselves to a safe distance.

Then, I'm reminded just how stupid humans can be, as Fem approaches Dio and crouches beside him. He flinches as he lays a hand gently on Dio's shoulder. I wince involuntarily as I imagine the pain Fem must feel at that touch. It has to be like touching lightning.

He asks something, and I can only just hear Dio mumble a response. They speak for a few moments, but I can't make out the words. Finally, Fem digs in his pocket as Dio presses himself up to sit on his heels. Fem hands him something, and he puts it in his mouth. After a moment, his arm drops into his lap, and he slumps slightly. The intensity of the magic in the air slowly lessens until it doesn't hurt to breathe.

I glance at Chiron and note that he's staring at Dio. Instead of anger, though, his face is full of concern. I join him, looking at his finger. "Can I help?" I ask under my breath.

He shakes his head, not seeming to notice the broken finger as he glances at me and mouths, "Now what?"

I gesture at his hand again, and he swears under his breath, repeating himself as though I'm the one asking the stupid question. Wracking my mind for an idea, I finally turn to where he's crouched, say, "Fem?"

When he leaves Dio's side, I lead us out into the hallway where we can have some privacy.

Fem is pale but otherwise seems composed. He glares at me as he says, "What?"

"Was that a sedative you gave him?" I ask.

Fem nods.

"Think he'll continue to accept them?" Chiron asks.

"Even if he would, that's hardly a good idea with his history of addiction," Fem says tightly.

"What is the alternative?" Chiron asks, his voice quiet.

Fem glances at Chiron's finger again and sighs. "Yeah, I think he will, but I'll have no part in drugging him."

"Then we'll move him to the stronghold, and I'll manage it," Chiron says.

Fem shakes his head and glares at Chiron. "You think I'll allow him to go with you? After what just happened, you can't expect that I'd trust you not to hurt him."

"You mean because he hurt me? You think I want to hurt him back?" Chiron growls.

"Well?" Fem snaps back, apparently not at all concerned for his own safety, as he now stares down an angry demon.

"As a fellow healer, you should understand," Chiron finally says as he meets Fem's glare. "I shouldn't have tried to knock him out like that. I'm lucky he just broke my finger. I wish him no harm."

Fem sighs and then nods as he says tightly, "Alright then, I'll talk with him and see if he's willing to go with you." He returns to the office, pulling the door mostly shut behind him.

"Are the medical supplies we sent with them still here?" Chiron asks.

"I believe so, why?"

Chiron shakes his head and turns and leaves the entry hall.

I pace as I wait, wondering if he's getting more sedatives. When he returns, though, his hand is wrapped in a bandage, his finger no longer at an odd angle.

My jaw tightens as I stare at him. "We have other healers," I growl.

"It's fine," he growls back. His face is slightly pale, but otherwise he seems all right.

Then the door to the office opens, and Fem emerges through

the doorway and joins us. "He's willing to go with you, but not as a prisoner. He also has some things that he wants from Lent."

Chiron tenses, "What does he want from Lent?"

Fem shakes his head slightly. He holds out a hand as though trying to soothe Chiron, and I wonder suddenly if Fem knows about their relationship. "Just some books, research things," he says.

"I'll collect them when Lent is back," Chiron says more calmly.

Fem nods. "Please be careful. I'm sure he'll try to save her."

"We will be," I say. Then Chiron and I return to the office.

He crouches beside Dio, moving slowly as though he's approaching a wounded animal.

"Sorry about the finger," Dio slurs slightly.

"I've had worse," Chiron says softly. "I shouldn't have tried to use magic to knock you out."

"Still. I'm sorry," Dio mumbles.

"Will you be able to keep it together while I transport us?"

"Fine for now," Dio slurs.

Chiron wraps his arms carefully around Dio's shoulders and then glances at me and says, "See you in the clearing." Then they disappear in the familiar cloud of shadow and wingbeats.

I follow quickly after, reforming a few yards away from them back at the stronghold. I help Chiron get Dio to his feet and support him into one of the small living spaces. We help him to the bed, and then I step away, standing just outside the door where I can see Chiron as he covers Dio with a blanket.

When he rises and leaves the room, closing the door behind him softly, he says, "Help me put up locking wards?"

I feel myself blanch. "You'll go back on what Fem asked of us?"

"I never told him we could honor that request," he says bluntly, his voice rough.

I swear until he looks like he might slap me again. In the end, though, I reluctantly agree.

We spend a couple of hours placing the wards. "Think that will hold him?" I'm shaking, and I realize I probably need some wine and a little more food.

Chiron shakes his head slightly. His expression is grim as he says, "Who knows. We have to try, though."

I sigh and then go to get something to eat. We can only hope that he won't fight us too badly when he eventually realizes that we've attempted to confine him to his room.

DO NOT SEEK BEYOND DEATH

As I'm led, bound with a hood over my head, I consider briefly that the routine this time seems to be different. I would guess that it has been about a month since I was last tortured. At least that's if you don't count lying bound on a bed, in a medical room, without pain meds for several weeks, as torture.

I'm brought back to the present as I trip, my legs giving out. The angels on either side of me don't seem to care, dragging instead of leading me. I'm jostled slightly as they change positions, likely going through a doorway. After a few more strides, they drop me, and I flinch as my knees and shins hit the floor.

After this much time has passed, even my freshest wounds are mostly healed, but I am far from free of pain.

As I wait in near silence, breathing through my nose, I try to relax. Of course, it's not that easy.

They have tortured me a few times since I agreed to join them. Each time has been different, so I'm unsure what to expect today. Unlike my last stint of torture here, where they asked me questions, this time they just seem interested in causing me pain.

Rex's words about atoning again cross my mind, and I flinch.

Just as I do, a cold wall of something strikes my back, and I gasp. I belatedly realize it's cold water and begin to shake. They throw sheets of water at me a few more times.

Some time passes as I flinch at sounds, still shaking, unsure what they're going to do next.

Eventually, I'm grabbed by the arms and dragged forward. They lift and press me over the rim of something, and I realize why when my head is submerged under water.

My body fights back instinctually, but my heart isn't in it. I'm exhausted, in pain, freezing cold, weak, and I'm not quite sure what I'm living for anymore. Because of that, I guess I don't try that hard to hold my breath. Liquid fills my lungs. I feel my body go limp, and I float away into blackness.

~

I open my eyes to the familiar vision of the little boy covered in gore. Blood-covered roses carpet the ground, seeming to grow and spread from past dreams even though they look dead. The sky is white as always, the light hurting my eyes even in the vision.

This version of the little boy wears a black crown with roses carved into it. At the front, two spikes rise, looking like horns. His eyes drip with blood, and the white orbs watch me as he gets closer. This time, he has both arms, but one ends at the elbow.

As he limps forward, I see that he's no longer missing part of a leg, but one is clearly broken. Then he opens his mouth, and that deep, masculine voice says, "You should not be here!"

I stay where I am, considering what to say even as he visibly grows more upset.

"Leave! It is not your time. I made you stronger than this," he commands.

"To return to what?" I finally gasp at him. Water gushes down my chin as I open my mouth. I choke slightly, eyes watering.

"The question you should ask yourself is what you will do to them if you stay?" He gestures behind him, and suddenly I'm in a nightmare as all of the people I care for, all those I love, appear behind him. They are all in similarly gory states.

Malam has a sword wound that has torn his abdomen open, and blood is leaking from his mouth.

Lent is gripping a sword that is impaled through Chiron's chest as blood drips like tears from his eyes.

Pepper has a significant amount of blood running from a wound on her head. I can't bear it after the first few, and I drag my eyes back to the little boy.

"You. Must. Go," he snarls.

Then something catches my attention, and I see Dio behind him, bound and gagged, blood leaking from multiple wounds. Despite that, he is focused on me with that familiar intensity. I know this is a dream but he seems so real that the broken shards of my heart threaten to cut me to pieces.

There is open desperation in his expression as he looks at me. His eyes seem to say, *You promised.*

I begin to move toward him, but the little boy steps in front of me.

"If you want them to live, THERE IS NO TIME," he yells.

Standing where I am, nearly touching him, I gasp, "What if I don't have it in me to be their savior? What if I don't have it in me to save humanity? What if I just want to be a girl who loves a boy?"

He sighs, and I watch his jaw tighten as he considers me as though I'm a problem he wasn't expecting to deal with."I will buy you a moment, *one moment*," he finally grits out. "Think hard and fast about the decision you are making because there will be no option to change your mind once that time passes."

I rush to Dio and, knowing I don't have much time, I leave him gagged.

His eyes eat me up as though he's starving.

"I love you, Dio," I gasp as tears run down my face. "I didn't get to say goodbye, and I think it's going to break me, so goodbye. He's right, I need to go. I need you to live for me."

Tears sparkle in Dio's eyes, doing nothing to change the desperation I see there. His body bucks as he fights his bindings. A muted cry tears itself out of his throat.

With tears running down my cheeks, I look at the little boy, and he nods at me.

~

There is a hard surface at my back, firm pressure on my sternum, and then water bursts out of my mouth. I'm no longer wearing the hood, but the light is too bright for my eyes, so I keep them squinted shut. Hands roll me over onto my side as I cough, gasp, and choke up water.

As I struggle to clear my lungs and get a breath of air, I hear a female voice say, "She has atoned, bring her to medical."

Someone picks me up off the ground and carries me out of the room.

It's clearly futile to hope to see Dio again, but the pain in my heart is somewhat eased now that I've at least been able to say goodbye in a dream.

When we get to the healers, for the first time in months, I'm given pain medication, and I quickly descend into a dark, dreamless sleep.

EXCERPTS FROM MALAM

I leave the latest conclave and head to the lift. Even in the poisonous state that it's in, I need to get some air. Mostly, I just need to get out of the stronghold for a bit. When the bell in the lift dings and the door opens, I walk out onto the street, blind to my surroundings as I consider how I got where I am now.

Shortly after we brought Dio to the stronghold, I realized that we needed to move up our timeline for getting our people to the coast. Thanks to Chaosta's research, we learned that a large body of water will increase the power of the storm and help with the magic. That should mean that we're able to clear more land, and the more land we clear, the longer it will remain despite the angels rebuilding it after they've defeated us. Of course, my hope is that despite the futility of fighting the other side, we might manage an arrangement with them for many of my people not to be killed.

I thought we had more time, but it was clear when she was taken that things were beginning to escalate.

I took a few days to come to terms with the upheaval that we would all be facing. Then I began to orchestrate the move.

Since then, my people have been working every minute of every day to make the arrangements. The logistics are that much more complex since we can't pull all of our people away from the farms. If we did, the food shortages would certainly become untenable, and that might give the angels a reason to break the truce before we're ready.

Of course, there have also been a lot of emotions to manage, a task I am ill-suited for. It took nearly a month for me to convince my people that the move needed to happen. There are still fights breaking out daily about it, but so far, no one has outright refused.

Unfortunately, I've also had to manage my own emotions about all of this. Well, mine and Chiron's.

At first, he tried to find a solution to get Chaosta away from the angels. I knew the moment that Bonum told me they were holding her that there was nothing we could do. I indulged Chiron for a while, letting him make up plans and hearing him out.

Eventually, he came to the same conclusion I had that any action we took would break the truce without the benefits of the storm. He's been extremely short-tempered ever since. Thankfully, I have been able to distract him by giving him mundane tasks to help with. He's also ill-suited for work like this, but at least his frustration over those tasks is keeping him from other, more painful emotions.

As the months stretched on, I knew I needed to make living arrangements for all of us. I delayed as long as possible because it meant talking with Dio. Thankfully, he has continued to accept sedatives and has seemed content enough to remain in a drugged state in his room. I had been mostly able to avoid seeing or thinking about him. Now that I needed to ask him a favor, though, I had no choice but to confront my feelings about this head-on.

When I showed up at his room, Casey was on the guard shift, sitting outside the room where she could see him through his open door. She was reading a book but glanced up, acknowledging me with a nod of her head before she went back to reading.

I was relieved to see that he was upright, sitting with his legs curled under him on the bed, leaning against the wall. His head was tipped back, resting against the wall, his eyes closed, his hands loosely resting in his lap.

As I walked through the door, he opened his eyes and lifted his head, slowly turning to face me. When I met his eyes and saw that the black of his pupils had taken over the irises, pain stabbed through my heart. "How are you doing, Dio?" I asked.

He turned and rested his head back against the wall, eyes closed as he said, "Fine.

"I'm sorry to bother you, but I have a favor to ask," I said.

"How can I help?" His voice was soft, but he wasn't slurring.

I was relieved by that, as I certainly didn't want to take advantage of him. Especially not with this monumental request.

"We need to move to the coast to take the next step in our plans. We will need to be able to house the fan club and all the demons we can spare. We will also need spaces to train. Can you help with the money to procure them?"

"How many floors?" he asked, otherwise unmoving.

"We need sixty floors if we can get them. No less than fifty," I said.

He was silent for a few minutes, likely doing the math in his head.

I had done it before I went to see him. The number was massive.

"Alright," he said. "Sixty should be fine. I can give the information to you, or sign, or whatever you need, I guess."

"Are you sure?" I asked.

"Nervos belli, pecuniam infinitam," he said.

My Latin is rusty, but my rough translation was that he was acknowledging the importance of money in fighting a war. "Thank you, Dio."

He opened his eyes, looked at me again, then. Despite the sedatives in his system, the intensity of the magic in his expression still stung. "I thought I told you I wasn't willing to be your prisoner."

I hesitated, wondering if I should just leave and get Chiron. Finally, I said, "We're just trying to keep you and Chaosta safe."

He closed his eyes and rested his head against the wall again. He was brushing his fingers against the base of his throat.

I waited, wondering if I would need to defend myself. After several minutes of silence, though, I left his room.

When I told Chiron later, he seemed surprised that Dio had mentioned it, but told me that he'd check with him and make sure he was all right.

In the end, the spaces were far more expensive than I expected. The buildings needed to be modified, and we had to pay to force some tenants out. When I apologized to Dio, he just said that he had expected it and it was ok. As though he wasn't bothered by the massive numbers.

While that was occurring, we continued to prepare for the move.

Pepper and I have been working closely together to arrange things with The Boys fan club. I really have to hand it to the band. I guess I hadn't understood the kind of numbers they would be able to attract. They currently add nearly 3,000 to our ranks, a massive number of human magic users. Of course, moving all those humans only added to the difficulty of this task.

Despite all our efforts, we still won't come close to even half the number the angels will bring to a battle.

That thought reminds me where I am, maybe because it was exactly that worry that drove me out for a walk. I glance around, and when I realize where I'm standing, my stomach twists.

My feet led me to Lily's old apartment.

I look up at the building, towards her window where I used to sit with her in the mornings. I can almost feel her in my arms, sitting on my lap with her fingers in my hair.

I really should let the apartment go, I think for the thousandth time.

She really doesn't deserve for me to trap any part of her here in the living realm. Shaking my head, I light up a cigarette and then stride off down a different street, altering my course since I'm not ready to go back to the stronghold yet.

Tomorrow is the big day, the first step toward the end of this, whatever that might be. While everyone else fusses and worries over logistics and how disruptive this might be to our farms, I carry the weight of the fact that this may very well be the beginning of the end for my people.

PART V

THE FALLIBILITY OF MEMORY

My mind wanders as I stand at the side of the courtroom. Court has been in session for hours and my feet have been numb for a while already.

I'm armed, my Angelforged blade strapped to my waist as is the way with angels. It is a weight that is still uncomfortable at my hip instead of my back, and a sword that still feels unfamiliar in my hand. My clothes are still a foreign, and uncomfortable, white in the already overly bright room. In place of the manacles, I wear a wide bracelet around my left wrist, concealing the scarred rune beneath.

Not that I'm free, the shackles that bind me now may be made of light, but they are iron-clad.

I'm here as a show of force more than anything else. An armed guard in a peaceful space. Not that my skills with a blade have slipped. Several months ago, they began to allow me to spar with other angels and I attend practice every day now, under the watchful eye of the sword-master.

I roll my shoulders, subtly stretching out oncoming stiffness from my bout this morning. Around me, the court proceedings continue as always, lawyers droning on as though they are putting on a spellbinding performance while most of the people cover yawns. Determining that there is no more risk than before, I let my mind drift again and think back to how I came to be bored, in a courtroom instead of in pain in a medical bed.

When I arrived in medical I was mostly kept unconscious for the next few weeks while my body healed. The healers took good care of me. After they determined I was healed enough to leave, I lived for a few months in what basically amounted to a cell.

I could hardly complain. At least I wasn't being tortured by the demons anymore.

While I was there, they began to set me small tasks, allowing me to demonstrate that I was as good as my word. At first, I was always accompanied by a guard. My hands were often still bound.

Eventually, the guard didn't follow me around. Then they began to allow me to train with a wooden practice sword. They tested my skill and then added me to the schedule for morning sword practice.

Eventually, I received a badge that marked me as a city official, specifically a city enforcer. When I received the badge, I felt a strange, slightly ill feeling in my stomach.

They also provided me with an apartment. It was novel to have my own, well-appointed living space for a while, although it has since become lonely.

Over these months, I have done nothing to break their trust in me. I have been treated, for the most part, just like the other city officials.

My shifts are from morning to evening every day. Each day I have a different assignment, although it is often in courtrooms across this part of the city.

Through my interactions with the various angels, it became

clear that none of them were informed about who I am. It seems that, other than Bonum, Rex, and the sword-master, most believe me to be simply another angel. Instead of a homing beacon like I used to be, now I seem to blend in, almost as though the trick I used to disguise myself has become a consistent state.

I also realized when I left the medical bay that I seemed to be missing memories of my past. I know vaguely that people existed who I cared about, and who cared about me, but I don't remember much of anything from before I saved Bonum. While I remember the demons hurting me in those dark rooms full of shadow after they captured me, those memories are blurry and feel distant. The fact that they decided to punish me like that for simply saving an angel still feels slightly odd but I can't remember why. The images of the angels rescuing me and getting me to their medical bay are more clear.

Despite some odd, occasional reluctance, I have found the angels to be unfailingly kind and good people. They have welcomed me with open arms, and I can't help but enjoy their company. In fact, I've even made a few new friends.

One day, I stopped at a new place for lunch during guard duty. I was getting some of my favorite spiced bread and dip when I bumped into another angel and spilled her drink. I expected to be scolded, but she was kind and just laughed good-naturedly. She didn't even allow me to purchase a replacement. She introduced herself as Hypatia.

I was getting ready to leave, heading back to my shift, but when I saw her sit down at a table and pick up a book I recognized, I said something. We ended up talking for a bit, and I made myself late. As I rushed out the door, she handed me a slip of paper with her contact information on it. Since then, we have become friends.

Then I met Simone under strangely similar circumstances. This time, we were in the cafeteria in the main stronghold, where I get most of my dinners after guard duty. Simone was carrying her tray out the door, and I wasn't looking and ran into her. I made more of a mess this time as food went everywhere.

Simone was angry and far less understanding than Hypatia, but as I helped her clean up and apologized profusely, she calmed down. As I waited with her in line again to pay for her meal, we started talking about my work as a guard. Somehow, that also led to a conversation about books, and suddenly I had another friend. Since then, I see both of them at least a few times a week. We rotate apartments and spend the evenings together reading.

As I remember that it's my turn to bring the food tonight, I am suddenly pulled back to the present just in time to see the changeover to the next case.

I glance around, again assessing if there are any threats. As I do, I see a face that seems vaguely familiar. I reach for a name, but it doesn't come to me. The human lawyer walks to the table at the front of the courtroom and begins to organize a pile of paperwork. I can't help myself as I stare at him. Despite the strange numbness and lack of memory, my heart pounds and my head feels fuzzy.

I realize my hands are clenched into fists and I force myself to relax, directing my eyes straight ahead so I don't keep staring. I reach again for the memory of who this is, but I can't find it.

I try to find something to distract me from the feelings banging through my chest and think of the book that I'm reading tonight.

Hypatia, Simone, and I all have very different tastes. Simone tends to read lots of love stories. Hypatia does as well, along with poetry and histories. I was reading some of the love stories, but despite not quite knowing why, I ended up spending too much of our evenings crying.

I glance again at the lawyer. I hear someone refer to him as Counselor Magnus, but it doesn't help my memory. His back is to me, but I can hear his voice. It is poised and powerful.

Tears prick at my eyes for some reason.

Swearing to myself, cursing the stupidity of all of this, I train my eyes up, focusing on the architecture of the ceiling. Or maybe I'm looking for help from a deity, whatever will help.

For a while, I manage to distract myself by thinking about what food I'm going to bring to our reading date tonight and where I might purchase it. When that topic runs out, I try focusing on the sword techniques I'm working on now. Finally, realizing it is an exercise in futility, I stare straight ahead and just try to ignore the emotions.

During the never-ending closing remarks, I'm finally able to get control of my emotions and return to a more normal calm. Then the court case wraps up, and people begin to filter out of the door beside me. I carefully avoid the lawyer's eyes, but I can feel him looking at me as he walks out of the courtroom.

"Chaosta?" He says as he nears me. His voice is full of surprise and his expression is guarded as he says, "What are you doing here, and why are you working as a city guard?"

I swallow past the sudden lump in my throat. I reach desperately again for where I might know him or what his name is. "Counselor Magnus," I finally say with a nod of my head. Thankfully, I'm saved from having to say any more, as the young man at his side asks him a question. The lawyer leaves with another long, hard look at me.

As he disappears out the door, pain ricochets unexpectedly through my chest. Still, I force myself to appear outwardly calm, standing by the door until the courtroom completely empties and I can leave. Breathing a sigh of relief, I head out the door and, after locking up, I walk out of the building to the street.

This particular courtroom is close enough to the stronghold, where I have an apartment, that I walked here this morning, so there is no reason for me to call a carriage. I enjoy the physical exertion of the walk and carefully pull numbness, like a blanket, around me.

Then, remembering belatedly that I need to buy the food I decided on earlier, I stop at a small store. Shopping goes quickly, and then I head back to my room to get cleaned up before making my way to Simone's apartment.

When I arrive at the door, I walk into the cozy apartment and set my items down on the counter as Simone calls a welcome to me from her bedroom. The space is cluttered, slightly messy, and well-lived-in. Hypatia likes to tease her about it since Simone works on a cleaning crew. I just find it comfortable, cozy almost, compared to the mostly bare space of my apartment.

I start to unpack the food I brought and then dig through cabinets and cupboards to find spoons and other things we'll need. I'm on the third drawer with no spoons in sight when Simone comes out of the bathroom.

Seeing me searching, she laughs, "You would think by now you would know that the stuff you need is in here." She walks around the counter and pulls open a drawer that I am familiar with.

"My memory isn't good, you know that," I laugh back as my stomach twists with the lie.

Simone is pale with dark hair that curls in a mass around her head. She has light blue eyes that are striking, and she's tall, even for an angel. Her face is soft, and she's often smiling. She tends to run hot or cold and has quite a temper, but is also a staunch supporter of her friends. She tends toward plumpness and loves food and wine.

As I take out the utensils, the door opens, and Hypatia walks into the apartment.

"Hey girls!" she calls out as she walks through the door. She drops an armful of books, bags, and containers of food, along with a couple of bottles of wine, onto the couch.

Hypatia is also pale but with blond hair and dark eyes. Where Simone is all soft curves with no edges, Hypatia looks as though she's carved out of granite. She also tends to be sharp and impatient, at least when she isn't doing something she loves like spending time reading with friends.

As I continue to get the snacks ready, Hypatia and Simone carry the items into the kitchen while they compare notes about their workdays.

I can't help but smile. Their joy is infectious.

I start to serve up the wine, catching the tail end of their conversation, which seems to be mostly Hypatia complaining about one of her colleagues.

"I don't know how many fucking times I need to tell him that if he tries to combine the solvent with the polymer that way, he will continue to get the wrong viscosity! Gah, he's so stupid," she says loudly as she takes a piece of dry spiced bread from the tray I'm arranging and pops it in her mouth.

"Have you figured out the issue with your part of the project?" I ask. I know she and her team have been stumped as they've tried to get a certain effect with the invention they are working on. They can recreate what they want on an individual basis, but have not been able to move it to production yet.

"No, it isn't solved, but at least I had another breakthrough," she crows. "Unlike that idiot who just keeps repeating the same mistake."

I laugh, but it's shaky at the unwelcome news of her breakthrough. I pour myself a glass of wine before heading to one of the couches.

Simone carries a tray over to the living space. Hypatia helps, and soon we are spread across the various seating in the cozy living space, reading and occasionally talking about our books.

After a couple of hours, I'm yawning, struggling to keep my eyes open.

"It isn't even that late," Hypatia scolds me.

"I've been dealing with some insomnia," I say with a frown.

"Anything we can do to help?" Simone asks softly.

"I think she just needs to get laid," Hypatia laughs.

I smile and shake my head. "Sleep has been a struggle for me for a while. I should probably get going, though, and try to get some rest. As you both know, I have an early morning getting beaten up at the sword range tomorrow."

"I still don't know how you, such a gentle and tiny little thing, can take all that abuse," Simone says with a shake of her head.

The blurred memories, supported by the network of scars that cover my body courtesy of the demons, crawl behind my eyes. *If only they knew,* I think to myself.

They persist with trying to get me to stay for a few minutes, but in the end, I pack up my things and head back to my apartment.

Walking back into the empty space, another wave of loneliness crashes over me. I can't take the time to think about it, though, I have a night full of reading ahead of me. I put my things away and, taking the appropriate books and other papers out of the back of my closet, I spread everything out on my floor and get back to work.

EXCERPTS FROM MALAM

I stand at the breakwater, looking out over the ocean, somehow missing Lily more than I have in the past several months combined. Perhaps it's the fact that I feel further from her and her memory than ever. Perhaps it's because I have been giving more and more of myself to our cause. Or maybe it's because I am not only missing Lily.

Whatever the reason, the familiar and yet unwelcome ache fills me as I look out at the beautiful scene. It's been a while, but I have stood at the edge of this water many times, in many places, over many years.

Fuck, I've been here when there was sand beneath my feet, and I was surrounded by wilderness.

My chest aches at the thought.

In my role as leader of the demons, I visit the various farms on a frequent basis. Because there are so many, it isn't a regular occurrence for me to be at any one farm, but there are many that line the coasts. Recently, though, I've been more focused on the work within the farms and have not taken the time to leave.

As I look out at the water, the waves bound, surf swirling as the grey, smoggy sky is reflected in the angry silver of the waves. I close my eyes and listen to the water lapping along the stone barrier. As I do, it is almost as though I can hear the song of a Siren. The sound is so long lost in my memory, though, that the feeling passes quickly.

I finish my cigarette and turn back to my walk, back towards the chaos of the new army training centers. Back toward work that, while of my creation, is still unwelcome mayhem.

We managed to purchase consecutive floors in three different buildings. They are near each other but not on neighboring blocks. We also managed to get the top block of floors in each building, so they are adjacent to our farms.

Each camp consists mainly of living quarters that house our army. The living quarters are small and cramped but clean, and they fulfill basic needs. At the top of each block of floors, we have a couple of floors we can use for training. We recently completed construction in all of those spaces to set them up well for their intended purpose.

The demons also completed some work on the farms above the three camps to create additional medical rooms and living quarters for our other elders and me. Chiron, as a trained healer, and I live in quarters at one of the farms, a farm that grows barley primarily. Dio is living there as well.

He has certainly become more stable. Under Chiron's watchful eye, he's actually been training fan club members and some of our people in both combat and coven magic. It was Chiron's idea to give him something else to focus on, and it seems to be working.

Under Dio's instruction, those magic users are making even more progress than they were previously. Hopefully, enough to at least not be a liability to us when we eventually end up in combat.

I briefly consider who will likely turn out to be a liability to us. As usual, though, the thought of her and what is likely happening to her brings so much pain that I shove the thought away. I can't afford that weakness right now. I need to help keep all of this moving forward.

As my feet move me nearer to the entrance of the building that one of our camps resides in, I sigh deeply and go to do just that.

BURNT

The wine is already starting to go to my head as Hypatia, Simone, and I descend into giggles about the statement Simone just shared with us from the book she is reading.

"The author deciding to compare that to food is an interesting choice," Hypatia finally gasps out between giggles.

"I blame the wine," I chime in, trying to catch my breath.

"Blaming the poor wine for the author's choice of words seems unfair," Simone gasps, and we all dissolve into giggles again.

As we all try to get control of ourselves again, I set my wine down.

I really don't need to get drunk, I remind myself.

Even as I'm considering if I could risk finishing the rest of the glass, a timer dings and Simone jumps up and goes to the kitchen. When she opens the oven, the smell of baked goods fills the room, and my mouth begins to water.

Hypatia goes to help Simone with the pastries. Deciding I'll risk it, I drink the rest of the glass as I watch the two of them in the kitchen. It feels cozy, I realize. As I watch them, I allow myself to enjoy the quiet safety that I've found here.

Simone carries a plate of sweet pastries over to the table in front of us. I almost instantly take one, tossing it from hand to hand as it tries to burn my fingers. "You'd think after almost burning my apartment down, you would be more cautious of hot pastries," Hypatia jabs at me.

I scoff at her. "It wasn't that bad."

"Oh, it was bad," Simone says, shaking her head.

"At least the fire crewmen who showed up were nice to look at," Hypatia says, lifting her eyebrows at us and eliciting laughter from Simone.

"I would say that, since it wasn't the first time, we probably shouldn't try to teach Chaosta to bake again, but maybe that's how we find her a man. Teach her to bake, she'll start the kitchen on fire, and then we can all get rescued by sexy fire crewmen," Simone laughs.

I throw a pillow at her, which just makes both of them laugh harder. Joy pings through my chest. Joy that feels less like a betrayal as the one-year anniversary of my capture approaches. Then again, I'm still not exactly sure why that joy feels like it ever *should* have been a betrayal.

Mostly, I've been trying not to think about the fuzzy memories or what I've forgotten since I joined the angels.

"Hey, I didn't do so bad the first two times," I say in a grumpy voice.

"Even the first two times! I've never seen baked goods so black," Hypatia crows, which makes all of us start giggling again.

After we each get our breath back and fill our mouths with pastries, we get back to reading.

After another hour or so, I call it a night. The wine is mostly out of my system, and I'm tired. As they grumble a bit that I'm no fun, I pack up my things. "Hypatia's place next right?" I ask.

"I thought it was yours?" Hypatia says.

"I really thought it was yours, but I guess I can take it if you want me to?" I say, hoping that she'll be willing to take it. I need more time with access to her apartment.

"Nah, if it's my turn, we can be at my place next time," Hypatia says with a yawn.

"I'm no fun?" I say as I point at her, and she quickly hides the yawn and throws a pillow at me.

As I get ready to head out the door, Simone calls out, "Hey, we should plan a group date, huh? There's this concert I'd like to go to, and it would be fun to get out of our apartments sometime."

I feel my body tense, but carefully hide it as Hypatia cheers and then says, "Yes! Let's go to a concert and get out of here for a night!"

"Sounds good to me! Let us know the time and place, and I'll be there," I say.

"Perfect!" Simone says happily, "I'll let you know in a couple of days when I see you both again and we can make plans then."

Bidding them both goodbye, I walk through the door into the hallway. When I arrive at my apartment, I put the food away and then head to the closet to take out my research.

At the door to my room, though I pause, I'm exhausted. Every night, I have been researching into the early hours of the morning and then getting only a few hours of sleep before waking up early for sword practice. After considering for a few moments, I decide I will get a full night's sleep and see if that helps.

Undressing, I drop my clothes to the floor. Then I climb into bed and curl up in the cold blankets, swallowing down that familiar feeling of loneliness yet again. I sink into sleep almost immediately.

~

Bile burns my throat as I find myself back in a now familiar memory. This, the session before I drowned, is a memory that has been haunting my dreams for a while.

I've just been dragged into one of the open, white rooms. My hands are fastened to the wall at a reasonably comfortable level for me to stand. The two angels who dragged me in here leave, and I'm left alone momentarily. I'm still in pain from my last session, the wounds not yet fully healed. However, a few weeks have passed since the last time I was tortured.

Moments pass that feel like years as I wait to figure out how they might hurt me today. Finally, a group of angels walks in the door. Two of them are carrying a case that they set down on a table, against the wall across from me.

As one of the angels starts to mess with the case, the door opens again, and Rex walks into the room. I note that, other than Rex, the others in the room are all wearing white coats rather than the typical uniform of black shirts and pants. As I watch them, my toes curl against the floor.

Rex and the others talk for a while, and then he moves to look at whatever is in the case. I am unable to look away from whatever horror I'm going to face.

From where I'm standing, with their voices pitched low, I can't make out the words, but I can make out the approval in Rex's voice, and on his face. Approval that certainly implies this won't be good for me.

Eventually, he walks over to me, and I brace myself, staring at the floor. Despite my effort, he moves to stand directly in front of me."Look at me while I talk to you," he says in a commanding tone.

I meet his eyes. I know better than to bait or resist him.

"You are in for a little treat today," he says, and he sounds pleased. "We have a surprise we have been working on for a while now. Since I discovered that the demons are training humans to use magic, I decided that we needed to be prepared to defend ourselves in our own way. After all, calling lightning down on my people in the street wasn't something to ignore."

My heart pounds in my chest.

"Initial testing on the target population is positive, but there has been some curiosity regarding what might happen if it were to be tested on you. After all, you are a singular being. One who contains the strength of each of our two peoples." He grins maliciously at me. "We even have bets on the result. Some of us, including myself, think it will finally eliminate you as a problem."

I flinch slightly, but at this moment, death isn't what scares me.

"The others think you will survive. If they are right, your value to us will increase, as it will mean you are particularly hard to kill. If that is the case, you will be close to atonement. What do you call that, high risk, high reward?" He laughs then, as though he's not about to potentially end someone's life.

Then he steps back, and one of the other angels pulls the item contained in the case out and levels it at me. I recognized the item as the weapon that did so much damage to the demons in past dreams.

As I did then, I brace myself as white energy bursts from the tip of the weapon and collides with my chest. Pure agony pierces through me, and I scream so hard that it feels like my throat will tear.

~

I wake, the scream dying in my throat as I recognize my bed. After all these mornings of waking from that dream, I just relax back onto my pillows, body shaking. My gut twists as I realize I'm running out of time.

I close my eyes and fight back a sob as thoughts of what I need to do crash into me. As I lay with my eyes closed, body shaking, I fight to remember as much of the dream as possible.

The first few times I woke from dreaming this memory, it instantly faded. At first, I was confused, I was so sure it was the demons who hurt me and not the angels. Then I realized that they must have some control over my memories to the point where they actually altered them. Most of the time, it is still the demons I see when I have flashbacks to my torture. This dream though feels like a key, one which keeps repeating. Just as I'm about to forget that the angels have ever hurt me, this dream appears again.

I'm sure it is a message. From whom, I don't know, but it is clearly important, and I need to do something about it. Despite the fact that by later today, I'll despise the demons again I know that I need to ensure their kind aren't completely wiped out. I lay in bed for awhile, my head aching from forcing myself, yet again, to memorize all the details of the dream. It will slowly fade again, but I've been remembering more and more about it as time goes on.

I finally look at the clock and see that it is time for me to get ready for sword practice, so I rise.

After cleaning up, I dress in my usual guard uniform. Hanging the badge that marks me as a city official around my neck, I leave the bathroom. After cleaning up, I complete the habitual check to ensure the strange scar on the underside of my wrist is still covered by the bracelet I wear. Confirming it is, I strap the Angelforged blade to my waist and then leave my apartment, headed for the sword range.

Walking into the familiar space is centering. As always, the sword-master is watching over a match between two opponents. I now recognize many of the angels who train here, and these two are familiar to me.

I move past them to the space at the back where there are

cubbies for our things. I place my badge and Angelforged blade on a shelf. Then I take one of the wooden practice blades and walk back to the edge of the mat, just behind the sword master. He nods, acknowledging me, and then goes back to watching the ongoing match. He occasionally gives instructions or encouragement.

His name is Alaris, and I quickly developed respect for his thoughtful coaching. I have become increasingly skilled at the sword under his tutelage. Coaching sessions with him are one of the few things I look forward to every day.

He has grey hair and striking cheekbones with dark eyes. His face is usually expressionless, and he is a terrifying and consummate swordsman, partially because of it. He is also extremely graceful on his feet, a style I have been emulating since I began to practice here.

The two in the ring swirl around each other, neither getting a blow in for a while. I watch the footwork, noting a hole I would have taken advantage of. I start to warm up, rolling my shoulders and bouncing on my heels as I continue to watch the match.

A few more minutes pass, and then Alaris calls out the end of the match. In practice, he doesn't identify a winner. Instead, opponents give each other feedback.

As they finish and leave the room, Alaris calls my name, gesturing with his head toward the cleared-out space on the mat. He looks around the room as I continue to stretch out. Then, with a shrug, he picks up a wooden blade and joins me in the ring.

I freeze for a moment as he walks closer, my heart pounding in my chest.

"Don't tell me you're scared, Cream Puff," he growls at me, but there's a smile on his face.

I take the position of the first form, and he closes in on me, towering over my small frame. I react carefully, letting my feet fall into the familiar pattern.

I allow him to lead for a while, letting my heart settle as my mind begins to flow.

The clashes of the wooden blades reverberate up my arm into my shoulder in a way that somehow further grounds me. My heart evens out, giving me a steady rhythm to dance to. In this state of flow, my body moves without conscious thought, my eyes going slightly unfocused as I take in the whole rather than the individual movements he makes.

In that place, I somehow catch a slight loss of balance and press my advantage, moving quickly and gracefully, until suddenly I blink the focus back into my eyes to see the point of my practice sword pressed to his chest.

For half a breath, his face remains impassive, and then the slightest grin spreads across it as I step back, lowering the sword. My palms start to sweat, and the rhythm of my heart picks up as I realize what I just did.

Instead of anger, though, he steps forward with his hand held out.

Looking down at it as though it's a test, I finally reach out and take it.

He shakes my hand once, firmly as he says, "Good match. It has been a long time since I've been bested. You do need to work on your overhand blocks. You leave an opening that may allow your opponent a strike under the right circumstances."

I relax as he gives the feedback, the familiar process beginning to return me to a calmer state.

Looking over my head, he gestures to someone behind me, "Come over here, Brachious, you could learn something from the footwork Chaosta has recently improved."

I step back into the middle of the ring and prepare myself for another match before starting a long day of guard duty.

EXCERPTS FROM MALAM

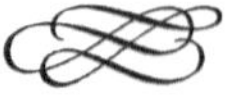

The two ex-farmers have only gone about half a round, and I'm already close to throwing one of the wooden practice blades at them. I've never seen such a timid, miserable display of sword fighting. Growling to myself, I step into the ring and stop them, unable to watch this travesty any longer. I reset their positions and, as patiently as I can, I walk them through the forms yet again. I must not be accomplishing the patient exterior I'm attempting, though, because they're both a little pale. I fight back yet another growl.

It's impressive I'm being as patient as I am, I remind myself. They should be flowing through the forms together easily and quickly by now.

As I take a few steps back, ready to get them going again, one of them, *Akasha,* I remind myself, swallows and looks like she's about to ask me something.

A snarl manages to escape my careful control, but I swallow the end of it and ask patiently, "What now?"

"I just don't understand how the movement from this form to that form leads to me getting a strike on my opponent?" she says, her voice a quiet squeak.

I rub my hand over my face, asking whichever of our gods might be available to help me retain my patience. I'm just about to respond to her question when I hear quick, sharp footsteps behind me. When I turn, I see Pepper striding up to me confidently. It has taken a while to get used to her energy, but I must admit, she's good at what she does.

Happy for any distraction, I tell the two demons in the ring to take a break and turn my focus to Pepper. She's wearing her normal fitted top and knee-length fitted skirt. Her hair is neatly piled on her head, and she is carrying a leather-bound book against her chest.

As she gets close to me, she says, "Malam, sir."

"Pepper," I acknowledge. "What do you need?"

"Roxana, Alexander's assistant, reached out to me about Dio. Since I know you want all communication for him to go through you, I told her that I would check and get back to her."

"How long ago?" I ask, unable to keep the anger, driven by worry, from my voice.

"Just now," she says, her voice bright and unbothered as though she didn't notice my tone.

"Give me the note, and I will take care of it."

She hands me a page with a neatly written name and contact information. "That should get you to Alexander's office. Roxana was the one who contacted me, but I'm sure it is Alexander who is asking," she says breezily and then asks, "Need anything else, sir?"

"No. Thank you, Pepper, I appreciate your help as always." I rub my hand over my face as I consider what to do next.

Pepper is already energetically striding away across the training space.

Deciding that I have time to consider, I return to teaching. I'm glad the day is almost done.

EXCERPTS FROM MALAM

My feet took me to the ocean yet again, so now I'm standing here, smoking and watching the waves as I consider the conversation I just had.

I just finished up a call with Alexander via one of our private terminals. Since he obviously doesn't have any context of who I am, I pretended to be an investigator who's looking for Dio.

I was shocked when he told me that he'd seen Chaosta. I was even more surprised when he mentioned that she was working as a city enforcer.

I knew the moment she was taken by the angels again that they would turn her into a liability for us. I expected that they'd drag her bloodied body out in front of us at some point, a point of pain to torture us with. Or maybe that they'd use her as a hostage. I never expected that they would turn her.

Suddenly feeling exhausted, I lean forward, resting my elbows on the concrete barrier and my head in my hands. Unable to think further down that particular path right now, I return to reflecting on the conversation with Alexander.

He said that when he saw Chaosta, he was surprised she was working as a city official since, last he was aware, she'd been accused of an attack on a mental hospital. He shared that he reached out because this was the contact information he had for her, and he was digging since something didn't feel right. He let me know that he was also looking for Dio.

In my fake role as an investigator, I asked him not to conduct his own investigation on this. I reassured him that *we* had it handled and told him that we didn't feel he was in any danger from Dio.

I asked that he share anything he learns, and he agreed. Of course, because I was meant to be with the city, I just pretended I was aware of Chaosta's whereabouts but told him that the case was sealed.

Pulled back to the present again, I put out my cigarette and stare out across the waves. I swear under my breath and then turn away from the view to walk back to the training camps.

I know that I should do something to prepare, that I should make a plan to limit the liability that I know we're now facing with my creation on the side of the angels. However, I cannot force myself to think about it right now.

Tomorrow, I lie to myself, *I'll think about it tomorrow.*

TO KNOW, NOT BE KNOWN

My palms are sweaty as I watch the clock on the wall in my living space. When I am confident that both my friends are at Hypatia's, I message them on my terminal to tell them that I got held up at work and will be running late.

Then I leave my room, my knees weak as I walk the familiar route to Simone's apartment. Her door is unlocked, just as I expected. I step inside, careful to act normal just in case she is still here.

Thankfully, the space is empty.

I go to the cabinet that I now know she keeps her badge in. My arms are heavy as I open the door and remove it. Tucking it into my pocket, I quickly leave the apartment, time counting down in my head.

As I walk to the lift and punch in one of the basement floors, I feel as though I might vomit. Eventually, the lift dings and the door opens. The air smells of food from the cafeteria located on this floor, and the scent of spaghetti makes me nauseous.

I walk past the cafeteria toward the security office, nervous but plastering a look of calm on my face. I'm ready to do this, I remind myself.

I have access to this space as one of the city guards, so I swipe my badge at the door, and the lock clicks open. I shouldn't have access to the badge replicator, but over the past few months, I have been able to figure out a way into that office.

Striding confidently through the space, I get to the end of the hallway and wait, counting in my head. Just as I begin to wonder if I've made an error, the door opens toward me, and I hide behind it, in the shadows.

The evening crew, whose shift just ended, leaves through the door and continues down the hallway without looking back. I wait until the last minute. As they round the corner, I swiftly catch the door just before it can latch closed and walk through into the more highly secured part of the suite.

I take a deeper breath to settle my nerves. The clock is still counting down in my head.

Other than the numbness that is now my constant companion, there is nothing helping me here. Those instincts that I can now vaguely, remember from when I saved Bonum have been quiet, not directing me since I was captured. I'm sure the control the wings have over me is restricting them somehow. At any rate, this is all me, and it's terrifying.

Shaking off fear at the thought of what a misstep might mean, I make it to the small office with the badge replicator. Pulling Simone's badge from my pocket and removing the clip, I place it into the machine and hit the correct button.

I start to gnaw on my lip, but catch myself automatically and stop as a muted ghost of a memory of Dio removing my lip from my teeth washes over me. These brief glimpses of memories are hard-won. After over a year of not having any access, I've slowly, painfully, been able to find some of them. In the same sort of way that I've fought to retain the memory of the angel's weapon, I've slowly clawed back bits of my old life.

I have very vague memories of the boys and of Malam and Chiron, but most of the memories I've fought to regain are of Dio. I hold them close to my aching heart, as though I can stitch the wreck of it together with these threads of memory.

After some time, and more noise than I am comfortable with, I have a copy of the badge. Sticking both in my pocket, I move around the desk and back toward the door. However, as I get closer to the opening, I hear voices. My stomach twists, and I drop quickly and tuck myself under the desk, hiding in the shadows as the footsteps and voices move closer. As they do, they become clearer until I can understand the words.

"...hear the rumors about the High Leader?" says a masculine voice.

"There can't possibly be any rumors about the High Leader I'd be interested in. I don't follow politics," says a second, masculine voice.

"How can you be on the security detail and not be inundated with political rumors?"

"Remember how I just moved to this region? We don't talk that much about politics if you can believe it." The tone is sarcastic.

A bead of sweat slides down my temple as they pause just outside the door of the room I'm hiding in. My heart is suddenly in my throat as I realize I left the lanyard for Simone's badge out on the counter.

"Well, you might be interested in this. It's not considered politics if the rumor is about the High Leader being in a secret relationship, is it?"

Bile rises in my throat, and my hands clench into fists. I say a quiet prayer to any deity that might be listening that the guards move on.

"Now that IS interesting. Why didn't you start with that?" says the second voice. "Who do you think it is?"

"I'm not sure, but there must be a good story there. It's been centuries since he last had a suitor, and that was very public."

I close my eyes and concentrate on breathing as my heart pounds. Thankfully, just as I'm beginning to wonder if the rising panic might consume me, the two guards move away. Their voices slowly grow indistinct again. I wait until I can't hear them and then count slowly to some undefined number until I can breathe again. I crawl out from under the desk, take Simone's lanyard, and go to the door.

Glancing out into the larger room that surrounds this central office, I scan for danger. Seeing no one, I stride across the space, but when I'm midway, I hear humming. I freeze as I try to identify where it is coming from and if it is moving closer.

Fuck. It's moving closer.

I'm in the open with nowhere to go. I stride forward and tuck myself against the wall at the edge of a doorway.

"Anyone he—"

His voice cuts off as I wrap an elbow around his throat and hang on until his body goes limp. I continue to hold pressure, not relaxing until I count to ten slowly. Angels are immortal after all. Once I'm confident that he's unconscious, I let him slump to the floor. I'm confident he didn't get a look at me, a fact I'm extremely thankful for.

I flee quickly from this space and back to the lift. Every moment, I expect to be discovered, and I can't begin to relax until I'm on the lift headed toward Simone's floor.

I swiftly return the badge to its place in her apartment. I'm careful to remember to reattach the clip. I run back to my apartment to hide the replicated badge and grab my food for tonight. Then I rush to Hypatia's apartment.

. . .

It's about an hour later, and the three of us are reading. Based on our conversation, I know Simone is at a particularly tense part of her book, and Hypatia is reading a history, so there hasn't been as much chatting as normal. My book, one about an adventure where the characters are in peril as they try to subvert a ruling group, just makes me anxious. Especially with the adrenaline from earlier still coursing through me.

I persist, needing something to do while the time passes.

Hearing a sniff, I look up and see Simone wiping at her face.

Hypatia has also stopped reading and is looking at her as well. "That good, huh?" she says and hands Simone one of the cloth napkins on the table.

"One of the lovers just got taken by the royal guards," Simone sobs and then, accepting the napkin, mops up her tears.

My chest constricts, and I say, "See, that's why I don't read that stuff. It's just too heartbreaking."

"Hey now," Hypatia says. "The painful parts just make it better and, once again, I think you might feel differently if we can find you a person to love."

"Speaking of that," Simone says with a quiet hiccup, "are we going to talk about our plans for the concert?"

"Not speaking of that," I shoot back, but the two of them just grin at each other conspiratorially. My heart pounds, and bile again rises in my throat.

"I have the tickets," Simone says excitedly. "Want to guess who we are going to see?"

The name of the only band I know, and can now vaguely remember, echoes through my head. I remain silent.

"Who?" Hypatia asks. She is clearly excited, bouncing slightly on the couch where she's sitting.

"The Amulets!" Simone crows, and Hypatia jumps up and hugs her.

I relax slightly. I wasn't sure what I'd do if we ended up at one of The Boys' concerts.

"How? They're impossible to get tickets for, and you know they're my favorite," Hypatia nearly screams.

I flinch at the loud noise.

"Sorry, sorry," Hypatia says, lowering her voice and sitting back down. "I know you don't do well with loud noises."

I shake my head slightly. "I'm fine," I say cheerily despite not feeling it. "When is the concert?"

Hypatia looks at me like she doesn't believe I'm fine, while Simone says, "Only about two weeks."

"You're my hero!" Hypatia cheers for Simone, but I note that she keeps her voice down.

Yet again, I am reminded that I don't deserve their friendship.

"Ok, onto the important question, what are we wearing?" Simone asks.

The rest of the evening devolves into conversation about outfits and a plan to go shopping. I stay longer than normal, my heart enjoying the closeness with the two of them. My head appreciates the distraction. Anything to avoid having to think about the cause of the panic that has been clawing at my chest since I escaped with the duplicate badge.

LINCHPIN

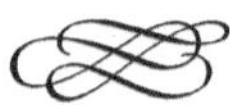

A few days have passed and, as planned, we are at a shop looking for outfits to wear to the concert. We are at this particular small shop at Simone's recommendation since she loves clothes. I was dragged here despite my quiet protests. I must admit, though, I'm having a good time.

We've already been shopping for nearly an hour, and the other two have already found things to wear. I haven't been able to find anything yet that doesn't show too much skin.

I have carefully kept my scars from the two of them. The questions that would arise about where they came from would be far too hard to explain, especially since those memories are still mostly inaccessible.

I'm pulled back to the present as Hypatia says, "Not sure why you are such a prude. You're toned as hell, with all that sword practice, and fine as fuck." She gestures at me as she says it, her eyes scanning my body.

"She just isn't comfortable showing skin, Hypatia," Simone says, irritation creeping into her voice. "I'm sure we can find something that will be less revealing."

Hypatia holds up a perfect top and skirt combination, and I reach for it.

"Absolutely not," Simone says, rolling her eyes, "The red is going to clash with her hair."

"I like it though," I say, pouting slightly.

Hypatia holds up a grey version, clearly proud of herself, and Simone looks at me, a question in her eyes.

"That's perfect," I say, reaching for it again.

"Aren't you going to try it on at least?" Simone asks.

Grumbling, I take the dress to the small room at the back of the shop and pull it on. Checking the mirror, I see that it does, indeed, cover all of my scars. It is a dark grey color, and the skirt nearly touches the floor. The shirt is fitted with long sleeves and a high collar, but because of the shape, it doesn't look too "Prudish," as Hypatia would say.

"Going to show us?" Hypatia calls out.

Feeling a blush creep toward my cheeks, I walk out of the room and show them the outfit.

"See?" Simone says to both of us, "I knew we could find something for all of us here."

With that approval, I return to the dressing room to get changed back into my things. As I do, I hear them mumbling something about how I'll have someone wrapped around my little finger. I flinch, and yet again, panic crawls in my chest.

I hope they aren't actually planning to try to set me up with someone. I don't think I can take that right now.

After I get changed back into my things, we go to the counter and pay for our items, and then leave the shop. As we walk to a busier street where it will be easier to get a carriage, I catch sight of something that piques my interest. It's a museum entrance that I noticed on the way to the shop earlier. "How would you two feel about extending our expedition?" I ask.

"What are you thinking?" Simone asks.

"Maybe coffee and a stroll around that museum?" I gesture to it with my head as we walk past.

Simone looks unsure, but Hypatia's eyes light up. When Simone sees that, she laughs and agrees.

"I think I saw a little cafe over there," Hypatia says with a broad smile.

I unexpectedly feel a similar expression on my face.

We get coffees and then walk back to the museum entrance. It's open and free to the public, so we don't even need to use our city badges to get in. Most of what is on display seems to be ancient human artifacts. Hypatia and I compare notes about things we've read in history books while Simone mostly follows us around sipping her coffee and occasionally pointing out an item or description.

The coffee is quite good and a rare treat. Angels seem not to drink it frequently, and, without access to specific memories about why, I still know I miss it.

Hypatia is looking at an exhibit with Simone looking over her shoulder. I'm walking down a hallway when the end exhibit, nearly in the dark, draws me in. When I get close enough to make out the small item on the podium, I freeze. Sitting on a white platform with a small placard under a glass case is a small, gold, filigree stake.

Staring at it, my head slowly fills with sound as though I'm standing in the middle of a crowd. The wings pulse slightly where they join my shoulders.

Memories I haven't had access to suddenly come flooding back as I remember a dream. I also remember conversations with a friend about something that was missing from a different magical object.

Suddenly, Simone's voice, close to me, catches my attention, and I quickly shake myself out of whatever state I was just in.

Masking my expression, I move to another case, trying not

draw attention to this object. I pretend to read the placard to buy myself some time.

"This is actually pretty," Simone says as she walks behind me and catches sight of the stake.

With an excuse to look more closely, I step beside her and read the plaque in front of the stake, which identifies it as a decorative hairpin. I nearly scoff before I catch myself. "That is pretty," I agree as the vision of it floating within the center of the small stone plays again in my mind.

They move on and, after a moment, I follow them. The wings slowly stop pulsing against my shoulder blades. Suddenly exhausted, I numbly participate as we walk through the remainder of the museum. I must do a decent job of hiding it, though, because my friends don't seem to catch on. They both thank me for the idea as we step back out onto the street.

I return the hug each of them gives me and then call a carriage to return home. My head is spinning, and I'm thankful to be able to head back to my apartment.

SOLELY RESPONSIBLE

I'm sitting in my closet with schematics, books, papers, and notes in my messy handwriting surrounding me. It has been several days since we shopped for clothing, and I saw the stake.

A few nights ago, when we met up to read at my apartment, Hypatia shared how close her team is to solving the last issue with production. Since then, I have been unable to focus on anything else.

Tonight we are meant to be at Simone's apartment, but I told the two of them that I had a headache. I'm in my closet because I was worried they might show up to try to make me feel better. As the end of the night approaches, that concern has thankfully failed to materialize.

Months ago, when I was finally allowed nearly full freedom and moved into this apartment, I spent a couple of weeks adjusting to the new routine. I was bored and didn't quite know what to do with myself. Then I had that dream about the weapon, and suddenly I had a purpose again. The memory faded quickly, but it was enough to give me some impetus to take action.

Then I had the dream again. The next morning, when I woke, I took some hasty notes and from there I built my plan. The action I needed to take was pretty clear. I needed to do something to prevent this weapon from wiping out the demons.

If the power of the weapon in my dream was even close to accurate, it certainly has the ability to wipe out their entire race. While I struggle daily with the painful memories of the demons torturing me, I know that is the influence of the wings. My belief in balance is stronger than the narrative the wings are forcing on me. Besides, my morals haven't changed, and I refuse to be part of wiping out an entire race.

It took me a while to figure out how to impact the weapon, but eventually I was able to identify Hypatia and Simone as my best options to get access to what I needed. I started out by befriending them, and I am filled with guilt that those relationships are based on a lie. Since then, I've been carefully working my way closer to a solution until finally, about a week ago, I had a breakthrough.

The weapon functions similarly to how a combat magic user causes damage. It has runes drawn into it and, when activated, it pushes magical energy through those runes to create an effect. In this case, it causes a blast of magic that will explode into the life energy of the targeted demon. The angels have found a specific magical signature that impacts demons with near instant death. This works similarly to how an Angelforged blade will poison and eventually cause a demon's body to turn to dust. This weapon just acts much faster.

In non-demons, it causes a significant amount of pain that is momentarily debilitating but not deadly. I shudder as I remember what that felt like.

After careful, calculated spying and subtle questioning with Hypatia, I finally came to the conclusion that I needed to impact the production of the weapon. I had to find a way to invalidate something so they won't work as designed. However, I need it to be subtle enough that it isn't caught until the weapons are put into use. I finally had a breakthrough regarding one of the runes that Hypatia mentioned.

Isa, with its meaning of stasis, is used in the weapon to ensure the bolt of energy doesn't activate until it hits its intended victim. I realized that if I could get the production equipment to mirror-image the rune and draw it backwards, it would invalidate that rune without the difference being visible.

After making that realization a week ago, I have been spending most of my time learning to code so that I can reprogram the production equipment. However, after seeing the stake at the museum, I knew I needed to pause that work.

I am not naive. I know my chances of surviving the mission in the weapons production plant are extremely low. I'm fairly confident that I can reprogram the machine while avoiding suspicion of tampering. However, getting out safely is unlikely at best.

I think there is a part of me that wonders if that would be such a bad result. It is the same part of me that has been wondering if allowing good and bright to prevail is ever wrong.

My focus had been entirely on how to disable that weapon. However, after I saw the stake, I realized that I needed to get it into the hands of that friend, so I changed my focus to infiltrating the museum. Thankfully, with minimum security, that should be fairly simple. Since it is less likely to end in my capture, that must come first.

My eyes blur as I continue to stare at the museum floor plan. My head is beginning to ache as I review my plan for what feels like the millionth time.

Finally, when I check the clock, the hands show the time I've been waiting for.

I change into my guard uniform and clip on my badge. Strapping my sword to my waist, I pick up the bag I packed earlier and hang it over my shoulder. Then I leave my apartment, taking the back way just to ensure I don't run into anyone I know. Exiting the building through the side door, I walk to a quiet street before catching a carriage.

When it pulls up outside the museum, I walk, as confidently as I can, into the building. As I approach the guard booth, I greet the current guard and let her know that I'm her replacement.

"Thanks for being early," she says as she starts packing up.

"Anything I should know?" I ask. It's the familiar shift change question.

"Quiet as always," she says and then, with her things packed up, she leaves.

I sit, tucking the bag under the desk, and wait.

As expected, after a few more minutes pass, the next guard shows up. The correct guard. He walks towards me, and I ignore him.

When he gets close, he says, "Hey, I'm your replacement."

I look up at him, surprise plastered across my face as I say, "I just got here. This shift is on my schedule."

"Well, that's odd," he says, looking confused. I pull up the image I prepared and point out to him how I'm on the schedule.

"I will never say no to a surprise night off," he says with a grin.

"Or you could take it, and I could leave?" I ask, acting hopeful.

"Look, I see your name right there just like you do. Looks like you're the unlucky winner tonight," he says. He's already turning and walking away.

"Ok, but you'll owe me," I say with a laugh.

He makes a rude gesture without turning around as he leaves.

I wait for about an hour, making one round to ensure the cameras see me in my guard uniform. Guard shifts are swapped all the time, so if anyone questions why I'm here instead of the guard on the official schedule, I'll have an easy explanation.

Once I get back to the booth, I get started on my plan. First, I divert a couple of cameras just slightly, making a slim path that I can conceal myself in. Then I change into black clothes with a hood and mask just in case I run into anyone or the camera catches something. Finally, I take the replica of the stake that I crafted out of glue, string, and gold paint and tuck it carefully into a pocket.

Moving methodically, I head for the case, watching the range of the cameras and carefully navigating to ensure I don't get caught.

There is one spot that is particularly tight, and I consider going back to move the camera a bit more, but I know I don't have time. My heart is in my throat, and I gnaw on my lip as I consider. Finally, deciding to go for it, I tuck myself against the wall and, in a quick movement, duck around the corner into the open room.

When I arrive at the appropriate case, I use the small tool I brought to separate the glass cover from the base.

Finally managing it, I lift the glass carefully and set it on the nearby case. I take the stake and swap it with mine. It is certainly not an exact replica, but hopefully, a minor change in this artifact, which is clearly not under any significant security, won't be noticed.

That done, I pull the adhesive out of my pocket and carefully re-secure the case. I can feel the clock counting down in my head, and before I can quite finish, I need to turn and leave. I pray silently to the dark gods I've slowly been able to remember as I navigate back to the security desk.

I re-dress in my guard uniform and tuck the real stake into my bag. Then I sit down at the guard station. I focus on breathing evenly until my heart finally slows and the sweat on my hairline dries. After a couple of minutes, I rise and walk the rounds, careful to be caught on camera in my guard uniform as much as possible.

The time passes slowly, and I'm exhausted by the time the end of my shift approaches.

The past few nights, I've barely been sleeping. I'm running out of time to figure out the last few things I need in order to disable or hinder the production of the weapons. An all-night shift tonight was certainly not helpful.

Finally, the other guard shows up to replace me. I give them my report and then take my bag and leave. I return to my apartment and conceal the stake carefully in the back of my closet. Then I change into the clothes I wear for sword practice and make my way to the practice range. I would love to skip it this morning and take a nap, but since I haven't missed a single morning so far, I know that could raise suspicion. Instead, I stop at the cafeteria and grab something to eat and then walk to the sword range, covering a yawn.

After besting Alaris a few weeks ago, the sword master has been using me to demonstrate different techniques with other pupils. After today, where I bumbled around and took a few hits, I'm sure he won't be doing that again anytime soon.

Gods, that was the worst I've ever fought in a practice match, I think to myself as I walk back to my apartment.

To his credit, he did look concerned after I took the second hit and asked if everything was ok. I said it was my insomnia again. He instructed me to get back to it, but after I was hit a third time, he told me to call in for my shift and get some sleep. I was happy to take him up on his offer, especially when he said that he would call my superior for me.

I finally get to my apartment and unlock the door. I eye my bed, but I have a task to complete first. Going to the closet, I take the stake and conceal it in a pocket. I leave my apartment headed for the lift. Punching the button for floor

111, I gnaw on my lip, hoping that Bonum is in their apartment.

Eventually, I find myself standing in front of the door I haven't visited since the day I was captured. I knock once, still gnawing on my lip as I wait. Moments pass, and I'm trying to decide if I should knock again or leave and try later, when the door opens.

Bonum stands just inside, a naked sword in their hand. They're wearing nothing but a pair of pants.

They blink and move back into the room as they rasp quietly but forcefully, "Get out of the hallway." I follow them into the room, and they close the door quickly behind me. "We both know you shouldn't be here, little bird," they grit out. Somehow, even their inflectionless voice portrays anger.

"I'm not exactly here for a social visit," I grind out past a clenched jaw. Clearly, the exhaustion is getting to me.

Bonum sighs and rolls their shoulders, "What then?"

I pull the stake out of my pocket and hold it out to them. "I need you to figure out how to get this to…" I fight yet again to access memories that I've regained.

Bonum stares through me, their shoulders tight.

Finally, I find the right name, and as I hand the stake to the angel, I say, "Lent. I need you to get this to Lent." His name feels odd on my tongue, and my chest constricts as I remember that I miss him without knowing why.

They accept it from me, examining it with their fingers as their eyes continue to stare through me. "What treasure have you found, Little Bird?" they rasp.

"We both know I shouldn't tell you," I say, mirroring their words back at them.

Bonum laughs, a grating sound like claws against a cage, and I flinch. "What damage will this cause to our people?"

"If I am correct in what I believe it to be, it will cause no direct damage to our—I mean your people."

They nod once, their expression suddenly calculating and then drop their hand to their side, the stake concealed in their palm. "Time to go now," they rasp at me.

"Thank you, Bonum," I say softly.

After checking the hallway, I leave the apartment and walk to the lift. I'm glad to be able to return to my room. Once there, I collapse in bed and finally get some sleep.

EXCERPTS FROM MALAM

I'm, yet again, trying not to lose my temper with a couple of idiotic farmers, turned soldiers, when I hear the sound of wingbeats. All of our floors have entries for crows, but so far, they haven't had much reason to be used.

Crows are beloved by our kind, and previously, they acted as our eyes and ears. Now that fewer of them exist, and we have terminals, they aren't often used to communicate. Normally, they communicate telepathically with us as the crow did when Chaosta was injured.

As this one flies unerringly toward me, though I note that it seems to be carrying something.

Suddenly concerned, I hold out my arm to give it a place to land. It drops the item on the ground at my feet as it wraps its claws around my forearm. I wait for a moment, but no vision arrives.

I reach for the item that it dropped. When I pick it up off the ground, I see that it is a piece of paper tied around a small, stick-shaped object no longer than the width of my palm.

Unwrapping the paper, I see a delicate, gold, filigreed stick.

Unsure what to think, and feeling the eyes of most of the training floor on me, I open the paper and read the message.

A gift for Lent

I don't recognize the handwriting, and while I immediately wonder about Chaosta, it is certainly not hers.

"What is it, Elder?" asks one of my people from the small crowd that surrounds me.

I shake my head and call out, "Back to practice, all of you. I will expect progress when I return."

Then I leave this space, knowing I need to talk with Chiron.

As I arrive at the lift, the crow takes off from my arm, headed for the opening that will take it back outside. I take the lift to the level set up for magic work. Stepping into the space, I orient myself. Groups of magic users, arranged in covens, are spread across this floor. I walk around the edge of the open room until I see familiar faces.

Chiron sits against a wall in a corner, watching the coven and Dio with a casualness that I know is feigned. This is nearly an obsession, his own unhealthy coping mechanism. Obviously, he is here for Lent. However, I personally know that he also continues to obsessively observe Dio.

I walk over to join Chiron and sink down along the wall to sit on the floor beside him. Looking out over the magic practice range, I survey the familiar scene. Covens of three or more people, both humans and demons, practice group magic. Most of them are working on nature magic, under the guidance of my people. They stand in small groups near each other or arranged in slightly larger circles. There is quiet chanting coming from some of the groups.

In specially marked spaces around the edges of the wide, open room, individual magic practitioners are dueling with combat magic or aiming at dummies. The space smells of copper from blood magic as well as the acrid smell of combat magic.

"Why are you here?" Chiron asks abruptly after I don't say anything for a few moments.

Passing him the item, I ask, "Do you know what this is?"

He looks at it, rolling it in his fingers a minute before saying, "No, should I?" He sounds irritated.

"A crow just brought it to me. It was wrapped in this note," I say as I hand him the small piece of paper.

He tenses as he reads it. Tightly, and very quietly, he says, "Why, the fuck, would this be sent to Lent?"

"I'm not sure," I say, also pitching my voice low.

"You aren't going to give it to him, are you?" he asks, a threatening note creeping into his voice.

"What if Lent knows what it is?" I ask. Out of the corner of my eye, I see him considering.

"I'm not willing to risk it," he finally says, running his hand through his tousled curls. He's staring at Lent, and the love shining in his eyes makes my chest ache.

"Then what?" I ask.

"I'll keep it somewhere safe. If it comes up or is needed at some point, I can give it to him. It just seems too random, like someone is targeting him."

I glance where he's looking and watch Lent. The coven is talking quietly about something. I suspect they're in the middle of working out some bit of magic because scrubbed-out chalk markings cover the floor where they're standing.

Glancing past them, I watch Dio coaching two people practicing combat magic. They're aiming various magical effects against shapes drawn on a wall, clearly not quite ready for the risk of sparing. Dio is standing behind a woman, talking her through something as she aims a blast of wind at the wall.

"How has he been?" I ask, jerking my chin toward Dio.

"About the same. Still sedated but not as much. He hasn't tried to leave. He seems to be focused on helping with our work, and he continues to make significant progress with those he is training. "

As Chiron speaks, I watch as Dio steps alongside the woman he's coaching. He's watching her, saying something when the entire practice dummy is suddenly covered in black flame. I blink, my breath halting in my lungs.

He's not even looking at the dummy.

I drag my eyes away from the strange, magical effect and see that the woman he's teaching is nodding to him calmly.

My attention is interrupted as I realize Chiron is watching me, perhaps waiting for a response. "Do you still think he'll try to go after Chaosta if we don't watch him and maintain the wards?"

I can't help but look back at Dio, and when I do, I note that the black flame is gone. Yet again, I can't help but wonder how effective he'll be in the upcoming conflict.

"Don't you?" Chiron says.

I hesitate, still staring at Dio as I say, "It's been over a year, he hasn't tried yet."

Initially, the plan was that he would help trigger the storm with the rest of the coven. Since he was replaced by Cal, I hadn't considered what role he might play. It's been impossible to know how he'd handle Chaosta's disappearance.

Now, as I watch him teach, I begin to wonder if I should include it in my plan. At least, he might take a few angels out before he's killed. At best, perhaps he can disable a contingent and stem the flood while my people kill them with our blades.

"All I can say is that if it were Lent who they'd taken, I wouldn't let anything stop me, no matter the time or distance," Chiron says with a firmness that makes my chest ache.

I glance at him and see that he's staring at Lent again.

Feeling my emotions threatening to bubble over, I realize that I need some air. I push myself up and bid him farewell.

I feel his eyes on me, clearly noting something I'd rather he not.

Fucking observant bastard, I think to myself.

He grunts at me, but then goes back to watching the practice in front of him as I escape.

I take the lift to the street level. Taking advantage of the break from training, I light up a cigarette. I realize, as I walk, how much more frequent the habit has gotten. An unhealthy way of dealing with stress.

We've all got our things, I remind myself.

SINGING A DIFFERENT TUNE

Leaving my apartment, I double-check to ensure I have my concert ticket and then lock my door. We're meeting out front so we can take a carriage together. Hypatia's boyfriend and Simone's girlfriend are meeting us there.

When I meet the two of them on the street out front, they're in high spirits. As we hail a carriage and begin the ride to the concert venue, my friends pull me along with them in their happiness.

It takes us a while to get to the venue, so we have some time to chat about our days at work during the carriage ride. Simone and I had our typical boring days, but Hypatia is bubbly with success. She shares that her team had a breakthrough she believes will allow the weapon to go into production in a couple of weeks.

Trying not to panic, I manage to change the topic to focus on the band we'll be seeing. I push down frustration at another late night and terror that I'm not going to get everything figured out in time.

As I work to control that rising panic, Simone tells us more about The Amulets. It sounds like the music is much different than the bits and pieces that I can sort of remember from the last concert I went to. I'm relieved when I learn that the lead singer is female.

Eventually, the carriage stops, and we step out into the chaos of a crowd of people flooding towards the entrance of the building. We somehow manage to locate Hypatia's boyfriend, who's named Noah, and Simone's girlfriend, Leah. Then we insert ourselves into the crowd that is headed into the venue.

The next several moments are chaotic as we follow the press of the crowd, somehow managing to stick together until we're inside. Hypatia, always sharp, uses her elbows and plenty of snarky comments to get us closer to the front, near the middle of the room.

Noah and Leah seem nice, and we manage to chat a bit as we wait for the band. It's tough to hear the conversation, but since we're pressed against each other by the crowd surrounding us, at least we don't have to shout.

After a little while, Noah lets us know that he'll be right back. I notice him wink at Hypatia, who grins conspiratorially back at him. Then he's pushing his way through the crowd away from us. Simone and Hypatia give each other a look, and I wonder what's going on.

Then the band walks out on stage. The feeling of being in this crowd is similar to distant memories. My head begins to ache slightly, the wings stinging slightly where they join my back as I struggle to remember. As the crowd surges, I'm thankfully distracted from my internal battle.

I see Noah making his way back through the crowd. When he gets to us, he puts a hand on Hypatia's arm and gestures with his head to a man who is following him.

I feel my chest grow tight as I realize they did indeed conspire to set me up. Noah and Hypatia both turn to me, grins on their faces.

"This is Asher. He's Noah's friend," Hypatia manages to yell out over the crowd just before the band starts playing.

I focus on breathing for a moment and take advantage of the disruption to subtly look at him. Like most angels, he has blond hair and blue eyes. He is slender and casually dressed, and I also note that he has kind eyes.

As the musicians continue to perform, I quickly decide I dislike the singer and the band. She does a lot of screaming, and especially with the volume of it, all I can think of is my own voice screaming, the sound reverberating against the hard surfaces of the clinical rooms.

Asher seems to feel as awkward about our unexpected circumstances as I do. After a bit, he also seems to realize that I'm uncomfortable, or more accurately, that I'm jumping out of my own skin.

Out of my peripheral vision, I see him glancing at me, and finally, he puts a hand on my shoulder. I flinch, and he quickly removes it. Worry crosses his expression. After a moment, he leans a little closer so he can speak into my ear and says, "Come on, it'll be quieter back here."

Not sure what else to do, and more than happy to escape even some of the trauma I'm feeling, I allow him to lead me through the crowd to the back of the room, where there is an open door. He steps through it, and I follow into a hallway that runs along the side of the venue.

There are a few others out here, including a couple who are making out. It's still loud, but he's right, it is better. At least it is quiet enough that I feel like I can breathe. As my heart begins to settle, I feel his eyes on me again, and I glance at him.

His expression is apologetic as he says, "Sorry for the ambush. I didn't realize you were in the dark about them setting us up, or I would have refused."

Surprised by his kindness, I look away and manage to choke

out, "It's alright, Hypatia and Simone are confident that I need a man in my life. I'm sure they think this is the best thing for me."

"You don't agree?" he asks as quietly as he can with the din occurring through the open door.

"It's complicated," I say as my stomach churns.

"Ah," he says wisely. "I can leave if you want?"

I shake my head, still not looking at him. I don't want to go back in with the others.

"We can both leave and get something to drink?" he asks.

Unsure what else to do, I say, "I'd like that."

He smiles, his face becoming more boyish as he does. The panic I'm still feeling recedes a little.

"Come on," he says, gesturing to me.

I follow him down the hallway and out of the venue. When we get to the street, I pause for a minute, feeling my knees wobble as thankfulness for the quiet crashes through me.

"Not your thing, huh?" he says.

I glance sideways at him and see pity in his expression. "It used to be," I say, fighting back the shadow of tears. "Tonight it was just too much, I think."

I don't dare tell him that his presence as a man, and an angel, is adding to it.

"I get that," he says. "Need a minute?"

I shake my head as I get control of myself again and follow him down the street to a small food shop.

"Do you like wine?" he asks as we enter the shop.

My chest tightens at the question. "Yes, please, I prefer red."

He nods and orders a bottle for us. Then we find a table and sit.

"Tell me about yourself," I say before he can ask about me.

"Hmm, well, I work as a manager at the central library," he says. "Not usually thrilling work by any means, but I love books."

A ghost of a smile crosses my face. "I'm not surprised they decided to set us up then."

"You too?"

I nod.

"What do you read?" he asks.

Searching my memory quickly for a safe option, I rattle off the names of a few benign histories just as the wine shows up. I feel tears prick at my eyes as I note that it's a Cabernet.

Asher thankfully doesn't seem to notice the tears. His face lights up as I name the titles. "What do you do for work?"

"I work as a city guard," I say.

"Well, our worlds collided just over a year ago now, when a couple of priceless books were stolen. I don't think you were one of the guards who showed up to investigate, though. I think I would have remembered you." There is a slightly crooked smile on his face, and his eyes are sparkling.

I mask a flinch at the flirtation and ask for more information about the books. When I learn they were old stories about magic, I get a strange sense of deja vu. Before I can try to locate the memory, though, he moves on to ask me more about what I'm currently reading.

Hours later, I unlock the door to my apartment and step inside. After we finished our wine and some food, Asher walked me back to this building. He lives in a different high-rise.

I, surprisingly, had a lovely time, and I could tell he did as well. We even set up a time to meet for coffee.

Thanks to the conversation and his kindness, the feeling of panic has nearly faded, which is good because I have a long night ahead of me. I sigh as I move to the closet, pull the books and papers out of where I've hidden them, and begin to set them up on the floor of my room.

EXCERPTS FROM MALAM

Panting, I lean my hands on my knees, sweat dripping from my forehead. I realized recently that without working the land and not having a sparring partner who could keep up with me, I was getting out of shape. I quit smoking and took up running instead, a healthier way to cope, I guess.

Once I get my breath back, I look out over the water. At least I have a beautiful route to run. I've been trying to get Chiron to join me, but so far he's refused. This last time I tried, he mumbled something about having plenty of activities that make him sweat. I'm not sure what he's talking about. He spends most of his time watching the others practice magic.

I'll keep working on it, I know it would be good for him.

Also, at this point, it would likely be good for Dio if Chiron let go of his self-appointed guard duty. Dio certainly hasn't given us any reason to believe that he's going to try to leave at this point.

Staring out at the water as I continue to catch my breath, a feeling rises in my chest, one that was unfamiliar at first but has been occurring with more frequency lately. It's a feeling of hope.

As I have been, I smother it. The only hope for my people is that, through great sacrifice, we might cause a slight shift in the balance.

Our army now numbers around 12,000 strong, including the fan club, demons, and other more experienced magic users who have joined us. That is still a small fraction of the numbers that the angels will have.

Along with the increased numbers, the skill of our army is rapidly improving. Despite that, there likely won't be enough time to get all of my people competent at wielding a sword. Most combat magic users only have enough strength to kill an angel or two at most before they'd burn out. The two are typically used in combination, but we're unlikely to have the numbers to put together enough contingents for any sort of useful strategy. Instead, I'm hoping we can rely on the covens and the magic effects they wield, which will affect larger areas.

At any rate, while we have no chance of winning this, I'm hoping I can preserve most of my people by surrendering at the right time. The critical piece really is the storm. The last time I asked Chiron how the coven was doing, he shared that he thinks they are close to having all the knowledge they need. He believes there are still some missing pieces, likely informed by some dream he had, but I'm feeling more confident that part of my plan will work as intended.

Unfortunately, all the progress meant I no longer had an excuse to avoid the topic I've been running from since I heard from Alexander. I finally had to come up with a plan to mitigate the risk now caused by Chaosta.

When I created her, I didn't give myself any way to compel her toward my vision of what balance meant. Other than ensuring she had some of both worlds, technology for the angels, and my life-force for the demons, I have widely left her to her own devices, especially more recently.

Unfortunately, based on the evidence, we must assume the angels have been able to turn her to support their side. In all this time I've had to consider, I have come to the conclusion that they are likely using the wings against her. The gift that Rex gave her so long ago, the *gift* that I now wish I had taken more seriously. I never got an answer from Bonum about why she might have felt weak when she fought the angels at my safe house. However, I suspect that they may have been trying to control her with them back then.

There's still a chance that they don't have magical control over her and instead are just using threats against those she cares about. I'm less worried if that's the case since I believe she will be unlikely to turn on us. Of course, that doesn't mean that she wouldn't still tip the balance in their favor.

If they're using the wings to control her, she will be forced to fully embrace their ideology, in which case we will have to disable her. Knowing I couldn't be the only one with this knowledge, I brought a conclave of elders together, and we have a plan to do just that. Gods forbid there comes a time where we need to use it.

Praying for forgiveness of these dark thoughts, I stretch my shoulders and then continue on with my run.

TANGIBLE NIGHTMARE

I grit my teeth against the memory that suddenly hits me. In it, I'm in an alley outside a concert that turned into a riot. Dio has me pinned against the outer wall of a building. His hand is tangled in my hair, and we're kissing each other almost desperately.

The memory fades, and a choked sob crawls its way out of my throat as some of the brutal pain escapes. The pain of this feels somehow worse than the pain of the torture I've endured.

I lean forward and rest my head against the table in the dining room of my apartment. I'm here by myself in the nearly empty space. In fact, if anything, it is even emptier than it was a couple of weeks ago. Back then, I still had all of the schematics, a copy of Simone's badge, and all sorts of tools and other things that I needed to pull off my mission. Now, all of that has been destroyed, and all I'm left with are a few books, some random food, and basic living items like my clothes.

I wish this were a night when I was planning to see my friends, but instead I'm alone here. In the past, I would have been pleased not to have plans because it would have meant an earlier start on research and more sleep. Now, as the pangs of loneliness batter against me, I just don't want to be alone. Being here by myself gives me too much time to think.

Since I won my fight to access memories of Dio, they have been mercurial. Sometimes I reach for them, and nothing is there. Other times, such as now, they assault me without warning. I have come to prefer the pain of those memories over the emptiness when they're hidden from me. Still, that pain feels as though it might slowly bleed me dry.

I swipe at the tears on my cheeks, trying to swallow past the lump in my throat and attempting to return to some inner calm. I try to remind myself of the success of my mission since those feelings have been a good distraction recently, but it is hard to think of that when my heart aches with loneliness.

I pulled off a nearly impossible task somehow. The knowledge of what it will mean when the demons eventually clash with the angels has been fortifying. It still helps to think about it, but as time passes, those thoughts are less capable of pulling me away from the increasing ache in my chest.

My self-assumed mission concluded just over two weeks ago when I snuck into the production plant using Simone's badge. I had studied the layout, including the security system and guard rotations, until it was so imprinted in my memory that I still dream about it.

I made it successfully past the gauntlet of security guards, a maze of hallways, and various security doors, only a few of which Simone's badge worked for.

Then I faced my first real challenge. The machine in front of me, the one they would be using when production started the following day, was slightly different from the plans I had been studying. Thankfully, I'd become proficient enough with coding that I figured out a workaround and was still able to reprogram it to make the machine draw the rune in reverse.

Then I successfully got through the next part of my plan. That got me far enough away from the machine, with my tools destroyed, so that it would have been unlikely anyone could have traced me back to the production equipment.

Finally, I took a leap and attempted the full escape, and somehow it worked.

There is a void where the work I was doing for that mission used to exist. A void I haven't been able to fill in yet. I've been trying to read more, but after all the late nights spent poring over technical manuals, I just can't. At least not outside of the reading I'm doing when I spend time with Hypatia and Simone.

Thoughts about trying to escape have completely faded out. I'm somehow aware of the oddity of that absence while still not feeling as though I need to take any action to leave.

When I began to win the battle to remember my old friends and Dio, I had hoped that maybe someone would show up to save me. However, it has been well over a year since I was captured, and I haven't heard anything from any of them. At this point, I'm glad. I can't remember exactly what they're working on, but I know it is something of critical importance. Far more important than my rescue.

Also, I wouldn't ask any of them to risk themselves on what is likely an impossible task. It is highly probable that if anyone did try, we would both end up dead. Or at least that's probably the best we could hope for.

As though considering a rescue attempt summons it, another memory fills my mind. I'm sparring against Malam, and he gets through my defenses and strikes my ribs. The breath is driven from my lungs, and I lean over, gasping and coughing. As I work to fill my lungs with air, Dio strides across the space and pins Malam with a vine. Seeing him defending me like that, rescuing me, shatters my heart all over again.

I stare at him, feeling as though I'm consuming everything I can, every bit of kindness, every bit of love that exists in this brief memory. It feels as though it will need to sustain me for a while.

The memory fades, but a ghost of a feeling of Dio's arms around me remains for a few more moments. I cling to it as though I'm starving, and when it finally, fully dissipates, I sob until I'm gasping for breath.

The thought I've been torturing myself with rises again, feeling as though it might choke me. I don't think I ever told him I loved him.

As the memories began to come back, I searched for that in particular. Surely I'd told him I loved him at some point. I still hope that I might be wrong, that the memory of it is just buried. Instead, I have an awful feeling that I never actually said those words.

There is no way for me to go back there, and it hurts so badly that it feels like my chest might cave in without the flames filling it. The pain crashes through me, looking for a weak spot, looking for worn threads where it might be able to tear itself free, breaking me in the process.

Eventually, the tears slow, and I get control of my sobs. Once again, I allow any memories about those people I loved to fade. I've made a decision recently. I need to let these memories go and allow the wings to alter my memories fully again. A greater risk than loneliness is that Rex will get a hold of these feelings and use them against me by hurting the man I love, or at least loved. I flinch as Rex's face, too near mine, rises yet again in my memory.

Then I go to the bathroom, clean my face, and get ready for dinner.

Just surviving this life can't be that hard, can it?

DIO'S JOURNAL - ENTRY 35

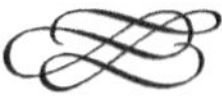

Annum:5617
Entry 35 - eripio

Earlier, I went to the edge of the ocean. I wanted to see if I would be able to escape Chiron's surveillance of me for a short while, and I managed it. The pain in my chest as I looked out over the water, and thought about how much Chaosta would enjoy it, almost made me wish I hadn't.

When I got back and opened up this journal to write, I realized how little I've documented in here. It's not that I haven't been writing. It's just that every time I sit down to do so, it turns into a letter to her.

It's been well over a year since I lost her, and the agony has increased every day. It was easier at first, when I was actually taking the sedatives, but since I got myself clean again, that agony has been hard to bear.

The only thing that's kept me going is knowing that I'm going to get her out of there. I've been working unerringly toward that goal and, while it has taken far longer than I would have liked, I'm nearly ready now.

A few months after I lost the love of my life, I had an awful and very realistic dream. In it, I was kneeling, bound and gagged behind a being I'm fairly certain was Cernunnos, the horned god.

He was talking with Chaosta, who was clearly badly injured. It also looked like they had been trying to drown her. He yelled something at her about needing to leave if she wanted to live. She said something about not wanting to be the one to save everyone, and why couldn't she just love a boy. Her eyes were on me as she said that, and I thought I was going to break something as I struggled against my bonds, trying to go to her.

Then she came to me and said goodbye. She said I needed to live. She told me she loved me. I didn't realize until I woke up that we hadn't said it to each other, not directly.

I woke broken from seeing her like that, but also with a renewed sense of what I needed to do. At the time, I was still taking the sedatives, but when I woke up, I resolved to stop. I knew I needed to be clean so I could think clearly. I'm still accepting them, of course, so Chiron doesn't realize something is up. I have quite the collection at this point. They're my insurance policy, I guess, if this fails and I don't die in the process. At any rate, since then, I've been working every minute of every day on my plan to rescue her.

I had been making some progress on figuring out the answers I needed to the magical energy requirements. Then I learned from a contact I'd cultivated that my asshole brother had reached out because he ran into Chaosta working as a city enforcer. My first feelings were relief that she was alive and wasn't still being tortured. Then I realized they must have some way of compelling her, and I knew that my rescue might be more complicated.

I also learned through those same channels that Malam and Chiron believe Chaosta has been turned by the angels and are preparing to disable her somehow. I don't believe for a second that the angels have been able to turn her. She's far too strong, far too willful for them to be able to manage that. Still, I needed to plan for her rescue to be more difficult.

Fuck, my back is sore. Scarred runes are painfully itchy as they heal, and I've had to inscribe several more runes for my plan to work. I also have a few new tattoos, but since I'm running out of space, I had one of the students practice by cutting a critical rune I need onto my back.

Oh yeah, Lent and the others came through for me, and we finally have a solution for the energy issue with magic against angels. This new rune on my back, Melyr, was inscribed with a Demonforged blade.

Because of the combination of a seeding rune and

the tool it was inscribed with, it should reduce the energy consumption of combat magic against angels. I certainly hope so, or this is even more of a futile mission than I expect. We have been working with the other combat magic users to do the same. At least I finally feel as though I was part of something that might actually help.

This will likely be my last journal entry before I leave to rescue her. I have my plan in place, and the runes are inscribed. Now I just need to make my way to the angel stronghold, where I assume she's still being held. Thankfully, I have that much more reason to believe she's there since I was able to look up Alexander's court case. It was in a courtroom within walking distance of the stronghold.

I hope I can return to this journal when I get back with her, but if I can't get her out, I've accepted that I don't really care if I live. Hopefully, Chiron doesn't beat himself up too much if I don't make it back. At least I'll be far enough away from everyone here, on the southern coast, that, even if she dies and I lose control, the damage will be unlikely to reach this place. If that happens, I'll also take a lot of angels with me.

Speaking of that, some of the new runes are also a contingency that I've worked out. If it seems as though we're cornered and there is no way for the two of us to get out alive, the magic will get her back here safely. Of course, that plan doesn't include my survival. It can't. I hope it doesn't come to that, but at least there is peace of mind for me knowing that she'll live. Especially with the odds that we'll be up against.

That reminds me, I need to write one final letter to leave where she can find it so that if she makes it back here without me, she'll have what she needs. It is important to me that she has a good life even if I'm not in it.

DIO'S LETTERS

Annum:5616

Dear Chaosta,

I can't believe you did this to me. I can't believe you didn't say goodbye. I know the angels have you. I also know if you'd stayed in the mansion or included me in whatever you were working on, it wouldn't have happened. I can't believe you could do this to me. Leaving the mansion without saying goodbye and asking the others to share that message with me was a fucking awful thing for you to do.

Did you really think that I wouldn't figure out you'd been captured? The least you could have done, when you sent that message, was to tell me you loved me. Or at least, I think you do. Right now, it's hard to believe that. Also, it hurts because I know I've been suffocating you and I feel godsdamned awful about it. Why you decided to share those specific words with me, I don't know.

If you had fucking given me an opportunity, I could have helped you. I've always admired how independent you are, but fuck, I'm not some helpless idiot, I know what I'm doing. Instead, you've taken that opportunity away from me. I'm so angry at you for that. I don't need to be your hero, but I would like to have had the opportunity to fight for you. I'd have liked the opportunity to fight for us.

Signed,
Dio Magnus

DIO'S LETTERS

Annum:5616

Darling,

I'm sorry to be writing you yet another letter. I know there have been a lot recently, but this one feels important. I just had a dream where I saw you, and it looked like you were being tortured. You came to me, said goodbye, and told me that you loved me.

When I woke up this morning, I realized that I can't keep living like this. I've been accepting the sedatives because they've been helping me keep it together, but after seeing you like that, I realized I need to get clean again. I need to make a plan and help you. I need to stop drowning in my own misery and get you out of there.

I already knew they were torturing you, seeing you in a dream like that, in that state—just seems like a *sign. It felt too real. I just hope it was actually only a dream. I have to believe it was and that you aren't that badly injured right now.*

I know I'll need to conceal this from the demons. If they suspect I'm not taking the sedatives anymore, they may make another attempt at subduing me, and in my current state, that won't end well. Fuck the godsdamned fucking delay that this has caused in getting you out of there.

I just need you to survive ok? Promise me that?

Love, Dio

DIO'S LETTER

Annum:5616

Hi Darling,

I've finally figured it out. Or rather, we've finally figured it out. That's really important, actually. Lent and Fem have been researching at all hours, and recently, actually, Reem and Cal have been helping as well.

We finally discovered the answer in some old tomes. We needed the information from the two Cal stole from the central library, but that didn't fully get us what we needed. Recently, he and Fem were able to obtain another ancient book from a different library, which had the final piece.

In that book, we found an ancient, forgotten rune called Melyr. We also discovered that it needs to be inscribed with the appropriate metal, in this case, a

Demonforged blade. Cal came through again and stole Malam's sword for me so that I can use it.

I hope Malam won't be too angry since I'm sure he'll miss it. After all, I'm taking it with me when I leave here to rescue you. I know you'll need to be armed if I'm going to have a chance of getting you out of there.

Anyway, I'm going to get some help to inscribe the rune since it will need to go on my back. Then I'll be mostly ready to come after you. I have just a few more arrangements to make.

The other guys don't know what I'm attempting, of course, I knew they'd try to stop me or tell the demons. I'd rather they not realize. I mean, I can walk right through that ward they set on my room, but I don't want any more bloodshed. I still feel bad enough about breaking Chiron's finger.

Every day that has passed has been agony. If I could have done this any quicker, I would have, but I won't risk you. I knew I needed to figure out how to kill the bastards before I came after you.

Fuck, darling, I miss you so much. I don't know what I'll do if you aren't all right.

With all my love, Dio

DIO'S LAST LETTER

Annum:5617

Hi Darling,

I feel like this is becoming kind of a habit at this point. Since there are so many letters, I know you won't get most of these, but in case you get back, and I'm not here, I need to leave you something.

I'm clear-headed, I have been for a while, but I don't think I said it specifically, and I need you to know that. It's important because I'm coming after you, just after I finish writing this. I'm so sorry, I know you don't want me to, but I can't help myself. I hope to get both of us out safely, but I know this is a massive risk.

I've done everything I can to insulate the others, and I have a contingency in place to get you out safely. Unfortunately, I haven't been able to find a contingency for myself, so if things go wrong, I may not be there for you anymore.

Just in case, I've left instructions for Pepper that the remainder of my estate should pass to you. There's plenty there for you to live comfortably for the rest of your life. If you don't personally want my parents' blood money, you can put it toward some good causes. I just wanted to make sure you're taken care of.

If I don't survive this, I need you to promise me that you'll be stronger than I am and move on. Please promise me that ok? I think I know how you'll feel about that request, but I mean it. I need you to move on for me. I just need to know that you live a full, happy life, and all of this will be worth it.

I love you with all my heart, darling, ab imo pectore.

Dio

ALSO BY CHARLI NILE

Runes to Rain

A Bright Blight

CONTENT INFORMATION

- Incorrect/overuse of psychiatric medications with ill intent
- Psychiatric "treatment" without consent
- Discussion of addiction
- Thoughts of suicide, implication of thoughts of suicide
- Drugs given without consent
- Violence
- Gore
- Torture - semi graphic (open door)
- Sex - explicit (open door)
- Bondage with consent

ABOUT THE AUTHOR

Charli Nile is an indie author of fantasy romance novels that feature pining men and strong women. She's also queer, polyamorous, and lives with her amazing wife and a tiny dog. She has been writing since she was a teenager, but only recently thought of publishing any of her work. Her younger self would be proud.

She is passionate about storytelling and loves easter eggs and foreshadowing.

She has been a voracious reader for her entire life and has been inspired by more books than she could ever possibly list here.

When she's not writing, it's likely she's spending time running or riding her horse. On quiet evenings, you will certainly find her reading.

www.ingramcontent.com/pod-product-compliance
Lightning Source LLC
LaVergne TN
LVHW100507110826
845146LV00002B/542

* 9 7 9 8 9 9 9 8 4 3 7 1 5 *